THE SHELL HOUSE

Jane Thynne was born in Venezuela in 1961 and was educated in London and Oxford. She has worked as a journalist at the BBC, *Sunday Times* and *Daily Telegraph*, and is a frequent guest on Radio 4's *Start the Week*. She is married with two children and lives in London. Her first novel, *Patrimony*, is also published by Fourth Estate.

THE SHELL HOUSE

a novel

JANE THYNNE

FOURTH ESTATE • *London*

For my mother and father

First published in Great Britain in 1998 by
Fourth Estate Limited
6 Salem Road
London W2 4BU

1 3 5 7 9 10 8 6 4 2

A catalogue record for this book is available from the
British Library.

ISBN 1-85702-856-2

Typeset by Avon Dataset Ltd, Bidford on Avon, B50 4JH
Printed in Great Britain by Clays Ltd, St Ives plc,
Bungay, Suffolk.

PART ONE

Chapter One

'Holiday reading,' said Jessica Leigh, dumping a thick file on Harry Everett's crowded desk. 'Something to browse through by the pool in Tuscany.' It was the last week before the recess. Up in a tiny office, along a thousand miles of carpeted corridor, high in a far turret of parliament, the politician and the lobbyist regarded each other with polite fatigue.

'Thanks, Jessica. I'll look forward to it.'

As usual Harry seemed keen to focus on anything but the concerns of Jessica's clients. Shuffling through a heap of papers with one hand, his back half turned to her, he picked up a ringing phone with the other and gestured with a wave that suggested she should sit down. Jessica searched in vain for a seat. The Palace of Westminster did look impressively lofty from the outside, with its furled stone arching into the sky and its butterscotch battlements shimmering in the heat haze, but it was no place to work, she thought. Her own office in Holborn, a cool glass cube in the air-conditioned comfort of Hughes Associates, was several times this size. It looked even bigger because she didn't clutter it. She liked things just so. Just a minimalist desk, a few slender filing cabinets and a chrome chair with black leather inserts. Actually the chair was uncomfortable and deterred visitors from staying long, but it was a thing of beauty, Jessica believed, so it stayed put.

Harry's office didn't even run to a chair. Perched uncomfortably on a windowseat she jiggled a little in her neat cream suit, crossed her sheer-stockinged legs and looked down through the narrow window at Parliament Square below. Across the parched and tawdry grass, weary flocks of tourists were milling like migrant birds. Sunbathing commuters, daydreaming holidays, were picking up their bags after the lunch break and making unwilling pilgrimages back to their desks.

Even in the plush panelled gloom of the Commons' Harcourt room, looking out over the lazy glitter of the Thames, their own lunch had been hard work. Harry Everett was a consultant to

Hughes Associates, the public affairs firm, but that didn't mean he felt it necessary to show any interest in the ambitions of AMCO UK, the company whose dealings Jessica was there to discuss. He was a genial man, a long-serving backbencher with a big, red perspiring face, a string of extra-marital liaisons and a raging appetite for political scandal. Jessica, who would have loved to swap gossip over the mushroom risotto, was instead obliged repeatedly to return the conversation to the business of her clients. Harry pretended to pay attention, but then he would ask a telling non-sequitur or a give-away irrelevance which revealed that he wasn't concentrating on DNA databases or bioethical research constraints at all.

Nor did Jessica have any faith that he would make headway with her bulging file of figures and data outlining AMCO's achievements to date, let alone take it on holiday with him. In truth she didn't blame him. The small-print was boring. But it was crucial that he achieved a semblance of under-standing on this issue – nothing too in depth of course – if he was to play any useful part in voicing her client's interests as the crucial human genetics bill passed through parliament next session.

Putting the phone down, Harry swiped a few drops of sweat that had been trickling down his brow and shrugged at her as if he could read her thoughts.

'I'll get on with this AMCO stuff as soon as I can. It's all here, is it? Everything I need to know?'

'Yes, it's all there.' That wasn't a lie, Jessica told herself. Harry would know everything he needed to as soon as she did.

Harry pulled his jacket off. 'Baking, isn't it? Are you off anywhere nice for the recess?'

Jessica sighed.

'No Italian villas unfortunately. I'm going to a place called Fallings in Sussex. A friend of mine is running a conference there.'

'Fallings? That was Lewis Appleby's home.' For the first time that day Harry Everett looked genuinely fascinated. 'I went to his funeral back in '96. He was an amazing old man – not just as a scientist of course. He was one of those icons of the left who always managed to unite the modernisers and the traditionalists.'

CHAPTER ONE

'There were two Labour leaders at the funeral, weren't there?'

'That's right. Lining up right next to all the old agitators. The only thing more amazing was that it was held in a church at all, given that he was a lifelong atheist.'

'Yes, but he was part of the British establishment, wasn't he? Isn't that what the Church of England is for?'

'I suppose so,' Harry Everett laughed and looked at her with fresh interest. 'So you're going to his home. They've turned it into some sort of conference centre, have they?'

'Kind of.' She didn't want to dwell on it.

'And what are you doing there? Don't tell me. A course of lectures on genetic engineering?'

'Harry, do you honestly think that's how I spend my leisure time?'

'Why not? An ambitious career woman like you, if that doesn't sound too sexist. You seem quite into the subject.'

'Actually I'm studying for a masters in computer science.'

'Really?'

'No, Harry. I'm joking. I may communicate entirely by e-mail but apart from that I barely know one end of a computer from another. And I don't know that much about genetics either. I'm just visiting someone.' Jessica jumped off the windowseat and made to leave.

'Oh. Well, have a great time. It's a good idea of yours, staying in England. Think of me hacking through the Tuscan hillsides, dodging the PM and all the other MPs who're taking holidays there.' He shook her hand. 'It was lovely to see you, Jessica, as always. We'll meet up in September, but you have my number if you need to reach me.'

* * *

Harry Everett finds me intimidating, Jessica realised suddenly as she left the Commons swinging her calfskin briefcase and walked briskly back to her car. Mingled with surprise she felt a little pang of anxiety. She didn't want to deter clients. Perhaps she should try to cultivate a more approachable air. Laugh at their jokes more. It wasn't Harry's fault that AMCO's business was technically complex. She'd felt much the same on her first meeting with the new American clients some months before.

She'd taken an instant dislike to Frank LeRoux, the tall, gangling executive with his barely concealed disdain for the English scene.

'Well, Miss Leigh. Take a good long look at the future.'

That was his way of introducing AMCO's sprawling, redbrick building on the outskirts of Slough. Jessica had regarded it dubiously. Whatever she thought about the future, and she had not considered it in that much depth, she certainly never expected it to look like this. Outside was a brick forecourt with a tiny fountain dribbling in the centre. Inside, a hushed, open-plan environment of computers gave way to a series of laboratories containing tomatoes, fruit flies, rabbits and mice.

Were it not for the prestige of handling a large and lucrative new account which she had only just been entrusted to take on, Jessica would have felt worse about this AMCO work. Like most big corporations nowadays the company was fanatical about confidentiality, but in this case that extended to Jessica, their own lobbyist, meaning that she didn't have a clear picture at all of the 'big project' they were so keen to keep under wraps in their brand new headquarters. Mr LeRoux had promised her she would be further briefed in due course, but the implication was clearly that they did not trust her to keep their work to herself. Annoyed by this, Jessica had done a little research of her own which turned up very little except to reassure her, through AMCO's track record on animal experimentation, that there would be no trouble on the anti-vivisectionist front. It was always tricky representing a client who had attracted the attention of the animal lovers but in this case, officially at least, the world's most advanced transgenic pig, which had wrinkled its wet snout at her and clattered its trotters disconsolately on the metal slats of its enclosure, should have nothing to complain of.

Climbing into her car she winced as the hot seat branded her back, and wound down the window. Perhaps Harry Everett was right. A week or two in the cool, green Sussex countryside might be very relaxing. It would certainly be good to get away from Hughes Associates, where the pressure to be seen working hard, even when most of the clients were away, was difficult to take.

She wondered what Fallings was like. Steve's sketchy description had made it sound like something out of a *Country*

Life advertisement. The house was Regency, with later additions, set in about forty acres of parkland with a little piece of woodland attached, a man-made lake and gardens that took paying visitors. The house itself had quite a history apparently. It had been in the Appleby family for generations and in Edwardian days they had hosted house parties which were visited by the king. Things must have taken quite a turn when Sir Lewis Appleby inherited, she supposed. Steve had mentioned there was a swimming pool. He'd told her to imagine they were staying in a country house hotel.

But then he would, wouldn't he? Jessica had been furious when he announced that his conference would effectively eat up all his vacation so they'd have no chance of getting abroad properly until the winter. It was bad enough that he lived in Cambridge most of the time, so they only saw each other at weekends. They'd had several inconclusive rows about this over the phone, but as Steve hated arguments, at least the non-academic kind, and tended to retreat into lofty silence, it was often hard to feel she had won her case. Sometimes she wondered how much Steve would care if they did break up. Recognising this familiar miserable spiral, Jessica swiftly checked her train of thought and got out the map. With her bags packed already and in the boot it should take no more than a couple of hours, mostly down the A3, to reach Fallings. With luck she could be there by tea-time. If her minor detour didn't take too long.

* * *

Jessica made her way through London to Battersea, where the rows of identical Victorian villas strived, and failed, to assert their individuality with wisteria and pastel paintwork and fancy metal railings. Away from the city streets it was a foreign land here, the pavements busy with mothers and buggies, dogs and children engaged in peaceable play, untouched by the purposeful hurry of office hours. Down a road which ran towards the common she pulled up outside a slightly shabby white house. Taking a parcel containing a toy rabbit with a large pink bow, she rang the bell.

'Jessy. Jessy.' A four-year-old girl opened the door by herself. 'We've got a new baby.'

'I know, Laura.' Jessica edged past the child, who was eating a melting ice-cream, and flinched from the sticky hands as from a leper's touch. The congealed drips were pooling on the hall floor. 'Where is she?'

'Upstairs with Mummy.' Laura's six-year-old sister lounged against the banisters, eyeing Jessica critically. 'She cries all night long. Daddy's in a filthy mood.'

Jessica was not surprised. She made her way round a rubble of pushchairs and boots. She never ceased to wonder at the amount of equipment needed to transport children as far as the shops. It would be enough to take ordinary people on a trek up Ben Nevis.

'What present have you got her?' The six-year-old scrutinised her parcel.

'A rabbit. Is that OK?'

'Yes. Most people have brought bears. She's only had one other rabbit.'

'Oh, well that's relief.' Jessica climbed the stairs in the direction of the crying. There were two sets of wails, rising and falling in dreadful, nerve-fraying counterpoint. Her sister was in the bedroom still in her night clothes, her hair a matted cloud, her eyes shadowed with dark circles of fatigue, rocking the new baby while a toddler howled abandoned on the floor.

'Oh, Jessica. Do take Clementine.'

Jessica picked up the toddler, who clung wet and chimp-like to her hip, grabbing one of her earrings and dripping a bottle of milk on her jacket.

'Sorry I couldn't get here earlier.'

'Don't worry. Come and have a look at little Holly. Three days old.' She stroked the baby's scrunched face, small as a fist. 'Holly, meet Aunt Jessica.'

'Not aunt, Rosie, remember. It makes me sound like something out of P. G. Wodehouse. I prefer first name terms. I can take the lack of deference.'

'Oh, whatever. Do you want a cup of tea? Pete's disappeared, needless to say. He's taking paternity leave a bit literally.'

As her sister attempted to cram her expanded form into some clothes, Jessica looked away and wondered what familial mutation had determined that Rosie should have four daughters by the age of thirty-one and she herself approach thirty with none at all. More than that, no plans for any. People talked of pregnancy making women bloom but Rosie, whose figure had grown rounder and stouter with each girl, seemed increasingly like a husk of the person she once was. Jessica knew it must be difficult, but she couldn't help noticing how her sister no longer seemed to realise the value of a good haircut, and wore clothes way beyond their season. Admittedly she had a bad start there, because whereas Jessica's sleek shape seemed to fit naturally into the rigours of a size ten suit, Rosie's untidy, amorphous frame had always seemed to rebel against the strictures of well-designed clothes, and she'd given in to loose, floaty things even before being perpetually pregnant. Yet as well as her sense of style, her promising legal career had also been forfeited to this concatenation of children, much to Jessica's disapproval. Rosie did try to stay in touch with the adult world, but when you talked to her about politics, say, or current affairs, every sentence was punctuated with baby talk, every conversation interrupted as she leapt up and down providing bottles and snacks, her mind scattered and wandering, like one gently demented.

In every way Jessica seemed to have been formed from a different template to Rosie. Thinking about it irresistibly brought to mind the image of their mother dressmaking, pins protruding from her pursed lips, her huge pinking shears crunching patiently round the pattern and the ponderous Singer jabbing away, as though she had shaped her children as carefully as her own flowery summer dresses. It had been a happy home, but the crush of children meant too little cash for holidays and school trips, and too many home-made clothes, a sorry situation which Jessica could just see being repeated in Rosie's life. Yet that was plainly what her sister wanted.

Jessica shuffled round the kitchen making tea, hobbled by the sobbing toddler pulling at her spotless linen skirt. Though she really had no idea what living with children was like, these visits provided an alarming glimpse. The house was far too small, its floors strewn with juvenile jetsam, its walls fluttering with scraps of drawing, its every surface littered with coloured plastic like the aftermath of an earth tremor. Below knee-level the impact of its inhabitants was even more evident: the walls were scarred with passing felt-tip pens and spattered with dried foodstuffs, the furniture imprinted with muddy hands. Jessica liked to think she had a natural empathy with children, and earnestly tried to chat to her nieces about the books they were reading and their schools, but in truth she was always glad to get back to her small flat, its cool aqua walls, its contents untouched since she left them, its serenity disturbed only by the familiar howl of police sirens as they screeched round the Notting Hill streets.

'So how are you? How was it this time?' Jessica handed Rosie her tea.

'Fine. Very quick. Apparently my insides are as elastic as a bin liner by now.' Her sister stroked the feeding baby's head.

'I take it this is your last?'

'Oh, I don't know. It's terrible to think of never having any more.'

'Really?' Personally Jessica found the alternative too terrible to contemplate. 'But what about Pete?'

'Oh, he loves children, so he'll go along with whatever I choose. We'd still like a boy.'

'My God.' Jessica regarded her with horror, like a participant in an Eastern-bloc breeding plan. She wondered if Rosie was jealous of her single state. 'If you lived in the old Soviet Union you'd have a medal for motherhood by now.'

'You sound as though I've put you off children for life.'

This idea was too close to the truth to risk any reply. Jessica watched the baby's pulsing, walnut head, its small pink body still curled like a spring leaf, and checked herself curiously for the nudge of maternal instinct. She was relieved to detect nothing.

'I can't think where Pete's gone,' whined Rosie, in one of her characteristic conversational U-turns. 'He'd better be back soon. The girls are Wild Forest Creatures today.'

There was indeed something feral about the two older children, who had come to lurk moodily in the room, with their ungroomed appearance, matted hair and generally mistrustful demeanour.

'Wild what?'

'Wild Forest Creatures. It's their speech and drama class. Pete's taking them.' Impatiently Rosie checked her watch. 'I hope he's back in time or I don't know how they're going to get there.'

Like a chessplayer forecasting a simple pitfall ahead, Jessica jumped to her feet.

'It sounds awful, but I'm going to have to get going. I'm meeting Steve in this place in Sussex. He's chairing a conference. I want to get there in time for the first evening's dinner.'

'Somewhere nice, is it?'

'It's a house called Fallings. You wouldn't have heard of it.'

'Of course I've heard of it,' said Rosie impatiently, a glimmer of her old, professional authority appearing. 'It was Lewis Appleby's home.'

'That's right.'

'He used to give talks on the BBC when we were teenagers. All about evolution and heredity. He must have been about seventy even then, ancient anyway, but I remember thinking he was ridiculously handsome. One of those men who age really well. All a total waste of course.'

'You mean . . . ?'

'Well he didn't appear to have a wife or children so draw your own conclusions.'

'I don't really know anything about him. I'm only going because Steve has decided to devote all his holiday time to this conference and if I don't go I won't see him. Frankly I just hope I'll be able to relax there. I could do with a rest. I can't tell you the hours I've been putting in on this new client.'

Rosie yawned resentfully and shuffled the baby like an awkwardly wrapped parcel on her lap. 'Well thanks for the rabbit anyway. It's very nice.'

The toy sat cockeyed on the floor where the other children had already fought over it, the large floppy ears now smeared with ice-cream.

'Holly's sweet,' said Jessica inadequately. 'I'll drop in for a bit longer as soon as I get back.'

Kissing the now sleeping baby, she made her way down the stairs to the door, snagging her stockings on a carrycot as she escaped.

CHAPTER TWO

'WITH MOST RIVERS *at less than a quarter of their usual level, and heading for the driest summer on record, experts have already predicted the drought could mean a radical reappraisal of all our lifestyles. But is the heat having any long-term effect on wildlife? This week naturalists reported the development of a mutated frog which they claim has adapted its amphibious system to reflect more time spent out of water. According to Dr James Miles the frogs are producing a thicker body slime which retains . . .'*

Jessica snapped the radio off. She wasn't interested in frogs. She tried to concentrate on the road. By her reckoning there were only a few miles to go before the turnoff and Steve had warned her it was easy to miss. Although the hottest part of the afternoon was past, it was still stifling. Heat shimmered above the ground, making it shift and undulate before her. In the fields crops withered in the cracked earth. At the side of the road she saw flies hovering over a dead crow, like a glistening wedge of coal roasting slowly on the verge and above, against a burning blue sky, a solo plane droned. Everything in the afternoon sun was still, expectant, too hot to move.

But at least the car was moving now. Outside Guildford she had hit roadworks – a dusty site where a rubble of cables and pipes spilled out on the Tarmac like a road kill. Cars snaked in a slow glistening trail, drivers fanning themselves with newspapers, and it had felt like hours before the relative peace of the B roads unfurled emptily before her.

No one would call Jessica a country person. She had spent her childhood amid the manicured lawns of a Surrey suburb where the family had started off in a cul-de-sac and progressed, with horrible symbolism, to a close. From as early as she could remember it was London that she had seen as the great escape. London was more an idea than a place at first, emerging gradually out of the train windows as the buildings grew taller, the people ruder and their accents coarser, their speech a riot of glottal stops and their words colliding into one another like a motorway pile-up. When she grew older and found a way to stay nights, she was ensnared by the city's unsleeping dream. The bars and clubs, the whole teeming scenery of meetings, transactions and trysts made her feel alive. She moved there as soon as she possibly could and years on she still loved it. In London the landscape was human, the greenery sophisticated into parks and only the graffiti bloomed uncontrolled.

The turning for Fallings came up suddenly but it was another mile down the Tarmacked track and through a beech wood before the path rose up and curved, allowing her to catch the first glimpse of the house before her. Almost immediately the road bent again, so that the house dipped seductively in and out of sight until she reached the long avenue, flanked by horse chestnuts, that rolled down towards its frontage.

It was certainly beautiful. Fallings was smaller than she had expected, little bigger than a manor, and far from the stately affair Jessica had pictured, but it emerged from its setting, flint grey and brown, as though carved from the dappled landscape itself. Even without its historical associations, the house had an air of romance about it. Twin columns beside the central doors pointed up the modest but perfect proportions of the bow frontage and tall windows, and in front there was a gravel drive, dominated by a large circular rose bed. To one side a laurel shrubbery concealed a rambling stable block, but the west wing of the house was its glory, a rolling, unspoiled vista facing out over the Sussex downs, the lawns saturated in the slanting afternoon sun.

The house wore its exquisite architecture like good cheekbones, a defiant distraction from the delapidations of age. Only a close inspection showed up the slightly flaking paintwork, the pocked velvet of elderly curtains or the crumbled pointing on the brickwork which signalled that Fallings was not being kept in the style to which it was once accustomed.

For a moment Jessica almost forgot her opposition to the notion of a landed gentry and found herself regretting that the ancestral Appleby line had died out with Sir Lewis, leaving Fallings to decline into the impersonal status of a conference centre. Besides which, if there had been a younger Appleby to inherit the place, she might now be enjoying a conventional summer holiday abroad rather than sharing her lover with a selection of students and foreign academics for the next two months.

On his death Sir Lewis Appleby had instructed that the house be given over to the continuation of his life's work and furthering the ideals outlined in his masterpiece, *The Elite of Nations* – a work which advocated improved international relations and bridge-building between the arts and the sciences. Fallings was administered by a trust, and its reputation for serenity and spacious accommodation had already ensured that it was block-booked at least a year ahead by think-tanks, conferences and summer schools. Sir Lewis had not been the kind of writer who wanted his home preserved in aspic, though there were plenty of admirers who would have made the pilgrimage to see the place where he had lived. He wanted Fallings to continue as a breeding place of thought and discussion, as it had become in his lifetime. At least, that was what a jubilant Steve had told Jessica, on the day he secured Fallings to host his Shakespeare conference.

Jessica parked the car and wandered in through the opened front door. The hall was pungent with the tang of polish, diligently applied over decades, the oak panelling rising in linenfolds to the ceiling where it looped round the room in a frieze of fat apples and knotted itself in fanciful florets under each banister. Past generations of Applebys lowered down from musty oils arranged round the central staircase. In the centre of the hall, pinned on an easel, a fluttering paper arrowed 'conference office'.

The office turned out to be a cupboard-like room containing a harrowed woman with a frizz of brown hair and spectacles who was shuffling through registration forms. Jessica recognised her vaguely as a research graduate from Steve's college, whom she had met drifting round some excruciating faculty party clutching a glass of bad white wine. Her name was Sarah something. She'd had her eye on Steve, apparently. She looked up at Jessica stonily.

'Oh, it's Dr Irvine's friend, isn't it? I didn't know you were going to drop in on us.'

'Yes. Do you know where I can find him?'

'Well, he'll be very busy at the moment. He's giving the

opening speech in the morning.' As Jessica continued to stand there she added grudgingly: 'He's probably in the library. Through the hall, round the corridor, last door on the left.'

A few stray, badly dressed Belgians were wandering along the corridor, muttering to each other, peering at the notice boards and jotting down times of the papers. With the provocative title 'Shakespeare, Man or Myth?' Steve's conference was likely to prove lucrative for his faculty, which was charging £1,000 a week from each international academic who attended – and there were plenty of takers. The long-running debate over the playwright's true identity, seen as an irrelevant distraction to many, was going through a spate of popularity. It was an obscure sideline of literature studies and Jessica didn't know that much about the subject, but she privately thought it objectionable that so many people couldn't take a simple glove maker's son to be the genius that Shakespeare was. That they couldn't accept he had the necessary education or experience or breeding to write the canon and preferred to think that an aristocratic lawyer like Francis Bacon or a blue-blooded dilettante like the Earl of Oxford were far more suitable contenders. Or they thought that if it was Shakespeare who wrote the plays, then he must have been an anti-government spy, or a secret Catholic, and not simply the part-time actor and writer he made out.

It was all a tiresome cocktail of conspiracy theory and snobbery, Jessica thought, but somehow she had never actually said so. Steve had chosen this conference to launch his own big discovery – the identity of a new contender for the authorship of some of Shakespeare's work. Steve's candidate was a London nobleman called Sir Edgar Avon who had apparently secretly collaborated with the playwright and left coded messages sprinkled throughout the plays. It was a case he had worked on for years – it could be the coup of his career, and Jessica knew better than to air her views on it just here.

The library was a long low room, hung with undistinguished oils, the gold embossed titles of thousands of books glinting in the gloom. Steve was sitting in one of the leather armchairs by the window, his angular frame relaxed, his long legs stretched before him, absorbed in the work on his laptop. As every time she saw him after a short absence, Jessica was struck again by the cool, masculine beauty which had first attracted her. He was tall – six foot four – and kept his spare frame punishingly fit. Steve was forty, but his only concession to ageing was the fashionable horn-rimmed glasses he had bought in New York and the faint recession of his thick dark hair above his temples. He had slender, sensitive hands, like a doctor or a pianist, a long, straight nose and precise, Wykehamist manners that had already secured him a place on numerous faculty committees. His clothes seemed eternally pressed. He was so absorbed in his work that he didn't look up when she entered, so Jessica went to stand before him, blocking his light. He squinted up at her.

'Hi! You got here at last. You do look hot.'

Looking down at him, Jessica became instantly aware of her shiny face and limp hair, her linen clothes concertina-ed with creases. She felt her voice emerging petulantly. 'Aren't you going to say hello properly?'

'Sorry. Of course.' He got up and placed his arms lightly round her before detaching them as though her disarray was contagious. 'Hello.' His lips brushed hers. 'It's just that I was expecting you earlier. I'm right in the middle of this now.'

'What's this?'

'Tomorrow's speech. We start at nine, and I'm only half done.'

'Do you want a cup of tea?'

'Well actually, Sarah just brought me one.'

'Is there anywhere I could get one then?'

An irritated, Germanic voice cut in from the other end of the library. 'Could we have some quiet in here, please?'

'I'm sorry, darling. I'm being thoughtless and you've had a long journey. Let me just show you up to our room then I'll rush down and finish this before dinner.'

Steve strode ahead of her down the corridor, carrying her bag as though it weighed nothing, and mounted the wide staircase which led up from the entrance hall. He pushed open a heavy oak door.

'Chairman's privilege, we're in the master bedroom.'

'Lewis Appleby's room?'

'Yes. Amazing, isn't it?'

It wasn't really. In fact, if Jessica had been feeling cooler, she might have pointed out that the room was more like a concert hall than a bedroom and the furniture looked as if it had not been moved since Lewis Appleby died. It was huge and underfurnished, its walls papered in peeling sky blue and hung randomly with landscapes. At one end was a wide desk, already overflowing with Steve's paperwork, and an ugly mahogany dressing table. A couple of massive armchairs in purple-sprigged upholstery were splayed in the middle of the room like someone's elderly relatives come to stay. At the far end a dark four-poster stood, done up in matching linen and soft as a giant marshmallow.

'I could fit my flat in here.'

'I know. It's great,' said Steve, sitting down at the desk. 'Thank God no one's tried to partition it up. They liked to do things on a grand scale when this house was built. It's probably got brilliant acoustics.'

Jessica wandered around, unconsciously checking with her fingertip for dust. Beside the bed hung a portrait of the man himself. The painter had posed him leaning against a tree, one arm crossed, jacket slung across his shoulder. Were it not for the fact that he held a cigarette, rather than a book of poems, in his hand, she could imagine him as a Holbein miniature, dressed in dark doublet and ruff, a monkish austerity issuing from the lean, ascetic lines of his face. A crest of chestnut hair stood out from his large, beautifully proportioned head and his famously piercing blue eyes stared levelly into the middle distance. His thin, mediaeval mouth did not smile. Beyond him, Fallings could be seen rising from a crease in the hills, like a castle in a *faux* Renaissance landscape.

It was not until Jessica sank on to the windowseat and gazed outside that she realised what really made the room special was the view. Against the stone-mullioned window the buds of a peachy rambling rose knocked on the glass like insistent little lips pursed for a kiss. Beyond the flagged terrace there were more roses in an arbour, whose pergola frames, bulging with blooms, led directly on to a long herbaceous walk, bordered on each side by a frothing mass of colour. At the far end of the walk, where the grassy path met the dark fringe of woodland, Jessica could make out a small, whitish building standing in a niche of trees. It had plainly been positioned so that the occupant of this room, whenever he looked out, would never fail to see it.

'What's that out there?'

Steve looked up from his desk. 'Sorry, Jessica. It's no good expecting me to give you a tour. I've been up to my eyes.'

'There's a little white thing, a sort of folly I think, in the clearing of the woods.'

'Uh huh.' He was bent over his laptop, erasing a line of text.

Suddenly the heat of the day, her fatigue and Steve's lack of welcome made Jessica want to walk out, slamming the door behind her in a childish rage. But she had long ago learned to avoid such dramatic gestures. Steve hated confrontation and what he called emotional histrionics. Even more, he hated discussing their relationship, whose very evocation provoked a tangible displeasure in him, as though it were some dull or reprehensible acquaintance he would rather not mention.

So Jessica never aired the flurries of irritation and dismay which regularly ruffled her composure. Spontaneity was a luxury she had been forced to abandon. She knew that this was the one area of her life where she was not in control and she disliked that, but she feared losing Steve even more. After all, she reminded herself, she and Steve were better suited than any other couple she knew. They had intellectual compatibility and mutual interests. They liked the same music and read the same modern fiction. In politics, art and culture they agreed on whom they disdained and whom they approved. And more important than all that, she admired Steve. Everyone said respect was crucial to a good relationship, and she did respect him. She admired his drive, his ambition and his keen, analytical mind. Not to mention that even after five years, just the sight of him undressing was enough to quicken her pulse.

She kicked off her shoes, shrugged off her crumpled jacket and stretched her thin arms, the late afternoon light behind her glinting on the gold filaments of hair. Then she laid full length on the bed, feeling the downy mattress subside beneath her. Steve remained undistracted.

'I can tell you're pleased to see me,' said Jessica, drowning in the depths of sprigged cotton.

One thing to be said for English lecturers was that they

were generally alert to linguistic nuance. Abandoning his desk with a barely detectable sigh, Steve came over to Jessica, sat beside her and kissed her, running his hands over her shoulders as though performing some invisible dusting. Jessica felt the moth's wing of his breath on her shut eyelid and sensed the clean, acid smell of his skin freshly showered and scrubbed. As his shadow fell across her she felt him tower beside her like a mountain, a huge flinty mountain of a man with a cold north face.

'Of course I'm pleased to see you,' he said.

'Have you missed me?'

'Don't go all insecure on me, darling. That's not like you.'

Jessica began to unzip her dress, but, sensing the slight freeze of his movements, she hesitated. He doodled a finger on the sleek skin of her shoulder blades but when she looked at him his eyes flickered away.

'What is it?'

'I'm just a bit pressed for time actually. I've got to get back to the speech.' Jessica turned her face away. 'Look, I'm sorry. I really am.' She heard the edges of his voice fraying with irritation. 'I know it's not a proper holiday for you and you're being very patient, but you appreciate how important this is for me, don't you? I mean it's a great platform for me to talk about Edgar Avon, there are people from all over Europe and America here.' He got up. 'Besides, it's not exactly Colditz here, darling. I mean, you can relax, do some serious reading. You're welcome to come to the seminars if you like. And maybe later we can talk houses.'

Jessica knew this reference to their much-delayed plan to find a home together was a bribe, as shameless as offering an old crust to a dog. Nonetheless she jumped up and gave him a Pavlovian kiss.

'Seriously?'

'Sure.' He hesitated. 'But meanwhile there is something you could do for me.'

She laughed. 'I thought you were too busy.'

He looked away. He disliked innuendo in women.

'No, the thing is, my brother's coming.'

'Alex?' At the memory of Steve's younger brother, Jessica's face fell. 'Oh no. Why?'

19

'I thought he could be useful in publicising Edgar Avon. Even if he doesn't write about it himself, he is a journalist after all. He can spread the word.'

Alex Irvine was a roving foreign correspondent. Jessica had met him only twice but somehow both times they had ended up arguing. She saw his attraction to war zones as dysfunctional. He had displayed ill-informed and simplistic views on her work in public affairs. His fiery, confrontational manner could not be more different from Steve's cool, methodical approach.

'I thought he was supposed to be in Africa or something?'

'No, he's back at the moment.' Observing Jessica's reaction he added: 'It's all right. He's coming tomorrow but he won't be staying long. A day or two at most. He wanted a break. I could hardly say no.'

'But he annoys you. And you're so busy.'

'Yes, I know. So I'd be terribly grateful if you could take him off my hands a bit.' Steve was halfway out the door now, his duty done. He smiled encouragingly. 'You know – you could talk to him, show him round, keep him company. I'd really appreciate it. Anyway he regards you as practically one of the family.'

CHAPTER THREE

FINALLY INSTALLED IN the gummy seating of the much-delayed 10.04, Alex Irvine tried bending his mind to the serious issues surrounding his balls-achingly long wait at Victoria. But it was no good. Privatised or not, British railways seemed to him uniformly awful. Their very petty-mindedness infected you, so you ended up whinging about stopping in tunnels and spilt tea in the buffet car like some old bank manager. Abroad, he never got worked up about train timetables. He remembered the fabulous, day-long journey he once took rocking through the rusty umber of the Moroccan countryside, a trip that should have lasted a few hours but for the nonchalant locals who would wave the ancient train to a stop at tiny stations and swing themselves up on to the roof. Then the soot-blackened machine would wait for an indefinite period emitting little grunts of steam from its flanks, before squealing into life and clanking on down the line. They had a different approach to journeys there. It was something to do with a sense of the infinite, he might have said if he was writing pretentious travel pieces, which he wasn't.

Out of the window he watched the shoebox houses in their plastic estates and attempted to quell the fugitive spirit within him. No sooner had he made up his mind to stay here, to stem the wandering instinct for good and settle to some other area of journalism, than he grew restless. And he'd really wanted to come back this time. He had wanted it, even though it meant renting a dank little hole in Pimlico and looking up old friends who turned out to be unemployed, divorced or dead or who had gone into corporate PR – the journalist's graveyard – or given everything up to run a pub in Wales. The thing was, he acknowledged yet again to himself, he'd been on the road for too long. Ten years he had spent like an addict following the source of his habit, drawn irresistibly to any place where shrapnel flew, guns were worn or firebombs thrown. It had started when, by a stroke of sheer luck and fresh out of university, he got a press place on the task force sailing to the Falklands, but after he had acquired the taste for it nothing could stop him. He'd gone on to the Gulf, Afghanistan, Tiananmen Square, Bosnia, Rwanda, Zaïre. He learned to dwell at the heart of things, in those cauldrons of madness and indecision where life was cheap and crisis hung like cordite in the air. He liked to picture himself as some strange subterranean creature, adapted for extremities and no longer able to breathe the mundane air of peace. The domestic hacks called his kind war junkies, and perhaps he had been, but this last trip – a nasty little guerrilla insurgence in Burkina Faso – was the first time anyone had suggested he was going soft or losing his taste for it.

It had been a routine misunderstanding. Some crazed bastard at a border crossing point hauled him out of the car, held a gun to his head and accused him of being a government spy. He'd been made to kneel down for two hours at the side of the road, waving his press card uselessly at the stony-faced nineteen-year-olds, wishing he knew the local dialect for 'journalist' and sweating with fear, before a senior rebel who knew a bit of English came by in a Land Rover, stole his cameras and reprieved him. That kind of thing was an occupational hazard of course, but for some reason he'd been seriously shaken. He'd backed out of the country and holed up in fleapit hotel just across the border where he stayed, trembling, for days before he got it together to return. He didn't know quite why, but something in him had changed. The reason was there, nagging just below his consciousness – some urgent new aversion to getting a bullet in his brain – but he couldn't put a finger on it. All he knew was when that happened you had to get out, or the fright made you do something stupid and that finished you.

This visit to Steve was something of a diversion. It was no good rattling round the office while they waited for him to carve his new niche. With a shudder he remembered his first day back at *The Nation*'s tower block just a few weeks ago. The task of finding him a new job had been deputed to the deputy editor, itself a very bad sign. Lois was a small, emaciated woman, armour-plated in Chanel, who buzzed round the office like a shiny, immaculate insect. Expressing her delight in having him 'back on board on the home pages' with a smile that wild animals might find menacing, she gestured round the expanse of neon-lit open-plan desk space visible through her glass cubicle and asked him where he would genuinely like to work. Fortunately he had not had time to answer before it emerged that the question was a rhetorical one. The deputy editor had already decided that it would be best for him, and for the development of his 'career' – the latter concept imbued with just the discreetest quizzical flicker – that he join the lobby, covering the day-to-day work of parliament.

Like all foreign specialists, Alex had always had a personal contempt for the job of political correspondent, cosying up to the MPs, cravenly churning out other people's propaganda. But that was the natural route for war junkies who had tired of real battles, he supposed, and he acquiesced to Lois' suggestion without protest. In future he would report on internecine ministry feuds, domestic squibs about tax and education and civil wars in Whitehall. He would meet deadbeat ministers and talk grandly afterwards about his sources, carefully observing lobby rules that dictated he left at least a day's grace before revealing their so-called stories. His new colleagues in the department included an odd, sardonic girl, formerly the shopping correspondent, who was known to be sleeping with a minister, and another ex-foreign journalist who had started his career covering the Vietnam war but now spent his days monitoring the activities of the House of Lords. Still, Alex was determined to be optimistic about his new life. He'd do all that was required of him and willingly, but the paper could hardly expect him to start in July, when half of the people who counted were on holiday and nothing was happening.

Besides, he was interested to see the home of Lewis Appleby. Clever, charming and charismatic, Appleby had been a minor boyhood hero of his. Not a cult figure of course, like George Orwell or even George Best, but in his books and on the radio he managed to convey his interest in human heredity and cultures as well as politics and social policy in a way that made Alex realise how the issues might interconnect.

Perhaps he could write some soft feature about Appleby's home. It was certainly more interesting than his brother's obscure find about Shakespeare which sounded to him like a lead balloon of a story, though he'd pretended a polite interest. Either way, a short stay should be pleasant. It was gearing up to be another scorching day and the place had a pool apparently. He only hoped Steve had ditched that frigid girl he was seeing.

If he was honest with himself, the chief reason for his visit was to spend some time with his brother again. It had always been just the two of them. Their mother couldn't have any more children, but they hadn't minded because they'd been so close. There were only eighteen months between them and before boarding school, living out in the country, they'd got on better than brothers, like real friends, huddled over Subbuteo in the house, spiralling away through the fields on their bikes or careering round with a football. Steve liked playing the older brother, being the one in control, and that was fine because Alex admired him. He used to admire everything about Steve – his mind, his physique, his technique with girls, the way he tackled a ball. The way he devastated women and charmed men. Alex, his stubbier, crosser, saturnine counterpart, possessed a blunter manner which often left people inexplicably offended, as though there was some obvious yet invisible etiquette he transgressed.

But now all that had changed. When they met now it was like communicating through fog, as though a mist of manners and platitudes had descended, behind which Steve inhabited his own suburbia of the soul. Sometimes it was more like visiting a solicitor than a brother. Alex started arguments like fires, trying to coax a spark of the old Steve out of him and sometimes he thought he glimpsed it in an evanescent flicker of the eye or a burst of temper or shared reminiscence. But the closeness never came back. When they met he felt himself wanting to embrace his brother, but instead all he got was a jocular slap on the back, and even then he knew Steve would have preferred a handshake.

Alex stretched his legs out on to the seat in front of him.

'That man's got his feet on the seat. Can I put my feet on the seat?'

'No, you cannot.'

The woman across the carriage, sitting with a boy of about six, looked up from her magazine and withered Alex with a single glance. He adjusted his position hastily and took out his paper like a passport verifying his adult status. He longed for a smoke and mentally traced the hard edges of the packet in his pocket, but he knew better than to try. A moment later he lowered a corner of the paper and winked at the kid. The child smiled back, checking to see that his mum was not watching. Alex contorted his face to a monstrous grimace. The boy, delighted, continued watching Alex with the frank interest children display for an adult who has descended to their level, waiting for further entertainment, until Alex was forced to return to his paper to divert the penetrating gaze.

★　★　★

Jessica wasn't used to being at a loose end. Her life in London was so packed, so busy with breakfast meetings and conference calls and client presentations and weekend working that she had to think hard about when she could find half an hour to dash to a supermarket and buy food, which was generally frozen or strangled in clingfilm or with a generous use-by date, and she scarcely ever found a window to wander randomly round clothes shops without very strict prior planning. Even relaxing was a seriously scheduled occupation, to be done by the book in a health club, or by following a rigorous work-out chart alongside the sweating merchant bankers and grunting celebrities who wrestled with the stainless steel in her gleaming, neighbourhood gym. Practically everyone she knew lived like this and meetings with friends almost always concluded with a devotional flick through mutual diaries, hunting out the next unoccupied hour, usually weeks hence, when competitive conversations about the hectic nature of their lives could resume. Steve, whose existence was equally parcelled out into pre-planned segments of time like so much processed cheese, approved. His work ethic chimed with hers, which was why when he was thinking of ways for Jessica to amuse herself during the conference, he suggested 'serious reading'. It didn't sound nearly so bad as relaxing with a novel.

It was clear to Jessica, though, that she had no choice but to attend the first lecture of the event, which was Steve's announcement of his Edgar Avon find. Even though Steve had insisted on reading it through to her the night before, declaiming from his side of the bed while Jessica's mind swooped and teetered on the brink of sleep, she still sat loyally at the back of the lecture hall to hear Steve present his argument to the world, or at least to the assortment of European and American academics there who shared his doubts about Shakespeare.

He held himself tidily at the lectern like a disapproving headmaster, surveying the ranks before him with a magisterial glance. He was saying: 'After all, are we really expected to accept that a grain dealer and merchant, and, yes, he may have been a very impressive man – for a country merchant – but a man with no heritage, self-taught, with little schooling, no record of attending university, or of foreign travel, was the sole originator of the canon? We know he was no stranger to collaboration – Christopher Marlowe's hand, you will remember, is seen in *Titus Andronicus* and *Henry VI* – and then we are confronted with this . . .'

On a screen beside him Steve produced a complicated acrostic spelling EDGR AVN which could apparently be found by twisting certain lines in *As You Like It*.

'How much more impressive than the so-called Baconian motto on the Shakespeare memorial this is! Am I really going too far in suggesting this can be taken as definitive proof that Sir Edgar was actively involved in guiding and helping Shakespeare?' he demanded.

The academics scribbled away in their notebooks. Shakespeare was put in his place. Jessica glanced at the day's timetable. After Steve, there was to be a man from Perugia University arguing the case for the Earl of Oxford. She'd sat next to him at the dinner the night before, listening to his carefully crafted banalities delivered in painful, fractured English. She decided that she could, after all, slip away unnoticed. Doing her best not to catch Steve's eye, she got up, closed the lecture room door behind her and trod the dark length of the corridor, swinging the small canvas bag containing her swimming costume and looking forward, in time, to a blissful swim.

The creeping dilapidation of the house's exterior continued unchecked within, but to Jessica who had grown up swaddled in wipe-clean Formica, her home a padded cell of Dralon and thick beige carpet, this was an aesthetically pleasing sort of decay. The parquet was splintered and the lino curled, bare brown patches spotted the stretches of rich scarlet runner. She followed the corridor round to the far north end, to in a room labelled in a yellowing card as the Red Dining Room and hung with a branching, dusty chandelier. Every patch of wall was festooned with photographs of Fallings' history, some of them brown and blotted with age, some more recent. The earliest featured a vast Victorian family, its fertile ranks extending like the empire, its individual faces reappearing elsewhere in a variety of groupings and poses. There was a panoramic picture of a house party, at the centre of which, in a wicker chair, sat Edward VII, a wide-hatted lady standing at his side with a small terrier frisking at their feet. The photographs then moved on chronologically, until they reached the point when Sir Lewis, then plain Lewis Appleby, inherited. There was a group of fat frowning men in tweed suits, no doubt discussing some crisis on the international scene and a posse of severe young men with slicked hair standing round stagily, faking conversation for the camera. One portrait commemorated the 1936 science conference which Lewis Appleby had inaugurated. Science was Appleby's vocation – his religion, he used to say. Unusually, that time he took centre stage in the group, his handsome leonine frame towering over his guests. Looking up at him, Jessica thought about why he never married. She agreed with Rosie. He was exactly the kind of man she would have fallen for.

Prowling on through to the deserted library she cursed herself for having brought nothing to read. Perhaps she should find something serious, as Steve suggested. She picked up a copy of Eliot's *The Waste Land*, then replaced it. It was too hot to concentrate on poetry. The sun was already slicing fiercely through the shutters in dazzling white bands. She felt restless. She would go outside and see the garden which was so highly talked of.

In London Jessica's flat was on the fifth floor of a handsome Victorian block and had no garden, just a balcony containing two regimented window boxes of geraniums and an outrageously expensive standard box tree. Like a prelapsarian Adam most plants were nameless to her and much of what was special about Fallings' garden she missed. She paid scant attention to the bells of convolvulus or the euphorbias' fleshy spears. The aching blue of the delphiniums, the vaunting clematis and brazen marigolds made little impression. As her bare shins brushed a border, the sharp scent of lavender pricked her nostrils, but went unrecognised. Yet even Jessica knew enough to see that the studied informality of this garden had been planned with the utmost care. The topiary, poised like dark chessmen in a giant's game, the sunken garden ranked with colour like a table laid for a rich dinner, the casual arch of a pergola writhing with honeysuckle and the swelling fruit trees trained around the walled garden; everywhere the designer's hand was plain.

The pool was at the far west side of the grounds, bounded by laurels, at the point where horticulture receded into parkland. She walked through the Italianate garden, where, from their niches in the tenebrous box, blank-eyed statues leant, like cows at a milking gate. She passed through a gate in a thin screen of hedge, but instead of the inviting waters lapping coolly as she had hoped, there was only an empty rhomboid, cracked and flaking, with a shrinking puddle at its base.

She peered down at the pool, whose sides bounced back the bold glare of the sun. Steve had not mentioned that it was out of use, though now that she thought about it, she realised that he had not been forthcoming when she had told him about buying a new costume the previous week. Yet somehow the water she had imagined remained so real and inviting, she felt she could almost step forward and put a toe in it, watch the light shivering over the ripples. She had thought of herself scissoring into its limpid depths, stretching her limbs through the lazy expanse of blue. Now it was not there she became conscious again of the merciless heat prickling on her skin. With a stab of irritation she turned to follow the grassy path that wound up the hill to the edge of the wood.

At the top of the path the ground levelled out to a plateau, giving a spectacular view of the house and gardens below. Jessica lay on her stomach, feeling the scorched spikes of grass scratch her naked legs. Stray curls of fair hair caught damply against her neck. From where she was she could see below her small figures coming in and out of the great French windows of the house, chatting under the rose arbour. It was a coffee break, evidently. Before her a drowsy wasp swam, snagging the heat-thickened air. After a while Jessica shut her eyes and felt the tide of blood surge through her body like a secret, enclosed sea.

⋆　⋆　⋆

'Mind if I join you?'

Beside her rose bare, browned toes and a pair of muscular hairy calves. Jessica, who had been dozing, propped herself up on her elbows. She did mind. She minded a lot. She shielded her eyes and squinted up at him.

'Oh, Alex. Steve said you were coming. You didn't half give me a fright.'

He squatted beside her. He was dressed in a pair of aged shorts and a none too clean T-shirt.

'Sorry. I've just arrived. Thought I'd take a quick recce round the grounds. Check out the facilities. I was planning on a swim but it doesn't look too promising.'

'I didn't see you in the house.'

'Well, I wanted to avoid the professors. I did peek in a room and saw Steve holding forth, some stuff about Shakespeare not writing his own plays, so I beat a quick retreat.' Jessica shut her eyes again. 'I'm not disturbing you, am I?'

With an effort, she reminded herself that Steve had especially asked her to look after Alex. She sighed and sat up.

'I almost didn't recognise you.' His gaze was as searching as a mine sweeper, his eyes travelling down her legs as though noticing them for the first time. 'Don't think I've seen you without a power suit and a mobile phone before. How's the world of PR?'

Nothing could be more guaranteed to annoy Jessica.

'It's not PR, it's public affairs. Which, as any experienced journalist should know, is a very different ballgame.' She had explained the difference before, and suspected he was trying to irritate her.

'Oh well, thanks for putting me right. Anyway, the job's going well, is it?'

'Fine. Thank you.'

'Are you staying here long?'

'Any reason why I shouldn't be?'

'Hey, look, hold it a moment. I was only asking.' He sat

beside her and took out a packet of cigarettes. Jessica refused one with a perceptible flinch.

She took a sideways look at him. It was hard to believe he was Steve's brother, a cocktail of the same parental DNA. His skin was tanned a light chestnut and his dark hair was both unrulier and more plentiful than his brother's. He lacked Steve's imposing height, but whereas Steve was compact and lean, Alex was broad and muscular. He was very keen on football too, she remembered, one of those men you saw in parks who didn't consider it undignified to puff round after a ball on a Sunday afternoon. Steve said he lacked intellectual depth, though Jessica supposed he must have fairly quick wits to survive in foreign countries, picking up cultures in a matter of days and then discarding them again like the dust on his boots. Maybe if she were in a jungle she would rate her chances of survival higher with Alex than Steve, but there weren't many jungles in greater London and anyway she preferred city-based holidays to anything involving a rucksack.

'I suppose Steve told you there was a pool too?' she said.

He laughed. 'Yes, he did. Funny that. Stupidly I forgot to ask if there was any water in it, so I suppose he can't be entirely blamed for misleading me.'

'What do you plan to do while you're here, then?'

Even as she asked it, Jessica felt a little cruel. She knew he wouldn't have a plan, but amongst her own friends being without a schedule, even on a short holiday, was unthinkable.

Strangely, Alex did not seem to appreciate that his aimlessness constituted a modern mortal sin. 'Oh, I'll just hang loose.' He regarded the distant house reflectively. 'I thought I'd like to write something about Lewis Appleby. His legacy and his house and all that. It's a shame my paper is so conservative because the left absolutely love him. He was tremendously catholic – "multidisciplinary" is probably what they call it in your world. What I mean is that apart from his own specialisation – which was amphibian heredity or something equally obscure – he was very into primitive societies and preliterate cultures. He was fascinated by tribes and their cultural systems. He actually met Claude Lévi-Strauss apparently, and from what I can remember he once agreed to some colleague of his bringing a family of American Indians, wigwams and all, right here to Fallings to see how integration into a different civilisation affected their reproductive and health patterns.'

'Whatever happened to them?'

'Oh, it never came off. It was 1946, just after the war. Couldn't get visas or something.'

Though she tried not to show it, Jessica was surprised how much he knew. But then journalists, like lobbyists, were adept at absorbing information rapidly. Perhaps he'd read up in an attempt to impress.

Alex added: 'He always said that it was his interest in science and what it taught him about people's potential which led to his involvement with the left.'

'There are a lot of old photos down in the house. I'll show you if you like.'

He smiled. 'Ah. Steve's asked you to look after me, then.'

'How did you know?'

'Oh, I know my big brother.' Alex seemed about to settle down beside Jessica so she sprang up, smoothing the grass off her clothes and began to walk back towards the house, forcing him to follow. 'Hold on a moment. I thought you were supposed to be looking after me.' As Jessica barely slackened her pace, he loped along in her wake. But after a few moments walking, he stopped again. 'Wait. I want to take a look at this.'

He was standing in a clearing of trees, set back from the path. In front of him was the folly which Jessica had seen from the window. She wondered how she could have walked past without seeing it, but then realised that it was designed like that – framed by a natural keyhole of beech and elm trees, so that it would be more visible from a distance than close up. It was entirely circular, shaped like a small round turret with a quaint pineapple dome supported by white marble pillars. But the astonishing aspect, as they looked more closely inside, was that the interior was made entirely of shells and fossils. Hundreds of different types and sizes covered the walls, placed in perfect, intricate panels and pictures. The whorls of cockles alternated with white mussels in a bulging snakeskin across the roof, sea urchins pricked out borders for slabs of black shale, marked with the delicate scribble of graptolites, ammonites spiralled like rams' horns round the window arches. Scallop shells formed pale petals and the basalt backs of molluscs ran in arching ossicles to the roof.

The artist who had wrought such perfection from natural materials would have been dismayed at how nature now threatened to overwhelm it. Tall fronds of meadowsweet thrust from holes in the floor, brambles and bracken leant through the window arches and the cracked windowseat running round the interior wall was dark with the must of dead leaves. The floor was filthy too, but beneath the dust a mosaic could just be seen, a tumbling tableau of shells fashioned into birds and animals, their corals and blues dull with the mould of age.

'Isn't this what they call a grotto?' Alex asked. He was sitting down and seemed to be preparing to smoke another cigarette. Jessica felt impelled to turn away.

'I think it's a folly.'

'OK. Fallings' folly. I like that. Hey, look down there, just behind you.'

Jessica turned and saw beneath her, half hidden in the bracken, a statue of a woman, a nymph perhaps, crouching down with her hands cupped. She was about two-foot high, her stone form lichened in turquoise and green. A tiny rivulet spurted through her hands, before trickling away into the undergrowth.

'A fountain,' said Jessica, delighted despite herself.

'It won't be a fountain this far from the house. More like an underground river rising to the surface.'

'You know about these things, I suppose.'

'Yes,' he replied simply.

They walked back down together. The heat was rising. A plane performed a lazy stitch in the sky. As they reached the garden and passed through the huge pyramids of yew, its bulk clipped to a velvety nap, Jessica could not help thinking of the Indian wigwams which might, had bureaucracy not intervened, have been pitched here in the heart of the Sussex countryside fifty-odd years before.

Approaching the house, Jessica could see Steve engaged in conversation with a group of people on the terrace, including Sarah from the conference office, who was dressed in something resembling a smock – if people still wore smocks – her hair scrunched into a bun. Jessica started to make towards him, but as he caught sight of her coming, Steve made a slight, delaying gesture with his hand, signalling that he was on official conference business and too busy to be interrupted. Jessica quickly altered her path and Alex, who had observed this but pretended not to, said: 'Where are these photographs you were going to show me, then?'

'Oh, I'm far too hot to do it now,' she said, pleased to have someone to vent her irritation on. 'I'm sure you'll find them yourself if you look round the house a bit. You're the journalist, after all.'

Chapter Four

ALEX'S BLACK QUEEN tipped Steve's king provocatively on its side.

'Check mate, mate.'

The gaggle of French professors who had hovered annoyingly over their shoulders during the dying minutes of the game dispersed, and Steve turned back to his notebook with a terse laugh.

'Thank God for that. I've got a pile of work to do.'

It was the third day at Fallings and Steve had at last found time to have lunch with them. His Edgar Avon paper had gone down well, so well indeed that he had been asked to submit an article for the following month's edition of *Literature Revised*, an influential journal whose hirsute editor was a prominent delegate at the conference. The importance of this magazine could not be overestimated, he had explained to Jessica, as he seized every spare moment to prepare the feature on his laptop. Given Alex's torpor with regard to the news value of the Edgar Avon find for his own paper, a well-written, properly argued piece in *LR*, as it was popularly known, was an opportunity not to be missed.

But he had agreed to a short break, sitting on a balconied terrace overlooking the gardens, where the drone of a motor mower required conversations to be conducted in a gentle shout. Wearing a clean straw hat, neat chinos and white shirt, he looked less than ever like his younger brother, whose own shirt was unbuttoned to the waist and whose chest was covered in a mat of curling black hair, so that he reminded Jessica of a short, brown bear basking in the sun.

Having disposed of a lunch of cheese and ham rolls, the staple fare provided for the delegates, to which Alex had contributed a few bottles of red wine, the brothers had engaged in a game of chess. Jessica was stretched on an ancient sunlounger, reapplying factor 25, which had not prevented her fair, freckly skin flushing pink.

'Look at him. He hates losing,' said Alex cheerfully. 'Chess is the one thing he can't beat me at. When was the last time you won at chess, Stephen?'

'I really wouldn't know.'

Alex winked at Jessica.

'Don't worry, Kasparov. You can blame it on those boffins distracting you.'

Indeed they were hard to ignore. Strolling the gardens and dotting the lawn, chatting or reading or tanning skin normally lit only by the library's halogen, the delegates were impossible to escape. Jessica felt that a perennial, shifting audience of other people was almost part of the landscape now. It was so long since she had been properly alone with Steve. Needless to say they had not had time to discuss the house-buying proposition.

Steve regarded Alex over the rim of his glass. 'So how long do we get the pleasure of your company? Aren't you needed in some civil war somewhere?'

'Well the good news is, apparently not. I'm being relocated to London.'

'Permanently?'

'Dangerous word in newspapers. Particularly when you're pushing thirty-nine.'

'Oh. Well, have you found somewhere to live?'

'I have found someone willing to take £300 a week off me for the privilege of renting a filthy, three-room windowless garret, yes. What's the matter? You don't look pleased.'

'No, of course I'm pleased. I just can't believe you've kept all this up your sleeve.'

Alex shrugged. 'I'm not sure how pleased I am. Though of course as my editor tells me,' here he affected a voice of Scots pomposity, instantly recognisable to anyone who knew the editor in question. 'Number three in the lobby is a very import-ant position, laddie. You're not so busy with the big stories, so there's plenty of time for uncovering the real scoops – poking your nose into the things no one else notices.'

'So it wasn't anything to do with – what's her name – Lisa? The aromatherapist?'

Alex yawned and stretched. 'The strange thing about women is, they love the idea of a foreign correspondent. They get a hell of a kick out of imagining you standing there getting shot at, they love looking at the holes in your flak jacket and poking around in your medical kit, but when you're actually out there and doing it, somehow they meet a merchant banker at a dinner party and decide that what they really want to do is marry him and live in a nice little house in Barnes.'

'Whoops. Sorry.'

'Don't worry. They invited me to the wedding.'

'Oh dear.'

'Besides, she was always wanting to go ski-ing.'

'You don't like ski-ing?' Jessica was surprised to find she and Alex had something in common. Ploughing expensively down an icy slope had never appealed to her, but unfortunately it was the one sport which Steve genuinely adored. He made a point of going at least once a year.

'On the list of my all-time favourite occupations, ski-ing is right up there with root canal dentistry.'

'You're well rid of Lisa anyway,' said Steve decisively. 'Airhead.'

'Thanks for that kind endorsement of my taste in women.'

'So what political scoops are you working on?' asked Jessica.

'Not much around at the moment. I was hoping you could tip me off.'

'Don't count on it.'

'Anyway,' continued Alex, 'isn't Steve going to be moving down to London soon?'

'Well actually,' Steve's tone became vague, 'it looks like I'll be staying up in my place in Cambridge for a while. To start with I think I'm going to be busy organising another one of these seminars. It's gone even better than I hoped.'

Jessica sat up, flushed with annoyance. 'Another conference?'

Steve tipped the last of the wine into his glass, avoiding her eye.

'The thing is, darling, there's been a lot of demand and summer is really the only time possible. I've had several requests already. I have to think of the financial benefits involved for the faculty.'

'But I can't believe you've got anything else to talk about. Surely with a subject like this you pretty much cover all the discussion points the first time round?'

Alex cut in. 'Oh no, Jessica. Single-subject seminars can get quite an obsession. What about those *Star Trek* fans? They hold conventions all the time. They even dress up. Hello, I'm Spock. Beam me up, Scottie . . .'

Steve turned to his brother.

'Well, I'm glad everyone finds it so risible, but out here in the real world the college has to think about any funding opportunity that can supplement grievously dwindling government support.'

'Whoa.' Alex spread his hands, as though deflecting physical contact. 'Sorry.' Heaving himself to his feet, Alex said, 'Perhaps I should be getting back to my project.'

Silently they watched him amble across the lawn, then Steve came up behind Jessica and laid a tentative hand on her head, like a priest administering benediction to a troublesome communicant. His impression of unappreciated forbearance was supplemented by low sniffs into a handkerchief, prompted by his allergy to grass cuttings.

'Listen, I know you're not happy about my plans for next year. And I should probably have talked through the idea of staying in Cambridge a while, but let's discuss it later, eh? I just don't need it right now. You've got to appreciate how busy I am, darling. You know I'm grateful for what you're doing with Alex. It must be a pain looking after him.'

Jessica looked over at Alex, who had run into a group from the Czech Republic and appeared to be teasing them, pointing in the direction of the pool and engaging in wild, explanatory swimming movements.

'It's not a pain actually,' she said stiffly, attempting to submerge her hurt. 'I'm rather enjoying his company.'

*   *   *

The strange thing was, it was true, though she was determined not to show it. After their initial meeting, Jessica had found herself accompanying Alex on what he had self-mockingly started to call his 'project'. He was assembling all the facts he could collect about Lewis Appleby, with a view to a retrospective piece in his newspaper's arts section. He had greeted the roomful of photographs with rapacious interest, and continued to mooch round the house, diverting Jessica with a series of anecdotes about Appleby's life, interspersed at her request with episodes from his own brother's youth, or what he facetiously called the Home Life of Our Own Dear Steve. It was while they were rooting through the library that he unearthed an old brochure, called *A Guide to Fallings*, poorly produced on speckled paper, listing the contents of the house and a sketchy history.

'Here we are. "The prospect of tribal diminution among the north American Metake group led Ronald Llewelyn and Lewis Appleby to initiate conversations in 1946 with the American government over the possibility of transporting an extended family to live in Fallings House, Sussex. The proposition, which would involve all expenses to be covered by Appleby, foundered on long drawn-out negotiations over visa requirements." God, look at this list of visitors. Dr Laurence Harvey, specialist on the African chimpanzee, author of *A Monographic Survey of the World's Great Apes*, published 1935, president of the Simian Society of Great Britain, delivered a short talk on the activities of the Congolese chimp tribes and their interrelation with man.'

Once he was interested, Alex really got into things, Jessica reflected. She supposed that was how he coped abroad. He immersed himself in whatever issue of interest was at hand. As he pored over the brochure, she lounged over the untuned piano, fiddling with the notes.

'You're not at work now, you know. You don't have to research everything.'

'Oh, I know, but it's fascinating, isn't it?'

⋆   ⋆   ⋆

That afternoon she sought him out again. He was standing in the morning room, a small, serene room with good walnut furniture, decorated in worn shades of eau-de-Nil and dominated at one end by a bay window enclosing the desk Lewis Appleby had once used to write on. In his hand Alex held a heavy silver picture frame, tarnished in a way that would have grieved those who once polished it religiously. It contained a black and white photograph of Appleby standing outside what looked like the gates of Buckingham Palace. Smartly attired, with his springy hair sleeked to his head, he regarded the unknown photographer seriously, the set of his fine features suggesting determined tolerance of a tiresome, but necessary formality.

Jessica peered over Alex's shoulder. 'You'd think whoever took the picture would get him to say cheese.'

Alex slipped the picture out of its frame and flipped it over. 'Yes, I thought that was it. "Receiving knighthood. 1953." For services to popularising science, if I remember rightly.'

'Wait a minute. What's that?'

Beneath the frame's bed of dark, pressed velvet, where the picture had lain, Jessica noticed a triangle of protruding white. There was no sign that the backing could be detached from the frame, but jabbing at it with her thumbnail eased it apart, revealing another photograph, face down and dog-eared. Jessica turned it over. The tiny figures were grey and faded, but Sir Lewis' patrician pose was unmistakable, as were the huge west doors of the house in the background. At his feet a large greyhound sat and beside him, turned slightly from the camera and squinting into the sun, was a woman with a pale, oval face and dark, shingled hair. Her throat was encircled by a single-strand pearl necklace and the skirts of her dress lifted in the breeze.

Alex looked over. 'How mysterious. I wonder who that is.'

'You'd think it was his wife, but he didn't have one. Anyway, she looks too young to be his wife. Perhaps it's a sister.'

'I don't think he had any sisters. Could be a cousin or something. Hold on a second, I know where I could check.'

He strode out of the room and down the corridor to the library, where a set of heavy red-bound volumes were ranked on a shelf. He returned holding one.

'*Who's Who*. You're right about the wife. There's no mention of a marriage, or any sisters, in his entry.'

'Maybe she's a lover. But she doesn't appear in any of the other pictures. And how strange that he hid her picture away. Perhaps she died and he couldn't bear to be reminded of her.'

'Perhaps he hated the sight of her.' Alex deflated the moment with a snort of laughter but Jessica continued to gaze at the young woman, with her earnest, slightly anxious face and her lips pressed into a suggestion of a smile. She looked so young, surely not more than twenty, but there was something private about her and self-contained. Her hand rested on the greyhound's head as if its slender bones could give support. She reminded Jessica of Millais' Isabella, with the watchful dog in the foreground and the doomed heroine with pellucid skin and distrustful eyes.

'Unless . . .' Alex dug in his pocket and brought out the *Guide to Fallings* brochure. 'There's a picture in here by someone called Katherine Appleby. Just let me find it.'

He turned to a black and white reproduction of Lewis Appleby, striking his Renaissance pose.

'That's it. Do you suppose it could be her?'

'That's the painting in our room. His bedroom as was.'

'Brilliant. I'd really like to see it.'

Almost as soon as she'd said it Jessica wished she hadn't, but she led the way up the polished oak stair to the master bedroom. She regretted not tidying up that morning; the sheets lay rumpled on the bed, clothes sprawled over them. She gestured to the picture and went pointedly over to the far window, which she opened to gaze up to the shell house on the hill.

Alex said: 'Oh yes. This is fascinating. Amateur but striking, don't you think? And there's the signature in the corner. I wonder if she was the woman in the photo.'

He peered at the picture for a while, before dawdling round the room. Jessica could hear him looking round the other pictures, and examining the furniture. After a few moments of this he came to stand beside her and following her gaze said casually: 'How long have you been with my brother now?'

'Five years.'

'Five years, eh?' He exhaled theatrically. 'That's some time. You must be thinking of getting married and having children.'

Jessica could not remember the last time she had been asked such an intrusive question. Was it the suggestion that she – the woman – would be the one wanting to formalise their relationship, or the faint implication that she was ageing a bit for childbearing, or, perhaps worst, his implicit realisation that she did indeed harbour the shameful, outdated, inglorious ambition of matrimony, though she did her level best to repress it. Who on earth did Alex think he was? An employer or something? She turned to face him, her voice tart with indignation.

'Steve doesn't want children, actually, and if we do decide to get married, I'm sure we'll let you know in good time.'

'He doesn't want children? Surely you wouldn't marry someone who doesn't want children?'

'What on earth has that got to do with you?'

'I'm interested in you.'

They were very close. She saw the dark pool of his pupil dilate, the slight flex of the nostril as he inhaled. The still air carried faint scents of the abandoned bedclothes behind them.

'Jess?' He reached forward and touched her arm, gently, experimentally, as though she were some feral thing, or an uninitiated Indian girl, breathing the unfamiliar Sussex air. He surveyed her face, as though contemplating her physiognomy for a sketch. Jessica knew she must move, but she was paralysed by his scrutiny. No one called her Jess.

'Don't mind me asking, but are you still . . . you know, in love?'

She neither moved nor spoke.

'I only ask because . . .'

With a rough movement she detached his hand and turned.

'Hey, sorry. Jess . . .?'

Marching furiously out of the room, she ran down the stairs and through the gloomy oak-lined hall out to the garden. She walked rigorously up the path that led to the woods, hardly noticing where she was going, until she reached the shell house.

She went in and sat there, outraged, glancing down at the window of the house below and wondering if he was still in the room looking out at her. Eventually she got her breath back but there was something else, perhaps her dignity, which she feared she might not regain. Scuffing her foot against the corrugations of weathered shells, she noticed that in the centre of the floor was a mother of pearl motif, bearing the entwined letters L and K, surrounded by a circlet of dancing griffins. She rubbed her shoe against it to clear the whole mosaic.

She was interrupted by the crunch of footsteps. Fearing it was Alex she looked round, but it was Bill, the chief gardener. She'd seen him before, dolefully poking at the cracked earth of the rose beds with his hoe. He looked about a hundred, the skin on his face creased and leathery as one of his old gloves.

'Oh, hello.'

'Afternoon.' He seemed about to pass by, but Jessica could not quell the urban imperative to make light conversation.

'It's an interesting little summerhouse, this.'

He paused reflectively, as though noticing it for the first time. 'It was once. Goes back a long time, does that. He was restoring it. Never got finished though.'

'Were you here when it was restored?'

'Uh. Long time ago now. Just after the war, it was.'

'Did he do the floor?'

'Uh huh.'

'What does the K stand for?'

'Katherine.'

'Was she his wife?'

'Aye.'

'So he was married. And was she the reason it wasn't finished?'

'Reckon so.'

'When did she die?'

'Don't know that she did.'

'But surely . . .?'

'She vanished. That's why he never finished it.'

'She vanished?'

'Disappeared. Like a thief in the night.'

'But why?'

'Dunno. It were a sudden thing. In '45. No one heard of her since.'

He turned his shoulder pointedly, as though physically deflecting any more questions, and lurched off, forcing Jessica to call after his retreating back: 'What was she like?'

He stopped and looked up. 'She was a lovely girl. I will say that for her.'

Jessica watched the gardener make his way down the valley along the path of the brook which Alex had said signified an underground river. It was strange to think of a waterway flowing freely beneath this parched veneer, irrigating the fractured earth. She had never encountered an underground river before, outside the classics class of course. Then it was the rivers of the ancient underworld, running their strange, powerful ways beneath the surfaces of human lives, infecting and controlling the destinies of men. Which could she remember? Acheron, stagnant and thick with reeds, where the boatman Charon rowed the dead. And the snaking, mortal water of Styx, circling nine times the bounds of Hades, giving invulnerability to some and to others death.

All that seemed a long way from Fallings, which stood below her, basking in the late sun, cupped in its hollow of hills as though the landscape had been designed with the house in mind, rather than the other way round. Above the fine symmetry of its roof, swallows were swooping and diving for invisible gnats and beyond them the western sky, edged with fire, promised the good weather would not end. All along the herbaceous walk honeysuckle, jasmine and stocks prepared to send their scents into the serene evening. A woman on the rose terrace was cutting flowers to replenish the large bowl in the hall.

And all this Katherine Appleby had left. She had simply vanished one day without trace. But why? Jessica closed her eyes, breathed in the green perfume of earth and mowed grass and wondered whether some great passion had prompted her urgent departure. And whether some answering passion had ensured that barely a trace of Katherine Appleby remained, bar a mouldering photograph of a pale-faced young woman and a single picture on the bedroom wall. If this was her home, Jessica knew, she would never want to leave it.

CHAPTER FIVE

AMCO WAS ONE of the world's leading pharmaceutical organisations, with a base in Washington and branches in Europe and Asia. It had built up its enormous fortune back in the 1960s on an arthritis treatment which came to dominate the north American market but for such a well-placed market leader the company also demonstrated an unusual degree of lateral thinking and vision. This had led in the past to initiatives like the confidential investments in cannabis-growth experimentation, during the period when it first looked as though the drug might be legalised, and it was similar foresight that prompted AMCO to channel profits early into a division of molecular biological research, in particular the field of gene patenting, before any of its rivals had extended tentacles that far from their normal patch. Now that the excitement surrounding the human genome project – the project mapping all the genes in the human body – had spawned numerous satellite research efforts, everyone had a finger in the genetics pie. But AMCO's work was always on the cutting edge, whether it be pinpointing the 'age genes' which might ultimately make ageing a reversible phenomenon, or working on a prototype for personalised DNA codes on a microchip the size of a fingernail. Innovation was AMCO's lifeblood and it was now concentrating its more exciting – some might say audacious – work in the more tranquil climes of the United Kingdom.

Warwick Saunders, the chief executive officer of AMCO, sitting in his award-winning glass and steel fortress in Virginia therefore was not pleased when, on the third day of Jessica's stay at Fallings, an article appeared on his fax machine from an English newspaper. The report, under the by-line Brent Southern, questioned the precise nature of the company's new research establishment in Slough and the motivations of the company in transferring more of its business to Britain. Due to the scarcity of real news in what the British press apparently called the 'silly season', Mr Southern's over-hyped scare story was given an enormous amount of space in the newspaper. The possibility that this speculation might frustrate AMCO's plans, or, worse, result in a cautious amendment to the human genetics bill about to pass through the British parliament when the Commons reconvened, was deeply unwelcome. Yet the CEO's reaction was no more dramatic than if a fly had found a way through his air-conditioned, bomb-proofed plate glass window to buzz round his desk. With a relaxed flick of the wrist he picked up a telephone that connected him immediately to the headquarters of AMCO UK. There a purring professional voice reassured him that the company had gotten on board a most prestigious Westminster lobbying firm for just such eventualities and that the firm was already 'on the case'. The woman heading up the lobbying team, Jessica Leigh, had assured them that her own political contacts would be more than ready to oppose any irritants in the forthcoming legislation.

★ ★ ★

What on earth had made Jessica disappear? Alex searched, about an hour after the incident in the bedroom, just in case she'd stupidly taken offence, in the way women did, but there was no sign. It wasn't until the evening dinner that he encountered Steve to ask him, and then he didn't know what to believe. Steve told him she'd left in a hurry. She'd found a message on her mobile phone asking her to return to London and sort out a 'bit of a mess' at the office. According to Steve it appeared that a big problem had blown up, though Jessica had no doubt she could calm things down. He, Steve, had not had time to enquire into what the problem was exactly. He had a lot to do himself, as Alex must have noticed.

This explanation disquieted Alex. He didn't know what to make of it. When exactly, he demanded of Steve, did Jessica say she'd be back? Steve didn't know. A few days or later? She'd only said she'd return when things were sorted out. When, after a fretful, unsatisfactory walk round the grounds, Alex finally returned to his room he found something of an answer. Slipped under the door – a strangely old-fashioned and inefficient method for a girl who communicated almost entirely through e-mail – was a note from Jessica. In a hasty scrawl it read: 'Re. your interest in other people's marriages. It turns out Lewis

Appleby did have a wife. She was called Katherine and she left without trace in 1945. How about that for your project?'

Alex gazed out of the window into the garden, the air heavy with the day's remembered heat, and up through the avenue of horse chestnuts to the far front gate of Fallings, uncertain what to do next.

PART TWO

Chapter Six

London, 1935

Katherine Scott stopped for a moment on the steps of the imposing house in Kensington with the shudder of apprehension that affects even the happiest of party-goers, before the maid opened the large black door and she heard beyond the harsh, intimidating cries of polite conversation, tussling over the niceties like a host of raucous crows fighting over a bun in the street.

It was Meredith Davenport's twenty-first birthday cocktail party. Katherine was hard put to imagine a more appalling prospect, but she knew that her grandmother, whose close friendship with Meredith's grandmother had ensured her invitation, would brook no opposition. Her mother, who said she didn't see why Katherine should go if she didn't want to, had paid for a taxi, perhaps because her father, who had said it would make a break from moping around the house, pointed out that the Davenport's home was right on the bus route from their own home in Chelsea. Her mother had made Katherine a new dress from a yellow chiffon she had been keeping for the summer, but it was cold for April and Katherine felt like a daffodil which had emerged unnaturally soon, awkward and etiolated among the more delicate stuff of spring. The wind carried in it a shiver of rain, and she hunched her navy coat closer round her, longing to get inside, and dreading it.

The party looked like being every bit as bad as she feared. The tall drawing room had been cleared, and a quartet of strings occupied one end, while waiters holding trays of champagne cocktails circulated among the assorted guests, most of whom seemed to be friends of Meredith's parents, greying politicians, ageing businessmen and their wives. Over their heads chandeliers suspended soft globes of light which shimmered off the walls, papered in watered silk of blue, silver and aquamarine at the behest, Katherine knew, of a fashionable

Parisian designer. Whole boughs of pink and white blossom had been imported and arranged in enormous urns in the corners, and above the main fireplace hung a photograph of Meredith by Cecil Beaton, her birthday present from her parents. Katherine guessed she would hate it. She was draped in a waterfall of frothy tulle and had been made to pose on a *chaise longue* like a film star, her arms resting on the raised end. Her straight blonde hair was smoothed neatly behind her ears and her gaze focused on something in the middle distance. Her face, normally self-assured and phlegmatic, had a tense, frozen look, like an antelope which knows it is about to be shot.

Looking around her, Katherine realised that Meredith was nowhere to be seen. She head the loud bleat of laughter that signified Lady Davenport, huge and jewelled as a great, ceremonial elephant as she progressed round the room, and she identified the commanding bray of her husband Sir Ronald, the MP. Though obviously a Conservative from the womb, Sir Ronald Davenport had become an MP only late in life, almost as if the idea had occurred to him by accident, but despite this had experienced little difficulty in getting elected. Persuading people to vote for him largely seemed to entail driving round his Derbyshire estate, with his wife or Meredith at his side, waving condescendingly at the locals, a prospect which Katherine thought would have alienated even the least radical among them, but instead seemed to endear him to them all the more.

Katherine accepted a glass of champagne from a silver tray and, hoping that milling around might pass for circulating, she eavesdropped on snatches of other people's conversation.

'She may look like a funny little Chinawoman but, my dear, when we dined at the Fort she was absolutely dripping with new jewels. He adores her, it's quite plain.'

'Lorne's planning a fabulous party for the King's jubilee, with everyone flying over to his villa in Rome the next day. We're so glad we're able to make it.'

Then through the thicket of guests she sighted May Barnes, a short, cheerful girl, with a reddish cloud of hair and an outdoor flush on her face, who had been at school with her and Meredith. May hailed Katherine gratefully.

'Hey, Katherine, you look jolly nice. Lucky you. I feel pretty dreadful in this get-up.'

May did indeed look peculiar, dressed in a dark halter-neck dress with tight ribbons which criss-crossed her back like a turkey trussed for the oven. She peered myopically into the crowd.

'Do you know many of these people? I can't see much without my glasses on, but my father said the specs and the dress together were just too much. I should never have listened to him because if the guest of honour does turn up, I'm going to miss him.'

'Who's the guest of honour?'

'Edward Tiverton. You know, he runs that new literary magazine. He's always in the gossip columns. He keeps a marmoset in his office. He actually brings it out with him sometimes, curled round his neck apparently, though I suppose he's hardly likely to bring it here.'

May stared soberly round the black-jacketed backs now forming in tight knots in the room.

'But why is Edward Tiverton the guest of honour?' asked Katherine.

'Oh, he's not really. Only as far as Meredith's concerned. Haven't you heard her talking about him? She's hoping he might introduce her to some of his bohemian friends.'

But neither the marmoset man, nor anyone remotely bohemian was in evidence among the older guests milling in ever louder circles. Before the two girls could avoid it, Lady Davenport bore down. She was upholstered in a tight pleated crêpe dress the colour of raw liver.

'Don't you two look delightful. Katherine, your grandmother was telling me how excited you were about the party. I hope we don't disappoint you.'

'No, it's lovely. The flower arrangements are charming.'

'Yes, they are. Very *au naturel*.' She turned threateningly to May. 'I understand you have a job, May.' From her expression, she might as well have understood May had a contagious disease.

'That's right. I'm working at the *Daily Mail*.' Knowing Lady Davenport's disapproval, she blushed. 'I'm not writing or anything. I'm an assistant on the women's page.'

'*Daily Mail*, eh? That's Lord Rothermere's paper, isn't it? Tom Mosley's friend.'

'Oh, he's not, not any more,' said May quickly, her heart sinking as the conversation assumed its predictable course.

It was true that Rothermere, the bluff, grey-suited figure whom May had glimpsed a few times climbing out of his Daimler and striding round the offices, had become known for his campaign in support of Mosley's fascist movement. Only the previous year *Daily Mail* readers had been given the chance to win a seat to watch a blackshirt rally at the Albert Hall. For a brief period some staff had even started to wear black shirts to the office, but the paper's romance had soured after an embarrassing event at Olympia, when Mosley's supporters turned brutally against communist protesters who were trying to disrupt the evening. Subsequently Rothermere broke off his support for Oswald Mosley, claiming that the paper's Jewish advertisers disliked it. Despite that, though, he was widely known to keep in touch with fascist leaders abroad. He had dined with Hitler, Goebbels, Goering and Ribbentrop in the Führer's official residence in Berlin. It was said he informed for the British government, but many of the old guard distrusted him. They included Sir Ronald Davenport, who at this moment joined them, his moustache bristling like a small, angry animal.

'You talking about Rothermere? I don't quite trust the man. He's a profiteer, always trying to get us to bankrupt ourselves with rearmament.'

May turned a serious face to him. 'You don't think he's right to be concerned?'

'Not at all. The man's friendly with Hitler himself after all, always telling us what a good fellow he is. He should know better than anyone that there's no real threat. Anyhow,' Sir Ronald seemed to recollect he was discoursing on serious subject with his daughter's friends, 'girls like you don't need to be worrying your heads about international affairs.'

He was right there, Katherine thought. Her domestic affairs were quite enough bother just then. On the home front, at least, there was every chance of civil war breaking out. She thought of the family she had left earlier that evening, then instantly tried to repress the image, like someone reminded of some dismal, inescapable chore. She could picture the scene in the drawing room of their tiny Chelsea home as well as if she had been sitting there. The squabbling siblings, continually roared at by their father as they drowned out the sound of the wireless, the pursed disappointment of her mother, like a card player trying to conceal the fact that she has been dealt a bad hand, the ill-tempered housemaid – whose moods were borne only because of the sheer difficulty of getting staff – summoning them to the dining room for steak and kidney pie. Katherine needed, no she ached to get a job. Not that there was any hope of finding any kind of job she liked, and indeed it would have to conform to the narrow range of occupations her parents approved of, but she simply had to find something. Because with a job, she could finally leave home.

As far as Katherine could tell, the idea of her leaving home had not crossed the mind of anyone in her family. Her parents presided over their children like a resentful colonial power, aware of their obligations to keep order and to monitor developments but unable to conceive that any of their dependants should want to secede. While the finite nature of all household resources – food, clothes, gas and the rest – were an incessant, grinding topic of conversation, the idea of Katherine as a solo economic unit, actually capable of earning a living, of entirely supporting herself, seemed not to have occurred to them. Therefore, after a limited foray into her affairs in which they quashed her ambition to attend university on the grounds of financial hardship, they had withdrawn, leaving the problem of her future as a preoccupation for Katherine alone. And the furthest she'd got was to realise that her own expectations and those of girls like Meredith were very far apart.

Though they had attended the same London day school, Katherine's fees had been paid by her grandmother, Lady Maud Myddleton – funding melodramatically described as 'blood money' by her father, though he did not noticeably hesitate to accept it. The financing of Katherine's expensive education was generally assumed in the family to be an act of guilt by her grandmother for her conspicuous failure towards her own daughter, Syrie, after she provoked enormous family upset by marrying Arthur Scott, then a young solicitor, encountered one morning when he was sent to deliver some documents to Sir Frank Myddleton's home. From what Katherine could gather, Arthur had been a friendly, romantic man with dreams far above his circumstances and ambitions which did not include the path set out for him of inheriting his father's firm and continuing his work on conveyancing and wills. At first, the lack of financial assistance from Syrie's parents had scarcely bothered them, indeed they laughed about it in their small, rented flat as they discussed Arthur's change of direction, a spot of travelling perhaps, or settling in America. But before they could decide on anything definite the first baby was on its way and then the Great War broke out, and somehow Arthur saw joining up as just the change he'd been looking for. Unfortunately, as the later, laconic Syrie put it, the war proved 'a turn for the worse'.

He did return to her four years later, for which Syrie knew she should be thankful, but the change in him was dismaying. His worldly impoverishment was henceforth matched by a personal dilapidation that she could not have expected. Like a parcel badly damaged in the post, her handsome, bold husband was transformed into an angry, aged, embittered creature. But unlike with a parcel there was nobody to complain to. Not only was he physically incapacitated, but somehow his horizons seemed narrowed, rather than widened, by his experience, so that he settled quite readily back into a slightly larger house and took up his life amongst the legal documents, with no suggestion that he would not carry on at it for ever. The only real change to their circumstances was the arrival of several more children among whom to divide their slender means, and the grand-mother's infuriating offer to pay for the oldest alone to attend an expensive school, though not, Syrie bitterly reflected, to buy any of the accoutrements. To condemn her grandchild to feel her inferior social status throughout her school-life must be, Syrie thought, an exquisite revenge.

Fortunately, with the resilience of youth, Katherine did not see it that way. Though her school had been a hotbed of snobbery and condescension, she was quick enough to cope, and there prevailed a sufficiently academic ethos that being always top of the class earned a certain grudging respect, as did the knowledge that she would be one of the few to stay on to eighteen. She was also close to her grandmother and got into the habit of visiting the old lady for tea and scones after school, her large, comfortable house being free of the stifling air of scrimp and save that characterised Katherine's own home. Katherine had never known her father as anything other than an irascible malcontent who reserved his life's enthusiasm for stamp collecting, so she did not miss his earlier incarnation. Nor was she aware that her grandmother might be paying her school fees as an act of revenge. Indeed she saw a role for herself, rather romantically, as drawing the family back together after a needless estrangement. Painstakingly she relayed all news of the Myddleton household back to her own family. She tried not to notice when the exploits of her wealthy cousins, the products of a more socially acceptable marriage by Syrie's sister, provoked in her parents bridling resentment or sniffy indifference.

Yet now that school had finished, and two years of art school had passed, it was becoming uncomfortably plain even to Katherine that grandmother's patronage would in future be more social than financial, involving evenings at the theatre and concerts, the occasional dinner and, worse, procuring invitations to painful events like this.

'You see,' continued Lady Davenport, exhaling a satisfied plume of smoke from her Sobranie cigarette, 'if we had any doubt at all about the international situation, we wouldn't be sending Meredith to visit some dear friends in Berlin.'

May was dutifully impressed. 'Berlin. Really? Lucky girl!'

Katherine did not doubt May's envy. She knew that May longed to travel. Obligingly Lady Davenport went on to provide a detailed itinerary of the family's plans. A visit to the family seat in Derbyshire would be immediately followed by a short break at their Monte Carlo home – a glorious villa overlooking the sea with gardens full of bougainvillaea and orange trees – after which Meredith was to be dispatched to Germany, entrusted to the care of the Bauers, some old family friends.

'What a wonderful opportunity,' said Katherine, while she thought what a waste it was. She could hardly imagine anyone less deserving than Meredith of a such a trip. Wherever in the world she went Meredith inhabited the same essential landscape – a terrain of wealth, smart hotels, beautiful cars and flurries of people to carry her luggage, fetch tea, meals or drinks, and draw her baths. It reminded Katherine of what they said about the king, how he thought the most natural smell in the world was fresh paint, because people always decorated their surrounding for his visits. Despite her stated craving for bohemian friends, Meredith had no real interest in other people's lives. People who weren't rich, that was.

'Aren't you a bit worried about the international situation?'

'Not a bit. Why should we be? She'll be fine and if, heaven forbid, she did get into any difficulties, you know Herr Ribbentrop is an acquaintance of ours, and I'm sure will be of every assistance. But where is she? I need to introduce her to some people.'

Lady Davenport sailed off to bully some more of her guests, leaving Katherine to wonder how long there was to go until dinner. She was just skirting through the party with her head down, hoping she would not be assailed by anyone else, when she came right up against Meredith.

Even in the earliest days of their acquaintance, when she was in the same shapeless grey gymslip as a hundred other schoolgirls, Meredith's sophistication set her apart. It was only skin deep, as Katherine always reminded herself, but then with Meredith the skin was quite something in itself. It had a flawless quality, as though sculpted from fine soap, and her long, slender limbs were accompanied by a thick coil of pale blonde hair and vague grey eyes, the colour of a distant winter lake. The worst you could say about her, as Katherine's father had, was that she looked as though she needed more exercise. But tonight, for her party, a rare touch of pink tinged her cheeks. She looked as exquisite as ever, older than her twenty-one years, with her hair curled on to her shoulders like Greta Garbo and wearing a backless, emerald satin dress, patterned with sequins and tiny serpentine straps which reminded Katherine very slightly of the sinister snake woman in Coleridge's 'Christabel'. As ever, she managed to make other women feel instantly oversized and clumsy beside her. Attached to her arm was a man, who Katherine immediately guessed to be the owner of the marmoset.

'Katherine, darling. Thank you so much for coming. Are you enjoying yourself?'

Meredith's voice was strangely languid, as though she were

on drugs or her deathbed. Katherine knew she cultivated this
tone, and hated it.

'Very much, thank you, Meredith, and many happy returns.
Your mother's looking for you.'

'Oh dear. She wants to exhibit me. Katherine, can you look
after Eddie for a while? You might have read his magazine. It's
called *Extremity*.'

Meredith's casual introduction was, as usual, laughably
deceptive. After all, everyone of their acquaintance knew
Extremity. Its colourful, hand-printed covers were the last word
in chic. The magazine had only been launched the year before,
with a grand 'Declaration of War on Our Cultural Frontiers',
but already it was required reading among their circle. It prided
itself on breaking taboos, which, as far as Katherine could see,
stretched to printing unreadable poetry, but despite its radical
political stance, it also carried a gossip page filled with the
antics of a group of writers, artists and actors with whom
Meredith longed to be involved.

'So you're Katherine. Meredith mentioned you.' He leant
forward and kissed her hand.

Meredith drifted away, laying a pale hand on Katherine's
arm. 'Be careful of Edward. He eats people.'

However carnivorous his reputation, Eddie Tiverton did not
seem too formidable. He was tall and foreign-looking, with a
brush of black, corkscrew curls and dark, smoky eyes, but
despite his immense celebrity he did not look in the least unfriendly. Katherine could just imagine why a marmoset might
want to curl round his neck. She decided it might bore him to
ask about his magazine, but before she could think of anything
else to say, he waved his glass at her and said: 'Let's go and fill
up on champagne. It's not often I get the chance so I'm making
the absolute most of it.'

They wandered into another room, in which were pillars
festooned with ropes of flowers, and tables set with linen cloths
crowded with glasses and champagne.

'Isn't Meredith lucky, going to Berlin?' said Katherine.

'I suppose so. Very intrepid of her parents, I must say.'

Sir Ronald and Lady Davenport did not strike Katherine as
the intrepid type.

'Why? She'll be in good company there, won't she?'

'Oh yes, I've heard the Nazis like an English Fräulein.'

'But she won't be going anywhere near the Nazis. She's staying with friends.'

'I rather think it's impossible to keep away from them just at the moment. Still, I'm sure Meredith can look after herself. What about you? Meredith has told me only the barest bit about you.'

She told him about meeting Meredith at school, and how their two families were not exactly close acquaintances. Then he explained how he had come to establish *Extremity* on a shoestring budget with a group of university friends. How to start with they were always convinced that the next issue was going to be the last but now they had more financial security which was good, except the more radical contributors argued that it was better for their political integrity to be always on the brink of bankruptcy, rather like the economic version of permanent revolution.

'I say it may be good for our politics, but it's not very good for the nerves,' he confessed. 'Thank God we've got some vile capital behind us now.'

As he talked on, dry, amusing, Katherine thought how he resembled the older brother she used to fantasise for herself.

'So what do you do now?' he asked.

'Not much at the moment. Unfortunately. I've finished art school and I paint a little but I'm hardly likely to get a job doing it.'

'Do you need a job then?'

'I want one, actually.'

'What sort of career do you have in mind?'

Katherine was not sure. She had simply thought of work with a capital w, just a way to get money, nothing so grand as a career. Before she could answer he said: 'You see, I might have a job. It's nothing much but I need a secretary. I bet you'd be awfully good. Maybe you could help design a cover for us. And it would be so original to have someone who was both intelligent and decorative.'

Though Katherine might have felt patronised, it was Eddie Tiverton's skill to make her feel as though she herself had inspired this original, stylish idea.

'Would you like to think about it?'

'Do you really mean it?'

'But of course.'

'Well, I think I'd love to.'

'Wonderful. Come to the offices tomorrow then, why don't you?'

At that moment Meredith rejoined them, linking her arm proprietorially in his. 'Sorry to leave you so long,' she said.

'Not at all. In fact I'm glad you introduced me to Katherine. It looks like she's coming to work for me.'

Meredith's cool grey eyes were suddenly sharp with mistrust.

'I told you he'd charm you into the ground, Katherine. You never offered me a job, Eddie.'

'You don't need one, Meredith. Besides, don't forget you've promised to write me a piece from Berlin.'

From across the room Lady Davenport was clapping her hands.

'Now, everyone, if you'd just move over to the Square gardens, there's a birthday surprise.'

The guests drifted out of the door and peered into the huge communal gardens, which were swallowed up in shadow. As the house lights dimmed, they discerned men moving about, black shapes scurrying with tapers, canes and equipment. Above them, a sprinkling of stars hammered the dark sheet of sky.

For a moment, everything was still, then the first burst came in a shower of red and gold sparks, illuminating the shrubs and trees around. A satisfied chorus of delight went up from the guests. It was fireworks. First the rockets went up, splintering the darkness, casting their wild, ephemeral light on the smart Kensington houses, then came the crash of the bangers and the slow fizz of roman candles, bathing everyone in their ruby glow. And though the combination of bright light and explosion brought grim associations for many of the older men, who would never again enjoy firework displays without unconsciously bracing themselves for the worst, Katherine, May and Meredith stood in the cold air entranced, their sophistication forgotten, their faces alight with youthful anticipation.

CHAPTER SEVEN

AT HOME, KATHERINE neglected to mention the acquisition of her first paid employment before she had made her way up the three flights of steps above a bookshop on the King's Road which led to the cramped offices of *Extremity* magazine. You never knew what might happen. Instead she had explained she would be spending the day with Meredith, which seemed at least partially true in that Meredith would be certain to hover in jealous spirit over anything she did in the company of Eddie Tiverton. After all, she could not really be sure if he had meant what he said about a job, and if he did, what it would entail and how much it might pay.

It did not bode well that when she finally pushed open the door, there was no sign of him. The office seemed to consist of three low-ceilinged rooms crowded beneath the eaves of the building, the walls painted in blue and pale green distemper. The only person to be seen in the place was a beautiful, fair-haired woman in a pale pink twinset, painting her nails on the desktop as she read a newspaper.

'Is Mr Tiverton here?'

'No,' she said curtly. 'Who are you?'

'I'm Katherine Scott. He said I should come here about a job.'

'Not another one,' said the girl, returning to her newspaper. 'You'd better sit down there. He's gone for some food.'

With a sinking feeling Katherine perched on the edge of a deep armchair, her handbag on her knees. Her smart heathery tweed suit was scratchy against her legs. She gazed across at the framed back issues of *Extremity*, hung along the wall. Looking covertly at the turned back of the other woman, another awful thought struck her. Suppose this woman was the secretary, and was to be sacked to make way for her. Or just as bad, that Eddie Tiverton had offered her the job last night in a drunken haze, and had forgotten all about it today. So convincing did this idea seem that she was about to get to her feet and leave when she heard clattering on the stairs, and he entered, wearing a black leather jacket which made him look like a New York gangster.

'Have you noticed, Sonia, that pie van is parked outside again? I'm convinced he knows I'm doing a lunch and he's there to pick off the guests who don't agree with my catering.'

The late night at Meredith's party seemed to have made little impression on him. His eyes were bright and lively with humour. Catching sight of Katherine, he beamed and dumped an armful of bags on the floor, holding out a hand.

'Wonderful. You remembered. I'm so glad you came. Have you already met Sonia?' As if he could guess what had passed he gave a grand sweeping gesture and said: 'Sonia Rees, Katherine Scott. I'm hoping she'll agree to be my new secretary.'

'Delighted,' said Sonia, looking Katherine up and down.

'I was rather worried you might be the secretary and I'd been hired by mistake,' volunteered Katherine in a rush.

'Hardly, darling . . .' Now that she stood up Katherine saw that Sonia had a kind of voluptuous, expensive elegance to match her languid drawl and wore a rope of indecently large pearls round her neck. 'I'm a commissioning editor actually.'

'We have to employ Sonia because it's her trust fund that's keeping us afloat,' said Eddie, in a stage whisper, 'but we try to keep her away from the politics because she's a friend of our fascist overlord.'

'Who?'

'The Prince of Wales.'

With his wrinkled little monkey face and his toothy smile, Katherine was none too keen on the future king, but nor had she thought of him as a fascist.

'Why do you call him that?'

'Because he's a Nazi-lover – going round saying we ought to mend fences with the Germans.'

Sonia took an exaggerated drag on her cigarette and puffed the smoke to one side. 'Oh, for heaven's sake, don't listen to him. They are a perfectly sweet couple and they're going to make very good monarchs one day and when they are I'll shop you for high treason, Eddie.'

'That's if we haven't dispensed with the lot of them in a Bolshevik coup first.'

Katherine was unused to this sort of badinage. She wondered how to return the conversation to the subject of her employment. Though it seemed to have been taken for granted that she would be working at the magazine, she would like to formalise her presence.

'If I'm to be your secretary, what would you like me to do?'

'Well, as we're having a lunch today, entertaining can be your first duty.'

Edward disappeared with an armful of daffodils into the back room of the office which had been given over to a kitchen, or rather there was a sink, a chopping board, a tiny stove with three gas rings and lino on the floor. For Katherine, who had imagined her job would involve ringing contributors and discussing the submissions of well-known authors, the thought of preparing a lunch was horrifying. None of the dishes she had been taught at school – duchesse potatoes, fish pie, queen of puddings – seemed appropriate. Agonised, she said: 'How many people will be coming?'

'God knows,' said Sonia. 'Could be two, could be twenty. Seeing as RSVP seems to have gone by the board nowadays and Edward dishes out invitations willy nilly to anyone he meets.' Here she cast a meaningful look at Katherine, who assumed she was included in this undeserving category.

'Because the problem is,' Katherine stumbled on, 'I can't really cook much. I mean I can do things like Victoria sponge and Cabinet pudding and white fish pie with puff pastry, but I don't really think I can cope with a full-blown luncheon. I wasn't really aware it was part of the job.'

'What's not part of the job?' called Edward.

'Katherine is querying the extent of her duties. She can do a nice fish pie, but she needs firm numbers.'

Sonia's was the kind of voice born to give orders to cooks and parlourmaids. Eddie reappeared looking doubtful. 'Well we shall just have to feed off delicious conversation then. That should be perfectly satisfying just so long as you've got some nice titbits of interest, nothing heavy, and plenty of juicy gossip to keep us going.'

An ear-splitting scream distracted them and Katherine muffled a shriek as she felt something warm and heavy drop on her shoulder. She realised it was the marmoset, but the shock of it, with its claws and mad, high pitched chatter made her feel quite dizzy. Watching her, Edward softened.

'Hey, don't worry about it. It's only Maugham.' He picked the animal up and stroked it gently. Following him into the kitchen, Katherine saw with relief a plate of red, bloody steaks.

'Only teasing about lunch by the way. I'm the chef.'

'Oh.' Cursing her naïveté she said: 'Do you always have people to lunch?'

'God, no! Only Thursdays.'

'Edward's still trying to prove that intelligent life exists in London,' Sonia called grandly.

The job was agreed. She would be paid a pound a week to act as Edward Tiverton's assistant, answering the telephone, typing, doing something called sub-editing and possibly helping with an even more technical activity called pasting the pages. She would also be expected, said Edward, to have 'hundreds of ideas' which she should air whenever they came into her head. It was better than she could possibly have expected.

She spent the morning in a blur of opening letters and answering the phone as best she could, while cooking smells rose tantalisingly from the kitchen. From noon onwards, the guests started to drift in. They arrived panting after climbing the stairs, some complaining loudly about the location of the office, all acting as if they owned the place, picking up magazines and newspapers, pouring themselves drinks from a tiny wooden cabinet at the back, putting their feet up on the table. Many of them, it appeared, were 'contributing editors', which put them on Edward's extensive payroll in return for the occasional book review, article, or in the laziest cases a thought about an article, which might one day appear in *Extremity*. Like Edward, many used their clothing to suggest a disdain for convention, which meant they looked unusually grubby, mostly in leather jackets with roll neck sweaters underneath and baggy corduroys. Everyone seemed very much at home. A black and white cat wove its way through their legs, earning a few caresses and Maugham hopped from shoulder to shoulder, but few of them took much notice of Katherine, and as Sonia did not bother to introduce her, no one came over to her desk to talk to her.

Soon, however, she realised that she was required to do very little anyway except listen. Lunch, which was fried steak accompanied by heaps of boiled potatoes and bread, made up for its lack of sophistication by being plentiful. Crammed around the table, fuelled by bottles of cheap red wine, they talked incessantly, mostly about friends, but Katherine could not help noticing they seemed extremely critical. A couple of writers who had decided to emigrate to America were being particularly reviled.

'Thank God they're going. We could do with a little less gloom round here,' said a tall, peaky man with a greased sweep of lank blond hair.

'I hadn't noticed much cheer from you,' said Edward.

'That's because it's my fate to be living in a dull, sterile decade which has been bankrupted by the excesses gone before it and is careering its way to war. Only a madman would be inanely cheerful. But at least I'm not boring. Old Emlyn could bore a channel tunnel.'

'What is this great attraction of the land of the hot-dog anyway?'

'Well, they're not just about to have a war, for a start.'

Another pug-faced man, who ate with his mouth open, was holding forth on the problems of contemporary English fiction.

'Please no more novels about people taking train rides to suburbia, or middle-class people living in genteel poverty in Ealing,' he appealed, the little doughy pouches of his face bunched in an agony of disdain. 'Same goes for all that stuff put out by women novelists. Who wants to know about standing in a queue at the butcher's shop waiting for a couple of pork chops?'

Katherine thought of her own family. She could think of no one more certain to qualify for precisely this type of novel. Yet how indignant they would be if they ever found themselves fictionalised. Even in a story their characters would not conform. They would behave in cross, contrary ways and refuse to co-operate with a happy ending.

'Brute Davis is an absolute personification of the genre. He should be taught in universities. How not to write a novel. Just think of all those poor trees that died.'

'Weren't you rather harsh on his latest effort,' enquired Edward, 'considering you were his best man five years ago?'

'Cruel to be kind, dear chap. One just does so much want to put him out of his misery. He tries to write, but you see, it simply doesn't work. The little characters lie dead on the page, flat as in their coffins, poor things. He coaxes one into a semblance of life, but by the time you get back to them they've expired of neglect.'

'Why does he bother, then?'

'Well, he says novels are the only way of having more than one life. They're his way of creating alternative worlds. The trouble is, all his alternative worlds are exactly like his own world. Everyone in his books has a rather dreary existence living in Palmers Green and worrying whether they can afford to keep two maids and a mistress. In the end they usually they get rid of the mistress and bourgeois moral order is restored.'

The wine flowed and the cigarettes sent their blue coils into the fading bars of afternoon light and the lunch guests showed no signs of going. It didn't look like work, but Katherine noticed that now and again Edward would note down a snippet of conversation on a pad by his elbow, presumably for transformation into a *pensée* or a Topic For Debate in the next issue. *Extremity* welcomed views from all sides, he had explained to Katherine, its only real targets were pretentiousness, hypocrisy and negativity.

'I say. I've got a new guest for our next lunch,' announced one visitor, a cadaverous figure with a red wool scarf which he had not removed throughout the meal. 'He's without doubt the most gifted poet of our generation. He's called Bryn Cadwalladar and I'll bet none of you have ever heard of him.'

'What's he like?'

'Absolute natural genius. Hates politics. He won't have any truck with this nonsense of poetry as propaganda . . .'

'What d'you mean? All art is political!'

'How can you say that?' cut in someone else. 'Art's a moral force. It helps with understanding the workings of the unconscious and gives us greater responsibility over our destiny, but to say it's *per se* political . . .'

'Well, either way,' finished the red scarfed man impatiently, 'it really doesn't matter much because he's certain to die before he's forty.'

'I have heard of him actually,' said the pug man. 'Rather

a horny-handed son of toil, isn't he?'

'Oh, worse than that, he's utterly sordid. He's always rolling drunk in some disgusting pub in Fitzrovia mouthing obscenities. A friend of mine from the BBC was thinking of offering him a programme but took one look and ran back to Broadcasting House. Bryn will insult you soon as look at you. Unless you're a woman that is, in which case he'll try and rape you.'

'It's rather a good job he won't live long then, isn't it,' said Sonia, who apart from Katherine, was the only woman present. Edward, however, nodded quietly and wrote the name down on his pad.

From her seat, squashed in on one of the table corners next to a silent, fat guest whose clothes could do with a wash and the cadaverous man who had a suspiciously consumptive cough, Katherine could see out of the garret window. Dreamily she watched the number eleven bus sail by, the bus she so often took herself on shopping trips down the King's Road. She felt nervous, but happy. Somehow, without realising it, she seemed to have stepped over an invisible threshold into another life, where the number eleven and the price of hats and the worry about whether or not to take an umbrella in case of rain – a prevailing concern of her mother's – simply did not feature. Instead there was benign quarrelling about literature, politics and art, as though what people said didn't just matter, it could actually affect the course of things.

The conversation was so raucous that no one seemed to hear a knock on the outer door, so Katherine slipped out to open it. The late arrival was tall, swathed in a voluminous dark coat and a trilby hat. As he took off his things, Katherine observed his pallid features, so fine they might have been cut out of marble and his blaze of springy, auburn hair.

'Dreadfully sorry I'm late. I'm Lewis. Lewis Appleby.' His large cool hand shook hers, his penetrating eyes were the colour of a chill summer sky. 'I don't think I've seen you here before.'

'I'm the new secretary.'

As she hung up his hat and coat she expected him to stride into the lunch room, but when she turned he was still there, watching her.

'And may I ask your name?'

'Oh, Katherine. Katherine Scott.'

'Have you worked here long?'

'One morning, to be precise.' She gave a nervous laugh.

'From what I know of Edward's crowd, I'm sure that's enough to get the measure of things.'

His effect on the other guests was immediate. They were like a group of boys whose admired older brother had arrived. Someone hastened to pour him a glass of wine, Edward went in search of more food.

'Well, we are honoured,' said Sonia. 'Shove up, everyone, please.'

Obediently they all shifted round to make room at the table, and Lewis Appleby ended up on the seat next to Katherine's. Though he said little, his arrival subtly changed the tone of the conversation. Politics began to be discussed seriously and in earnest. Someone mentioned the German re-armament and the recent reintroduction of conscription there, and opinions instantly divided. There was a vocal minority in favour of accommodation with Germany, including a fey young man called Angus Ffrench, whose abbreviated upper lip and receding chin reminded Katherine of a shark, and who said he did not know why there was such a fuss about fascism.

'It's the most civilised nation on earth after all. My father went just last year and had the most glamorous time. He was received by Ribbentrop and a whole posse of lovely marching storm troopers who stomped around everywhere as an escort.'

His remarks drew a savage response from other guests. In particular, Robert Erskine, a gypsyish-looking artist with moody brown eyes who drew the magazine covers, was passionate: 'My God, Angus. It's an obscenity, the dalliances of people like you. Have you any idea what's going on out there?'

Generally, however, the guests seemed mildly amused that their political opinions divided between opposing extremes. One languid young man, no more than twenty-five, commented: 'I wouldn't be surprised if one day half the occupants of this table were asked to execute the other half. The question is who will be on the side of the victors?' Everybody laughed.

Throughout the conversation, Katherine could not help observing the new guest. The way he sat, his large head bent, allowing the ebb and flow of talk to swell around him, gave him a strange air of *gravitas*. He was, she decided, one of the most handsome men she had seen, his fine, aquiline nose, high forehead and thin, sensitive mouth exuding a sort of nobility. He was – she cast around for the image – like one of the fallen angels from *Paradise Lost*.

Though he had become the centre of attention, Lewis Appleby didn't promote his own views but sat, making his way through a pile of steak and potatoes, listening to the exchange of fire around him. Seated as he was beside her, Katherine knew she should talk to him, but knowing practically no one, and having very little in-depth acquaintance with either literature or current affairs, she was at a loss for anything to say. Suddenly he turned to her: 'And what about you, Miss Scott? Where do you stand on the re-arming of Germany?'

'Oh, I'm not a political animal.'

'Wasn't it Aristotle who said man is by nature a political animal?'

'I can't remember. What I mean to say is, I don't get much chance to be political in Chelsea. Though as far as re-arming goes, I suppose I'm against it.'

He laughed, as though she had made some particularly clever joke and said: 'I entirely sympathise. For the past few months I've been confined in a small room utterly immersed in amphibian reproductive systems so I'm totally out of touch.'

'Is that what you do then, study frogs?'

'Yes, though they're not my sole area of expertise. I'm a biologist. I work at London University.'

'Wasn't it Pope who said the proper study of mankind is man?'

He smiled wryly. '*Touché*. He was probably right, but then biology is all to do with what it means to be human. Part of the reason we study amphibians is for what they tell us about man.'

'Isn't that rather demeaning to the frog?'

'Now you put it that way, perhaps yes.'

At that point he was called on to adjudicate on the relative merits of Laurence Olivier and Charles Laughton and it wasn't until just before he left that they spoke again.

It took another hour to dislodge the rest of the guests – a task Edward had quietly deputed to her. The last to leave, the fat man, who turned out to have gout, had to be winkled from a deep, shabby armchair and physically hauled to the top of the stairs, down which he peered as though it were Beachy Head, muttering over and over, 'No. I simply can't.' When eventually Katherine shoved him down and pushed him out into the darkening afternoon, he asked her to lend him some cab fare and she pretended not to hear.

Back in the office she asked Edward: 'Who exactly is that Lewis Appleby?'

'He's a biologist,' said Edward reflectively. 'Our only scientific contributor, as it happens, and no philistine. I wish he'd invite a few of his colleagues actually. The magazine needs a bit of cultural cross-pollination.'

'Oh, come on, Eddie. Katherine asked who he was. That's no answer.' Draped comfortably in an armchair, her legs looped over the ends, Sonia looked up at her with an enigmatic smile. 'Yes, Lewis Appleby is a terrifyingly clever scientist and he writes books about frogs, for goodness' sake, but he also happens to live in the most beautiful house in Sussex, he's rich, thirty-five and unmarried and that's quite enough for a load of my girlfriends to be in love with him.'

'Really?' Katherine bent her face to her desk.

'Why? What did he say to you?'

'The awful thing is,' said Katherine, 'he asked me to lunch.'

Chapter Eight

Meredith opened her burgundy hand-tooled, leather-bound notebook again and stared down at the blank sheets, wondering what to write. She had brought the notebook specially, to contain the 'Letter from Berlin' for which Eddie had asked, but so far she couldn't think of a word. Eddie had said travel writing was very much the thing just then, just to make sure she illustrated her interior journey as well as the details of city life, local colour, mood, tension, political movements and so on. Could she keep it short, about three thousand words? What on earth did he mean, her 'interior journey'? Meredith didn't have a clue. All she knew was, this visit was not turning out to be nearly so much fun as she'd been promised.

She glanced in the gloomy baroque mirror which hung opposite the desk and her smooth brow puckered as she instinctively moved a hand to her hair. She wondered whether if it was longer she might look a little more artistic. Meredith was too young for lines to mar the fine translucent skin but the sheer weariness of being in a foreign city and having to be polite to people had left shadows under her cheekbones and a subtle darkening beneath her eyes which she hated, unaware that it only increased her grave beauty.

Crossly she looked out of her front room window, down the gravelled drive which led through tall iron gates to a long, grey street, with its fashionable villas set back from the road, all slightly different in their styles, but all uniform in their affluence. The house itself was all right, she supposed, if not exactly tasteful. Set in the smart Dahlem suburb of Berlin, it was overstuffed with huge pieces of Biedermeier furniture which crowded the rooms like large, ponderous guests at a party. The furnishing zeal continued outdoors, where a tennis court and swimming pool jostled for space with a proliferation of topiary in the garden. The Bauers, the married couple who lived here, had met Meredith once or perhaps twice, at least a decade before. Olive Bauer, a plump, flaxen woman in her early thirties, was in fact Irish, the daughter of an old army friend of her father's, who had problematically fallen in love with a handsome young man called Oscar, a manager in a large industrial firm, when he passed on a working visit to England. Despite initial obstacles, their unlikely romance smouldered dangerously on, until Oscar's breeding and his bank balance together were eventually judged sufficient compensation for his unfortunate nationality and a marriage went ahead.

Yet somehow, even Meredith could tell, years of star-crossed love had not translated into untrammelled marital bliss. The lean, good-looking Oscar had acquired a corpulent ripple round his midriff and a ruff of fat round his neck. He also flourished a ratty little moustache, of the kind favoured by senior National Socialists, which aged him and looked faintly ridiculous. Olive had got fatter too, and bored. Though she had formed some firm friendships among the wives of her husband's colleagues, acquired a little dachsund, Lotti, and become a popular figure among her wealthy, card-playing set, who thought it chic to acquire a few words of English over coffee and cakes, she missed her home. She relished the prospect of a little first-hand gossip from England, no matter who brought it. In truth she could hardly remember Meredith when Lady Davenport had first written, suggesting the visit. She hadn't taken much notice of her when they first met, and had only a faint recollection of a rather stand-offish little girl in pigtails, stalking round her father's estate. But by all accounts she had grown up a beauty. Oscar's family was pleased too, thinking that the prospect of a visitor from England signalled that nothing was quite as bad as the Nazi party and the communists and everyone said it would be. Indeed it was rather fashionable to have an English visitor. Some of the most senior people in the party, after all, were zealous hosts.

The problem was Frau Bauer had got pregnant. And ill. Not that it was anything life-threatening, or that her problematic pregnancy had caused Meredith more than a second's concern, but with her hostess laid up Meredith's chances of going out, seeing the celebrated Berlin night life, with its restaurants and bars, indeed of having any fun at all, were seriously diminished. She looked down at her ivory jersey suit and buttoned shoes – specially bought for the trip – and scowled. When she thought of the treats that had been proffered she felt cheated, really. She could have stayed on in the Riviera where there were plenty of parties even this late in the season, but everyone had said how interesting Berlin would be. Even her father, who thought Hitler was an awful little Austrian who had got quite above himself, said it was admirable how Germany had picked itself up by its bootstraps.

That on its own would not have been enough to prise Meredith on to an aeroplane and towards Tempelhof airport, however. She had to admit to herself there was only one person whose approval she craved, Eddie Tiverton. He had said it would be a fascinating experience to visit Berlin, and she felt sure he meant that Meredith would be the more fascinating person for it.

Given that the quality of her companionship had seriously dwindled, Olive had not even been particularly apologetic. She lay confined in bed like a rotund little farm animal, wearing a frilly nightdress and full make-up (she had never quite gone along with the Nazi fashion against cosmetics), with Lotti beside her and a huge pile of magazines and chocolates, despite the fact that she was on a fish and vegetable diet. She was fascinated by the story of Mrs Simpson and the Prince of Wales and asked endless questions on the same theme, seemingly insensible to the bored exasperation in Meredith's answers.

'I hear she goes everywhere absolutely wreathed in jewels. Is she very beautiful? Is he hopelessly infatuated?'

In a flat monotone Meredith fed her the stories of the London scene and the Jubilee celebrations and how the King's Road had been one shimmering mass of red, white and blue. She wasn't really surprised that Olive was so hungry for diversion, given the calibre of the German Frauen she had been introduced to. She had already endured two bridge parties, where most of the women were overdressed and used perfume like a lethal weapon. One in particular, an enormously bosomy woman with a shiny, airtight silver dress like a Zeppelin ship, had taken her aside and attempted to regale her with the joys of the new regime but Meredith's aesthetic sense alone had biased her against it.

Olive may have been an invalid but as she lay there in the light of her pink tasselled lamp, taking endless telephone calls from her friends, she didn't seem to be suffering especially. Nowhere near as much as Meredith was. Meredith had seriously considered wiring her parents and demanding to bring forward her leaving date, except for this beastly 'Letter' thing she had to write. She'd make it up, she thought resentfully, if only she could imagine anything. But she absolutely could not return without it, for to fail Eddie was unthinkable.

Her thoughts were interrupted by Hans, the Bauers' old manservant, tapping on the door with a tray of coffee. She watched him lay it on the side table before waving him away with an irritated sigh. Telling Eddie she could not complete his commission would be too awful. She had so looked forward to attending one of his famous lunches, boasting about the sights she had seen.

Yet what was there to boast about? Meredith was so swathed in the cloak of her own preoccupations that it seemed impossible to reach imaginatively out and observe the life of real Berliners. Friends had told her that Berlin was the most cosmopolitan city in the world, but the long, uniform streets seemed so dreary to her and the poverty was impossible to ignore. Even the famous Unter den Linden did not live up to its name, after Hitler had most of the lime trees cut down to make more room for his processions. She could write about the politics, she supposed. She had seen a march of Nazi youth the other day and thought they looked rather smart, their colourful banners waving in the breeze as they sang the '*Horst Wessel*' song and people along the street giving the Nazi salute with their right arms raised. There were a lot of these marches and meetings, and there seemed to be a restless tension, a sort of mild hysteria about the place. It was a very different approach to what she knew in England. No such gleaming faces and fanatical enthusiasm were in evidence when she accompanied her father on his tours of duty round the Derbyshire Conservative Associations. She tried to remember the details of what her brothers referred to as 'the German situation'. Peter was by far the fiercest about it, saying that since 1933, when Hitler banned other political parties, the country had become a 'police state' and now that conscription had been restored, it was plain Hitler was preparing for war. But Hugo was far more cautious, claiming that the Nazis just wanted to get their country on its feet again and if it wasn't the Nazis it would be the communists so what was wrong with that? Either way, dinner at home had for the last year been absolutely dogged by arguments over the Germans, but mercifully the women usually went out at the point when voices were raised. Her father said that too many people were getting absolutely obsessed about the National Socialists.

Oscar, who was a kind and considerate man, had tried to occupy her. When she wanted to see the tourist sights he showed her the ruined hulk of the Reichstag and the Brandenburg gate. They sat and drank lemon tea under the fluttering swastikas at the Café Kranzler, they went to a concert conducted by Herbert von Karajan and he even drove her out in the car to see the huge neo-classical stadium that was being prepared for the Olympics the following year. More than two thousand workers were being employed round the clock on its construction, he explained. They had taken a year alone to demolish the old stadium, which had been built for an earlier Olympiad and never used. The new place would be the grandest ever to host the Games and a symbol to the whole world of the new Germany. He was terribly proud of it, as if he had been directly involved in its commission and planning, though when she questioned him closely it emerged that all his firm was supplying was the metal sheeting and rivets. As they drove there by the beautiful Grünewald, with its faint drifting fragrance of pine, they saw the street approaching the site being widened and huge green flagpoles already lining the way, bearing blood-red swastika flags to impress the hordes of expected visitors.

★ ★ ★

Hans tapped at the door again, arousing her irritation afresh, but this time he held a telegram in his hand.

'*Bitte? Fräulein Davenport. Ein Telegramm.*'

'Oh. Thank you, Hans.'

She looked immediately at the sender – Ralph Kingsland – and frowned before she remembered. Oh yes, a friend of Hugo's. The telegram was not very forthcoming. In fact it was positively noncommittal: 'Heard you were here. Would you join me for a drink at the Hotel Adlon? Will be in the bar on Saturday at seven. If not, no matter.'

Meredith had heard of the Hotel Adlon. It was across the Pariser Platz from the British Embassy, very smart, and quite the place to stay. Perhaps she would go. It was something to do after all. Ralph Kingsland had been at school with Hugo and had stayed once in the holidays with them when she was about thirteen. She leant back in her big chair, thinking about him. Ralph. A name like a fox's bark. And he even resembled a fox, being a big, russet-headed boy with a sharp intelligent face and a quick wit. A scholarship boy. She remembered how she had beaten him at tennis. He'd been ever so surprised.

She was making her way down to find Hans, to enquire about telegraphing a reply, when she came across Dr Reichmann leaving Olive's room. The doctor, whose daily attendance on Olive seemed wildly excessive to Meredith, was a slender, stooping, earnest-looking figure with a thick shock of black hair threaded with grey which fell into his eyes, prompting a nervous habit of running his fingers constantly through his fringe. His face was pale and the eyes so darkly circled that Meredith, who rarely reflected on the well-being of others, assumed he had been up late with a patient. To her surprise, he indicated that he wanted to speak to her, addressing her in heavily accented English.

'Will you enquire please of Frau Bauer if she wants me to continue visiting her?'

Meredith was surprised. 'She's not completely well yet, is she?'

'No . . .'

'Then why on earth shouldn't she?'

He looked at her strangely.

'You know I am Jewish, Fräulein?'

This made Meredith uncomfortable. 'Well, I'm sure she's very happy with your services.'

As they made their way down the stairs he said: 'You live in England, yes?'

'Yes. I'm just over here on a visit.'

His eyes gained a perceptible tinge of warmth. 'My sons are in England. In London.'

'How nice. Which part?'

'They are living in the north of the city, in Hampstead.'

'Oh, parts of Hampstead are lovely,' said Meredith politely, though she barely knew it.

'Yes, it sounds beautiful . . .'

They had reached the front door.

'Well, good day, Fräulein.'

'Goodbye.' She watched the slight figure trudge up the gravelled drive, then turn left up the long street which led eventually to the city centre.

★ ★ ★

For want of any other diversion, the next day when the doctor visited Olive, she lingered deliberately on the stairs. Between two fingers she twirled her thick blonde hair, which Olive had persuaded her to have cut shorter in a blunt, shining bob. Meredith did not like the style. She thought it made her look like one of the heroines of a Wagner opera. The second she got home, she would have it waved.

'How is Olive?'

'Oh, she's fine. You don't need to be worried about her. Just keeping an eye on the blood pressure, you know.'

Dr Reichmann hesitated in a conversational way so she said: 'Would you like some coffee?'

He seemed startled and looked at his watch.

'I don't know, Fräulein. I mean, yes, that would be most kind.'

She led him into Olive's luxurious morning room, with its pale silk carpet crowded with chairs and occasional tables and every surface covered with picture frames and little pieces of Meissen and tiny porcelain trinkets. The chairs were done in an expensive gold material, to match the curtains, which Meredith considered a touch vulgar. The doctor sat down awkwardly, as though he might leave an imprint, and placed his large, worn bag close to his knees. When Meredith asked Hans for coffee he looked straight ahead of him, not glancing at the servant.

'So your sons are in England. When did they go?'

Almost as soon as she said it, Meredith wondered if she had made a *faux pas*. She knew the Jews were leaving if they could. Oscar had told her in quite matter of fact terms that they were being encouraged to emigrate so that the German people could resume the occupations and take over the property that they once enjoyed. Even before then she had been aware that things were bad for the Jews in all sorts of ways. She had seen the signs outside hotels and bars saying '*Juden Unerwünscht*' and one day she had seen a group of youths throwing stones at a Jewish shop, while a policeman stood idly by.

'My sons left two years ago.'

'And are they also doctors?'

'They hope to become so. One is just sixteen, the other twenty-three.'

Meredith looked at him, startled.

'Sixteen. Oh, but that is so young. Doesn't your wife miss them?'

'Yes. Very much. So do I.'

'Can I ask why you . . . ?'

'Why we did not go too? I could not leave my parents. But that was no reason for our children to stay.'

When it had been decided that the brothers should leave, he explained, the family home was sold at the same time. It had been in a good location, just off the Ku-damm, but it went for a tenth of its value to an Aryan family. The rest of them moved to a much smaller place in a poorer part of Berlin. That in itself had affected his practice. Patients liked a doctor with a good address.

'Of course, we are no longer allowed to be doctors,' he added. 'What I meant to say was medical practitioners. Pfffft.' He made an abrupt, exasperated noise with his mouth. 'You look surprised, Fräulein. That at least is good. I despair for what is happening to this country of mine. It used to be anger, but now my anger has turned into despair. It is like the decline of the terminal patient, whose reactions begin with denial and anger, then move to despair, before ending in acceptance and peace. Except that I hope I will never reach the final stages.' Banging his hands on his knees he drained his coffee cup and got to his feet. 'Now I had better go. I must attend to the patients I have left.'

As he reached the door, he hesitated and stood with his hand on the knob.

'Despite that, if you would be so kind, you must ask Herr and Frau Bauer if they are happy for me to continue visiting Frau Bauer.'

'I said I would. I will. I'm sure there'll be no problem.'

'And, Fräulein, it has been a great pleasure meeting you. I wonder if I could ask of you an enormous favour.'

Meredith looked at the small figure before her, starved of the common nourishment of human courtesy and goodwill, his hair so dark it gleamed like the skin of an aubergine, the eyes bruised by fatigue. She felt a curious mixture of attraction and shame. It seemed impossible to refuse him.

'Sure.'

'I wonder if I could give you a very small package. For my sons from their mother. If you could tell them that we are thinking of them. Letters, you see, go astray . . .'

Meredith found herself in new territory. It was a bit much that she was being asked to act as a postman, but her natural manners were offended by what the doctor had just told her and the indignities that a professional like himself was being subjected to. Though she could not at that moment think out the logistics, how she would get to Hampstead herself and seek out these boys in order to deliver the message, to refuse such a request would be to ally herself with those who were behaving badly. She simply nodded.

'That is very kind of you. I will bring it with me tomorrow.'

* * *

The next day was Saturday. It was scorching hot and Meredith went for an early swim in the pool, but came in and changed hurriedly in order to catch the doctor. She could tell he was there from the murmuring coming from Olive's bedroom, but when the door opened, she was surprised to find another, older man emerge, large and white-haired with a gold watch chain and a highly polished briefcase. He engaged in a whispered conversation with Oscar in the hall downstairs. When he had left she said: 'Where's Herr Doktor Reichmann?'

Otto turned pleasantly. 'Oh hello, Meredith. I hope you had a good swim. That's the new specialist we've engaged.'

'Didn't Olive like Dr Reichmann?'

'Of course Olive liked him. But Herr Doktor Speigel is the acknowledged expert on mothers-to-be. You would not forgive me if I did not get the best Berlin could offer for Olive and Baby. And he has been very encouraging.'

'What about Dr Reichmann then? Will he be coming back?'

'What? Oh, I don't think so. No.'

It must have seemed quite incomprehensible to Oscar that this information caused Meredith to turn with a sulky air and march back up the stairs to her room. When she got there, the door was open, and Hans was standing by the bed. He held out a package to her.

'The doctor. When he came this morning, he left this for you.'

'He did come then?'

'Yes. Herr Bauer explained he would not be needed, so he asked if I could pass this to you.'

Meredith thought she saw a complicit glint in Hans' eye. She wondered if he were a Jew also. He certainly did not look like any of the anti-Semitic caricatures she had seen on posters round the city, but then nor did Dr Reichmann.

'Thank you. I'm grateful.'

The package was small, tightly wrapped in brown paper, with a Hampstead address written in clear, black print. Meredith tucked it into the wardrobe right at the bottom, beneath the smart twin-sets she had barely had the chance to show off and the silk drape, bias-cut evening dress she had not had the opportunity to wear. Somehow she felt glad that she would be in different company that night, even if it was only a courtesy cocktail with Ralph Kingsland, no doubt pumping her for news of Hugo's dull set and the season and relaying thrilling information about the import/export business she had vaguely heard he'd started.

CHAPTER NINE

KATHERINE WRIGGLED HER shoulders against the red plush of the theatre seat and looked up at the gilded ceiling from where garlanded putti peered down on a sea of bobbing, expectant heads. She knew she should be feeling unalloyed pleasure – everyone had been raving about the lean, compelling John Gielgud's performance in *Romeo and Juliet* and she knew it was practically sold out – but instead she had an unsettling feeling of anticipation, as though she were sickening for some mild, childhood disease. She felt she had lost the reins of her life, which was now careering off in directions beyond her control. And all in a matter of a few weeks.

Beside her sat Lewis Appleby, waiting for the play to begin and studying the programme with his peculiar fixed concentration, as though marking an exam paper. How extraordinary that they should be there together, enjoying an evening out just like a real couple. After the theatre, if their few previous outings were anything to go by, they would have a quick supper, then he would hail her a taxi home and bid a swift goodnight, which succeeded very well in maintaining the deception she had mounted on her parents that she was spending the evening at the Battersea flat of May Barnes. Lewis didn't know anything about that of course, indeed he rarely asked about her family, and she was more than happy not to fill him in.

But as the lights dimmed, heads bent and the murmuring voices dropped to an expectant hush, the same disturbing doubt recurred to cloud her pleasure. Why on earth should someone like Lewis Appleby be interested in the company of twenty-year-old Katherine Scott? She was not what you would call beautiful, though nor were the slender oval of her face, her straight nose and grey-blue eyes entirely plain. Her mid-brown hair, cut short and waved on to the nape of her neck, sprung joyously from the prison of its style whenever she ran her fingers distractedly through it. She was the sort of girl whom people said looked 'well' or 'intelligent', rather than 'lovely'.

So the idea that Lewis should be interested in her was a puzzling thought, and it went without saying that Katherine was not the only person to have had it. From the first day, a week after their meeting at the *Extremity* lunch, when Lewis appeared at the office to take her to lunch, little ripples of curiosity and rumour began to spread throughout the staff, and beyond, among contributors and their social circle. Sonia Rees had been the first to air her fascination, fingering her pearls in puzzlement.

'No offence, Katherine darling,' she enquired in her loud Home Counties drawl, 'but what on earth does he see in you?'

Equally mystified, Katherine took no offence. In their brief acquaintance she had grown to like Sonia far more than first impressions led her to expect. After her initial, glacial demeanour melted, Sonia began to treat her rather like a younger sister and during the frequent lulls at the magazine, made more frequent by Sonia's extreme idleness, she had co-opted Katherine in her favourite occupation – going through newspapers and magazines picking out gossipy items about men she had almost married. There seemed to be plenty of them, including a Greek with a shipping line, an ageing aristocrat and an Irishman who owned a string of race horses, and it was hard, Katherine found, to comprehend exactly why Sonia had turned them down.

'He proposed once. On the Riviera, it was, after Belle Livingston's dance,' she would murmur as she flicked the pages, squinting at a small, smudgy photo of someone in black tie. Or, of a duke's son reported to be paying some huge sum for his new wife to renovate their yacht: 'He once told me that the only alternative to my love was to join a contemplative order and let his younger brother inherit. Now look at him.'

Sometimes, the sight of former lovers turned Sonia quite philosophical. 'Not marrying people is such a frightfully irritating mistake to make. One remembers them proposing, prostrate at one's feet, begging and adoring, yet the next time one sees them it's in the *Bystander* and they're being tremendously rich and fêted for their talent. And all the time the promising young thing one has become attached to dwindles into an embittered middle age.'

'There goes Our Lady of Perpetual Disappointment,' jibed

Edward, in a reference to Sonia's Catholicism. 'Don't listen to her, Katherine. She'll sully your youthful optimism.'

Katherine felt genuine empathy with Sonia's missed opportunities, though, and couldn't help wondering why, given her private income and by all accounts a glittering débutante life, she had plumped for Peregrine, the army officer who gaily acquiesced in his own nickname of 'Plank' ('as in thick as' Edward explained).

'I suppose he'll want us to breed before long,' Sonia announced one day, a short associative jump from discussing the imminent arrival of kittens for the office cat.

'Don't you want children?' asked Katherine, intrigued, wondering how, as a Catholic, she had avoided breeding so far but not knowing enough about the subject to ask.

'It isn't a question of wanting. It's mandatory. Peregrine wants an heir,' replied Sonia, as though she had said he wanted a haircut, or a new pair of shoes. 'There's the family to think of.'

'That's right. Someone's got to be lumbered with that freezing pile in Monmouthshire,' explained Edward from his editor's desk. Since the death of Peregrine's father, the couple had come into a craggy, windswept ancestral hall, entirely unencumbered by electricity. Sonia's rigorous attendance of the London social scene was now interrupted by long intervals in Wales, where Peregrine lavished all his love and energy on his inheritance.

Though painfully aware from close observation of her own parents' marriage that the romantic myth was fraying at the edges, Katherine had never heard anyone discuss their feelings for their spouse so freely. She listened with guilty amazement as Sonia explained that her husband, the last in a line of minor Welsh aristocracy, was a dullard and a world-class bore, who only tolerated her working at *Extremity* because he was too dim to read it and recognise its radical politics.

'The only way I cope with marriage is by accepting every single dinner or party invitation that comes my way so that by the time I get home I'm too tipsy to talk,' she told Katherine dramatically.

'People always seem more appealing when you're drunk,' said Edward, 'but no one finds drunks appealing unless they're drunk themselves.'

'Well, there's no need to be appealing to Peregrine anyway,' sniffed Sonia. 'He's far too busy talking about repairing the estate buildings or extending the pasture land or nagging me about going down to Wales for what he calls a nice long stay. Just the thought of it makes me practically weep. All those awful wet hillsides with miserable sheep and their silly Welsh bleats. And the locals, you simply can't imagine. There's no social life, of course. You have to be absolutely desperate for a weekend to traipse out as far as Monmouthshire for a visit; it's not on anyone's way, so only the worst sort come and see us and they stay ages. Really, I'd rather watch paint dry.'

Evidently needing some distraction from her own affairs, the topic of Lewis Appleby was too good for Sonia to resist. She seized on the idea of his 'courtship' and played with it like a cat slowly killing a mouse. Each time she returned to the subject her tone veered unflatteringly between astonishment and unrestrained curiosity.

'He's been unattached for some time of course. He was with Ethel Denvers for years, you know the American girl with the diamond family, but he threw her over apparently. Then there was Amy Townsend, but that was only a fling after her husband left her, and of course he had a thing with the Fettes woman, you know, the historian, Jean, or Joan was it? They say he likes them very brainy.'

Then, with a quizzical look at her, she would continue in a faintly admonishing tone: 'Really, Katherine, a lot of women would kill to be seen with Lewis Appleby. What's your secret?'

After a few days of this, Edward took pity on Katherine. 'Has it not occurred to you, Sonia, that perhaps he just enjoys her company?'

He evidently did, for he asked her out several times, even after their first lunch when she had been so nervous she could barely speak. She had no idea where they would be going, and, with only Sonia's description of his background, thought it might be somewhere impossibly grand, for which she could not hope to be properly dressed. As it turned out it was wet, she had to wear the old mac she'd had at art school and lunch turned out to be a chop at a café in Chelsea, watching the rain stream down the windows while he asked her about her work and the magazine and her painting. Katherine had never before been out with a man of such age and sophistication. She watched the way his long fingers lit their cigarettes, the flame leaping from the tip of his gold lighter, the way his eyes would stray absently from her face as they talked, the lines under them bespeaking some unbearable sadness. ('Unbearable sadness? What's he got to be unbearably sad about?' Sonia had questioned sharply when Katherine confided this small detail to her. 'Inheritance tax?')

He did not seem to doubt that she would want to be with him, though he seemed to have little time for Eddie's other friends. When she chatted about the people she had met through *Extremity*, with their outspoken political sympathies ranged at each end of the spectrum, he gave a dismissive flick of the hand.

'Oh, these radical creeds are so exciting to the young. Communism, fascism, and the rest, but they're dangerous.'

'Why?'

'They need enemies to keep going. They feed on hate.'

'Where do you come down then? You have to take a stand, don't you?'

'Pragmatism is the only political philosophy I'd swear by. That and looking after your country. Why do you ask? You're not on one of those bandwagons are you?'

'No.'

'Good. That's what I like about you. You're free of serious prejudice.'

Katherine did not necessarily think that this did full justice to her views, but, given Lewis' passing confirmation that he did actually like her, she decided not to argue. She clung to this comment all the more, because throughout their meetings he had given no physical intimation that he regarded her as any more than a casual acquaintance. Indeed he had barely touched her. The odd steer of the elbow maybe, the brush of a hand on her shoulder, and just once he had bestowed the briefest of farewell kisses on the cheek. But nothing more. Was this what courtship was like then? She felt scarcely flesh and blood with him, hardly a woman at all, more like something abstract, an alibi perhaps. She imagined some caricature policeman saying: 'He spent the evening with a young lady, m'lud. She was a cast-iron alibi.'

Katherine didn't tell anyone this of course. She rather enjoyed revelling in the envy of Sonia and the new-found attention which visiting contributors would pay her on account of her alliance. But each time he turned up at the magazine's offices and enquired whether she would like to come for dinner, or to a film, she felt a greater, dragging sense of disquiet. This wasn't how she had imagined it would be.

That evening he was just the same. Throughout the play he sat rigorously at her side, watching with a tiny frown, as though he were observing some esoteric ritual fostered by a faraway tribe. After an awkward time in the interval, during which Katherine ate an ice, and Lewis read a newspaper which had been folded away in his pocket, they watched the second half in similar silence. Afterwards, they went out of the theatre and he stood on the steps, apparently oblivious to the crowds parting around him.

'I suppose we should have some supper now,' he said slowly, as though pondering some particularly intractable algebraic problem.

Suddenly, for Katherine, the stark contrast between Lewis' abstraction and the conventional passion of Gielgud's Romeo was tauntingly obvious. She hadn't asked Lewis to take her out. She had not, even in the skewered terminology of her father's world view, exactly 'thrown herself' at him. He obviously found her dull. Compared to this she would rather be at home with her parents, with the younger children pestering and asking for help with their schoolwork. Almost.

'Well, actually, I don't really want supper. I think I'd better be getting home. Thank you so much for the play, Lewis.' She swivelled on her heel and headed to the Strand, where she hoped to catch a bus home.

She managed to get halfway down the street before she heard the pounding steps behind her, and he caught her up. He put his hands on her shoulders to stop her.

'Do you have to walk so fast?'

'Please let me go.'

His eyes crinkled in amusement, but his tone was grave. 'I'm extremely sorry. Please don't go. I've been terribly rude. The fact is, I've been absolutely absorbed in an idea for my next book.'

85

Though the streets were fairly full of people leaving theatres and restaurants and public houses, it was dark where they stood, at the entrance to a side street off the Strand, in a void where the two adjoining pools of lamplight failed to meet. Katherine looked away, shuffling feet which were aching in her highest heels.

'It was unforgivable of me but I thought you understood. You're different from other women I've known. I thought you didn't mind going without constant chatter. Come here.'

He pulled her towards him and made to kiss her, but either surprise or embarrassment at her own petulance caused Katherine to push him away.

'No. Please, don't.'

He took a step back, stiffly. 'Sorry. You looked very fetching like that. In the darkness.'

'I don't know if I should take that as a compliment.'

There was a pause, then they both laughed, and the awkward moment seemed over. Linking his arm through hers, he said: 'Do please come and have some supper with me.'

'Well . . .'

'Let's just hop into the Ritz.'

Katherine, who had never been in the Ritz, let alone hopped in there, was instantly cautious.

'Oh no. It's far too . . .'

'You're right, much too fusty. All right, what about the Café Royal? You've time just for a quick dinner.'

Later, when they were seated on the spindly gold chairs waiting for a waitress to arrive, he said: 'You know, I was rather hoping you'd agree to come and visit my home. This weekend would be good, because there's no one coming down then.'

'Fallings?'

The instant she said it, she knew her tone betrayed her. She knew that she could not conceal her wide-eyed, touristy delight at the prospect of seeing the house whose setting Sonia had so lovingly conjured for her – the façade with its elegant, flinty beauty, the lawns sweeping away to distant woodland, the famous garden with its unrivalled collection of rare, old roses. But even as she thought of it, she knew her hopes were quite futile. The chances of her parents allowing her to visit unchaperoned the home of an older, unmarried man were virtually nil. Even given their love–hate relationship with any people richer and more landed than themselves, they did not share the liberal outlook of the *Extremity* offices. And why was it good that no one else should be there? While she was pondering that, Lewis, as if reading her mind, added: 'Is there a friend of yours who might like to come too?'

★ ★ ★

So it was that the following weekend Katherine had her first sight of Fallings in the company of May Barnes. May had been only too pleased at the invitation and had chatted irrepressibly all the way down in the train, seemingly oblivious to Katherine's nervous silence. But when they reached the station and Lewis met them off the train in a little open-top red Buick, to her relief he seemed subtly changed from his London self, somehow less preoccupied, rejuvenated in an unfamiliar open-necked shirt and worn old sports jacket. She sat in the front seat beside him as they sped along, her hair a dark flag in the wind, exchanging shouts in the streaming air. When they breasted the hill and got their first sight of the house before them, Katherine, who had been training herself to confine her reactions to polite interest, could not conceal her enthusiasm.

'Oh, it's wonderful, Lewis. The most beautiful place.'

He seemed gratified. 'Isn't it? It's where I come when I need to work properly. There's some special ingredient in the air which aids concentration. A sort of extra oxygen, it seems like.'

'Is it old?'

'It's been in the family since 1687. The Applebys were farmers to start with, so originally this was just a farmhouse. Then one of my ancestors diversified into the tea business, began importing tea and got richer, so it became a little more grand in the Georgian era. Then there were Regency additions and a little bit more was stuck on at the end of the century. But after that came Lloyd George and his death duties, with the result that since my father died, it's badly in need of repairs and I'm going have to think seriously about shutting it up. The house is rather large for just one person to be rattling about it.'

Anxious to divert him from these melancholy speculations, Katherine said: 'The gardens are wonderful.'

'Yes, aren't they? They were all my mother's work.

Fortunately for me, as it turned out, because they were my inspiration.'

'You mean you're interested in gardening?' asked May politely from the back seat.

'No no, I mean that my mother introduced me to botany, and it was by way of plants that I became interested in biology. A bit like Gregor Mendel.'

'The monk who studied pea plants?' ventured Katherine, her memory hazy.

'That's right. Peas were what he used to discover the whole basis of what is now called genetics. How we inherit character-istics from our parents.'

May, in the back of the car, could not catch all the conversation. 'Do you grow peas then?'

'Not at all actually. My mother thought them rather more suited to cottages. There are some in the kitchen garden, I think.'

They pulled into the drive and he unloaded their bags from the car. Katherine had not known what to expect – she had half imagined some aged retainer would be there to greet them – but instead Lewis pushed the heavy oak door open himself and took them into the dark, shiny hall, showing the carved wood and the scrolled oak on the stairs with unguarded pride. He was right – the place did seem cavernously large for one person, smelling of vacancy and old varnish, yet his affection for the house was evident. As they went from room to room, May and Katherine's expressions of delight at the tapestry chairs and the fireplaces and the ornate ceilings were quietly accepted by him, as though they were expected, and no more than due. When he showed them his study, a long room perfumed with the must of old books which lined the shelves from floor to ceiling, and furnished simply with a desk and a pair of scratched leather chairs, Katherine longed to look over at his papers, to see what he was writing, but felt his eye upon her and did not dare. Then there was the library and as they cooed with admiration and he mounted a ladder to fetch down some precious ancient volumes, Katherine caught her reflection in a spotted, pewtery mirror. She saw a gawky figure, younger even than her age to look at, in a dull blue dress and cardigan, with windswept brown hair and she felt a momentary stab of dismay. She looked like a girl on a school outing being kindly shown around by the host.

'I'll show you two to your rooms, and then we'll find you some food,' said Lewis. 'There's no one here to get lunch but Mrs Mullins has left a picnic. It's too cold for a swim, but afterwards I thought you might like to see around the grounds. There's a farm attached to this house, I can show you. If you know anyone who wants a retriever, there're some new puppies just arrived.'

Their rooms were on the south side of the house and May and Katherine waited until he was out of sight before allowing themselves to explore properly. May's room was exquisite, papered with tiny knotted flowers and flooded with sunlight. Katherine's room, painted light green, was dominated by a huge bed. In one wall was a small door which she assumed to be a cupboard until she opened it to find her own white-tiled bathroom, with a huge, claw-footed bath, big enough to sink in, and a handsome panelled shower.

She hadn't known what to pack, not that her wardrobe afforded her much opportunity for variety. May said she was wearing the riding jacket she'd brought in the hope that horses might be available. Katherine urgently hoped they weren't.

'Let's pray there's no one else turning up. I haven't packed anything remotely suitable for a dinner,' she said, excavating the scant contents of her suitcase which looked all the more paltry spread across the expanse of the bed.

'I daresay he wants to keep us for himself. Perhaps he's planning to seduce us both in turn,' giggled May, bouncing on the mattress and adjusting her stockings. She seemed to be treating the whole thing like a huge joke. Katherine did not know what to think.

To their surprise when they descended the stairs, however, they found a group of people standing in the hall with tennis racquets. A freckle-faced girl in her twenties with hair tied back in a ponytail and two ginger-headed men, obviously brothers, grinned up at them.

'This is Antonia and Simon Franklin, they rent the farm,' said Lewis. 'And this is Simon's brother Robin. They've come up to use the court.'

The young couple seemed on sociable terms with Lewis. The young man called Robin turned to the girls and said:

'Either of you two any good with the old racquet? We could do with some more players.'

'Ooh, I'd love to,' said May without hesitation.

'Great! Doubles. You've made my day,' said Robin. 'We've got plenty of spare racquets to choose from.'

'Do you want to play, Katherine?' Lewis was eyeing her impassively, his hands on his hips.

'Er, no. I'd love to see round the grounds, if that's all right.'

'Fine. We'll join you lot later, then.'

★ ★ ★

Had he engineered this, diverting May so that he could get her alone? If so, he showed no sign of it. He strode ahead of Katherine, causing her to walk rather breathlessly, slightly faster than normal, as he pointed out each aspect of the grounds.

'That's the knot garden. It's from a design of one at Hatfield House . . . That woodland over there was planted well over a hundred years ago, by my great grandfather. At one point they thought of making their own tea crates, but they grew the wrong kind of timber . . . That's an outhouse I'm having converted for a laboratory.'

They walked away from the house up the herbaceous path, to where the woodland met the grounds and as they passed through the trees he said: 'Here. There's something I want to show you.'

It was a ruined grotto, almost like a summerhouse on the outside, round and made of white stone, supported by classical pillars. As they stepped inside, it took Katherine a moment to realise that the elaborate designs which covered every inch of the walls were composed of shells. Or mostly they were, because centuries of decay had dulled them and wide patches of plaster showed through where shells hung off or had fallen underfoot. Lewis swept his hand over the cobbled curves possessively, as though they were flesh.

'One day I'll restore this. It's our shell house. It's one of the finest examples of early eighteenth-century shell work surviving. It took thousands and thousands of shells to build it; they had to ship them in for years from Jamaica and Barbados. The housekeeping records from that period are still in the library and they have all the details – it makes fascinating reading.

Considering what care it took to construct, it deserves someone taking an effort to restore it, too.'

Katherine touched the shells tentatively, afraid to dislodge any more. The place was studded with them, wide scallops and razorshells and tiny black whelks, forming flowers and crosses and diamonds, arching over the windows in elegant swirls, set in fantastic shapes. Despite the neglect and the dirt, their ribs and ridges still gave off a pearly glimmer in the afternoon light, the slate glint of mussels, the coral conches and oysters' oily swirls recreating the far, opalescent sea cave they might once have occupied. Katherine imagined the shells shuffling for years in the underwater tide, before being netted, dried and purged of the living creatures within them. And now they were meeting their final decay as white shards to be crunched underfoot. Already the floor's design was entirely destroyed. She picked up a conch and pressed its pink sibilant lip against her ear, hearing the shell's eternal tinnitus.

'If you can hear the sea it's because it's only a few miles south from here. This grotto was placed in a direct line between the house and the coast, though the woodland grew and obscured any view you might have had. See here.'

He gestured to a panel in the wall studded with fossils. Some were recognisable sorts of things, like scallops, snails and corals fractured and riddled like brains, but others were merely the ghostly shapes of something once alive, imprisoned in rock or their faint carapaces imprinted on hunks of flint, fragments of frozen memory.

'These are all local,' Lewis explained, running his finger along them. 'The coast near here is particularly rich in finds from the cretaceous period – that's around a hundred million years ago. I used to find them on the beach when I was a boy.'

'What a wonderful place.' She regarded the shell in the palm of her hand, feeling with her finger its cochlear depths, tracing the pattern of intricate emptiness.

'Yes. It's very appealing.' Lewis was surveying the ceiling. 'In the eighteenth century they were very taken with improving nature through man's artistry. They liked the idea of control it gave them, the notion of perfecting what God had provided. Shells and fossils were a particular fad apparently, because of their precision and symmetry. Elena Appleby loved them anyway.'

'Was she the person who built it?'

'Yes. She has a rather romantic story. She was the daughter of a French nobleman who came to live in England and married an Appleby ancestor. She grew up by the sea, and shells reminded her of her childhood, so they said. Unfortunately, it ended rather unhappily for her because she fell in love again, with a merchant, one of those supplying the shells as it happened, and planned to run away with him. As it turned out their affair was discovered.'

'What happened to her?' asked Katherine, transfixed.

'You mean did her husband murder her in a fit of passion?' He regarded Katherine with an amused eye. 'Nothing so dramatic, I'm afraid. My ancestor, Roderick Appleby, confined her to base and refused to let her travel to London any more. They do say when she died her ghost returned to haunt the house, though I assure you I have never heard a squeak out of it, if it does.'

'Do you believe in ghosts?'

He looked at her for a moment, then burst into laughter. 'What do you think?'

They walked back down to the house, passed through the kitchen garden whose walls, beneath a burst of blush pink clematis, created a sheltered sunny spot, and opened the gate to the fields beyond. The farm was almost a mile from the house, through some uncomfortably muddy grassland, and up a long track. He took her to the stables, where the promised puppies were, cushioned in a corner deep with hay, rolling over their mother and chasing their tiny tails, all sharp teeth and excited ears. He knelt to caress them.

'Aren't they grand? There girl,' he patted the mother, 'let's have a look at your little ones.' He took hold of one dog, the biggest of the litter, who had jumped up to his knee, and held him up in the air.

'What about this one, Katherine? He's a fine fellow. Would you like to have him?'

'Oh. Not really, I couldn't.'

'They're pedigree, you know. No mongrels.'

Katherine picked up the tiniest of the puppies, a black and

tan ball of fluff who had been sniffing her foot.

'This one's gorgeous.'

'He is, but you don't want him. That's the runt. This one would make the better pet.'

Katherine looked at the puppy, wriggling and whining in his large hands, with its rolls of plump skin.

'What's wrong with the runt?'

'He might not survive, that's all. Here take this chap.'

He handed her the large puppy. 'No. Really, I don't want it.'

He gave her a quizzical look, put the dog down without a word, and meandered out into the sunlight. Katherine hurried after him, cursing herself for spoiling the moment for the sake of a silly argument. A tendency her father had noted and was always particularly keen to criticise.

Fortunately Antonia, Robin and Simon returned for tea then stayed late, lounging on the lawn, playing card games and smoking cigarettes. The Franklins were a friendly couple who had thrown up jobs in London to come to the country and run a farm.

'We're so lucky we met up with Lewis. It's a treat for us to be gallivanting round his tennis court,' Simon told Katherine. 'The idea was that we would both write fabulous novels at night, but the fact is there's such a huge amount of work to do on the farm that by the evening we're so wrecked we're normally capable of nothing more than downing a few glasses of drink and collapsing in bed. We've just thrown the towel in and hired help, which we can't afford, and we're way behind with the rent, but it does mean we have rather more fun.'

It turned out that they had horses, and were planning a ride in the morning, much to May's delight. With this in prospect, after supper May excused herself early, pleading exhaustion due to country air. She left Katherine and Lewis in the huge drawing room, a banked fire sinking into its embers in the ornate stone fireplace.

Lewis sprawled on a chintz sofa before the fire, his legs extended, his features softened and enigmatic in the flickering light. Katherine sat before him on a small needlework chair. He'd fetched them brandies after their coffee and she savoured the invigorating fumes with their mysterious, masculine potency. Around them the old house creaked and eased into rest. In the grate the logs spat and shifted and from outside came the sharp yelp of foxes and an owl's odd swooping cry. Katherine had viewed May's departure with a quiver of apprehension. Since the episode in the Strand he had not touched her again, and she wondered if he had taken it as a definitive rejection.

'You look very serious, Lewis.'

'Do I? I'm sorry. I'm thinking about what will happen to this place when war comes. We'll have to shut it up, I suppose. The taxes are hard enough to cope with as it is.'

'Don't you mean if war comes?'

'Oh, it's coming all right, I'm sure of that. The question is, how do we prepare for it? How do we ensure that we're not looking the other way, or cowed into defence when it arrives? The whole country seems to be sleepwalking and the danger is it's going to wake up to find itself in the midst of a real nightmare.'

Just at that moment, Katherine thought, war could not seem further from this quiet house, embedded in its setting like a stone jutting from a mossy hill. Fallings was like an anchor, mired in the mud of its fields, caught in the cleft of the Sussex downs.

'Well, I don't think there'll be another war. Far too many sensible people are devoted to preventing it.'

'That's what I like to hear. Incurable optimism. Mankind's most valuable characteristic.'

He rose and approached her, pulled her to her feet and encircled her in his arms. She laid her head against his warm chest and rested there for a moment, before he pulled her gently back to study her face with his pale, searching eyes.

'I hope I've been an adequate host. You are all right, aren't you?'

'Yes. I'm all right.'

'Well, I suppose I should say goodnight then. Is there anything you need for your room?'

'No. It's all lovely.'

He bent down and gave her a chaste kiss on the forehead.

★ ★ ★

The next morning she woke very early. She had decided against drawing the velvet curtains in her room and the sunlight was dancing on her face, prising her eyelids apart. Around seven there was a tap at the door and an old, smiling woman, whom she took to be Mrs Mullins, came in with a cup and saucer.

'I've brought you tea, miss. Breakfast is ready down in the dining room when you feel like it.'

But after she had scrubbed her skin, scrambled into a dress and cardigan, drawn a comb through her hair and run down the stairs to head for the red dining room, he was standing there already, dressed in a thick woollen jumper, waiting for her at the front door.

'Good. You're here. I had Mrs Mullins wake you early. Let's leave breakfast till later. I want to show you somewhere special.'

The air was so fresh it stung the face. At this hour, when the ashy blue of dawn was still receding, the grass cobwebbed with dew, the silence unbroken by tractors or dogs, Fallings was possessed of an almost mathematical calm. Everything was in its right place, architecture and environment matched like a perfect equation, conveying a cloistered air of academic serenity. Even the grey sculpted griffins along the rose walk seemed intellectually focused, their faces contorted into sombre little frowns of concentration. As they walked up towards the wood which Lewis Appleby's great grandfather had planted, Katherine thought that this place, with its life, its own traditions, history and rituals, seemed almost more real than herself. Its gardeners knew which roses went where, which trees in the orchard gave the best fruit, which summer bedding plants belonged in each position, as they had for generations before. Katherine barely knew what she would be doing from one day to the next.

Lewis walked with the assurance of one who knew his land like his own flesh. In the woods, the wide path winding between the pines was shaded in a green sepulchral light, the air stirred only by the rustles of birds and small creatures. They came out in a small clearing where a narrow pond glinted. Something, a frog or a fish, disappeared with a gulp at their arrival, leaving a wrinkle in the surface like linen. It looked so fresh, she could almost feel it clothe her limbs. She bent down and put a hand in but the water was sharp as a scalpel.

'Oh, it's cold.'

'No, it's wonderful. Very bracing. I used to come swimming here.'

For a moment Katherine's future seemed to stretch out before her like the dappled surface of that pond, untrammelled, waiting for action or intervention. But when she looked into it, the water receded into mottled depths, like a clouded crystal ball. She felt strangely separated from herself, as if she was watching a character from a long way away, one for whom she had only sporadic sympathy.

'Do you like Fallings, then?' he asked, looking into the pond.

'It's the most beautiful place I've ever seen.'

With anyone else, it might have been a polite exchange of courtesies between host and guest, but Katherine knew this was far more than a routine pleasantry. She knew her answer was an all-important expression of consent. It was only then that he bent to her, grasping her shoulders a little too tight, and gave her a hard, surprising kiss.

Chapter Ten

Ralph Kingsland curled his hand around another scotch and soda and reflected just what a spoilt, arrogant, unappealing person Meredith Davenport had been. He had fortuitously avoided her company since they had met, years ago on her father's drab, rain-sodden estate, but by all accounts her personality had not undergone any kind of sea change. It pained him to remember that holiday, the first after his mother died, when he had been invited down to Hugo's home out of pity while his father closeted himself in the house, withdrawing into his grief. It was a bleak time. His previous holidays kicking his heels round his parents' Victorian vicarage had barely equipped him to cope with Hugo's overbearing family or the sheer scale of the Davenport stately home. His lasting impression of it was as a huge, redbrick monstrosity surrounded by thousands of tussocky acres where rugged little sheep grazed in the constant drizzle and where some days he had quietly locked himself away in his room and some nights he had cried silently before sleep. Hugo was a good friend, decent, self-deprecating and always on for a laugh, so it amazed Ralph to meet this awful sister with all her airs and graces. She could only have been thirteen, but the adult woman was already visible within her. And first impressions had proved right, according to the odd magazine photograph he had seen of her since. She grew up thin as a rake with high Slavic cheekbones, eyes like chips of flint and that haughty, mannequin beauty which came with a look sour enough to curdle cream. She was athletic enough – she beat him at tennis once, he remembered, walking off the court with a tiny smirk of satisfaction, her neat French plait and her white dress barely ruffled. But it was not that which prompted his avoidance of Meredith all these years. If he was honest, his dislike of her was linked to an episode he preferred not to recall.

It had been another of those rainy afternoons during his stay when he had planned to retire to his room and finish a long, humiliating letter to his father, begging to come home and relating the horror of the Davenport household and the ghastliness of the family members. To his surprise as he opened the door to his room he found Meredith there, the unfinished letter spread on the desk before her. She gave no sign of whether she had read it, bar a secretive smile as she passed him and walked silently out of the room. Understandably Ralph never challenged her over the incident, nor did she ever mention it, yet still the thought of it alone was enough to make him feel positively aggressive.

This was not good, however. It was almost seven and she was due to arrive. He looked around the bar of the hotel to ensure she was not already waiting. It was a high-class place, spacious and quiet, with tall glinting mirrors, thick carpets and velvet curtains to shut out the bustle of the Berlin streets. Neatly uniformed bell boys manoeuvred cases almost as big as themselves up and down the stairs and smart waiters glided to and from guests bearing huge, foaming tankards of the local beer. The hotel attracted a big international clientele, as well as foreign correspondents and staff from the British Embassy across the way, but that evening the waiters were being particularly attentive towards the group of men in brown shirts and black boots – stormtrooper members of the SA – who were occupying a couple of tables in the centre of the room, drinking and laughing with loud disregard for the conversations of others.

He saw her first, and so had the advantage, as she hesitated in the doorway of the bar, scanning the faces for one she recognised. Caught unawares she looked less glacial and poised than he remembered – her bloodless features softened by a slight tan. She carried herself in a proud, upright way, which Ralph perceived as superior, though it was in fact the legacy of early ballet lessons, abandoned when she grew too tall. She wore a tight-fitting suit of some dark blue material that showed every detail of her scrawny form and she'd had her blonde hair bobbed short, like a German, but otherwise she was unmistakable. He wondered why she did not come over directly until he realised that his was not the only face turned towards her and that perhaps he had changed himself since then.

Ralph was not a man who thought much about his appearance. When he ran his hand over his close-cropped copper hair and splashed cold water over his sharp, freckled face in the morning, he looked as sleek as an otter shaking the drops from its pelt. But he did not waste time gazing into the mirror. Something about the extreme self-reliance forced on him when his relations had dwindled to one bred in him an air of utter assurance. He had women, now and then, when he wanted them, friendly, uncomplicated types, but he never stopped to consider whether his lean frame with its tough punctuation of muscle was attractive to them. He was simply not used to worrying about what women thought. Yet as he sat there in his pressed linen suit, fixing another French cigarette into his ebony holder, he realised he must present quite a change from the rumpled, miserable sixteen-year-old Kingsland whom Meredith had last seen.

Reluctantly he lifted a hand and she stalked over, proffering him her hand with a tight little smile.

'I'm so glad you could come.'

'Well, I was just passing, so I thought I'd look in.'

This was not entirely untrue. Meredith had also embarked on a shopping trip so that if the drink with Ralph Kingsland was a complete disaster, she would not have wasted her journey. She had rather enjoyed exploring Leipziger Strasse, a big Berlin shopping street, bounded on one end by Goering's newly erected air ministry and beyond it the bustle of Potsdamer Platz. She had tried on numerous hats at one of the big department stores there but liked none of them. There was something so dreadfully hearty about Germanic fashion, and the current vogue for dresses inspired by old folk costumes was too awful for words. After a brief restorative coffee at the Café Berlin she had walked lazily up Wilhelmstrasse, the political heart of the city, where the chancellery, justice, foreign and other ministries were sited, to the Hotel Adlon, careful to ensure she was not there on time. Now she installed herself in a plush velvet armchair, took one of Ralph's cigarettes and bent her head to his neat gold lighter. He ordered her a pink gin.

'I had no idea you were here.' She still spoke with that maddening drawl, which she presumably equated with sophistication.

'Yes. And when I heard from Hugo you were visiting, I thought I must look you up.'

Even though he'd practised this line, it still sounded unconvincing. Ralph recalled Hugo's politely restrained amazement when he had called requesting his sister's address in Berlin. She eyed him, curiously.

'It must be . . .'

'Eight years,' he said a shade too swiftly.

They discussed Hugo's lack of progress at the stockbroking firm where he worked. The thing about Hugo was, everyone loved him, but his life of golfing and weekend parties with other stockbrokers was not the ideal material for gossip.

'And what exactly do you do now?'

'Well, I have a little business importing and exporting books throughout Europe. I bring in books wanted here, and I take back with me all the latest foreign finds and distribute them to a circle of booksellers.'

'How interesting.' The wide eyes held his gaze steadily, the insolence in them submerged deep beneath their cool, grey surface.

'It is a bit at the moment actually. It's getting rather hairy in fact. All sorts of authors are off the menu – or more particularly one sort . . .' She looked blank. 'You've heard about the book burnings here, haven't you? The ones the Nazis organised in Opernplatz a couple of years ago? The destruction of literature antithetical to the spirit of the Reich? It means it's become awfully difficult to trade in a great variety of German literature – no Thomas Mann, nothing written by Jews or leftists . . .'

Meredith shook her head airily. No, she had not heard of this. Ralph realised that he had an uphill task in hand. And yet . . . perhaps this made things easier.

'Are you enjoying Berlin, then?' he asked.

Meredith was still unsure. She could hardly tell him she was bored to tears.

'It's wonderful. I met some people from the British Embassy at dinner the other night and they were very impressed with the regime. They said it had quite transformed the city.'

'Yes. Indeed it has.' That much was true. 'Have you seen much?'

'Not really. Olive's pregnant,' she said this accusingly, as though the conception of the young Bauer had been actively orchestrated to frustrate her plans. 'And she's ill with it, so I've been left with Oscar – her husband – taking me round.'

'Oh dear. Nothing serious I hope?'

'What? Oh no, I don't think so. She seems perfectly all right to me. But it means I haven't been able to see half what I hoped for.'

'How tiresome for you. Are you staying long?'

'I'm here for another week. I'm completing a piece for *Extremity* magazine.' Even though it was hardly worth it for Ralph Kingsland, she knew this would impress him.

'*Extremity*, eh?' he looked at her with fresh interest.

'Yes, Eddie Tiverton – the editor – wants me to be a regular correspondent. Have you met Eddie?'

'Afraid not.'

'Oh, he's simply wonderful.' Days of unloading Eddie's virtues to Olive, in the absence of any other diversion, had elevated him further in Meredith's mind, bestowing on him the looks of a young Adonis, the wit of Oscar Wilde and a dazzling literary glamour his friends would not have recognised. The fact that Ralph Kingsland didn't know him – well, he hardly moved in those circles – meant she could embroider as much as she pleased. 'Eddie's tremendously talented himself, considering how young he is. I'm sure he's going to be very famous one day. He's friends with all the major writers – people whose books you've probably sold,' she added generously.

Something – the eulogy for Eddie Tiverton, or the slight to Ralph's trade as bookseller – stirred his aggression again. He felt a cruelty coming on.

'And what angle are you taking in your piece?'

Meredith was not keen to expand on this topic. She paused to blow cigarette smoke out of the side of her mouth.

'Oh, my personal impressions of Berlin, my interior journey, that sort of thing.' She turned her attention to her gin, her eyes flitting round the room to signal that she was slightly bored.

'And where has your interior journey taken you?' He seemed deadpan. She could not tell if he was mocking her.

She gave a sigh. 'Well, it's a tremendously complex picture, Mr Kingsland.'

'Oh, Ralph, please.'

'Are you always this inquisitive, Ralph?'

'Only when I'm interested, Meredith.'

101

If Meredith was not ready to paint a true picture of her time in Berlin, then nor was Ralph Kingsland. In particular he had omitted to tell her about the private 'detective agency' established by Sir Robert Vansittart, the permanent under secretary at the Foreign Office, through which a string of businessmen in Europe liaised with the British secret services in charting the rise of German militarism. Sometimes the men back home arranged for newspapers to take on a foreign correspondent, to feed back information, sometimes they were interested in more mundane enterprises, like Ralph's modest book business. Most of the men were German opponents of Nazism, but others like Ralph were merely much-travelled Britons, fluent in German and well placed to observe the build up of German forces, to examine their preparations, if such they were, for war, and the readiness of their munitions, aircraft and naval industries to reinforce any aggressive intent. Hitler had recently been boasting of the strength of the Luftwaffe and his comments had alarmed Whitehall enough to redouble its efforts to gain intelligence on German air forces. Though the Versailles treaty only allowed Germany defensive weapons, everyone knew that tanks, artillery and aircraft were being assembled. Estimates of the number of trained German pilots varied wildly, as did assessments of the time it would take to build up a front-line strength of aircraft. The Foreign Office was anxious to get a clearer picture and Ralph had been more than keen to co-operate. Since Baldwin's election, Ralph felt with relief that Britain was sure to move faster in rearming, and that was a badly needed move after the crazy naval accord which had allowed Hitler to build up the German navy, in open defiance of controls in the Treaty of Versailles.

In this line of work any snippet of information could be useful – one agent had even been detailed to bring back packets of condoms, to assess the quality of the rubber content. Ralph's present task was considerably less amusing. The name of Oscar Bauer had come up because of the division he controlled in Roteberg's, the industrial component manufacturer, which was believed to be making parts to put the Luftwaffe on a war footing. He was known to be friendly with some of the senior people in the Nazi party, in particular Joachim von Ribbentrop, Hitler's cold, domineering minister of foreign policy, who lived practically opposite the Bauer home. He was also known to have an Irish wife, and a brother who was married to a Jewish woman. It was possible, just possible, that a useful link might be made. Once it emerged that Bauer had a young English girl staying, and that she was a past acquaintance of Ralph's, his fate was sealed. It was up to him to engineer a meeting with Bauer and extract as much information as he could. The only question was, how? Would he have to invite the Bauers out, with Meredith, or would he, through her, be able to inveigle an invitation to the house? Either way, it involved being quite nauseatingly nice to Hugo's dreadful younger sister, but he supposed that was all in the line of duty.

'Have you had a good summer up until now, then?'

'Oh yes, I had a marvellous time at Cannes. There were parties practically every night. Letty Feldman – you must know Letty, everyone knows her . . .'

'Afraid I don't.'

'Well, she had the most brilliant ball, stretching over a whole weekend and everybody drove down from London.'

'Really.'

Dimly, Meredith detected that she had misjudged Ralph Kingsland. Everything in her breeding encouraged her to look with a certain superciliousness on him – although he was a school friend of Hugo's, he was, after all, a scholarship boy. His father was something very low down in the church, a vicar wasn't it or a curate even? Anyway the family hadn't a bean. Yet now he looked so much more attractive, socially at ease and far better dressed than he had all those years ago. Although he had always had an introspective, dangerous look to him, the vulnerability that had once been etched so plainly on his face had been replaced with something else now – a sort of sardonic mockery. It was a look she had never encountered before, especially on the faces of young men and least of all ones who had invited her out for a drink. It was confusing, really.

Abruptly, she decided to leave, even though it meant disappointing Olive, to whom she had idly portrayed the evening as some sort of romantic encounter. As she rose to her feet, Ralph looked up. The girl appeared to be going and he had not yet managed to secure another meeting with her. It infuriated him that he had to do it. She would assume he was desperate to spend more time in her empty-headed company.

'You can't leave yet.'

'I can, I'm afraid,' she said coolly. 'I'm expected back.'

'But . . . perhaps we could have dinner?'

'I'd rather not, thank you.'

'I was hoping you'd let me show you round town. As you've not be able to get out as much as you thought.'

'Well, I've seen quite a lot, and I've only a week left.'

'But there's so much else to see. The zoo, for example, is delightful.' He leant forward and took her hand. 'Please?'

She hesitated. 'Perhaps.'

'Tomorrow then, will you come here? About lunch time? We can walk in the Tiergarten.'

Meredith was back on firm ground. She was used to the spectacle of men imploring.

'I suppose I could spare the time.'

★ ★ ★

She would be late, or course, Ralph thought. She was the kind of girl who regarded punctuality as the preserve of postmen and railway guards. He was therefore dressed only to the waist, shaving, with a white towel round his shoulders, when a knock came on the door at twelve thirty the following day. Assuming it to be a maid, he stayed in the bathroom and shouted through the door, '*Komm.*'

It was Meredith. Dressed in a soft beige crêpe-de-Chine suit whose clinging folds emphasised her small, high breasts and narrow waist, with a straw hat trimmed with pink wax flowers over her hair, a tan leather handbag dangling, she stepped into the room with proprietorial ease and took a good look round. She had been keen to see Ralph's room. She had hoped it might be one of the suites, but it was just a small, rather poky space, on the wrong side with no view.

'Oh, it's you. I'm not quite ready yet. You'd better sit down.'

He watched her through the bathroom mirror as she perched on an armchair, crossed her long, slim legs, played with her necklace and daintily examined her nails. There was an air of presumption about the girl, as though it were her own room. After a while she jumped up and strolled around, picking up his possessions and inspecting them. She examined his silver hairbrush and scrutinised a small photograph frame which he took everywhere, containing a picture of his mother when she was twenty-five, her face as yet unlined by the years of worry and illness. Carelessly Meredith put it back in the wrong place and moved away to flick through some papers on the small, mahogany desk. They were part of a report Ralph was compiling for his man at the Foreign Office – just a scrawl of jottings as yet, but not something he wanted her to see. He strode out of the bathroom, half naked.

'Have you quite satisfied your curiosity?'

Unabashed, she fingered the photograph again. 'Is that your girlfriend?'

'None of your business.'

Though she did not show it, the vision of Ralph Kingsland, semi-clothed, seriously dented Meredith's composure. Something about his chest with its dusting of red-gold hair brought forcibly back the memory of the tennis game all that time before. He had really played rather well, and were it not for the fact that she practised regularly morning and evening, she could not possibly have taken the match. He had been so fit, running round the court much faster than she, but his eye let him down. How cross he had been when she'd won. He was plainly not a person accustomed to losing. Well nor was she. Involuntarily a smile flitted across her features.

'You don't have to be so shy, Ralph. I think she's beautiful.'

He strode across and tidied up the papers, folding them carefully into the draw.

'You don't have a particularly high regard for people's privacy, do you?'

She knew he was referring to another incident, long ago, something more than today.

'I suppose not. But then I'm very good at keeping a secret. I've never liked people who blab everything they know.'

'And I've never liked young women who think they know more than they do.'

'Oh, some men are scared of a girl with her own opinions. Or so I'm told.'

Ralph flushed with annoyance. Her confidence – far beyond her years – was so infuriating he wanted to shake her. Then before he knew it, he realised that it was not anger that flashed through him at the sight of Meredith leaning against the chair, with her defiant, smiling eyes. It was something far more dangerous. Within the gloomy confines of the small hotel room he felt his breath coming faster and the rush of blood within him. He had an overbearing impulse to take the girl as she stood there taunting him, tear off her clothes and press her down on the bed until she cried out beneath him. Almost as soon as he had the thought, he was appalled by it. She was young, she was Hugo's sister, it was unthinkable. And yet . . . he could see she had thought it too. For a second they stood there, staring at each other, then he turned away and said tersely: 'Go downstairs. I'll meet you in the foyer.'

★ ★ ★

The incident had an unsettling effect on them both. Ralph was a hot-tempered person by nature, but the sudden aggressive desire for Meredith and the absolute need to contain it made him a testy companion that afternoon. Meredith, too, seemed preoccupied. Passers-by observing the tall, tight-lipped man, hands thrust into his jacket pockets, and the beautiful, silent girl at his side would hardly have taken them for a couple on a pleasant sight-seeing stroll. The turbulence of Ralph's feelings seemed all the more chaotic in contrast to the peace of the afternoon, as the sun blazed down on complacent Berliners taking their afternoon constitutional through the Tiergarten. Everything was clean in this city, everything in order, the lakes kept in their place by tidy greenery, which was in its turn circumscribed by spotless, well-defined paths. In a shady corner of the park they passed a couple of stormtroopers, with a small truck containing various cans of paint. They were decorating some of the benches in yellow.

'Why on earth are they doing that?' said Meredith.

'It's for the Jews. So they don't sit in the best benches.'

One of the brownshirts smiled at Meredith. He was the kind of man she could imagine touching up the paintwork in his own family home on a Sunday afternoon.

'They do go to such extraordinary lengths with the Jews.'

'These lengths? I'd say they've got some lengths to go yet. They're not going to stop with yellow benches or boycotts of Jewish shops and businesses. I wouldn't be surprised if they banned Jews from being German citizens soon. They're talking of it.'

'But why?'

'The biological material of the German nation needs cleansing or some such Nazi party nonsense. No wonder they're clamouring for passports abroad.' Realising he was straying into political waters, he tried to steer the conversation back to the mundane. 'But you haven't told me. What about the Bauers? It was very good of them to spare you today. Are they as you remembered them?'

'Oh, they're perfectly nice,' she said dismissively. 'I think Oscar was quite relieved I'd found something to occupy myself. Whenever he's stuck with me he always looks rather desperate to get away.'

'He's busy at the moment, then?'

'Supposedly. It's impossible to get any sense out of Olive. I did ask a bit about his job, but when Olive said his company made things like rivets and I said it didn't sound very riveting, she hardly even laughed. It sounds like the dullest job on earth to me.'

'Why is he so busy?'

'I don't know. Important meetings, he says.' She looked up at him. 'Oscar's friends are National Socialists but he never comes out with any of that stuff about the Jews.'

'Of course not. Nor would most well-born Berliners like him. You see, the people in this city are sophisticated – they're not the Führer's type of people at all and he's not theirs. All these banners, all these endless marches and parades are for show – Berlin is the showcase and it's people like you they're showing off to. And while they may not like what the Nazis stand for, they're frightened of the communists, people like the Rote Frontekampfer Bund, and they worry what would happen to them and their property if the commies got control.'

'But if they don't go along with the nastier end of the politics, it doesn't really matter, does it?'

He looked at her seriously. 'Whatever the Berliners may really think, it's bound to get worse here. They've just appointed the most unpleasant anti-Semite, Wolf von Helldorf, as chief of the Berlin police and they've given him a specific brief to purge the city of Jews and communists. There're violent incidents happening practically every night now, Jews getting beaten up, Jewish shops being attacked.'

He stopped himself. He was spouting like an idiot. He mustn't say too much, indeed he may have said too much already. Fortunately Meredith preserved her faintly distant air and did not question the extent of his knowledge or notice that he had halted mid-flow. They came to a café beside a small lake and ordered cakes and iced coffee topped with a thick crown of cream as they watched the people enjoying the water and the sunshine. Pleasantly she said: 'I wonder if you could do me a favour.'

'Of course.'

'You said you delivered books . . .'

'Not deliver exactly, but distribute. Why?'

Meredith had brought Dr Reichmann's parcel with her. As she took it out of her bag, she explained the conversation she'd had with him, then smiled sweetly.

'I thought as you were in that sort of line, you would know Hampstead and could possible drop it off when you're next passing.'

'Surely you could just put it in the post?'

'Well, he wanted it delivered personally. So that one could pass on some sort of personal message.'

'What message?'

'Oh God, I can't remember. That their family is thinking of them, sort of thing.'

It disgusted Ralph, both that Meredith perceived this task as a tiresome errand, and that she assumed she could easily fob it off on him. But he had other priorities than this girl's character defects, which were numerous.

'All right. I think I could do that for you. In return, I wonder if you would do me a favour.' She looked slightly surprised. 'I'd be awfully glad if you'd let me come with you to the Bauers' house. They sound so interesting. I'd love to meet them. That is, if Frau Bauer is well enough . . .'

'Really?' The idea of the Bauers as stimulating company was novel to her, but she had given up trying to fathom Ralph. Perhaps he was lonely here, or perhaps he was actually concealing an interest in her behind his convincing show of indifference.

'All right then. Olive is perfectly happy to get out of her bed for dinner. I'll get her to invite you, but I warn you, they might get some of their awful friends round too. Two English guests in a month will be Olive's idea of heaven.'

When he had put Meredith in a taxi for Dahlem, Ralph walked back to the hotel with a quite extraordinary sense of satisfaction. If anyone had asked him, he would have said it was due to the smooth accomplishment of his task, to secure a meeting with Oscar Bauer. He would never have admitted, even to himself, that it had anything to do with the prospect of another encounter with the infuriating, empty-headed Meredith Davenport.

Chapter Eleven

'Oh damn.'

May Barnes brushed the spilt coffee off her skirt as she remembered her lunch date. She was due to meet Katherine that day. May had hardly given another thought to her visit to Fallings, except to recall the sweaty, exhilarating horse ride which had left her thighs so sore, until that morning, a fortnight later, just as she was eating her breakfast – boiled egg and toast with one cup of coffee. Now there was no time to fetch another coffee or change her skirt – the jacket mostly covered the stain – or to consider why the thought of meeting up with Katherine made her vaguely uneasy. She barely had time to consider anything before dashing for the bus and standing all the way amid a fug of people who obviously didn't look too closely at the advertisements for Lifebuoy soap.

The day was already going badly. She had woken late and dressed in haste, subduing her spiralling red hair with grips, slapping on a lipstick too dark for her pale mouth, and choosing her grey tweed suit, which was hot and itchy. May always made this kind of mistake. She was not the type to spend too much time looking at her reflection. She was not under any illusions about herself. As her mother said, what with her hair and her glasses her looks did her no favours and her best asset was her knees. This was just May's luck, as her knees, although prettily smooth and unknobbled, were sandwiched between hefty calves and sturdy thighs and concealed practically all the time beneath her skirts. Her father, who rarely contributed to conversations of this nature except to snort, had intervened to tell May that her best asset was not her knees but her brain, yet the interruption earned him such contempt from Lavender Barnes that he returned swiftly to his paper.

Anyhow, it was best not to think about one's intellectual abilities when employed as a junior in the women's department of the *Daily Mail*. The page was held in considerable esteem – the *Mail* had been the first in Fleet Street to institute a women's page – and Giselle, the formidable editor who controlled May's destiny, was well aware of her position as guardian of an institution. She never hesitated to remind May that she was lucky and May accepted this, even if her duties largely consisted of running errands for Giselle, doing her shopping and deterring visitors to the office who were not sufficiently interesting to merit her attention.

May's luck had started when one of the paper's senior men who had been at Oxford with her father told him of a vacancy for a junior and her father risked his wife's annoyance to tell May. When to May's amazement she got the job, her mother had turned out to be surprisingly pleased, mollified by the thought of her daughter's close contact with the world of culture, Paris shows and other intensely female preoccupations.

Her father of course, who sensed May's true ambition, knew that the staples of the women's page were no attraction for his daughter. He was the only one who might have guessed that after she arrived each morning and made Giselle's china tea in a small brown teapot kept specially and put it on a tray with a slice of lemon and one biscuit, May contrived a reason to escape from the office and wander through the bustling, dark corridored Northcliffe House, where the yellow-globed lights shone night and day, and where she could glimpse through swing doors the forbidden world of the newsroom, in which serious looking men in shirtsleeves bent over their typewriters or jumped up suddenly, picking up their jackets from their chairs as they dashed out on a job.

It was always men she observed, yet there was a handful of female reporters, too, very distinguished ones, of whom she had heard. There was Margaret Lane, who had got an interview with Frau Goebbels, and a couple of other women, whose careers provided a secret inspiration for May. She knew if she stuck it, working her regular eleven till six stint, then someday Giselle was bound to let her have a stab at the kind of piece that graced the pages – how the new 'afternoon silhouette' should be worn with attractive leg-of-mutton sleeves, a wide belt and high collar for 'neck importance', how to complete an evening toilette in just half an hour (finger waving the hair and covering it with a small oil-sprinkled silk square while making up) or how the Jean Harlow blonde was now outclassed by the Vivien

Leigh brunette. That would be a start. And there was the odd ball or party where one might be sent for a write up. But it was a long way from foreign reportage and sometimes just the thought of the haul ahead was enough to dent even May's imperturbable good humour, albeit momentarily.

Still, her strength was making the best of things, and the best thing about working on this page was the presence of James Chumley, a gaunt, sad-eyed twenty-five-year-old with a cadaverous face and melancholy manner which concealed a lively sense of humour. Strictly speaking he was attached to the gossip column, but his talents were frequently borrowed by Giselle when someone was needed to cover glamorous dances or the doings of the glitterati. Perhaps as a result of attending so many social occasions, he had adopted a fey manner, which was totally at odds with his suburban origins – his father apparently owned a draper's shop in Redbridge. That day as May sat in the office, absent-mindedly biting her nails down to the quick and messily eating a currant bun, he poked his head round the door. He was supposed to be filing a report for Giselle on the ball he had attended at the Greek Embassy, in honour of Prince George and his bride Princess Marina of Greece. May unconsciously beamed with pleasure when she saw him and automatically took her glasses off.

'How were the Greeks?'

'Darling, too awful. "Timeo Danae . . ." and so on. The women practically had whiskers. The men were far more beautiful, but that, I suppose, is the Attic tradition.'

He paused, his hand lingering on her table, 'Where's Lady Bountiful?'

'Giselle's with the editor.'

'I have to speak to her about this frightful nudist piece she wants.'

'Nudist?'

'Oh, it's all the rage, didn't you know? All our readers are running off to join nudist colonies. I had to go and meet some poor woman who went because her husband wanted to join and she thought she'd better accompany him and she said it was simply dreadful. The men outnumbered the women three to one, and they had to sit in some freezing hut in the New Forest, with all the men self-consciously averting their eyes.

She said she'd rather they looked at her straight. I do think all this back-to-nature stuff is the end. Whoever said natural was best?'

'That's rather daring for the page, isn't it?'

'Rather drab actually. I just wonder whether she'll consider these people amusing enough. He's a schoolmaster in Clapham.'

Amusing was the universal term Giselle used to denote acceptability on the page. It meant interesting, chic, respectable and avant garde all in one.

'How's your friend Meredith?'

Meredith Davenport, despite being only twenty-one and doing nothing with her life, was considered highly amusing. Her party had been featured in full in James' gossip column, accompanied by the Cecil Beaton photograph.

'In Berlin, I think. Lucky thing.'

'Brave thing, more like. A friend of mine has been living out there but he moved recently. Said it was getting rather rough.'

'I can't believe that Meredith would go anywhere rough. Roughing it's not her style.'

'I suppose not . . .' his eyes lingered on her vaguely, as though contemplating her possession of any useful gossip.

'Are you doing anything for lunch?'

'Blow. I am rather, I'm afraid. I'm going out.'

'Anyone I know?'

'Um, I don't think so.' The disappointment of having to refuse lunch with James was sharp. 'Katherine Scott.'

His eyes glinted with interest. 'The girl who's running round with Lewis Appleby? So she's a friend of yours, is she? Tell me, are wedding bells in the air?'

'I really don't know. I could ask.'

'Oh do, darling, do. And let me know straight away.'

★ ★ ★

Other than to tease her friend about her relationship with a much older man, May had honestly not thought much about Lewis Appleby. She was well aware that a man like him would never normally have looked at her and that he had only sought her opinion throughout their stay because of the presence of Katherine. Though he had been perfectly courteous to her, it had been a distinct relief when she had escaped to play tennis with his friends and left him alone with Katherine, as he plainly desired. There was something rather intense about him and his penetrating gaze. She knew he was political, but in a different way from all the other friends of Eddie Tiverton she had met. They were either virulently anti-fascist, or pacifists, or leant dramatically to the right. None of them were moderates and they considered it a virtual crime to be apolitical or to sit on the fence. Yet Lewis Appleby made everyone else seem rather childish, as though they were merely striking poses, or adopting flamboyant opinions for effect. He and Katherine were alike in some ways, though no one else saw it. They were earnest about life and ideas. There was an underlying seriousness about them. But he was far too old for her. Perhaps that was what Katherine wanted to talk about over lunch. May rather hoped not, because she was absolutely useless at doling out romantic advice.

★ ★ ★

When they met at one o'clock, at a Lyons corner shop, her suspicions were confirmed. Katherine was looking thinner than usual, but more stylish. She'd had her hair done short and was wearing a close-fitting lilac dress which brought out the blue in her eyes. A gust of perfume eddied around her. She barely stopped to ask how May was or whether she was enjoying the newspaper job. No sooner had they ordered their sandwiches and cups of tea at a table by the window than she started talking in a rush.

'May, I've something to ask you, and I don't mind at all if you say no.'

'Fire away.' Now she was sure it was about Lewis. Katherine had a tentative, guarded look about her.

'You know you once asked if I knew anyone who'd like to share the flat?'

'Yes.'

'Well, I do. I would.'

'You're sure? How would your mother cope without you?' May was well aware of the semi-invalid status of Katherine's father and the help she gave with a set of unruly siblings.

'Oh, she'd cope fine. She'd be glad of the space but she can't bear the idea of me living somewhere completely – you know –

strange. And of course I'd pay the going rent. What do you think?'

'Well . . .'

May's flat was another boon from her father, who decided that when she started her job she deserved a little independent life. It wasn't much really. Its position in the middle of a redbrick mansion block which looked out on to Battersea Park was the best of it. Inside it was dark and smelt of varnish. The paintwork was chipped and cracked, the walls bore round brown damp rings and the curtains sagged from their rails. When she had first taken possession there had been a pungent, lingering reek of alcohol and cigarettes, and a few ashtrays scattered around still full. But with a through wind and a little decoration it became rather jolly. She whitewashed the walls herself, put an angle-poise lamp with pink shade on the table, and had stuck up some pictures of seaside scenes and photographs of her family everywhere. She was supposed to pay her father rent for the flat, which was why she had briefly tried to fill her spare room, but he so frequently 'forgot' when payment was due that the second bedroom had slowly accreted a pile of clothes, books and odd *objets d'art* that May had uncovered at weekend markets. Meanwhile she had grown accustomed to the single life. It wasn't all that lonely, given that downstairs was a family of three whose children, all under five, made a terrible racket charging down the stone stairs on their way to outings in the park and dispelled any sense of solitude. May loved children. Whenever she saw them, she couldn't resist touching the baby's fat cheeks, soft as rose petals, picking him up to smell his honey breath and stroking the hair of the older boy and girl. She volunteered endlessly to baby-sit, but the mother, shy and tired-looking, never liked to presume enough to take her up on it.

Now Katherine would end this pleasant solo existence, and she would have to accustom herself again to sharing. But being a wholly generous person by nature, and aware of the pleading in her friend's eyes, May was unable to refuse. She determined to look on the bright side.

'All right. When would you want to move in?'

'This weekend?'

'That's great. Then we can go out on Saturday night and see a film. *The Private Life of Henry VIII* is playing locally. I'd love to catch that. That is, unless you're already booked?'

'No. That would be lovely.'

Katherine visibly relaxed, May thought, and perhaps a spell in the flat would restore her to her old self. The spiky schoolgirl who could outwit several of the mistresses, who excelled at Shakespeare adaptations and whose artwork was good enough to frame, was now distracted and alive with nerves. She forgot things as soon as she was told, and jumped from subject to subject without absorbing any of the undercurrents of conversation. May wasn't qualified to judge, but she supposed this state of extreme preoccupation was something akin to love. And indeed Katherine did seem to startle when, remembering her promise to James, May added: 'And I want to know everything about Lewis Appleby.'

CHAPTER TWELVE

ON THE DAY that she left her parents' house Katherine took a last look at the tiny bedroom she shared with her middle sister, Ellen, who was even now unsentimentally transferring her possessions to the space vacated by her. Outside the window a hibiscus bloomed, its cream papery buds uncreasing like a débutante's taffeta and the sight of it provoked in Katherine a euphoric sense of anticipation, which was hardly even dented when Syrie came in complaining about Arthur, whose compulsive hoarding of stamp albums was threatening to crowd out what space remained in the dining room. Katherine said she would come back in a few days time for a visit but Syrie said Katherine should not be surprised to come back and find her mother dead of exhaustion, with all she had to put up with. Then, before Katherine could stop her, Syrie had picked up a photograph tucked in her daughter's small case and held it at arm's length. It was a wedding picture of Syrie and Arthur, her father gazing at his bride with the long-lashed mute appeal of a large gun dog, while her mother stared ahead with the same, compressed, mocking smile on her thin mouth with which she was now scrutinising the picture, making Katherine think that perhaps their relationship had not been changed that vastly by the war.

'Don't think you can forget your family that easily,' was all Syrie said as she left the room.

★   ★   ★

May was cooking soup when she arrived, her normally pink face flushed fiery red as she bent over the saucepan quizzically, testing the brownish substance with a worried air.

'Thought I'd do lunch!' she announced brightly, as soon as Katherine had deposited her two bulging suitcases, but once her friend had sat at the small kitchen table, and taken a few sips of the soup, with its sharp competing flavours of salt and alcohol, May herself burst out laughing.

'Oh, it's no good, Katherine, I was intending to be so hospitable and do a lovely meal, but my cooking is absolutely hopeless. Does "tsp." mean teaspoon or tablespoon? It could be either, couldn't it? It's not at all clear. We can't eat this. We'll either have to make do with egg sandwiches, or go out and buy something.'

Laughing as they walked to the baker's to buy bread and macaroons, the two girls found that they fitted together almost at once, like a well-made jigsaw, their common interests clear, their intimacies and privacies well defined. Far from having to listen to endless conversations about Lewis Appleby, May found herself coaxed to talk about her own office life and her friend James Chumley.

'He's such a good journalist. I mean even the simplest little things in the paper, they just leap off the page at you. But he's not going to stick at it long.'

'Really? Why not, if he's so good at it?'

'He wants to be a real writer. He's already done loads of short stories. He showed me some.'

'Are they romantic?'

'Well, not exactly,' said May, as though pondering something puzzling. 'He says that bourgeois subject matter is important for getting in touch with reality and that he intends to concentrate on things like trimming the hedge or waiting for the postman, which simultaneously illuminate and dramatise the decay of capitalist life.'

'Are they good?'

'Not really,' she said, a little sadly. 'I do hope he doesn't chuck the journalism in. We'd miss him dreadfully. I mean his contributions on the gossip page are practically required reading.'

'It sounds as though you rather like him, May.'

'Oh, not in that way, of course. I just think the office would be a frightfully dull place if he left.'

* * *

If Katherine scarcely spoke of Lewis Appleby, that did not mean she was not thinking of him. She hugged the thought of him to herself like an awkward burden and treasured his image like a puzzle she could not put down. She admired his beautiful, square jaw which gave his face a conviction of absolute rightness and was stirred by the intensity of his eyes. But the absence of any physical affection between them was troubling.

Since his urgent embrace in the wood at Fallings he had barely touched her, though he was more attentive than ever. Sometimes he regarded her utterances with an air of humorous tolerance, but at other times he had the ability to make her remarks sound penetrating and well-considered. When he tried to explain his experiments and the theories behind them – about embryology and mutation and segregation, about things called genes which lived in cells on chromosomes, and the ways that a species could evolve and adapt to an environment, Katherine would find herself drawn in, almost as though she were a student, or someone who actually understood. Occasionally he broadened his approach, telling her that all human behaviour, from what he called religiosity, to criminality and aggression or happiness, were simply manifestations of biology, and when more was known about genetics, more would be known about man.

He worked in a laboratory in South Kensington, but she rarely went there. It had been tacitly ruled out as a place to meet, and she was glad because it was an alien world to her with its benches and test tubes, the acid aromas and stoppered poisons ranked behind their glass cases. But one day, a few weeks after she moved in with May, he was going to be late and he asked her to meet him there. It was a drab, rainy afternoon, and the sound of her heels clicking down the high Victorian corridors with their smells and discoloured lino floors sounded distractingly loud. When she passed through the swing doors which led to his own space he gave her a swift wave and smile and asked her to wait. He was working, utterly absorbed, head bent over his notes, hair awry, the knot of his tie halfway down his shirt. The afternoon light coming slightly greenish through the thick lab windows lent a submarine gloom to the air. Her movements felt slowed and dreamy, too, as though she were drifting like a random cell on a slide. She wandered over to a tank in the corner and peered in. A fleshy pink creature about five inches long was pushing its way through the water, flipping and turning, its lidless lizard eyes regarding her without fear. She watched it, fascinated, until she realised with a shudder what it resembled. It was like the schoolbook pictures of the embryo baby, still in fishy freefall in the womb, at a stage when it was hard to think of it as human at all.

'It's an axolotl.' He came behind her and put his hands on her shoulders. 'A unique creature, capable of metamorphosing from an aquatic life with gills into an amphibian. It was recently discovered that if you feed these things thyroid extract they lose their fins and the gills get absorbed back into the body and they become able to breathe air. It was a very important discovery.'

'Why?'

'Well, it proved we could change the nature of living entities. Some people said we'd discovered the elixir of life.'

'Must make you biologists feel like God.'

His eyes shone with excitement. 'Oh no. It makes us forget God, more like. But it's important not because of how it makes us feel, but because it shows people what science can do. In a very clear and dramatic way. People have to know about science, it's dangerous if they don't.'

'Dangerous? Surely not?'

'Oh, yes it is. Power gets concentrated in too few hands. And just now we're discovering so much. There's just so much we're capable of.'

She turned away from the embryo creature in the tank and meandered over to his desk. It was covered with his papers of neat writing, his tiny, regular script stitching across the page.

'It's important what you're doing, isn't it?'

'Uh huh.'

'Does it bother you that people never think of scientists in the same way they think of artists or writers? I mean as far as their personal importance goes. Scientists don't get their names up in lights. No one cares whose cocktail parties they go to or which restaurant they've been seen at or . . .' she kept her back turned from him 'what's happening to their love life.'

'Well, we're not a generally glamorous bunch,' he responded absently.

'I suppose it's as if, once something is discovered, it takes on a life of its own and becomes independent of its finder. Whereas if you're a painter, say, or a poet, your work is always linked to you.'

He regarded her seriously. 'That works both ways of course. An artist's work can be judged – and adversely affected – by his life. But with scientists the individual and his life – his personal morality and all that – is entirely irrelevant. The work stands on its own. The science is infinitely more important than the scientist.'

She looked up at him. Such eyes he had. She would love to paint them. 'Well, you're more important to me than a whole sea full of axolotls.'

'How sweet you are, Katherine.'

He reached down and brushed her lips with his own. It was a fleeting gesture, as though he might have been moistening a stamp, but encouraging, Katherine thought.

★ ★ ★

It was a major relief to her that Lewis had not followed up on his polite intention to meet her parents. Visions of that encounter were enough to make her shudder whenever she allowed herself to entertain them – Arthur bitter and wandering, boring everyone with his time in the trenches, Syrie resentful and determined not to be patronised, anxious to let their guest know that she was once on a very different social footing even though she was now pouring tea in a cramped, dark little parlour, shackled to a mad invalid. The children would be in and out, anxious to get a good look at Lewis, impertinent and giggling. But as the weeks went on Lewis entirely failed to mention them. It was almost as if that whole dimension of Katherine, the parental annexe and sibling department, did not exist. Eventually, recklessly, she asked whether he ever wanted to meet them. His answer astonished her.

'Oh, didn't I tell you? But I know your family already. I mean not all of them of course, but the Applebys and the Myddletons have been friends for generations. I've met your grandmother several times.'

'You never mentioned it.'

'She was a great friend of my late mother. I've visited her home once or twice. But you're right, Katherine, perhaps we should meet again. Why don't you arrange something?'

'Fine. I'll telephone grandmother, shall I?'

An appointment for tea was fixed the following week. There

was a knowing air in her grandmother's voice which sounded as though she had been expecting the call.

'He said he knew you,' said Katherine. 'Or his mother did.'

'Lewis is such a nice man. Yes, I did know his mother, we were very close for a time. She lost her older son in the war, so he was such a consolation to her. I'm delighted you've met him, darling.'

Though she was relieved that it was her grandmother's home and not her parents' which they would be visiting, Katherine always felt a little tinge of guilt when she entered the portals of that house – the sheer cliff face of black polished door with its Georgian fanlight, the vast, black and white marbled hall, always furnished with cut flowers, leading off to the powder blue morning room and the drawing room in pale, porcelain green. While at home she dismissed her mother's resentment out of hand, when you compared her present confined quarters with those she had grown up in, a certain degree of disgruntlement seemed quite forgivable.

The maid took them into the drawing room, where grandmother was waiting before the fire. Her faded face crinkled with pleasure at the sight of him.

'My dear Lewis. I can't tell you what a pleasure it is to see you again. How is Fallings. As beautiful as ever?'

'Wonderfully so. I'm desperately thinking of ways to avoid shutting it up. But it's quite unacceptable to keep such a huge place for one person.'

'You should make more use of it. Just think of the parties your mother used to have.'

They murmured pleasantries as the maid handed round Earl Grey tea, triangular sandwiches and cakes. Then grandmother said: 'Now tell me, are you still beavering away with those frogs or worms, or whatever?'

'Oh yes, various amphibians. But the work I'm doing at the moment has implications well beyond the laboratory. It's more about the mechanisms of heredity. A science called genetics. I'm writing a book about it.'

'How fascinating.' Lady Myddleton made it sound so convincing.

'In fact I've been thinking of bringing together several people from different fields to talk around the subject. There's a couple of chaps I'd like to invite from abroad. The only question is the venue.'

'Why not use Fallings? You've just said you wanted to make more use of it?'

'Oh, I don't think it would be really appropriate. A family house . . .'

'It's hardly a family house if you've got no family in it. And you don't seem in any hurry to have one, Lewis, so I'd have thought it was perfect.' Mortified at this remark, Katherine lifted her eyes enough to see that Lewis had taken no umbrage at all. Instead he was gazing ahead of him, a little plate of cake perched on his knee.

'You say that, Lady Myddleton, but it's out in the country. Do you think it's an entirely suitable place?'

'Of course. Absolutely wonderful. I'm sure a lot of those academics would benefit from a bit of country air.'

He turned to her. 'You know, Katherine, I think your grand-mother has solved a problem for me. Using Fallings to plan a better society. I can't think of a finer use for it.'

'Who would you invite?'

'Oh, zoologists and biologists, mainly. Perhaps a politician or two.'

He rarely talked about his fellow scientists but Katherine recalled one man, a Dr Harvey, who had made a life's study of the African chimpanzee. She had remembered him because Lewis said the man had his own pet chimpanzee which he had reared from a baby.

'And would you discuss amphibians?'

'Oh, not animals, no. We'd be talking about people. Population planning.'

'What's that?'

'Well, it's about improving our national stock.'

'But why would you want to do that?' she asked.

'Why ever not? Look around you. Everything from livestock and crops to the roses we grow in the gardens at Fallings has benefited from our understanding of heredity. We're getting improvements all the time – fatter pigs, better milkers, corn that resists disease. What people are now asking is whether our species should evolve for the better too, and whether we can direct that? Whether man should have a hand in controlling his own place in nature and his own destiny.'

'You mean like vaccination programmes?'

'That certainly. Whatever it takes.'

'Those are rather dangerous waters, aren't they? I mean they sterilise people in Germany for being the wrong stock. I read about it.'

'I don't think that's really appropriate, dear.' Her grandmother sounded almost sharp, though whether it was Katherine's reference to sterilisation, or the generally risky topic of human reproduction, she could not tell. But Lewis was not to be deflected.

'Not all techniques of population planning are negative. A lot of what I'm thinking about involves nutrition and education. Or, to put it another way, instead of too many people having children with nowhere to put them and nothing to feed them on, we could be encouraging reproduction from the better fed and better educated. That doesn't sound a bad thing, does it?'

'I suppose not.'

'Exactly.' He smiled. 'And what we want to do is plan for that to come about.'

As Lewis went off with the maid to fetch their coats, Katherine approached Lady Myddleton for a kiss. Pressing Katherine's hand with sinewy rigour, the old lady's face bent forcefully towards her as she issued her benediction. 'What good taste you have, my dear. I do like Lewis. He's so appropriate for you.'

★　★　★

When she returned to the flat, James Chumley was there, sitting before the gasfire with May, eating cheese on toast. They had just come back from the news cinema and were talking about the pictures of hunger marchers they had seen.

'I don't know how people can act as though everything's getting better when there are still so many out of work.' James spoke bitterly, an edge of disgust in his voice. 'They say it's still one in four men in Scotland. And as many in Wales. And here we have Mosley spouting on about his "national plan" whipping up hatred and making everything worse.'

'How was your grandmother, Katherine?' asked May.

She told them about Lewis and her grandmother turning out to be old friends.

'I don't know why you're surprised,' said James. 'People with big houses are always immaculately connected. How is Fallings? Does he spend much time there?'

'Not really,' said Katherine, buttering toast. 'In fact he's decided he wants to use the house more. He thinks it could be used to produce a better society.'

'What on earth does he mean? Is he going to sell it?' said May.

'No no, not that at all. He's talking about science and improving the population. He's going to hold a conference at Fallings.'

'A conference! How exciting!' May could always be relied on for enthusiasm. 'What will they talk about?'

'Vaccination programmes,' said Katherine, trying to remember what Lewis had said. 'Improving national nutrition and things.'

James got up to leave. 'My dear, the best way Lewis Appleby could improve national nutrition is to take in some of those hunger marchers and give them all a good breakfast.'

Chapter Thirteen

Oscar leant back and patted the dome of his stomach.

'One thing I will say for my wife is that she has become a real German when it comes to food. She knows my special favourites, don't you, dear? If I'm not careful I'm in danger of growing fat.'

Privately Meredith marvelled at the modesty of his self-image but Olive, whose spreading pregnant belly was easily overshadowed by her husband's, smiled back triumphantly.

'It's so nice to have a man who eats well. You know, Meredith, since I've lived here I can honestly say I don't miss English food in the slightest. Not even a plate of my old nanny's rhubarb crumble and custard would be enough to tempt me back.'

Exactly how difficult could it be for Olive to cater for her husband, when all she needed to do was issue instructions to a bevy of kitchen staff? Meredith knew for a fact that her friend could not cook and had not even done the Cordon Bleu cookery course in Paris which had been threatened for Meredith herself. Still, she wished Oscar would not go on about it. Just the thought of the Kassler Rippen, the dish of smoked and pickled pork chops they had just eaten, was enough to make her feel queasy. The amount they ate! The wide wooden dining table had practically groaned with the food laid out for the four of them, the stacks of creamed potatoes and dumplings, which she had ostentatiously refused, the dessert cake, fruit and the wines, then coffee and brandy. There was a plate of ripe peaches, swollen and gold, and plums heaped in a dish, dark as bruises. Everything in the room seemed excessive in its abundance, from the stout yellow candles oozing down their golden candelabra and the arched ebony figure of a negress set on the silver cigarette box, to portly Oscar with his flushed face and even the pregnant Olive herself, bursting from her dress with its square-cut peasant neck, her hair braided in voluptuous blonde loops.

126

Yet Olive's positive mood was far preferable to her usual sessions of sentimental melancholy about the life she had left behind and the change of heart was obviously down to one person – Ralph Kingsland, who, Meredith had to admit, was a perfect guest.

When Meredith had mentioned, casually, that Ralph might come to dinner, Olive predictably, had been delighted. She swiftly smothered Oscar's more cautious concerns about his provenance and his occupation.

'Who cares what he does, Oscar? Don't be so stuffy. He's a friend of Meredith's family and he's English anyway, so don't invite any of those Nazi friends of yours. Why not forget what they think for once? If they're not worried about you having an Irish wife, they won't worry about a few British visitors, will they?'

Olive frequently took this childish tone with regard to her husband's political allegiances and even Meredith knew it must be irritating. As the daughter of a politician herself, she knew that politics itself was a subject to be strictly avoided in polite conversation. While Oscar was not a party member, he had several important contacts (as Olive never tired of telling her) and Meredith was well aware of the popular feeling against the British. If a German family had English guests to stay it would not go unnoticed. So while Meredith herself was bitterly regretting the day she agreed to come to Berlin and longing for her return home the next week, she appreciated Oscar's gracious hospitality. Though frankly, she thought, his wife was more of a liability than a whole houseful of Brits.

If he had doubts about playing host to so many foreigners in his own home, Oscar concealed them admirably. When Ralph arrived he neglected the customary Hitlergrüss, and instead seized his hand and shook it forcefully. Ralph, who looked even more lean and sinuous beside the rotund Bauers, excelled in his turn. She was vaguely startled to hear him speak in fluent German, until she remembered someone telling her that he spoke five languages. She was relieved, when after a few initial greetings, they all switched to English for her sake. Ralph spoke admiringly of the emergent Olympic stadium, without even knowing, until informed by Olive, that Oscar's firm was practically masterminding the project. He brushed Meredith's cheek with a light kiss in greeting, and asked how her travel article was going.

'What is this? You are writing something about us?' asked Oscar.

'Meredith has been invited to contribute to a very prestigious British magazine,' said Ralph. 'It's quite an honour actually. She is giving her impressions of Berlin.'

'I hope they are favourable. There is so much nonsense in the foreign press just now. So much envy.'

'Oh, I haven't even started yet,' said Meredith, annoyed. She smoothed the flat satin of her damson evening dress, selected to display her lithe frame to best advantage. How intriguing that Ralph had managed to irk her within moments of his arrival. It was almost as if they were engaged in some personal psychological duel. Even in conversation with the others, his sharp eyes kept darting towards her.

Olive, at her most coquettish, placed Ralph next to her at the table and leant close to him, as though in private conversation.

'I'm surprised Meredith didn't mention you when she first arrived,' she murmured winsomely. She had got the impression, from what Ralph had told her briefly in German, that an enduring friendship existed between himself and Meredith, that their families were so close they were practically cousins.

'As soon as I realised she was here, I got in touch.'

'You are an old friend of the Davenports, yes?' asked Oscar.

'We go back a long way.'

Meredith regarded him thoughtfully. She simply had no idea what he was playing at. Was he trying to pretend they were lovers? It really was most curious. She didn't really know why she was going along with it, though she would, while it suited her. He arched a coppery eyebrow at her and smiled fondly.

'We had such a good walk the other day, didn't we?'

'Wonderful,' she breathed. 'Really lovely. It was great to catch up on all your news.'

When the coffee arrived Oscar offered Ralph a cigarette from the silver box, and Ralph, seeing the look on Meredith's face, passed it to her. She took it gratefully. Oscar was becoming boring in his pronouncements about how women should not smoke, which although they were ostensibly directed towards his wife, were evidently meant to include herself. She saw him flicker with disapproval and felt even more rebellious.

'Did you know your friends are ruining Ralph's business, Oscar?'

Oscar looked startled. 'Oh. Why is that?'

'Well, he can't import any more books by Jewish writers. They've gone and banned them. Isn't that right, Ralph?'

'I wouldn't say it's ruining the business,' Ralph said smoothly. 'A minor hiccup really.'

Meredith would not give up, 'But that's crazy, isn't it, Oscar?'

'Ach. It's not as simple as that.' He seemed uncomfortable. Then, as if looking for some justification, he added: 'I employ many Jews myself, in my branches in Norway and Sweden. I have some very good Jewish reps.'

'But not in Berlin.'

Oscar's kindly face wrinkled in dismay at the tack the conversation was taking. 'You know, Meredith my dear, Berlin has been practically run by Jews in the past. In fact there are more Jews in Berlin now than ever before. They are moving here from the country. They don't like it out in the villages apparently.'

'It doesn't look much fun for them here either.'

'Oh, do let's talk about something less dreary.' Olive led them into the drawing room, plumped herself in the middle of a sofa, kicked off her shoes and put up her swollen ankles.

'Make yourself comfortable, Ralph. I'm afraid ladies in my condition can't stand on ceremony. Besides, I have to tell you, tonight is something of a celebration for us. My Oskie has just been made deputy director of his entire division. He now controls three factories, Munich, Dresden and Berlin. Isn't that tremendous?'

'Congratulations, Herr Bauer. What is it exactly your division does?'

'Manufacturing,' said Oscar.

'He's being far too modest,' Olive interrupted. 'It's not just the Olympic stadium – Oscar's secured a contract to supply equipment for most of the road building in Berlin.'

'Your firm must be delighted,' murmured Ralph.

'It's an admirable project,' said Oscar. 'Already around 10,000 unemployed men have been given work on the autobahn. When they are finished we shall have a ring round the whole city.'

'And he's personally drafted in extra steel workers for another government commission,' continued Olive irrepressibly.

'Olive, please, Herr Kingsland doesn't want to hear these boring details.'

'But I'm so proud of you, dearest. Imagine, five hundred extra staff! And it's all down to you.'

'Enough of me.' Oscar gave a strained smile. 'Where are you staying while you are in Berlin, Mr Kingsland?'

'At the Adlon.'

'Aah. Nice.'

'Yes, very nice.'

Just because he was staying in the Adlon, haunt of the better-off foreign guests and traditional meeting place for the international press, so much so that the rooms were said to be bugged by the Gestapo and the staff were rumoured to be spies, did not mean that Ralph had not seen another side to Berlin. He had many times walked through the poorer districts of the city, Wedding and Neukölln, the industrial districts with their enormous barrack-like blocks where hundreds of families lived crammed together, their tiny, filthy yards swarming with children, and where mothers with sprawling families sometimes rented out beds in the daytime to male labourers with nowhere to sleep. Look in the little bars at the corner of every street there and among the workers downing tankards of Weissbier, the local brew, communist sympathies were openly discussed. It was still possible to see flags displaying the hammer and sickle hanging from the tenement blocks, sometimes right alongside a swastika. In some parts of the city he had seen a man fall over with hunger while waiting for a trolleybus. He had passed fights in the street and respectable workers standing with cardboard signs around their necks advertising themselves for work. He did not think a hundred autobahns would be enough to solve what he had seen.

'The best thing about you being here,' said Olive, 'is that I don't need to feel so guilty about being unable to entertain Meredith properly. You really are a weight off my mind. Perhaps you can take her out dancing. I know that's what she most wants to do.'

'I'm afraid I have to return to London in a few days, for business. I don't think I'll be back before Meredith has to leave.'

'But what a shame. That's terrible. She will miss you, won't you, Meredith?'

'Oh, I will.'

Ralph gave Meredith a straight look. 'And of course, Frau Bauer, I will miss her too.'

★　★　★

After the meal, Oscar offered Ralph a lift back to the hotel in his car but Ralph said he would walk and catch a tram. When Meredith said she'd accompany him, to get a breath of air, Olive and Oscar exchanged glances. Oscar's was cautious, poised to dissuade.

'It's getting cold out. And really I don't know if a young woman wants to be wandering about the streets at this time of night.'

'You go on, dear,' said Olive. 'Remember, Oskie, what you are always saying about the streets being quite safe now.'

Picking up her beaded cardigan, Meredith thought with satisfaction that it was her turn now to take Ralph by surprise. But if he was surprised, he did not show it. He offered her his arm as if it were the most natural thing in the world. Outside the streets were quiet. Above them a bone-white moon burned in a tranquil sky and in the shadows around them the villas of Dahlem were shuttered behind their gates.

Ralph, too, seemed to withdraw into himself. He was thinking about the special friend he planned to visit immediately before returning to Britain. His friend was a most distinguished man, with decorations from his war service in the British airforce and the unusual asset of having been educated in Germany, which meant that in his later diplomatic career with the British government he had been able to move with ease in the highest official circles in Berlin. Goering liked and trusted him, it was said. Ralph's friend knew all sorts of people working in companies throughout the Netherlands, Switzerland, France and Germany. He had acquaintances in Prague and Vienna, many of them refugees from Nazi persecution. His friend had recently received unsettling news from a contact in the German air ministry, so when Ralph visited his unassuming house in the wooded countryside close to the border, he would be extremely interested to hear that Oscar Bauer's engineering division, known suppliers to the Luftwaffe, had employed an extra five hundred men.

Meredith's clear, sardonic voice broke the silence.

'I'm sorry to hear you'll miss me.' She was unbearably curious. She had been expecting that he would ask to see her again, especially after tonight when he had seemed so jovial, and had acted so familiar. It was odd of him to become shy in private. As they reached the corner of the street he stopped and removed his arm. He had no further need of her.

'Well, yes. Indeed I will. But meanwhile thank you for a most enjoyable evening. Really, you mustn't come any further.'

'Fine, then.'

'I hope you have a safe journey home.'

'And you.'

'Do please convey my thanks to Frau Bauer.'

'Perhaps we will meet again in London?'

'Perhaps. Yes.'

He smiled slightly, leant forward and kissed her glancingly on the cheek, so that she was aware of the light scrape of stubble on her skin and a waft of his sharp cologne. Then, before she could speak, he had turned and was gone. Meredith shrugged her cardigan closer around her and regarded his retreating back. It was infuriating. Who did he think he was that he could play with her? She felt the void opening up between them with the yards on the street and it seemed as though her whole body throbbed with a bitter frustration, a new sensation she did not identify or understand.

CHAPTER FOURTEEN

FOR SONIA IT was as though the doings of the Prince of Wales and his lady friend, which took place in yachts and Mediterranean villas and grand country houses, had imbued Katherine's own quiet romance with a borrowed glamour. Always a keen supporter of the Prince of Wales' right to marry and reign, Sonia had kept them updated on his summer spent cruising round France and revisiting Vienna and Budapest. She had been invited to the Simpsons' small but impossibly chic flat in Bryanston Court and reported that the tiny woman with the strong jaw, thin as a rake but elegant as one of her own enamelled Fabergé eggs, was just the thing the stuffy old royal family needed. A breath of fresh American air. And it was plain the prince adored her too, quite enough to conquer any obstacles in their path. Katherine and Lewis, of course, did not have any obstacles in their path. Or none in the eyes of the church and Sonia Rees.

'You're telling me he wants you to host a house party? How exciting. But don't think I'm angling for an invitation.'

'It's not a house party,' said Katherine. 'It's more of a work thing. A science conference.'

'He wants to show you off to his colleagues. What could be more romantic? If you need any help just you ask.'

'You're scarcely the expert, Sonia. I thought you never entertained in Monmouthshire,' interjected Eddie Tiverton from across the room.

'No one wants a house party in a Welsh tomb,' said Sonia funereally.

★ ★ ★

The day of the conference dawned dull and very soon rain began twirling down from an ash-grey sky. Across the lawn the fir trees poked their branches through a creeping mist. The wood reminded Katherine of the poem she'd learned at school, with its line 'vapours weep their burthen to the ground', but she could not for the life of her remember the next line. Fires had been lit in all the fireplaces, in an effort to warm the house up, and Mrs Mullins had brought in two girls from the village to help out. Katherine was vague about her own duties.

'I can't possibly join in the discussions. I don't know the first thing.'

He laughed. 'Just be yourself. I want everyone to meet you.'

There was quite a range of people coming. Lewis had asked some of them to prepare papers on their latest work. One man was going to discuss patterns in the inheritance of intelligence and there was an American talking about a programme in the United States to control drunkenness among the poor. Another scientist, who had corresponded with Lewis, sent a paper on inherited deformities in twins.

Katherine's deliverance came with the arrival of the second guest. Dr Laurence Harvey had brought his own chimpanzee, orphaned in the Belgian Congo and raised by the doctor himself. The animal travelled in the back seat of the car, from where it gazed with anxious eyes, through the bars of a large cage. Its arrival caused some consternation.

'I'm not touching it,' muttered Mrs Mullins, with a nasty look. 'It'll carry diseases and all sorts. It's bound to be covered with fleas.'

Set down in the hall, the chimp surveyed them with its oil-brown eyes, then it jumped up, bared its teeth and rattled the bars of the cage, sending Mrs Mullins and her helpers scuttling across to the other side of the room.

'It wants to get out.' Katherine unlatched the cage and pulled the animal out. It sat on her hip, the muscular thighs clinging tight, the long arms looping themselves round her shoulder, chattering away. She cradled the small, hairy body, heavier somehow than a human child, and smoothed its leathery pink feet.

'Why don't I look after him while you're busy?'

Dr Harvey leapt gratefully at her offer.

'That would be so kind of you. He does get nervous, somewhere new.'

'Well, if you're sure, Katherine . . .' said Lewis doubtfully.

'Oh, I am sure. And I'll try and listen in at the back.'

But it was hard to pay much attention. Everyone was sitting

in the library and she heard only the odd snippet of the conversation as she wandered in and out, feeding the chimpanzee with the fruit Dr Harvey had provided. She missed most of Lewis' talk about improving the post-war population, hearing only snatches.

'There's no doubt now that we're witnessing a grave decline in national intelligence. This latest survey of schoolchildren makes worrying reading. But what we need to know is whether it relates to family size or income. To my mind this is genetic degradation and the country needs a plan to reverse it.'

'But how can you plan things like that?' someone asked.

'If you can plan an economy,' said Lewis, 'then you can plan a population. Winston has had some valuable thoughts on this.'

* * *

That night, sleeping in the huge room on the south wing that she'd had on her first visit, she was woken by a cry. It was a high wailing lamentation, rising and falling, with an ancient, plangent tone. Drawing the sheets around her in her half sleep, Katherine dreamed it was the ghost of Elena Appleby, the young French woman who had fallen hopelessly in love with the seaman bringing her shells. How that long-dead woman must have yearned for the taste of salt on his skin, the sweat of the sea, and longed for her lover's rough, hastened embraces as they met to discuss the shell house, planning their elopement in hushed whispers. And how terrible her grief must have been on being found and confined to a lifetime of sewing and gardening, or escaping to her shell house to relive her passion.

* * *

The next morning at breakfast, it emerged that everyone had been woken. The culprit was the chimpanzee which had been crying and howling in its cage.

'Does it always make that racket?' said Lewis, handing a plate of kippers to Dr Harvey.

'It's being in a strange environment. He's not used to it,' said Dr Harvey, holding the animal protectively.

'It's worse than having a child. Couldn't you get a nurse for it?'

'Just wait till you have a child, Lewis,' said Dr Harvey, feeding the animal his toast. 'You'll understand.'

★ ★ ★

Having crowded round on the terrace for a photograph, the last guests left on Sunday afternoon. Lewis was delighted by the success of the weekend. Katherine had never seen him so buoyant. He suggested a walk through the grounds before he drove her back to London, so, linking arms, they wandered across the north side of the grounds to the chapel, a tiny place of fourteenth-century origin, older than the house itself and rebuilt at intervals whenever severe dilapidation or fire struck. On the outside wall there was a memorial plaque and she stopped to look at it. It commemorated Clive Appleby.

'That's your brother, I suppose.'

'Yes. He died on the first day of the Somme.'

Katherine remembered what her grandmother had said about the brother, and how his mother had doted on Clive.

'It must have hit your mother hard.'

'It destroyed her really. It affected me pretty deeply too. I was at school at the time and I remember him being mentioned at morning chapel. He was just one in a long line, of course, but even then I suspected that the loss of Clive wasn't something I would ever get over.'

'What do you mean?'

He turned to her, and she was startled to see his customary confidence clouded with emotion. 'You won't understand this, but I can't tell you the shame I felt – I still feel – in being too young to take part in the war. It never leaves you. After Clive died, it was as though I could never match up to him and that did something to me too, I suppose. It made me want to do something equally worthwhile, something that was equally for the good of humankind. To better mankind, if you like.'

'Through your scientific work?'

He seemed to be talking to himself. 'We're only raw material, you see, we can be improved. I'm a great believer in amelioration.'

They walked away from the memorial, then Katherine said: 'What do you mean, we can be improved?'

'The war wiped out the flower of a generation – we all know

136

that – but we forget that it left a surplus of poor specimens behind. Unless we do something to correct that, to reverse the degradation of our country, it will go on through the generations. It will affect our ability to fight another war.'

As he laid bare his vulnerability, this crack in his normal demeanour, Katherine caught the bright sheen of tears in his eyes and experienced a surge of feeling for him.

Silently he took her hand and led her inside the church. Outside, the walls and brickwork, with their differing styles, emerged like an architectural palimpsest of changing centuries, but inside the church seemed more an enduring record of the Appleby family itself than a place devoted to God. Plaques marking the burial of long-dead ancestors were set in the walls, their births and deaths recorded in the Bible on the lectern. From the roof blank-faced angels leant in chilly benediction and in the nineteenth-century stained-glass window a recent member of the Appleby family, perhaps Lewis' grandfather, engaged the attention of Christ in a lordly fashion as though pointing out that He was trespassing on private land. Standing beneath the window in a pool of jewelled light, Lewis seemed to regain his self-possession. He ran his hand over the backs of the pews and savoured the mouldy air, as though sampling some fabulously expensive claret.

'I love this place,' he said.

'Why?'

'I like the thought of all my ancestors, the unbroken blood line, all collected here. There's something sacred about it.'

'But, Lewis, you don't even believe in God.'

'I don't. And I know it's funny. But I believe in family.'

As she stood there the thought of the ancient bodies imprisoned around them, with their gleaming skulls and skeletal hands clawing empty air, felt horribly oppressive. The chill in the chapel's musty atmosphere clutched at her. Katherine was relieved to get out into the bright afternoon, up the worn path in the tiny graveyard, on to the field.

Lewis looked back at the chapel. 'All the Applebys are buried there. And are married there, come to that.'

He turned to her slightly, conversationally, as if commenting on the weather.

'That's where we'll get married.'

'What?' She halted in her tracks as though physically struck.
'That's where I want us to marry. That is, if you'll have me.'

She faltered to a stop in her tracks. Her foot played nervously
with a tussock of grass. In a neighbouring field she noticed a
sparrowhawk diving from the sheer sky like a bolt of flesh and
feather towards a mouse rustling in the ground beneath it.

'I don't know if I can.'

'Do you mean you don't want to?' There was genuine
surprise in his voice.

'Well . . . I mean . . . do you love me?' The words sounded
thick and clumsy as they came from her mouth, like biting on
cardboard.

He laughed. 'What did you think? Of course I love you.
Doesn't that go without saying?'

'No, it doesn't. I need you to tell me. Why?'

He studied her for a moment, as if pretending to search for
a reason, then said: 'There's something perfect about you. I
thought it the first moment I saw you. Something fresh and
untainted.'

'But, Lewis, I'm not sure if . . .'

'Don't, Katherine.' He put a finger to her lips and looked
down at her, so certain of everything, as rigorous in his rightness
as a fossil lodged in rock. 'Please trust me. You must marry me.
We're a perfect match.'

CHAPTER FIFTEEN

THE DEATH OF Ralph's father, in his final year at Oxford, had left him alone but quite comfortably off. If he had been so inclined, he could have pursued a life of some indolence, but eventually he invested the money to start the book business and spent much of the rest on a flat near Buckingham Palace, an odd, neo-classical place with a grand pilastered entry that belied its modest proportions. Inside there was really no more than a wide studio, from which steps led upwards to a bedroom, its doorway covered with velvet curtains, and a small bathroom. A well-equipped kitchenette, streamlined and new, extended like the prow of a ship over the yard at the back. The whole of one wall was given over to shelves of his book collection. Even when he was away from them, he could recall each book bodily, knew its precise weight and texture, as well as its aspirations, ambitions, context and achievement.

There was a woman, a Mrs Sorrentino, who came in when he was away to re-arrange the dust and generally pry around. Not that there was anything there to pry into. The compartments of Ralph's life were so tightly sealed that one might assume his own feet would not know, unless it was absolutely necessary, what his hands were doing. It was a habit he had learned in childhood and would never shake off. Discretion cloaked him like a second skin, so much so that the men and occasional girlfriends who visited when he was in London had given up probing too deeply into his travels, his job, or, God forbid, his feelings.

Despite his own secretive ways, he disliked any deviousness in others. He favoured girls who were open and uncomplicated. The last one who had been in the flat had indicated her willingness to be seduced by going to his large double bed and bouncing up and down on the Chinese silk coverlet. Ralph had cheerfully obliged. He had a liberal, unconventional approach to sex. He liked it, yet if there was no girl around he was quite capable of going for months without doing anything about it. If absolutely necessary there was always his good friend Virginia who would be persuaded to suspend the platonic nature of their friendship for an evening. He had never, to his knowledge, been in love.

The day he returned from Germany he walked into the flat, made tea, put some Bach cello music on the gramophone and laid down on the worn green sofa, feeling an immense stress lifting off him. It had been a difficult trip this time. After he had seen his friend and discussed the evening with Oscar Bauer, he had driven across the border, through France and taken the boat train. It was hard going back to Germany. Each time it was worse. Though he had been disturbed by what he saw in Berlin, it was nothing to what he had witnessed in Bavaria. A new order and firm government was just what the country needed, people said there. Yet he had seen the firm hands of governance wielding sticks which beat against the backs of Jews. In Munich he had seen the good citizens of the new order turn their fat backs when thugs abused a Jewish family in a restaurant, the father ushering his children out before they had finished their meals and the mother trying to shield their ears from the foul language shouted after them.

The past few years had given Ralph ample opportunity to form his own views on the continental situation. After university, finding himself alone in the world, he had spent a carefree year studying languages at the Sorbonne, perfecting both his French and German and making contacts of various nationalities who were to serve him well when he came to travel further, in Italy, Spain and Austria. Staying with local people, talking in inns and restaurants, he came to witness at first hand the extent of unemployment and insecurity, as well as the tension and rising apprehension at events in Germany. His travels abroad also widened his perspective on his native country and when he came back to Britain his old school and university companions seemed to him blinded by complacency, the country itself stagnating in a misguided belief in its own moral superiority. He was alarmed at the lofty disdain with which politicians viewed entanglements on the continent and dismayed at the gradual disarmament which had been practised by successive governments since the war. There seemed, in a Britain still numbed and bereaved by the Great

War, a determination to avoid more battle at all costs.

He was thinking about this when he began to unpack his suitcase and a heavy, tightly wrapped bundle rolled out from beneath one of his suits. It was Meredith's book, of course, for which he must act as postman. In an instant the memory of Meredith as he left her, brow knitted like a small, cross child, staring after him from the corner of the Dahlem street, disturbed the insulating calm of the flat. A sour sense of unfinished business arose. When would he get time to deliver the bloody book?

Annoyed, he turned to open his mail, which he tended to regard as generally unwelcome intrusions from the outside world. On the top of the pile was a postcard from a girl called Sally, holidaying in the south of France. 'Wish You Were Here!!!' she had added, with three suggestive exclamation marks. Did she really? He was quite genuinely surprised that anyone should wish his company – he had certainly given Sally no thought at all since a few months earlier when he had closed the door firmly behind her slightly dishevelled form very early one morning. Strangely, almost intuitively, after the Sally episode he remembered Virginia saying: 'You want to be careful. People will think you don't like women.'

That was a strange thing to say of a man who entertained them so freely, Ralph thought, yet those in his social circle did consider him a little sadistic, just a bit dangerous in the way he seemed to enjoy women's discomfiture, the way, they whispered among themselves, he sometimes liked to tie their hands in lovemaking. Ralph himself didn't care what they said. The truth was he didn't dislike women, he just found it hard to stay interested in them. There were obvious exceptions like Virginia, who was too keen on her life in the civil service ever to contemplate a more serious affair, which was probably why he got on so well with her.

* * *

They normally talked in the Mayfair office but the next morning Pennington wanted to meet at his club. He'd stayed there overnight, having gone to some theatre late the night before and been unable to get back to his home, somewhere outside Dorking, so he'd asked Ralph if he'd mind joining him for breakfast. Walking up Pall Mall, dressed in a dark Savile Row suit and looking just like the stockbroker he might have been, Ralph felt oddly piqued. It wasn't as though he was paid for what he did. He was young and came well down in the pecking order, else no one would have dared ask him to turn up for breakfast, but even so there did not seem to be any thanks for what he did. God knew why he did it really, yet it was he, not the Foreign Office man, who had initiated contact. Though these thoughts were turning bitterly in his head, nothing but calm good cheer was discernible in him when Pennington emerged in the lobby and ushered him into the gloomy brown-painted dining room.

He was famished, and ordered a full cooked breakfast, determined to get the most out of his meal in vengeance. Around them elderly men grappled with the opened sheets of *The Times*, as though struggling to erect vast white flags of surrender above the expanse of breakfast table. Ralph distrusted the newspaper of late. It had been going pretty soft on the Nazis, he thought, despite the excellence of its correspondent in Berlin. Even at that time in the morning, Pennington's diplomacy was at full force. He was charming, talking easily about last night's performance of *The Doll's House* – 'Frightfully depressive, these Scandinavians' – for an efficient few minutes before switching to the subject of Bauer. Ralph said he had already informed their friend in Germany, but for Pennington's sake he repeated the details about the manufacturing strength recruited in Oscar Bauer's factory and the new government orders he had secured. As the effects of fried egg and good bacon entering his bloodstream began to revive him, Ralph's bad temper gradually subsided, not that his companion would have known anything about it.

'Listen,' said Pennington, stroking his moustache gently like a small, domestic pet. 'There's a man I'd like you to meet.'

'I'm not going back for a while, I'm afraid. I've got practically no business there as it is. The publishers in Berlin can't understand why they keep seeing me.'

'No, no this man's British. A scientist – name of Lewis Appleby. You don't know him, do you? He and a couple of friends are coming down for a spot of fishing this weekend. We have a very useful stretch of trout river on our land.'

'How nice.'

'Yes, quite.'

'Is Appleby . . . er . . .?'

'No, he's not one of us in any official sense. Though he could be useful.'

'Why?'

'He just seems to have good ideas, you know. Now, everyone's pitching up first thing Saturday. Can I count you in?'

Ralph had nothing planned. 'Very kind of you. It could be a nice day out.'

'Precisely. A bit of fresh air. That's what I thought.' Pouring Ralph more tea, Pennington continued pleasantly: 'How did you find it over there?'

'Getting nastier. What's the Foreign Office view?'

Pennington exhaled, to signify resignation. 'They say Herr Hitler's doing well with the economy. He complains a lot about Versailles and the fact that the Deutsche Volk have not been treated fairly, etc, etc, but he admires England. He's impressed by the Empire, you know. There are certainly some in our office who think he's not a totally bad thing. And he does of course keep issuing proclamations assuring us of his peaceful intentions. Others think if Goering took over it could be perfectly workable.'

'Have you read *Mein Kampf*?' asked Ralph shortly.

'I haven't, since you ask. Very difficult to get in translation.'

'Oh yes,' recalled Ralph, who had read the book in German. 'Hitler was tricky about authorising British and French versions. Probably because he doesn't want us to realise just how limited his commitment to peace really is. You've seen these Nuremberg laws? Banning Jews from public life and stripping them of German citizenship?'

'Mmmn, of course. Very unpleasant.'

Pennington wiped his mouth, and moved his chair back, signalling the regrettable necessity of observing office hours. He was an odd young fellow, this Kingsland – it was impossible to know what he was thinking. He had no family and no dependants, which made him dangerous, but they said (and they should know) that he was utterly dependable. He was bright too, apparently – he'd learned several languages and taught himself some more. Pennington liked him, in as much as you could like any chap who gave away absolutely nothing about his personal life. He'd been at Pennington's old college at Oxford – his tutors had been quite enthusiastic about him – and that had to count for something, even now.

★ ★ ★

After they parted Ralph walked up to Piccadilly Circus and hailed a cab. Hampstead was way out of his usual ambit, but he had no other engagements that morning and he'd decided to get the thing done before he forgot about it. For a short time he had considered posting the book, but remembering what Meredith had said about a personal message for the recipients and her own obvious insouciance about its fate hardened his resolve. The message was, from what he could remember, that their family was thinking of them. Even if the brothers were out, and he was ardently hoping that they were, leaving the parcel with a short note looked better than abandoning it to the mercy of the Royal Mail.

At the top of the street he let the cab go, then immediately regretted it as it started to rain. A conker smashed against his shoulder like a spiked green grenade, spilling its glossy treasure on the ground. The rain swept against the tall, handsome faces of the houses, big, affluent buildings which were not, Ralph thought, the obvious place for a couple of refugee brothers to end up.

Number 35 was shabbier and more neglected than its neighbours. Net curtains dropped against the windows and rampant Michaelmas daisies peered over the fence. It was clear that what had once been a large, family house was divided into flats. Seven bells were ranked with names beside them. He pressed the one marked Reichmann and hoped for no answer.

He was counting on the brothers being out. Surely at ten o'clock in the morning they must reliably be about whatever business they had secured.

The door opened and a man of about Ralph's own age stood there, rubbing his eyes.

'I'm looking for the Reichmanns.'

'*Ja*. Yes, you have come to the right place.' Dark, watchful eyes in a pale face.

144

'Are you,' – What was the first name? Had he even been told it? – 'Herr Doktor Reichmann?'

'It's been some time since anyone called me that.' The man laughed. 'But tell me, how can I help you?'

'I have a parcel for you, from your father.'

In his grudging performance of this errand, Ralph had not stopped to think what impression the parcel may have on its recipient. The effect was immediate. Emotion filled the man's face, his eyes widened in excitement and alarm.

'What? Please, I'm sorry, do come in.'

He led Ralph through a dank hallway to a first-floor flat. Inside, the smell of gas fire mingled with the aura of damp and the bare furnishings of the room could be taken in at a glance. There was a card table and two armchairs, their covering sagging and split as though awaiting surgical intervention, and through a door was visible a bedroom, with a couple of narrow beds. The man gestured towards one, adding: 'Forgive the state of the room. I was in bed – I work night shifts.'

'No, not at all. Let me introduce myself properly. My name is Ralph Kingsland. When I was on a recent trip to Berlin, I met a friend of mine, a young woman called Meredith Davenport, who had been passed this by your father.'

Ralph proffered the brown-paper parcel. 'She is staying with a family who are attended by your father. He asked if she could let you have this . . . directly . . . and pass on the message that your family are well and thinking of you.'

He had embellished the message. Were they well? He could not remember. There must be a letter in the parcel, with more details.

All this time Ralph had been standing holding the parcel, while Reichmann stared at it. Then, taking it, he opened it swiftly and said, 'Aah.' Ralph tried to see what was inside. A Bible, it looked like. 'The family prayer book. It has the names of our family in it. It is a sign that he does not think I will be returning.' There was a letter in the book. 'Do you mind?' The man sat on the chair and read it. After a while, during which Ralph shuffled awkwardly round the room, he put down the letter and said: 'Please. You have been so kind to bring this to me. Let me give you some coffee. My name is Martin Reichmann. You must forgive my English. It is not so strong.'

* * *

Unwillingly at first, then with growing interest, Ralph heard the story of Martin Reichmann and his brother Rudi. It occurred to Ralph, once Martin had begun to speak and it was plain he would not be returning to sleep, that they should converse in German. At the sound of his mother tongue the other man seemed unnaturally grateful. He looked at Ralph and his eyes filmed for a moment – 'What a pleasure to speak German! Rudi insists we speak only English together' – then he went on in German.

'It was the boycott in 1933 that did it, the day the storm-troopers prevented people from patronising Jewish shops. My parents said they could tell from that day on that it was going to get worse. Berlin had always been a moderate city, always a bit cosmopolitan and sophisticated, you know? And most of our friends said that what was happening in the rest of the country would never happen in Berlin. We had all lived there for ever, for generations. But my father said it was still no atmosphere for young men to grow up in. Some people were looking up any American or English acquaintances, asking for advice on emigration, and luckily my father had relations here. He had been to England when he was a young man – he has cousins who live up in the north – and he had a sort of love affair with this place. An anglophile, I think you would call it. He really liked it and I suppose he saw me, a young doctor, just starting on my medical career, as he was then. My mother comes from Vienna, she is a passionate, emotional lady and she was very much against our going. But father persuaded her that Rudi and I would flourish in England. And as they only had two sons, they could afford to send us. If there had been more of us, perhaps it would have been hard to split us up. Anyhow, we went to Liverpool initially, but then it didn't work out – I didn't speak English and my cousin's wife did not want us living there while I had found no work – but my cousin knew of a man, a travelling salesman, who was vacating this place. My housekeeping skills are not particularly strong . . .' he cast a rueful wave around the litter of the room, 'but it suits us very well.'

Martin had secured work on the night shift at the Royal Free hospital, Rudi was admitted to a local school.

'He is very bright. His English is fluent already and he teaches me. I want him to go to university and then I'm hoping that eventually I will be able to build up a practice and he can join me. The Reichmann brothers.'

'And your parents?'

'Obviously, I was hoping that we would be able to join them, when this dreadful dictatorship is over. But in his letter my father says it will be a long road before that. He believes there will be a war. So, if necessary, I will raise the means to get them out of Germany and bring them here.'

Ralph remembered a joke doing the rounds in Berlin. 'The Germans are a medical miracle. They are the only country able to walk upright without a backbone.' Immediately he said it, he regretted it, but to his relief Martin laughed.

'It will get worse,' Martin said.

The two men looked at each other with complete under-standing, then Martin drew his hands across his eyes in a gesture of weariness. Ralph made polite moves to go.

'I'm keeping you,' said Martin, springing up. 'But I do want you to know my gratitude for taking the time to visit me. Are you are ever planning to return to Berlin?'

'I may be.'

'Then I would be grateful if I could meet you again and send a message back to my father.'

'Of course.' Ralph shook hands. 'It has been very good to meet you.' He meant it. On the spur of the moment, he realised he would like to see Martin again. 'I wonder if you'd like to meet up for a drink sometime?'

Chapter Sixteen

'Men,' Lavender Barnes frequently said, 'are aggressively tribal.' There being no men in the Barnes household except May's father, whose obvious domestication, slippers, and unthreatening way with gardening implements was assumed to disqualify him, it was hard to tell if she was right. But for May, an only child growing up with no brothers, men had taken on an increasingly exotic aura, like a rare pet, such as the lean, smooth-coated Doberman their neighbours had kept. Not exactly dangerous, but demanding and difficult to understand.

Now she found herself thrown into the company of men more than she had ever imagined, she was beginning to understand a little more, but not enough to challenge her mother's fundamental diagnosis. That day she was sitting in a pub at the east end of Fleet Street, within sight of the gloomy fluted portals of St Paul's and earshot of the hustle of Ludgate Circle. The pub was one especially favoured by journalists from her newspaper – different papers for some reason tended to patronise different pubs – and this she assumed was part of the tribal thing her mother had talked about. And even here in the pub, an invisible gender divide seemed to operate between the men and the women. It reminded her of what someone had told her about Japanese women speaking a slightly different version of the language from their males. Around the front of the pub clutches of secretaries chattered, their talk rapid and high, punctuated with swoops and eddies of laughter, while at the bar some newsroom journalists she recognised stood, tipping back their pints, their conversation ponderous and sporadic, as though merely incidental to the drinking.

May chose a seat at the dimly lit back of the pub, where the grubby afternoon light only just made its way through sooty windows, smoothed her hair – it always needed smoothing and never looked anything but untidy – fixed her hair slide yet again and carefully put her glasses away in her handbag. She wanted to look her best. It was only lunch with James, just a friendly lunch with an office companion, as anyone else would have observed, but her heart was racing. He was late of course. Where was he? She peered around her. It was already ten past.

When he arrived, pushing the flopping hair out of his eyes, his charm instantly offset any possible offence.

'I say, I bet you'd given up on me. I would have done, I'm sure. I'm awfully sorry I'm late. I just couldn't get away.'

May, who had been scrutinising her watch at the moment he came over, blushed, and feeling the red tide rise up her chest and neck and spread irrepressibly over her face, dipped her head.

'What'll you have?'

'Oh, gin and it, please.'

As James dashed off to the bar, May realised, with a quick spurt of disappointment, that he had brought someone with him. The other man edged round the table and held out his hand.

'Seeing as James neglects to introduce us, I'm Will. Will Mason.'

'I'm May Barnes.'

She knew the name, but for the moment she just couldn't remember how. She had certainly never seen him before. Will Mason was tall and lean, with grizzled, gingery hair combed forward across his scalp and ivory skin. He had watery green eyes which appeared to swim myopically, like reptiles behind opaque glass. He wore a trench coat with upturned collar and a dandyish cravat tied with a dramatic flourish. James must have mentioned him at some time but she had no idea when or why. He sat down, so there was no doubt he was staying.

'I hope I'm not barging in on your lunch. James said it was just a gossip session and the more the merrier.'

'No. No that's fine. How do you know James?'

'Well, to be precise I met him when he came over and poked a stick in my face. I spent the rest of the day having the wound bandaged. We were six years old at the time. Our first day at school.'

'Oh, I see.' That must be where she had heard of him.

'But since then, we've seen each other quite frequently. Or as often as we can when I'm over here.'

'Over from where?'

'Paris is where I'm living at the moment.'

Of course. The Will Mason. Painter. She had heard James talking of him, and had seen his work in James' flat – landscapes, seascapes and portraits painted with jewel-like colours that were primitive and dramatic, exuding a strange subconscious air of fear.

'So you two have introduced yourselves,' James returned with the drinks and three ham rolls. 'Will's over here to try and persuade a gallery to recognise his genius and hold an exhibition. I'm going to see if I can't craft a small paragraph about his glamorous life which might help the paintings sell.'

Will Mason's life did seem to be the kind James Chumley dreamed of. Since leaving university he had drifted around rootlessly before settling in Paris, where he spent his days painting in a studio off the Boulevard St-Germain and his evenings drinking with a crowd of poets, painters and philosophers. He had met Picasso and visited his studio in Montmartre.

'What's he like?' asked May.

'My dear, meeting Picasso was like a religious experience. When I saw his use of colour, so potent and mysterious, I knew that nothing in my life would ever come close to it. Nothing could be as real as what he portrayed.'

He knew Braque and Miró, had explored cubism and surrealism, and experimented with abstraction but forsaken it in favour of his own brand of realism. His work didn't make much money, he explained, but he didn't want to compromise himself with any kind of career.

'You lucky devil,' said James. 'How inspiring it must be to work in an atmosphere like that.'

How inspiring it must be, thought May, to have ideals on a private income. But Will was amused at his friend's envy.

'You don't have such a bad life, James. Parties every evening, cocktails at the Italian Embassy, dinners at Quaglinos, scavenging at rich men's tables – you practically never need pay to eat. Then there are the first nights at the theatre and the country weekends with the honourable so and so. It doesn't sound too deeply deprived.'

May, who frequently endured a biting commentary from James of his own social life, was aware that this butterfly existence was precisely what he found so unsatisfactory. Perhaps Will knew too.

James frowned in consternation. 'But that's just the trouble, Will. London society isn't exactly an intellectual powerhouse. There's no heart and soul to it. No ideals. And though I may trade in gossip, I'm still a journalist, remember? I do retain some peripheral awareness of the outside world. Hunger. Unemployment. It's not all champagne and canapés here.'

'My dear, you think things are better on the continent? You want to come and visit me.' Will scrutinised his empty glass. 'Britain seems a surreal paradise in comparison. Certainly rich enough to afford me. Which reminds me – I must be going. I'm to meet this dealer in Cork Street at two o'clock so wish me luck.'

When he had left, James turned a shining face to her.

'Well? How did you like him?'

His face seemed suffused with enthusiasm at the meeting with Will. Perhaps it was a male thing, May thought, some unconscious recognition from like to like, their shared past rising up to bind them.

'I thought he was very interesting.'

'I knew you'd like him. You and I like the same types, don't we?' Unaware of May's irrational pleasure at having their personal tastes bracketed together, he continued: 'I was rather hoping to ask you a tremendous favour, actually.'

'Of course, what is it?'

'The thing is, it's Will's birthday and while he's over here I rather wanted to do a dinner for him, but as you know I live in a broom cupboard and I wondered if you'd lend us your place. I mean I'll do all the food and everything, but I'd be awfully grateful if you could invite some nice girls and provide the seating arrangements and the roof over our heads. If you hadn't anything else planned, that is.'

'That's a wonderful idea. When is it?'

'A bit short notice, I'm afraid, it's this Saturday.'

May had been planning to spend the following Saturday visiting her cousin, Irene. She lived just outside Brentwood, married to a doctor who spent practically all his time answering house calls, with the result that Irene remained in provincial isolation along with nanny, maid, cook and four children. There was nothing better May liked than to be there, entertaining Irene who was starved of London life, playing with the older children, cosseting and kissing the new baby, with no one particularly fussing over whether she was comfortable, or needed more tea or lunch, but just allowing her to fit in as part of the family. She was looking forward to it so much she practically ached.

'Fine. Saturday would be fine.'

★   ★   ★

Naturally Katherine had not breathed a word of her engagement to a soul. For a start she was not entirely sure she was engaged – how were you supposed to feel when you first trussed up your future with another's? – or that the engagement would be followed by a marriage. No heavily jewelled ring yet manacled her finger. His proposal had seemed so unlikely, simultaneously so casual and yet so formal, that for a few days she was still able to sit at her desk in the *Extremity* office and pretend that nothing at all unusual had taken place. Marriage to Lewis and life at Fallings were so far from what she had imagined for herself that she found herself directionless, heading into uncertain territory, some wild distant outpost for whose extremes she would be ill-equipped. Yet it had to be admitted that there was something luxurious about falling in with Lewis' plans and succumbing to his controlling spirit. She had never before felt wanted by any man, or necessary to anyone else's scheme of things. It was just that Lewis himself seemed not so much a different type from her as practically another species.

When he rang and said he planned to place the engagement in *The Times* the next week, and that it would doubtless be followed by obligatory family meetings, she knew that once it appeared in print this dreamy, elusive state she was in would be submerged by the sheer bureaucracy of it all, and the proposal would be no longer hers to disbelieve at leisure, but the business of family, friends and the world, a morsel for them to dissect and quarrel over. So she was determined to say nothing until the announcement appeared. Yet her abstraction soon attracted the attention of Sonia, whose eyes, like those of a circling predator seeking minute deviation from the norm, instantly registered her languor. She homed in on Katherine, ravenous for detail.

'You've got your head in the clouds this week. That man has swept you off your feet. I can always tell. God, what I wouldn't do for some romance.'

This sense of hazy disorientation was hardly what Katherine had pictured as romance, though the image of herself being swept off her feet and hoisted into the air, shoes kicking impotently as she was uprooted and held aloft by some giant arm, did seem somehow appropriate. She went up to Oxford Street after work one afternoon and looked in the window of a bridal house. It was a foggy day and the swirling mist at ground level added an air of unreality to the slim sheaths of satin, which emerged like lily tubes in the window with tiny froths of lace spilling from their edges. Katherine tried to picture herself walking up the aisle of the little church at Fallings, smiling complicitly the way brides did smile, as though someone had just explained the point of a joke which they had previously not understood. There would be her younger sisters, perhaps, as bridesmaids, fiddling and whispering behind her, her father, a faltering, silenced figure in the front row and Syrie, mouth serrated in a grim lipstick stripe, a living martyr to the marital condition. Syrie had said little when first told of Katherine's friendship with Lewis, only flared her nostrils expressively and noted: 'He's a bit old for you, isn't he?'

Curiously, although she had been reluctant to tell her mother about Lewis, Katherine found her predictable dissatisfaction with the state of affairs and her total absence of romantic enthralment reassuring. She was certain that her mother would fail to furnish her with the traditional advice about packing a trousseau or hiring a cook or, most particularly, sex.

Her mother's advice on that topic, had it been proffered, would have been of the 'grin and bear it' variety, with a sinister nod towards men's essentially bestial nature, but as far as Katherine could see that was scarcely necessary. Lewis had gone so far as to express his desire for several children, yet the issue of physical intimacy remained dauntingly unexplored. The odd embrace aside, it was hard enough to imagine herself alone in a bedroom with him, never mind in a bed. It was just so hard to tell how he felt. Lewis was in love with her. He had said so himself. Yet when she went through her mental stack of schoolgirl images, it was impossible to picture him as a Mr

Rochester at the altar, staring down at her with raging, hungry eyes, or even as a predatory Mr Darcy, recently tamed. It was as though he regarded their marriage as – she struggled to find a word – unsurprising. Part of the natural order of things.

No sooner had she thought this, than Katherine chided herself for it. It was a fault in herself – this feeling of separation and solitariness. It was her own nature which seemed to cut her off from others, or at least placed a veil of bloodless scrutiny between them. With Katherine, feelings hesitated before they came out, like an emotional stammer, and then emerged blurred and changed so that nothing was ever as sharp or immediate as she had hoped. It was as though she was receiving a simultaneous translation of life, and in the interpreter's voice she recognised the wry, chiding accents of her mother.

The weekend before the engagement became public knowledge, Lewis was going fishing. She had watched him fish once before and he had attempted to instruct her, but she had shied away at the landed trout, secretly horrified at its mad squirming on the grass beside her, before the glassy-eyed flipping was brought to a sudden end as Lewis administered the priest – the silver hammer used to dispatch it. Though she knew she would later be eating the fish with appreciation, she had stroked its lustrous scales sorrowfully and her sentimentality had been roundly mocked.

She was secretly pleased, therefore, that he was going off fishing without her. It meant she could stay in London and help May with the dinner party. Unlike May, she knew the work of Will Mason and was rather excited at the idea of meeting him. And there was something so relaxing about May's company. Since they had shared the flat they had each increasingly enjoyed the time they spent together. They had daringly had their ears pierced by a chemist, to the horror of May's mother. They frequently took trips to the theatre or to the cinema, or, at Katherine's behest, to the National Gallery. And Katherine loved hearing about life at the newspaper, which seemed intensely sophisticated, though May grumbled at her slow progress. The writing career she had imagined for herself seemed to extend no further than captions for women's fashions, and selecting household tips and cookery hints, though considering the amount of time she spent combing the recipe books for ingenious ways to do lobster, or strawberry whip, they had certainly failed to make much impression. May regularly scorched and burnt her way through a variety of unappetising meals in their tiny kitchenette.

'The thing is, I can do basic things, like beef and bacon, but I just can't see how to put them together with other things,' she lamented. 'Whenever I even think about it my mind goes blank. But then if God had meant us to make soup, he wouldn't have given us tins.'

Given that Will Mason lived in Paris and was probably used to wonderful French cuisine, Katherine was relieved to hear that for the dinner party May intended to make kedgeree, one of her few foolproof dishes, and that James was bringing a large amount of beer and champagne to wash it down.

'Who on earth are you going to ask?'

'Oh, all the usual suspects,' said May. 'And there's Etta – the daughter of one of my mother's friends – she'd love to meet Will Mason. I remember her talking about his work. But she's terribly young and green, I don't want to be accused of corrupting her.'

'He can't be that wicked.'

'Just wait till you meet him.' May recalled, with a prickle of distaste, the way his watery eyes slid over her. 'There's something about him I don't entirely trust.'

'How enthralling. I'm sure Eddie Tiverton would like to meet him.'

'And if we have Eddie Tiverton and your friend Sonia, I suppose we ought to invite Meredith Davenport.'

'Why? She'll only put a damper on things. We're not grand enough for her. Besides, I think she's still in Berlin.'

'She's not. I spoke to her the other day. She was full of this commission from your friend Eddie. She'd be awfully hurt not to come.'

Katherine grimaced. 'Perhaps it'll be too short notice for her. I can't believe Meredith Davenport has nothing fixed for a Saturday night. How did she like Berlin?'

'It sounds like she had a fabulous time, lots of dancing in jazz clubs till dawn and that sort of thing. Her friends there sound pretty fearsome, though. One gave her a swastika to wear in her buttonhole. I told her to throw it away.'

'How awful. It makes her sound like that Mitford girl.'

May sighed. 'Oh, she's all right. She would never have worn it. The thing about Meredith is, she's incapable of taking things seriously. Despite her father, she simply can't imagine that politics isn't some parlour game where you dress up in different costumes, then change sides halfway through. She doesn't realise how it affects people.'

Chapter Seventeen

It should have been a very enjoyable day. From early in the morning it promised to be fine weather, one of the clear, warm days which appear like the ghost of summer, after summer itself has been buried by frost and rain. As Ralph drove down to Surrey the sun beamed from a high, blue sky, gently tattooing his face and casting a sharp splash of shadow where the car passed. For half an hour he wove through the suburbs of south London until he reached the countryside itself, where patches of land stood blackened as battlefields by the burning of stubble. As he neared Pennington's place he passed through a narrow tunnel of trees which arched overhead and enclosed him in a net of shifting, aqueous light, as though an army of fir and oak was advancing and reclaiming the inroads of cultivation. It was as English as Ralph could imagine. Opening the window and feeling the motoring breeze, he savoured the land's almost physical embrace.

Pennington was there to greet him, striding forward to shake Ralph's hand and introducing him to the other guests, pressing a sherry upon him and ushering everyone on to the terrace, which showed a distant prospect of the river they were to fish.

'From what I can remember it's absolutely bulging with brown trout,' said Lewis Appleby politely.

'You've come at a good time. End of the season and they're literally swimming on to the bait at the moment,' said Pennington.

Ralph took a covert look at Appleby. He was tall and good-looking, with a kind of aristocratic austerity that made him stand out from the other guests and an air of assurance as unmistakable as his tweed jacket. It was an attitude Ralph recognised with a shudder, the same impenetrable veneer of charm possessed by all the Old Etonians he had met, which successfully deflected deeper analysis. Just a single gesture was enough to signify the grand house and lands, the centuries of money and privilege, the assumption that other people would do what they were asked. The sight of Appleby aroused in Ralph unwelcome memories of landed homes he had visited during his schooldays and an old familiar unease at the hands of their inhabitants, as though he were being ranked and assessed.

It was not until they had gathered their equipment, nets and baskets together and were tramping down to the river that Ralph elicited any more concrete information about him.

'Good chap, eh?' said Pennington, who had fallen in beside him.

'How do you know him?'

'We were at school together, though I was four years older. I was the same year as his brother Clive. Clive was a great friend – killed on the first day of the Somme, like so many of the others. It was terrible for his parents of course – losing the heir whom they absolutely idolised. Tough on Lewis too, I suppose. He inherited the family seat – a lovely place called Fallings.'

'What does he do?'

'Marine biology is his specialisation, as far as I can remember. London University.'

'So these useful ideas you were talking about are in connection with marine biology, then?'

'Oh, good heavens no. Far more general. He created quite a little storm with a magazine piece calling for a more scientific assessment of the decline of national virility.'

They were a catholic selection, six of them all told. As well as Pennington there was Clarke, another Foreign Office man who worked in the Spanish section – a dark, thickset fellow with a dry wit and an obvious problem with the bottle, judging by the amount of sherry he had already downed and the hip flask he brought along. There was Briggs, a scientific colleague of Appleby's who worked at the Galton Institute and whom Ralph had already written off as dull, and an American journalist called Elmer Hutton who had met Hitler and regaled them with an imitation of the little man's rasping shout, and described the way his pale eyes seemed to burn through you, then switch off.

Surprisingly for a dictator, Hitler was also, said Hutton, enormously indolent. 'Most days he don't even get up until lunch time. When he goes back to the that mountain place of his, Berchtesgaden, he spends the afternoon watching a movie, and doesn't get down to anything serious until the evening.'

'It's hard to be alarmed about anyone truly lazy,' ventured Briggs in a nasal twang which Ralph found instantly annoying.

'That's rich,' crowed Clarke. 'That's just what the British establishment would love to believe. No one has to do anything about the Nazis, because although they are fanatically obsessed with the aggrandisement and self-determination of the German people, they're far too idle to do anything about it.'

'Don't worry, Ralph,' said Pennington quietly. 'We're all pretty much of the same mind here.'

Ralph felt curiously reluctant to join the conversation. Any suggestion that the German threat was overestimated was passionately opposed by Hutton and Clarke, the Foreign Office man. Pennington, freed of the caution that fettered him around Whitehall, worried openly about the government's tendency to ignore the growing tension and spoke warmly of Churchill.

At lunch, when they shared a basket of game pie and smoked salmon sandwiches, political talk resumed. Lewis Appleby mentioned Abyssinia, where Mussolini had crossed the frontier, and spoke disparagingly of the League of Nations.

'If it strengthens him then he will be formidable in a pact with Hitler,' said Hutton.

'If he makes a mistake and gets himself bogged in a long war Hitler wins too, because with Mussolini weakened, Herr Hitler can get on with seizing Austria,' added Clarke.

'But aren't you forgetting those assurances of peace he gave recently?' protested Briggs.

'When he tore up the Versailles treaty you mean?' said Hutton. 'Listen, fella, when I was last in Berlin I saw Goering's bombers flying in formation over my own rooftop. The only question in my mind is not does he have aggressive ambitions, but just how far they stretch.'

Ralph, being a relative novice at the sport, had landed three fish, far fewer that the rest of them. Lewis, who had taken his fish away from the river to gut them, squatted down beside him. He had caught ten and used his knife on them in swift succession, the blade neatly expelling the bloody waste.

Ralph said: 'I hope your wife likes trout.'

'I'm not married.'

Ralph felt a momentary embarrassment at his mistake, then a fragment of fellow feeling. Of course – Appleby was the last of his line, alone in the world like Ralph and without an heir. Then he shook himself contemptuously. There was an aeon of distance between a man like Lewis Appleby and himself. As he watched him walk away to the others he felt a curious wave of antagonism. Lewis Appleby was the type of man who ran this country, whose ancient blood silted up the veins of the establishment. Beneath the smooth good manners he was used to getting what he wanted and having his views heard respectfully, despite the fact that his knowledge of ordinary people and the way they thought and felt was undoubtedly nil. Still, if Pennington thought Appleby could be of use, then good luck to him.

★   ★   ★

Meredith was looking forward to the dinner for Will Mason. Her father had lent his driver, Charles, to take her to May's rather drab little flat, and though most of May's friends were hardly scintillating, she had actually heard of Will Mason and she knew Eddie Tiverton was to be there. Perhaps it was the thought of Eddie that prompted in Meredith a brilliant idea.

'Could we pick up a friend of mine first, Charles? I'll give you the address.' What a tease. That would teach Ralph Kingsland to walk away from her so casually. She would invite him to the party, where he would meet Eddie, who could be relied upon to be absolutely charming and deeply intelligent and with any luck he would realise what he had missed. She felt gay, intoxicated with excitement and the prospect of playing the two men off against each other. She shivered, growing chill in the fabulous backless evening gown that her mother had seen and failed to resist in that year's Paris collections. Beneath the silvery chiffon her small breasts goose-pimpled with excitement. When the Bentley stopped she said: 'That's fine, Charles. Drop me here and if I don't come straight back, then he's in and we'll make our own way to May's flat. So if you could meet me there at eleven, please.'

Ralph did indeed look gratifyingly astonished when he opened the door. His chin was grizzled with a day's stubble and he wore no tie. She caught a hint of alcohol on him. It happened

160

that he had telephoned Virginia, asking her if she wanted super, but got no answer, so he had lit a fire and was settling down to read. He had already downed a glass of whisky and had another by his side. With his early start, and the day's exercise, he had started to doze.

'What do you want?' he said.

'Aren't you going to invite me in?' Meredith arched her eyebrows as if at a serious social transgression.

'If you want to, come in,' he said indifferently, standing aside.

Meredith stepped into his sanctuary and gazed around her. It was quite unlike any other bachelor flat she had seen. It was quite dramatic, almost like the inside of a church or temple, with its one large, high-ceilinged room supported by decorative pillars, the whole of one wall dominated by rows of leather-bound books, their gold-embossed titles glinting in the light of a large fire. The lighting was low, two brackets of candles leant from the wall and the heavy tapestries hung around gave a theatrical feel to the place. She could see a staircase leading to what she assumed was the bedroom, obscured by a long velvet hanging. It had a distinct male scent about it, but there were none of the army prints, or pairs of boots, or hunting bric a brac she had found in other men's places.

'Are you going to offer me a drink?'

'All right. What will you have?'

'Whatever you've been having. Only not so much.'

As he poured her Scotch, Ralph said: 'Is this just a social visit?'

'I wondered if you'd like to come to a party with me.'

'When?'

'Now.'

'It's very kind of you but I can't tonight.'

'Oh. Are you expecting a visitor?'

'No.'

She settled herself on the green sofa, accepting her drink. As she did she let her sable-trimmed wrap slide from her shoulders, knowing how closely he was watching her. Dulled by drink and fatigue, Ralph could not take his eyes off her. She looked as lithe as a mermaid in her little grey slip of a dress, the buttons of her nipples clearly visible beneath the thin material. Round her neck a row of diamonds hung, glinting against her white skin like the speckled underscales of a fish.

'What a marvellous place. It's very artistic.' She lit a cigarette and checked her lipstick. 'So how did you enjoy your evening at the Bauers? You never told me.'

'Fine. Thank you. I returned the favour and delivered the book.'

'What book?'

'The parcel you asked me to deliver. I took it to Dr Reichmann's sons in Hampstead. It was a Jewish prayer book.'

'How exotic,' she said lightly.

'According to the son, Martin, it was a sign from their father that he doesn't expect them to return. It's a pretty sad tale.'

'Gloomy for you.'

'You're not really interested, are you? But then perhaps I shouldn't expect it from a girl like you.'

His sharp tone made Meredith apprehensive. Despite this room's sensuous opulence, its glittering candlelight darting off the cut-glass tumblers and the huge silver cigarette lighter, there was something threatening about it, like the lair of a feral beast.

'How terribly unfriendly you are. Is this how you treat all the women you entertain?'

'Which women did you have in mind?'

'Oh, Hugo says you're a tremendous ladies man.'

Was there a hint of snobbery in her accusation, the slightest suggestion of someone below the salt? He watched her jump up and finger the row of first editions stacked in order in the high, beechwood shelves. She stopped and removed a particularly fine Baudelaire, then put it back without looking at it.

'Are they amazingly valuable?'

'Yes.'

'Should they be this near the fire, then?'

'It keeps the damp out of the air. That's bad for books.'

She turned coquettishly.

'I've heard collecting is a sort of disease. A mental condition. One that mainly affects men.'

'A sort of madness, you mean?'

'An imbalance of the brain.'

'Do you think I'm mad then?'

'No. Just a little untamed.'

She was teasing him. She walked towards him provocatively, her eyes alight, lips puckered slightly at the edges in a droll smile. As she came close she saw the russet stubble, a stippling of red and gold, blurring the sharp planes of his face. He stood, almost a foot taller than her, regarding her with cold green eyes. He was thinking how right she was. How beside her alabaster shape, the shining hair held back from the face with a diamond slide, the arms fine and rounded, there was something rough about him. He could feel the sweat of the day's fishing still dried on his skin.

'What do you mean by untamed?' He reached out to her neck and ran a finger where the faint indigo vein made a line. She did not flinch.

'You're secretly rather unsocialised, aren't you? As though you're quite capable of behaving in polite society but you'd prefer to be locked away in your room.'

Locked in his room – as he had been that terrible summer when Meredith's family was supposed to be consoling him in grief. Meredith hardly knew what she was saying, but her flippant remarks re-ignited the sense of social exclusion which had been with Ralph during the day. Like that summer, when he had first seen Meredith, understood her taunts, but had not known how to reply. At that moment all the taboos he had erected around the girl, the invisible barrier of her age, her innocence and her family connections crumbled beneath his violent sexual urge. If he was unsocialised, he would damn well act that way.

Her teasing eyes widened momentarily in alarm as he took hold of her bodily, scooping her legs up in his arms, amazed at how light she was, and carried her up to the bedroom. Shouldering aside the velvet curtain, he laid her on the silk coverlet and swept a hand down the narrow ripple of her ribs to where the belly dipped and rose. He removed the necklace, heavy and precious in his hand, and peeled back the straps of her dress to lay her flesh bone-white and bare before him. There were no more flippancies from Meredith now. She was full of fear and excitement, but because she did not know what was coming she had no words for it.

Ralph pressed her down beneath him, parted her legs with

his knee, wrenched down his trousers and pushed into her with force, feeling the long suppressed urge fulfilled. Under him he saw her eyes close and her perfect mouth part and inhale as if in supplication. Into Ralph's mind came the thought of the fish Lewis Appleby had gutted. How after the deft knife's incision, the claret ropes of intestine, the strange fruit of organs and the heart's fat purse spilled on to the grass. He penetrated her more deeply, causing the first invisible let of blood within, then he felt her legs arch and cling around him, and heard her cry out, 'No.'

★   ★   ★

Afterwards Meredith felt that all her breath was stifled within her and could only escape in tiny gasps. She lay tensely beside Ralph, who was on his back, staring at the ceiling. After a while he said: 'That was what you wanted, wasn't it?'

'How can you say that?' She began to cry softly, stifling her sobs so that he would not notice. He did, of course, register the tears but even while he was thinking how best to respond, the exhaustion of the day and the drink overcame him and Ralph fell asleep.

★   ★   ★

For a moment Meredith hesitated outside the door of May's flat. Earlier the partygoers had danced to 'Blue Moon', 'Cheek to Cheek' and 'Red Sails in the Sunset'. They had started on beer and progressed to brandy and now they were circling, swaying, singing along with the gramophone to 'Love is the Sweetest Thing':

> *Love is the greatest thing*
> *The oldest and the latest thing,*
> *I only hope that fate will bring*
> *Love's story to you . . . oooo.*

Meredith laid her cheek against the cold door. She could feel her own body against the insides of her clothes, as though raw nerve ends stood out unfleshed. One stocking was laddered. The damp, bruised ache between her thighs began to hurt more. She was blooded now. She thought of the expression in its other use, how when she had first ridden to hounds at seven, the master had daubed her with the blood from the fox's tail – gently he anointed her, with just the neatest little spot of blood on the face, like an Indian bride. This was a worse violation. Did it show, what she had just lost, and what she had gained?

After she had left his flat, without waking him, she hailed a cab. Her first thought was to go home to a bath, yet the driver was due to meet her here in another hour. So she rubbed her eyes, brushed her hair and reapplied her lipstick. When May opened the door, Meredith half expected some sign of shock or dismay, as thought her experience was printed incarnadine on her skin. But May, looking bohemian in her black velvet trousers and red peeptoe shoes, was charming and tipsy, wandering away to find drink, gesturing vaguely that Meredith should find the others in the drawing room, apologising that they had eaten before her arrival. Standing at the door to the room, Meredith felt as though she was observing the party from a great distance. Someone had placed a red-fringed shawl on the lamp, casting a boudoir glow on the room and beautifying the faces of the couples dancing. James and Will were staging a mock waltz. She saw Eddie approach her and put his arm round her.

'Meredith, darling, well done.'

For a single, surreal moment, it was as though some bizarre congratulation was being proffered. As though the huge truth that stood in her mind, the dominating scene blocking out all else, could not but be visible to others.

'What for?'

'For the piece of course. "Inside Berlin, An Outsider's View". We'll need to do a little work on it, but I think we can make the next issue. Perhaps a little less about the stylishness of Nazi uniform but the part about the Jewish doctor was very moving.'

'Oh good,' she said faintly.

Eddie was so kind. He went off into one of his routines, his tinder dry wit sparking into a shower of impersonations and teasing stories about another of his contributors. Katherine was there, and another tall blonde girl, laughing heartily, and a timid little thing called Etta, no more than a schoolgirl, staring at Will Mason with undisguised awe. Besides the thin, gingery Mason and the foppish James Chumley, Eddie was like a Greek god, with his dark spirals of curls, the fine, straight profile, expensive cologne and languid, laughing grace. But for the first time, Eddie's striking looks did nothing to rouse her. Meredith could hardly focus on him, so absorbed was she with a confusing welter of anger and indignation. Just who did Ralph Kingsland think he was? How he would pay for this. Dully she accepted several brandies and as they began to circulate her body's deep maze of veins, the confusion cleared. She felt a desperate urge to get away from May's flat. She did not want to be at this party, thronged with beings from another planet, but nor, she realised, did she want to be at home in her bath. There was only one place she wanted to be and that was lying on a green silk Chinese coverlet, looking into the pale face of Ralph Kingsland, which would mirror, of course, her own fulfilment and desire.

Chapter Eighteen

MARCH THE WEDDING was set for. Lady Myddleton objected, saying it was a malevolent month, prone to rain and biting winds, coupled with the Lent problem, which meant there could be no flowers in church. It was most unnatural and why not Christmas or earlier in the year? As soon as she heard her mother's objections, Syrie instinctively sided with Katherine, so the little chapel in the grounds of Fallings was set for Saturday the seventh, and the slow wheels of an English wedding were put in motion.

As it turned out, the delay served them well, because the king died in January, plunging everyone into mourning and subjecting everyday life to a small, but distinct lacuna. Katherine's grandmother wore a black armband, the newspapers appeared with heavy black borders and the theatres and cinemas closed. The new Edward VIII walked behind the coffin with five other kings as well as representatives from Nazi Germany.

'Goering wanted to come but said his safety could not be ensured in the face of Jewish hostility. What tosh,' commented Sonia, who was reading from the paper. 'Now there's a wedding to copy, Katherine. When Goering got hitched with that actress last year, it was the works. Stormtroopers as guard of honour.'

'Oh, I don't want anything too theatrical,' shuddered Katherine.

★ ★ ★

Will Mason returned from Paris in February, having finally found a gallery to show his canvases. His work was, he freely and proudly admitted, deeply unfashionable, in that it shunned the abstract influences of the day in favour of more figurative style, but on the plus side there was plenty of it to go round – more than two hundred pictures, all told – and he was, he stated, among the best of his generation. There was evidently some truth in this, because despite the unfashionability of Will's style, several of the best-known critics had accepted invitations to the opening. But one evening newspaper, known to be reactionary in its approach to modern art, had jumped the gun and published its own review, suggesting that the public were being hoodwinked by Will Mason with 'a child's seaside drawings masquerading as art'. The review had made James unusually nervous. Outwardly he looked smooth as ever in a soft grey hat and smart suit, but his customary, world-worn ease had deserted him.

'All I ask is that he doesn't drink tonight,' he commented several times to May, who he had asked to accompany him. 'Especially if there are going to be other critics around.'

May knew of Will's problem and tried to sympathise but it was hard to concentrate on anything else because, for the first time ever, James had taken her arm just as though they were on a date. Her exhilaration quite obliterated her doubts about the figure-hugging, leaf-green dress she had chosen to wear. May's mother swore by the traditional advice that green or orange were the only suitable colours for redheads and May, whose fashion sense was as confined as her cooking skills, miserably followed this dictum. Yet she couldn't help thinking, as she surveyed her two-toned wardrobe, that knowing as little about fashion as she did, green certainly seemed to make her skin even more sallow and liverish than it already was, and no shade of orange, from terracotta to carrot, did anything but emphasise the flaming frizz of her hair.

James, however, had not mentioned her dress, so that was all right. He was hurrying along concentrating solely on Will's well-being with a fervour, May thought, which did their friendship credit. To their dismay the first thing they saw when they entered the narrow little gallery, a few blocks behind Regent's Street, was Will Mason with a glass in his hand and a high flush on his face, which was normally pale as a corpse. The party had already been going for an hour, and the packed mass of people had merged to a single floundering octopus of shoulders and elbows and heels, trapped in a space too small for it.

To avoid any confrontation May steered James towards the paintings which were arranged like theatre sets around the gallery walls. Having only seen his work in passing before, she was surprised to realise how powerful they were, how pure, with their clear colours and unworldly, almost childlike vision. She scrabbled in her bag for the glasses she had earlier forsaken, and the soft blur of her surroundings became sharp and clear. There was a selection of paintings, done when he had taken a house in Normandy, which portrayed much the same settings, little, whitewashed buildings, a wild sea lashed with waves as high as houses, tall cypresses and dramatic figures. In one, titled *Icarus*, a young man in the foreground stood like a god, a pool of feathers at his feet, hands loosely crossed on a naked, muscular torso so exquisite that May averted her eyes. There were similar beautiful men elsewhere, mainly workers – fishermen putting out to sea, a woodsman wielding his axe, and a barrow boy selling tangerines whose colour leapt from the thick oil. The women were less interesting somehow. Whether mending nets or gutting piles of silver fish, they were faceless, monolithic figures. They reminded May of the bulky, humourless heroines of Soviet propaganda.

James stood miserably at her side. 'Look at him,' he said. 'His flashing eyes, his floating hair. You can tell he's drunk the milk of Paradise all right.'

Even from across the room it was clear Will Mason was intensely drunk. He had cornered a noted newspaper critic and could be heard berating the man for his 'legendary' lack of discernment, causing nudging and giggling all round. Suddenly noticing James and May in the crowd, their faces aghast, he broke off and approached, deserting the critic and weaving through the packed guests with infinite care, as though on a ship in bad weather.

He stood very close to her. 'Ah, you've brought the mysterious May.'

Sensing something personal coming, May blushed and the fierce scarlet patterned her pale face like a map of empire. Looking her up and down, he said: 'You know, Miss Barnes, I think you might make a picture. Would you consent to be painted?'

May felt the heavy marble of her limbs, and every flattened angle of her glowing, moon face. She could practically feel herself transmogrifying into a fisherwoman under his eye.

'Thank you, Will, but I don't know if I'd make a good model. I'm hopeless at keeping still.'

'You can't be worse than James. Lie him down on a sofa with nothing on and he can't keep still a second without fidgeting or complaining that he's getting cold.'

James turned pink. 'Oh, do shut up, Will. That's quite enough. Isn't it time you laid off the bottle? It can't be good for sales.'

'What do I care about sales? They're all philistines, the lot of them. All of you,' he waved his glass in mock acknowledgement to the onlookers, who politely looked away.

James took his elbow, but was shaken roughly off. 'Steady on, Will. They can't be philistines if they're thinking of buying your work. And besides, it's an important evening for you tonight. Think of what you've achieved.'

Will gave a laboured frown. 'Oh? Which achievement in particular were you thinking of? Total obscurity, absolute fucking poverty, the status of a rag for critics to wipe their toffee noses on? The English wouldn't recognise a genius if he punched them in the face. Which come to think of it is a bloody good idea.'

'Nonsense. Don't get carried away.'

'And what about you?' There was a gleam of hatred and self-destruction in his eye as he turned on James. 'Frittering your life away on that ridiculous fascist rag. "The Duchess of Hoity Toit was seen dining with Lord Arse last night and all London is agog." You claim to hate all that stuff, but if you're going to write it why do you avoid the best gossip of all? When did you last mention the Simpson woman carrying on with the king? Oh, it wouldn't do to let the readers know what's really going on, would it? We are a newspaper, after all. Christ, I remember when you used to talk about writing, James. Real writing. Where's the great novel now, eh?'

James absorbed the words like body blows and failed to respond. The gallery owner was hurrying towards them, nurse-like, proffering a glass of water as though it possessed medicinal properties, his face betraying the long-suffering air of one anticipating further artistic behaviour. Suddenly May realised that she would have to take command of the situation.

'Come on, James, I'm going. Will's got other people to talk to. If you want to come with me, you'll have to come right now.'

She had thought of a little Italian restaurant she had been to, just off Jermyn Street, which was cheap without being particularly nasty. To her surprise, James let himself be led passively out of the gallery and silently through the streets. When they were settled inside and had taken their first mouthfuls of spaghetti, he looked at her gratefully and said: 'Thank you, May. There's absolutely nothing I can do about him. He'll regret it like hell in the morning. I'm glad you understand.'

She was not sure if she did entirely understand, but she knew that something had changed between them that night. Her earlier exhilaration had gone, to be replaced with a feeling of dull confidence. Men were such babies sometimes, May thought, and although she was not too skilled with men, babies were her speciality.

CHAPTER NINETEEN

MEREDITH ENJOYED VISITING Ralph's flat. She loved its forbidding mannish air, its sense of exclusion from the dull world outside, in which people behaved in predictable ways, operated by the silken strings of etiquette. Outside, men sent you flowers, and met your parents and tried to tell you how badly they had fallen for you. Ralph did none of those things. But the thrill of her first, illicit, sexual liaison, and the force of her infatuation, had obliged her to turn his disadvantages to virtues. So she told herself that it was romantic to carry on an affair without anyone's knowledge, mostly to stay in the flat but otherwise to pretend, whenever they found themselves at parties or restaurants or the theatre together, that they were old friends who had just come across each other by chance, and were delighted to have more company.

She assured herself it was a sign of his ease in her company that he did not cosset her, the way other men had, but allowed her to mix her own drink from his small cupboard, that he was happy to pick up a book and let the conversation lapse when they were together and that he did not pretend to be in a good humour when he was tired or moody. She grew interested in his first editions and asked questions about them which roused his enthusiasm and penetrated his unresponsive veneer. She put all the force of her considerable personality into finding out more about foreign affairs, which seemed to be an interest of his, and developing some views of her own, beyond the simple Conservatism she had absorbed with her nursery teas.

She had confidence in herself because she knew there was one thing which could be relied upon to break the dam of Ralph's reserve. She recognised that he regarded her as an unfortunate vice, rather like too many cigarettes, but one that was quite impossible to resist. Whenever she chose she could tease him until his chill self-sufficiency collapsed from the need to take her again and just for a while a glimpse of a more tender, earnest man emerged. His hunger for her flesh was a raging appetite, despite all his obvious previous experience. She felt more sure of it than her own delight, however much she savoured the acid tang of his sweat at close quarters, his narrow buttocks with their shadowy concavities and the novel but quite endearing vulnerability of a man unclothed.

The excitement of a physical relationship had been her chief preoccupation until February, when something unavoidable arose. She had been shopping for a suit to wear at Katherine Scott's wedding. She used the couturier her mother always used, a tiny French woman called Mademoiselle Susanne. She had known Meredith since she first fitted her for tiny embroidered party dresses with pin tucks and smocked bodices, and now she counted on the Davenport mother and daughter as reliable customers each season for some of her more expensive French evening dresses. Though Mademoiselle Susanne always preferred to see the mother because she spent more, as a couturier and an artist there was no competition between clothing the mammoth mama or perfecting the beautiful daughter with the twenty-two-inch waist. That day, however, taking Meredith's measurements for the baby-blue silk suit they had selected that so set off her buttery blonde hair, she noted with disapproval that the girl was losing weight.

'You have a lovely figure,' she chided. 'Please don't follow these fad diets and get any slimmer. Before you go you must sit down right there and I will fetch you coffee and a piece of my lemon cake.'

'Oh no, please, don't,' Meredith struggled back into her clothes. 'I haven't been able to keep anything down. I feel extremely queer.'

Mademoiselle had seen a lot of ladies in her tiny shop. It was a cosy, confessional place with its apricot walls satin-tented like an Arab's home, its gold-framed mirrors specially selected for the emaciating quality of their reflections. She had heard of more infidelities, insecurities and adulteries there than any priest and her penance was delivered only very indirectly in the size of her bill.

'Miss Davenport, what can be the matter with you, I wonder?'

'It'll clear up soon, I'm sure.'

Madame sat down beside her on a little chair. 'Do you mind

me asking, my dear, completely between the two of us, do you have a young man at the moment?'

'What's that to do with anything?'

'I wonder,' she looked at the girl's face, always pale, but now shadowed with dark circles and faintly puffy. 'Do you think you should see a doctor?'

'No.'

She hesitated, then with deliberation added: 'If you need help, my dear, you can always ask me, you know.'

Meredith grasped her meaning. It confirmed with a heavy thud of terror what she had already suspected, but not allowed herself to think. So it was obvious to Mademoiselle Susanne, and frankly if she knew, you might as well put it in *The Times*.

'No need. It's a touch of tummy flu. My mother has the same,' she said, making a face, then, as quickly as was decent, hurrying out of the shop.

★   ★   ★

She was due to meet Ralph at the flat. They had seen each other on and off for four months now and there had been times when they had arranged to meet and he'd returned late, to find her fuming on the doorstep, and times when she'd forced herself to walk away. With a man like Ralph, it was fatal to let him know she cared. That afternoon, however, he was in and welcomed her inside with a mock bow.

'Very honourable of you to call.'

He loved making a joke of her Hon. title. But Meredith was in no mood to reciprocate.

'How was your trip?'

'Fine. I'll be going back to France next week.'

He came towards her and stroked her hair – a prelude, she knew, to a kiss. His appetite for her was sharpened by a week away and for a moment she allowed herself the luxury of his embrace, feeling him harden in anticipation.

'I thought you might like to take me out,' she said, her voice unnaturally high.

'There's only one place I'd like to take you.'

He was removing her fur stole and slipping the jacket off her shoulders but as he made to undress her, the horror of it was too much for her. She could not forget the glint in

Mademoiselle's beady dark eyes, the complicit way she had offered her 'help'. Meredith pulled away from him and burst into tears on the sofa.

Disconcerted, Ralph reacted in a way that appeared insultingly casual. He turned his back on her and began to mix drinks.

'Oh, my God, histrionics. I can't cope with women crying, I thought you understood. Here, have some Scotch.' She took the glass, sniffing. 'What's the matter, anyway?'

She drew a breath, then told him. How gratifying it was, almost a pleasure, to shock him for once, to see his face slowly pale with alarm when the words sank in. To see how empty his calm reassurances about prevention really were. Well let him suffer for a bit. Meredith gave in to the luxury of sharing her anxiety.

'What are we going to do?' she wailed.

'Don't you know anyone else who's been fixed up?'

'Of course I don't. People I know don't get into these situations.'

'You could see your doctor.'

'And have him tell mamma and papa straight off? Hardly.'

'There are pills you can get.'

'Where?'

'I don't know. A chemist. I could ask around.'

'Ask around! My God, why don't you take out an advertisement?'

He fell silent, crossing his legs before him and placing his hands in his pockets.

'Mademoiselle said she could find me some help. God, it's so tawdry. Having to go to your dressmaker when you're in trouble. I simply can't. She'd tell the world.'

As if preparing for such exposure, Meredith blew her delicate nose and raked her hair behind her ears. After a long pause Ralph took out a cigarette and lit it, looking stonily across the room away from her.

'What do you want me to do?'

The unanswerable, distancing male response, she thought. How typical of him.

'Oh, I don't know. Help me, I suppose,' she said crossly.

'I could marry you, if you like.'

For a moment she could not believe she had heard right,

then she just had to laugh. It was the way he said it. The time-honoured offer in tones so curt and formal, with no more emotion than if he was offering to help her into her coat or across the road. She was laughing so hard, she could hardly get her answer out.

'Well, how romantic. You'd never have proposed to me in a million years without this.'

Why should he lie? It was true. She was the last girl on earth he'd think of marrying. But as he looked at her face, lit up with laughter that masked her misery, the idea momentarily appeared less repulsive. How mercurial she was – one moment dejected and the next amused, a blend of sun and thunder like an English spring. That proud snobbery in her, which he hated, that effortless arrogance imbued by her breeding, made her so independent even in this woeful state. And even pregnant and tear-stained her beauty was breathtaking.

'You're right. I wouldn't have asked before.'

'Then no thank you.'

He admired her for that. He came and sat beside her and placed his arm round her and the girl's touch and smell stirred in him a transitory, and now quite unacceptable, urge for sex.

'You know, I think I do know a doctor who might be able to help.'

★　★　★

May could not think when she'd been happier. The job offer was completely unforeseen and quite unexpected for someone who for the past year had written little more than captions about evening bags and notes on the correct use of fish knives at dinner parties. To think she would no longer be required to make Giselle's tea or collect her groceries. The new job brought with it a desk of its own and a pay rise. And all because of a chance article.

The piece on the sensational young artist Will Mason had not even been her own idea. After the opening of his exhibition the gossip columns were full of the moment, late in the evening, when he had eventually come to blows with one of his critics. The paper whose man had fallen into a fight with Will published a piece attacking his work, which it said represented a flight from reality and in its surrealist qualities discriminated against ordinary people in favour of the complacent middle-class art buyer. The attack sparked an answering defence in that newspaper's chief rival to the effect that Will Mason was a refreshing addition to the experimental modernists who prevailed just then, his self-conscious naïveté masking an underlying boldness of form, line and colour, and that he was a pioneer everyone should be proud to call British. Other papers joined in, broadening the row with full-scale attacks on the decadence of modern art, countered by excited celebrations of flourishing new ideas. According to Katherine, *Extremity* magazine was hastily preparing a piece about Will for its next issue. Many of the exhibits at the show were snapped up. Thus, in just a few weeks, Will Mason went from inconspicuous to controversial, and showed every sign of progressing to cult. When the topic of Will arose in the office May recalled her own reaction to his powerful, intriguing pictures.

'I don't think he is being deliberately avant garde or iconoclastic. He's the kind of artist who simply doesn't care what his contemporaries are doing. It's his own vision that matters to him.'

'You're talking as though you know him personally,' said Giselle loftily.

'I do actually. He came to dinner at my place on his last birthday.'

'But, May,' Giselle's mask of heavy make-up creased into a smile that would frighten small children, 'why didn't you mention this before? You really knew him before all the fuss. Ring him up at once and tell him you want to interview him. We'll call it "My Friend Will Mason".'

True to James' prediction, Will was suitably contrite about his behaviour at the party and willingly ushered May into the tiny Covent Garden studio flat James had found for him. It was just one room on the top floor of a tall building, with long sloping attic windows which let in an ethereal, northern light.

'So pure and melancholy. It's the best possible light for my painting. To be south-facing would be my ruin,' he remarked, waving his arm at the canvases crammed on to every available wall space. May stood at the door and wondered where to sit. There was only the bed, which was embarrassingly evident and unmade, or the sofa where she knew James had once lain.

Instead she went to the window and gazed out at the street below. 'It's such a lively situation, sir,' commented Will, adopting the falsetto of the agency woman who had let him the flat. 'We're right next door to the Communist party headquarters, so you can see a lot of awfully angry-looking communists stamping in and out all day, slamming the door behind them.' Lapsing into his own tone he added: 'Dreadfully badly dressed Communists. I can't imagine why James wants to be one.'

'Does he?'

'Oh, my dear. Hasn't he told you? In fact I think he's joined already. He tried to get me down to one of those anti-fascist marches the other day where they all got beaten up by big policemen's truncheons. He said I ought to paint them, would you believe.'

May knew the march he was referring to, down in the East End of London. The fascists and the communists had been equally pitched and the police had doled it out to both sides. But James had said nothing about being there. May couldn't believe that he would conceal something so important about himself from her. What their relationship – as she liked to think of it – lacked in reciprocated love, it made up for it in sheer depth of mutual knowledge. They often talked about politics.

'I think he would have mentioned it.'

'Perhaps he thought it wouldn't go down too well in the office. Not too much sympathy there for the reds.'

'No, he would have said. He's not afraid of people knowing his views.'

'Of course. Yes. You're probably right. He tells you everything, doesn't he? But why, then, is he pestering me to join this Marxist outfit – the International Artists Association? And he's always talking about how I should paint more unemployed men and servants and so on. How I should reflect poverty in my work and take my social responsibilities as an artist more seriously. I told him, James, my art is a political act in itself. I'm throwing off the shackles of form dictated by a past generation, liberating line and colour, enshrining idealism. But he'd much rather have pictures of disgruntled milkmen or miners or what have you.'

★   ★   ★

Will seemed to have no regrets about his behaviour at the

exhibition. Gaily he enlarged on how the critic had deserved his punch, and how the ensuing controversy had sold far more paintings than a whole sheaf of respectful notices ever could.

'Being written about isn't all bad. In fact, I'm getting quite addicted to it. If they go on writing about me, then I might not bother to go back to Paris at all.'

'Oh, I'm sure you'd find it easier to work there,' she murmured, wondering why on earth she should mind the idea of Will staying in London.

When she had finished her interview she closed her notebook and took out the camera she had brought with her to photograph Will.

'Could you stand still a minute?'

'A photograph, how lovely. But you don't want a dull head and shoulders. Remember, darling, art is all about perspective. Let me think of something.'

Dramatically he arranged himself against one of his canvases, and gazed sideways, looking intense and committed. 'Now take your camera down there, you'll need to kneel.' As she framed him in the viewfinder he said: 'By the way, I never thanked you properly for that lovely dinner you gave for my birthday.'

'Thank James really. It was his idea.'

'I know you think I behaved in a perfectly ghastly way to him the other night,' said Will, suddenly grave. When she did not contradict him, he said: 'The thing about James is, he's always been so wretchedly sensitive about these things.'

'He cares about you.'

'Oh, I know. And a little too much I think.'

'Probably,' she said coolly.

'But what about you, May?'

'What do you mean?' The elaborate business of taking photographs enabled her to avoid his eye.

'I was quite serious about that modelling. I'd still like to do a portrait of you. You're extremely paintable. I'm not like James, you know. I do actually like women.'

★ ★ ★

Shortly after May's account of 'My Friend Will Mason' appeared, alongside her moody shot of the artist in his studio, she received a telephone call from a man called Ernest Davies,

who said he was setting up a news magazine and would like to
see her. Mr Davies' office, in a narrow, dusty building off Fleet
Street, was not inspiring, but his vision was. He was a small,
excitable Welshman, and no sooner had May stepped through
the door and settled in a chair before his desk than he sprang
up and launched into his subject, his eye glittering, in a way
which reminded May irresistibly of the Ancient Mariner. But it
was impossible not to be caught up in his enthusiasm.

The first thing he did was to slap May's article down on his
desk dramatically.

'Magnificent.'

'Well, thank you. I tried to write it as truthfully as I could.'

'Not the words, Miss Barnes. I'm talking about the picture.'

'Oh, that was just a last-minute thought, really. I just
suggested that I take some and see how they come out.'

'We think alike, Miss Barnes. You see it's the image, and not
the printed word, which I believe to be the news medium of the
future. You're seen *Life*, the American magazine, of course.
Well, my backers and I are planning to establish a weekly paper
here which also takes the possibilities of photography seriously.
I can see you're interested.'

'Er, yes,' volunteered May, unnecessarily.

'And you're right. You're right! Look at all the excitement
over the television service the BBC has set up! That's all because
people want their news illustrated, as well as reported. The
power of the image is awesome and untapped. It's the future.
That probably comes as a blow to you, doesn't it? No more
jobs for journalists, I can see you thinking. We'll all have to turn
photographer. But no. I'm not the sort of man who wants to
make journalists redundant. I'm a journalist myself! I'm not
saying that the news reporter's notebook will be entirely
supplanted by his camera.'

'But,' interrupted May, 'we already have photographs in
newspapers, don't we? Like that one.'

'Very good point, Miss Barnes, indeed we do, but I believe
people want to see news as it happens, as it really happens,
rather than as the great and the good would like us to see it.
That's exactly what the new photography can do. It's un-
obtrusive, it's candid, it shows us the politicians and the film
stars when they are off their guard. It's realism, if you like. It

tells the truth, do you follow me? That's why I liked your picture of the artist fellow. It had a new perspective about it, something personal.'

Though the premises were down-at-heel and the office fixtures seemed pretty much non-existent, May was quite carried away by the notion. When he showed her some of the pictorial magazines from America, and some dummy pages from the magazine he wanted to establish, it was plain it could be highly successful. One shot showed a group of young working women, factory girls by the look of them, making the final adjustments to their outfits as they set off for a party. There was a backstage theatre shot of Vivien Leigh coming off stage, her face contorted in a comic grimace quite different from the glacial gaze she adopted for the flashbulbs. And there was the sombre stare of a small boy among a forest of adult legs, waiting for the funeral procession of the late king. The pictures were captivating, quite unlike anything she had seen before. They seemed, as Mr Davies had said, to offer a new perspective – one that was intelligent and unestablishment, that showed all of Britain, rather than just the accepted version.

'Do you have any other staff?' she asked gently, when he offered her the post of features editor.

'You're an observant lady, Miss Barnes, and the answer is not yet, but before very long they will be banging on the door for the privilege of working here. Who would want to remain part of the past, when they could be part of the future?'

'Who indeed,' murmured May, wondering what her father was going to say.

★　★　★

'It's such a marvellous idea,' she told James, who had taken her to the pub in celebration. 'I'm to commission features and take a hand in writing them. I'll be given some interviews to do and select which pictures to use. Even if it doesn't catch on at first, the American backers have agreed to fund our losses for a year, so we've plenty of breathing space.'

'Cheers.' They clinked glasses. 'So, now we've celebrated your news, May, I've got some news of my own. I'm leaving the paper!'

'No!'

'Well, it'd be no fun there without you, would it?'

'Don't be silly.'

'All right. The thing is, I can't really stand it anymore.'

'The gossip column?'

'Oh that, of course. You get a first-hand insight there into the way the country's going. The dreadful complacency of this place. And the fact that those who please to call themselves the ruling classes shut their eyes to what's really going on. Now that unemployment's gone down a bit, and we're in a so-called recovery, it's quite all right to forget about men out of work or people going hungry.'

He looked at her uncertainly, his hands furiously crumpling a cigarette packet on the table between them.

'I haven't told you much about this. I didn't know what you'd say. But I joined the party, Will told you. I just think there's got to be some sort of stand against fascism and they're the only ones who seem to want to pull together as a society.'

'But James, what are you going to do?'

He laughed. 'That's what I'm not sure about. I thought I might travel a bit. Go abroad. See what's happening.'

May felt a spiralling void open up beneath her. 'You're going to Paris? With Will?'

'No. Well, not like that. Though Paris is one place I'll be heading for because I have been offered some work filling in for one of the American radio networks. Helping out at the bureau there. I probably won't be able to keep body and soul together, but at least my mind will be nourished.'

All May's elation at her new job crumpled. Even as she'd accepted the post, she'd been thinking about sharing the news with James. That was the best bit of it really – talking over the implications of the new magazine, laughing at the comical Mr Davies, savouring the excitement of it with him. Fearing that she might cry, she steepled her hands to hide her face.

'May, what's the matter?'

'It's silly, it's the gin, it goes right up my nose.'

He brushed away his hair with his hand, in a characteristic way he had. Ever since the night of Will Mason's exhibition there had been a new understanding between them, something deeper and more serious.

'You know, May, I don't mind telling you, I'll miss you more than anyone else I can think of.'

'I'll miss you too.'

Awkwardly he drew her hand away from her face and patted it. Then he reached across the narrow in table and kissed her, a quick peck, just on the side of her mouth. As she raised her swimming eyes to his, he added: 'It'll be frightfully lonely without you. The truth is, you're like a sister to me.'

Chapter Twenty

THE CROWN PUBLIC house on Hampstead Hill offered a welcome prospect against the chill wind of a spring evening. A glimpse inside showed a ruddily lit interior, warm, ochre wallpaper, heavy varnished bar and soiled velvet chairs. It was a decor with no pretentions, promising nothing to spoil a night of relaxation, loud chat and hearty drinking and Ralph was getting to loathe the sight of it. Every aspect of that pub – the sweaty face of the barmaid and the roaring quartet of drunken office workers – reminded him of the night last week that he had met Martin Reichmann.

They had met at the pub several times since their first encounter, and each time until the last had been enjoyed by both, bar the habitual squabble when Ralph insisted on paying for the drinks. For Martin, to discuss his childhood and his home while ensconced in the warmth and safety of a London pub was a delight he had not expected in his alien and lonely new life. Sometimes, when he was at the hospital, or trudging Hampstead's elegant streets, it was as if his past had been entirely wiped out and there was no one except his brother to whom he could talk about it. Rudi was usually too busy with his books and his preparation for the scholarship examination to medical school to engage in nostalgic contemplation. So the advent of Ralph, with his almost fluent German, his knowledge of Berlin and his burning detestation of the Nazis was a joy. But better still was talking of nothing at all, just craning over the snooker table in the saloon bar where Ralph always won, or sitting for an hour at the chessboard where Martin would get his own back.

Last week's meeting was not so comfortable an occasion. Several times, reflecting on his new-found friendship, Martin had told himself there was nothing he would not do for Ralph, but he hardly expected his private vows to be put to the test so soon. When Ralph came back from the bar and asked him straight out if he knew a doctor who would take care of an unwanted pregnancy for a friend, Martin was troubled. But on reflection his image of Ralph was not shattered. After all, it was just like Ralph to help someone out in any way he could.

As it happened Martin did know the name of a doctor who could be prevailed upon for such things because a woman brought into the hospital badly haemorrhaging one night had explained she had seen doctor such and such earlier that day, and the senior nurse had told him that man's occupation with a knowing air. Martin was loathe to recommend this abortionist to Ralph but what else could he do?

The following Saturday evening they were to meet for a drink and a meat pie in the hour before Martin's shift started. When he entered, Ralph was already at their usual corner nursing a drink, the way his eyes dipped to the tabletop and the hunch of his shoulders bespeaking unhappiness.

'How did it go?'

'Fine,' said Ralph.

Fine. In as much as she had not died, and it was over and no one had found out. Otherwise there was nothing that could be described as fine about the experience last Tuesday morning when she went up to the cold, brass-plated Harley Street clinic and the doctor had relieved her of a baby and a hundred pounds. He had agreed that Meredith should come back to his flat later – it would hardy have done to let her parents know what was happening – and she had arrived at his door like an unwelcome delivery, pallid and unsmiling. Firmly, as though dealing with a recalcitrant child, he led her in and made tea. Until then, fastidious distaste and resentment had been at the forefront of Ralph's emotions about the affair, though he had, of course, paid for the operation and gone through the correct motions of gentlemanly concern. But curiously she never tried to make him feel guilty, as other girls might have done. Nor did she attempt to enlarge on the experience when she returned, except to say that she had lain on a leather couch and concentrated on the lampshade above her while he fiddled about and gave her something unpleasant to drink. Afterwards he assured her it would all be over in a few hours, so she should go home and expect some 'discomfort'.

Though Ralph too hoped she would go home soon, Meredith had showed no signs of moving when she finished her cup of tea. As he was going out, he was eventually obliged to leave with her still curled up on his sofa, vague and distant, reading a novel. Nor had she gone when he got back two hours later, but by then the discomfort the doctor had spoken of had evidently set in. Sheet-white and sweating, sobbing quietly with pain, she lay on his bed. He noticed the jade silk antique coverlet lay crumpled, ruined by rusty stains of blood. The sight of her appalled him.

'How do you feel?' he asked uselessly. 'Shall I call someone?'

'No. I'm . . . fine. I'll go soon.'

In that instant his resentment vanished. To see her crushed and battered and know that he was responsible was unbearable, but he did not know how to respond, other than being a competent nurse, fetching aspirin and tea, cleaning her, stroking the hair from her brow and going out to hail a taxi when she finally felt well enough to leave. He leant at the front door as she collected her things stiffly, without speaking or looking at him.

'I'm sorry,' he said.

She lifted her eyes in acknowledgement and walked past him. That had been four days ago and he had not seen her since.

★ ★ ★

He told Martin: 'It was all right. She says to thank you.'

He wondered how she was now. That morning her father's chauffeur was driving her down with May to Sussex, to Fallings, to see Lewis Appleby marry Katherine Scott. That was a strange match, apparently, of different ages and backgrounds, though he was assured they were deliriously happy. He thought again of Appleby and his smooth, autocratic manner. People like that thought nuptial bliss was their birthright. Ralph fleetingly imagined marrying Meredith, but the vision simply failed to come to mind. He could only picture her wide, red-rimmed eyes and their startling absence of reproach.

Martin lit a cigarette and offered him one. He had an air of urgency about him.

'You've heard the news, I take it?'

'What news?' Ralph had not listened to the wireless all day.

'Hitler's reoccupied the Rhineland. The troops arrived at dawn. Goose-stepped their way in.'

'My God. What will the French do?'

'Britain is urging France to wait and see. The BBC says Hitler's proposed a new treaty guaranteeing twenty-five years of peace.'

'No one will believe that.'

Martin lifted his dark-lidded eyes, his face heavy with scepticism. 'They'll do nothing. They'll say he's just re-occupied his own backyard. Britain doesn't want to get involved.'

'If it goes any further . . .'

'What is there to be done anyway? Declare war?'

★   ★   ★

Engagements were as catching as measles of course, so Lavender Barnes was absolutely thrilled by the prospect of a bride-to-be living in her daughter's flat. She prodded May remorselessly for details and took to dropping in unannounced. Given the contagious nature of nuptials, this event was sure to prompt May's own immersion in the affairs of lace and lists and going-away outfits. Lavender thought her daughter should go on one of those slimming diets beforehand and she certainly needed her hair completely restyled. Afterwards May would give up her job and there would be some darling babies – Mrs Barnes shared her daughter's enthusiasm on that score – and her help and advice would yet again be absolutely indispensable.

Despite Lavender's imaginative projections, however, May showed no symptoms of a fiancé and Katherine was most unforthcoming about her own wedding, except to say (astonishingly) there was very little to be done and she hoped there would be as little fuss as possible. It was a small affair, and the organisation would be jointly handled by her mother and grandmother. As that pair had not seen fit to co-operate for the past fifty years, that should be worth watching, Lavender thought shrewdly. But May was delighted to abandon polite enquiries about food and guest lists and restricted herself to giving Katherine something blue – a tiny sapphire pendant in the shape of a flower, encircled by a ring of opals – on the day before.

'Not that you need to be superstitious,' she told Katherine as she admired her present. 'You've had enough luck already.'

'How do you mean?'

'Well, marrying the man you want of course, lucky girl.'

* * *

May had not seen Fallings since the morning the previous year when she had visited with Katherine, and she was overjoyed to arrive. It was not just that the place was a picture – it was perfect wedding weather with a duck-egg blue sky and scattered blossom spiralling in a gentle breeze – but the journey there had been absolutely interminable. Meredith, looking listless but exquisite in an aquamarine suit, sat in virtual silence for the entire two hours and proved quite impossible to coax into conversation. Anyone else might have been offended but May assumed it was something to do with that man Ralph Kingsland who Meredith had been seeing. She had met them together once or twice and although she knew little about Ralph, they were plainly a perfect match, both tough as nails and totally self-possessed. For a moment, and against her own fierce resolution, she allowed herself to imagine how it would have been to arrive with James instead, exuding his easy charm, his wit and steady stream of banter. James was the sort everyone warmed to, he had charisma, he was absolutely the opposite of Meredith, who made one feel positively awkward and clumsy. But James had left London a couple of weeks before and understandably could give her no idea when he might return.

The wedding was at two, so they hardly had time for a quick cup of coffee before it was time to leave the house for the tiny chapel on the borders of Fallings' grounds. Clutching their hats to their heads against rogue winds, the guests picked their way through the grass path, smoothing down their smart clothes and shaking from their shoes the clinging earth underfoot. Meredith stalked on ahead when May was joined by Antonia and Simon Franklin, the couple who lived at the farm and who had allowed her to ride their horses. Behind her, May glimpsed the *Extremity* editor, Eddie Tiverton, walking with a blonde woman and another man, then, to her surprise, Will Mason appeared at her elbow.

'I didn't expect to see you here.'

'I didn't expect to be asked actually.' He was dressed

flamboyantly, and sported a scarlet cravat and an anemone in his buttonhole. 'But I'm extremely glad to be here. I adore weddings. I love the primitive ritual of it all. It must be something about the spectacle of lovers enmeshed in the harsh nets of formality. Sexual love subdued by the trappings of tradition.'

'I didn't realise you knew Katherine that well.'

'I don't. In fact I haven't seen her since that night you introduced us at your flat, remember. But we're both artists and that does bring a certain intimacy. We had the most interesting conversation.'

'About art?'

'Mmm art, yes, perspective and so on. I say, isn't the house marvellous? Did you get a good look at it? The reception should be jolly.'

'Yes, it should.' They had reached the churchyard. Looking up through the yew trees, dark as ink against the bright sky, May said levelly: 'Have you seen James at all?'

'Yes, I saw him just before he left last week. Though it's hardly goodbye, seeing as he's living at my place in Paris.'

'I thought he was going to look for his own lodgings?'

'Well, I'm delighted to hear it because I can't be expected to work with writers cluttering up my space. I say, are they the Scott family, do you think? The mother with the bad teeth and the screaming laugh? And what about all those children. Are they Catholics, d'you think? Oh, I love this sort of do.' He took her arm as they walked into the church and guided her towards a pew. 'When are you going to get married, May?'

★   ★   ★

If Katherine had ever thought seriously about her own wedding, which she hadn't except to hope that it wouldn't be embarrassing and to wish fervently that half her family would be unavoidably detained, she would probably have chosen a few moments in a registry office followed by a good lunch.

'I don't want anything grand,' she had confessed earlier to Sonia.

'Not do anything grand?' screeched Sonia. 'What's the point of marrying a country house then? What a waste.'

In fact apart from the hall which was ablaze with hothouse

flowers and several crates of vintage champagne which waited in the kitchen, ready to be dispensed by Mrs Mullins and her girls, her fears of overbearing grandeur were quite groundless.

Her father, coming to her to give her away, had sat in the library with her, feeding her sips of brandy from a silver hip flask that he'd had in the war.

'It's what men used to do before they went over the top,' he said cheerfully, while Katherine wondered whether he had given any thought to this comparison. Nonetheless, after a little while the brandy did have a strange, floaty effect, so she seemed to glide through the ceremony and the aftermath with very little effort at all.

She had chosen a close-fitting suit of ivory silk, with a bouquet of spring flowers and her hair was clasped tightly to her head, giving her an unusual air of sleek sophistication. When she reached the altar Lewis gave her an approving look before resuming his position, ramrod straight, listening to the vicar as though the marriage service was a long, rather involved anecdote in which, if not careful, one might miss a vital detail. When he came to pledge his vows Lewis smiled at her with a degree of assurance which seemed quite enough for both of them.

Even the reception – a tense interlude of polite talking, watching her mother and grandmother exchanging their spiky little smiles and posing for the photographs – went fairly swiftly. To eat there were beef or smoked salmon sandwiches, little bowls of pink and yellow sugar almonds on the tables and the wedding cake, surprisingly black and bitter beneath its veneer of icing and fragile, confectionery roses. Around the legs of the guests wandered the young dog which Lewis had given her that morning as a wedding present, a silvery greyhound with mournful bulging eyes and silk ribbons in his collar, his sharp claws clicking on the parquet floor. Katherine bent down to caress his trembling chest, taut as a warm bowl of bones, and felt the heart inside beating nervously as her own.

It seemed hardly any time at all before the guests started to drift away in the early evening. Lewis took her hand and they went out on to the terrace. It had been decided they would spend a few days of honeymoon there, rather than go away. Beneath the rose arbour, he put his arms round her waist, drew her towards him and whispered: 'I was proud of you today.'

There was something possessive, almost proprietorial in his touch. He curled a lock of her hair between his fingers then drew his hand down across her chest as though she were a work of art he was admiring.

'You know, you belong to me now. And to Fallings.'

Katherine looked up at the sloping lawns as they receded, beyond the lozenges of light from the library windows, into the towering darkness. She tried to picture her future children playing there, but the image escaped her.

'I was thinking I might paint the house soon.' Art was the way she had of taking charge of experience, and making it her own. 'And if you could stand still for long enough I could put you in the picture too.'

Lewis regarded her, the jacket of his morning dress slung over his shoulder, his thin mouth pursed in a smile.

'All right. And how would you show me?'

Katherine tried to recall what Will Mason had said; something about life being made up of millions of perspectives, and we could never escape our own but we should try to see other people's. That was the gift of the artist – to see the others.

'I'd try to show what you were thinking.'

'Really? Do you know what I'm thinking now?'

She turned away from him. 'You're probably thinking it's getting cold. Let's go back inside.'

'Not yet,' he said. 'Come with me. Just a quick walk.'

He led her away from the warmth and light of the house right up to the hilltop clearing where the shadows lay, indigo and violet, around the ruined shell house. Katherine looked at the little building, its broken shells giving off an iridescent glimmer in the early moonlight, and she quivered a little, thinking of the other Appleby bride, Elena, whose ghost still roamed Fallings' vacant spaces. Though her face was warm from the quantities of brandy and champagne she had drunk, her flesh prickled.

'What are we doing here?'

'Sit beside me.' He had spread his jacket out on the smooth grass. 'It's such a beautiful view from here.'

He was right, the house did look lovely below them, all lit up with a ribbon of dance music leaking out of an opened window, the clattering of china just audible from the kitchen on the south wing. As she huddled against Lewis for warmth he turned to her and loosened one by one the small ivory buttons that led up her suit, freeing her breasts beneath. Katherine shivered as he ran his hand up her leg, circling with his fingers and caressing her. In the darkness he had become strangely anonymous, hardly like Lewis at all, just a formless shape beside her, stroking and probing with increasing urgency until he was pushing her down beneath him and hefting his weight above her.

'Lewis. Not here . . .'

'Quiet.' He stopped her mouth with a kiss. 'You mustn't stop me now. I've waited so long for this.'

It was both him and not him. Even his voice had deepened to a hoarse gasp of desire. As his body strove heavy and pale above her, the sinews of his neck standing out like cords, she sensed the faint rip of her bridal clothes beneath and then a sharp pain sever her resisting flesh.

Her limbs struggled against his weight, then surrendered like lead. She felt removed, yet all her sensations were sharpened, so that she seemed aware of the tiny machinations of the earth beneath them and the sifting of the chill wind in the branches above their heads. She felt as distant as the desolate moon, viewing this random violation far below it. So this was what the Bible called carnal knowledge. Only it was not so much knowledge, Katherine thought, as a kind of estrangement.

When he finished he said: 'Are you all right?'

'Yes. Fine.'

'But you're cold?'

'Very.'

'We'd best get you back then. I don't want you catching a chill. I expect you could do with some supper.'

He was himself again. He wrapped an arm around her and took her back down the lawn to the wide, lighted windows of the house. As they moved into the familiar, comfortable surroundings, where the maid was waiting to serve them supper and the drawing-room fire was stoked, Katherine felt her usual sense of admiration towards her clever, new husband return. She was really so lucky to have married Lewis. She felt guilty that she had not responded to his needs as warmly as a new wife should. Later that night, as she waited for him to join her between the icy sheets of their bed, she told herself it was probably always like this. That for just a fleeting moment, every bride feared she had married a stranger.

PART THREE

CHAPTER TWENTY-ONE

'I CAN HARDLY believe I'm seeing this.'

Frank LeRoux waved the offending newspaper in the air before thrusting it disdainfully on Jessica's pristine desk.

'AMCO is deeply disappointed, I don't mind telling you, that just a matter of months after we initiate a relationship with Hughes Associates for the express purpose of keeping our important business confidential in the medium term, until we are ready to publicise it, this wildly uninformed, ignorant and biased account of our activities appears in the press.'

Jessica tried to maintain cordial relations with all her clients, especially the large, important ones whose handsome, six-figure fees kept the company afloat. But it was hard, very hard, when faced with someone like Frank LeRoux. He didn't seem to understand the notion of a free press, or the idea that libel and aspects of privacy aside, British journalists could write pretty much what they liked about you, without revealing their sources. Someone had given him the idea that in Britain, unlike America with its first amendment protection of free information, certain aspects of one's business were outside the ambit of journalistic interference. She certainly wished she was outside the ambit of client interference. LeRoux had turned up unannounced at the office at nine o'clock that morning, just as she was drinking a much-needed espresso, looking down the list of phone calls from journalists and trying to get on top of the crisis.

'I understand that, Mr LeRoux. But you must also understand that British newspapers are interested in a company as prestigious as AMCO setting up over here and of course they want to know your motivations. Now if you'd agreed to the interview and briefing for science correspondents I outlined in my strategy document, perhaps we could have directed and controlled that interest. But it's certainly not too late.'

LeRoux sat down on her chrome chair, mediaevally uncomfortable, and regarded her coldly. Jessica went on.

'We don't want to act too fast of course. You don't want to

look like you're reacting to this piece. Just to let other papers know, when they enquire, that there have been long-standing plans to hold a meeting sometime soon, say next week, and maybe a guided tour round the science park . . .'

'No.'

'I really would advise . . .'

'If I need any more advice, Miss Leigh, I'll ask for it. Briefing the world's press about every little aspect of our business is not our method, much as our rivals would like it to be. I don't know how many other clients you have in the highly competitive field of commercial biotech – I understood when we hired you that this was a world you were familiar with – but broadcasting confidential details about work-in-progress to suit some left-wing journalist is not the way we do things.'

The brow-beating was having its effect on Jessica. She gave him the most conciliatory look she could muster.

'In that case, is there anything AMCO would request that we do?'

'Clear up the mess. Redirect attention. The American president is coming over here next week, as you may have noticed. Tell them to examine his biodiversity bill. Tell them there's rumours of another sex scandal. Tell them anything you like, except our business. I'm sure you'll manage fine.'

'Certainly. Perhaps, in that case, we should talk later . . .'

'I'll call you.'

He got up to leave, almost colliding with Jessica's secretary who was bringing him coffee. The secretary raised her eyebrows as he retreated down the glass-partitioned corridor, entered the see-through lift and slid balefully downwards.

'They say the client's always right.'

'They hadn't met Mr LeRoux. Here, give me that.' Jessica took Frank LeRoux's coffee and drank it gloomily.

★   ★   ★

It was a sheer relief to get home, ten hours later, after a day of stalling the press and avoiding calls from her other, less critical clients. The neighbourhood was coming alive for the night, with the boys sitting out on the steps playing music, as the heat throbbed from the cracked pavements. But up in her fifth-floor haven with white blinds pulled down on the windows and the soft lighting illuminating a delicious interior of eggshell blues and greens, of clean, uncluttered surfaces and simple wooden floors, the outside world simply fell away, its only ambassador the ruby eye on the answerphone blinking reproachfully.

Jessica took off her suit and had a long bath before dressing in comfortable jeans and a white shirt, opening a can of Coke, and stabbing the answerphone button, expecting AMCO.

'Hi! It's me here.'

Rosie's voice, dressed in bright friendliness, failed to disguise its subtext of aggrievement.

'I simply can't remember whether you said you would be back by now or not, you know pregnancy shrinks the brain, but if you are could I ask an awfully big favour? You see we thought we'd take the baby to see Pete's mother and it's hours in the car and I simply can't stand it with all four, so is there any way you'd be a star and take three of them this weekend? It's only for Saturday really. I know it's an awful lot to ask but I'll do the same for you someday. They love your flat. They're always talking about your animal collection.'

Her collection. Jessica looked up at the little group of animals ranged on a shelf beside her. They had taken years to amass and each one was precious to her. She liked to think about the people who had made them; romantically she imagined them as tribesmen on some distant African plain, quick-fingered Indians and impassive native Americans, silently carving round a distant fire. The animals looked back at her with their familiar faces. There was the quizzical sandstone monkey, the jade elephant with its inlaid trunk and the early clay buffalo. The Inuit reindeer, made from a single walrus tusk, was broken now, following a session with her eldest niece. On the phone a squall rose in the background and her sister's saccharine pleading gave way to more characteristic exasperation, reflecting her general suspicion that the world was conspiring to provoke her.

'Oh God, there's the baby now. Listen, Jessica, I don't know if you'll actually get this message, so if you do, please call me or I'll have to make some other arrangement.'

Given the choice Jessica would probably rather have opted for another negative client encounter with Frank LeRoux than a day coping with her nieces. It was another world, the one

Rosie lived in, where nobody worked at weekends and single people simply had far too much time on their hands. Jessica loved the children, but the thought of combining them with a weekend's work was just impossible. For the meantime she decided to pretend she hadn't got the message at all. By rights she should still be on her holiday with Steve in Sussex. Correction. By rights she should still be on holiday with Steve in the South of France. Why hadn't he phoned?

At the thought of Steve, the emptiness in the flat, which a moment ago had been so exquisite, seemed to sound out an emptiness within her. Her beautiful room lost its lustre. Even her lovely furnishings dulled because they were perfect, so much in harmony with her own taste. There was not, as in many of her friends' homes, a single compromise item, no hopeless table or mismatched chair chosen by two people and representing in its very imperfection their union and hopes, their willingness to subjugate the ideal to the reality. Would there ever be?

Jessica looked at her face in the mirror, still bright and flawless after her awful day, and smoothed the loose hair from her forehead, wondering how long it would be before her inner anxieties marched across it in lines and creases, making her face a map of her cares.

At that moment the doorbell rang. That was why Steve had not rung! He had come to see her, she realised. Fallings was only two hours away after all. She pressed the intercom with joy.

'Hi. It's me. Just thought I'd drop by.'

'Alex. What on earth do you want?'

'If you let me in I'll tell you.'

With slight disdain she heard him puffing from the five flights of stairs as she unlocked the door. He stepped past her, creased and stubbled as usual.

'At last. It's like getting into Fort Knox.'

'Great. A journalist. Just about the last person I want to see.'

'I've had friendlier greetings in Beirut.'

'Well, sorry. I've had a horrible day.'

'Want to tell me about it?'

'No thanks, I'm tired. I was just about to get an early night.'

'That's a shame. I was just about to ask you out to dinner.'

'Nice of you, but no.'

'Oh dear.' He began to roam unbidden round the flat, like a

prospective purchaser. In the kitchen he approached her animal shelf and scrutinised a couple of the items casually. 'Cute little things,' he commented, as though they were a line of teddy bears on her bed, then, wandering into the kitchen, he asked: 'Why don't you offer me a drink now I've come all this way? I bet you've got lager.'

She poured him a bottle of the cold beer she kept for Steve on the rare occasions he came to the flat, though in general he preferred wine.

'Why *did* you come all this way?'

He plumped down on the sofa, recently re-covered in a delicate shade of aquamarine, and Jessica found herself hoping fleetingly that he wouldn't put his feet up.

'Oh, the charms of the country house were beginning to fade. And I wondered why you left in such a hurry.'

'I'm flattered at the interest, but it wasn't anything for you to worry about. There was a slight crisis with one of my clients, an American company called AMCO. They needed me on hand.'

'It's a bit dramatic to call you back from holiday, isn't it? I mean I know you're a high flyer . . .'

'Yes. It was a bit.'

She sank on to the sofa beside him. Apart from her secretary, she had spoken to no one sympathetic all day and suddenly it seemed impossible to have a willing listener and not tell him about AMCO and their ludicrous reaction to a single, speculative newspaper story. She poured it all out, concealing the undignified side of her meeting with Frank LeRoux, yet when she had finished Alex was annoyingly nonchalant.

'I saw Brent's piece. I didn't know you had anything to do with that company or I would have read it a bit more closely. Why are AMCO being so aggressive about it?'

'I don't know. Perhaps they don't like ill-informed speculation about their business. It's a very sensitive area, biotechnology, and they really are at the forefront of it.'

'Perhaps they're hiding something.'

'Now that's exactly why I didn't want to see a journalist. All these juvenile conspiracy theories are driving me mad. It's that mentality that's created all this fuss. In fact the Americans would say that an uneducated attitude to science is holding Britain back. The public thinks of Frankenstein's monster or

Brave New World and the journalists don't bother to equip themselves with enough knowledge to disabuse them. It's easier to spin a scare story.'

'Perhaps you'd like to educate me.'

'I suspect that would take too far long.'

'Well, seeing as I'm ravenous and the inside of your fridge looks about as full as my knowledge of biotechnology, why don't you disabuse me over dinner?'

'You must be joking. And have you pump me about AMCO?'

'Science is out of bounds then. I promise.'

'Sorry. I said I was tired.'

'What about later this week?'

'You're certainly persistent, aren't you? Besides, who gave you my address. Did you ask Steve?'

'I'm a journalist, remember.'

Jessica had plainly not missed the sheaf of correspondence she had left behind in her room at Fallings, then. It was a stack of phone and water bills, plus letters from accountants and clients that she must – incredibly by Alex's standards – have intended to tackle on holiday. He read them all religiously but they were dull, dull, dull. The only useful item was the phone bill which supplied her address and number.

'Well, let's say later this week. I'll take your mind off your crisis.'

Aware of her reluctance he debased himself by adding: 'We can talk more about Steve,' and was rewarded – or punished – by seeing her eyes brighten.

'OK then.'

'Friday?'

'Sure. Friday.'

As he went out he said: 'I meant to say. Thanks for the message you left me about Lewis Appleby. It's intriguing. Did you hear any more about why the wife vanished?'

'Nothing. The gardener told me. He said no one knew what had happened to her. But that she'd been a lovely woman.'

'You're sure there weren't any details you forgot?'

'Yes. I'm telling you, Alex. That was all he knew.'

'People never tell you all they know.'

'I take it you're still thinking of doing a piece about Appleby then?'

'Absolutely. It's coming up to the centenary of his birth, which is always a good peg. Here was the man who had everything – a brilliant mind, the admiration of his peers, fame, integrity, public respect . . .'

'Everything except a wife, you mean.'

'You see – we even think alike.'

CHAPTER TWENTY-TWO

'ARE YOU WITH us, Alex?'

A well-manicured talon chiselled his shoulder with precision. Alex jumped and turned hastily, like a person contemplating some petty crime. It was the deputy editor, a midget in Armani.

'Sorry, Lois. I was miles away.'

He had been gazing out of the window, his eyes taxi-ing vacantly over the rubble of London scattered thirty floors below the newspaper tower. Before him the city's edge expanded trashily, the gas stations, cranes, sink estates and low-rise hovels converging at random, like filthy foam on a tide. The offices on the west side of the building which offered far views of the real, architectural London of Fleet Street and St Paul's, a reminder of the joyful days when newspaper people still worked in the city proper, were taken by the most senior executives. Alex's department got to look down at the apology for urban planning on the eastern outskirts, where the slinking streets and ramshackle terraces cowered beneath the planes from the City airport rising to better, brighter climes.

It was strange living in one place. The past ten years of his life had been spent flying from one country to another, crisis to crisis, against a background blur of ever-changing scenery. There was barely any routine, unless you counted the simple one of hitting the ground, finding a hotel and bar and hoping one or two of the other foreign boys were on the road with you. The newspaper itself had for him been represented by a voice on the end of a phone, this office only an alien environment of random activity and flashing green computer screens, where he dropped in for lunch twice a year and caught up with the sex and the sackings. Weirdly the idea of having his own desk one day had taken on a surreal attraction for him during those long years in Africa and Asia. He had even imagined a desk, with the odd photograph sellotaped to the computer terminal and a surrounding circle of gossiping colleagues. Only now that it had come to it, it was not like that at all. Now there was no such thing as one's own desk. The place you sat was your workstation and a new scheme called 'hot desking' disenfranchised the journalists from their routine positions on the grounds of efficiency, enforcing rootless movement and constant competition for a seat, like tourists reserving sun-loungers round the pool.

Behind him the deputy editor permitted a brisk smile to cross her face.

'And how are you getting on?'

Even one as unaccustomed to workplace nuance as Alex could recognise that this query was not rooted in a compassionate concern for his well-being.

'Oh, fine thanks. I've just been hitting the phone, making a few calls.'

He had been making some token attempts to form political contacts, trying to cut through the high-minded disdain for the press, and the 'no lunch please we're working' brigade, to those old-fashioned politicians who still liked the idea of spilling the beans over a drink. But it had been uphill work. No one knew him yet and behind his back his new colleagues would have been guarding their patch, nursing their own contacts and damning him with faint praise. The politics at the newspaper were fiendishly complex. The place was like some office Bosnia in its shifting enmities, departmental coups and historical feuds. Fathoming which executives were secret rivals was often worse than working out why one East African tribe was dedicated to obliterating the other. Even when allegiances were overt, they could often turn into treacheries overnight, as in tinpot dictatorships where plotters seized the radio mast and television station to broadcast propaganda hostile to the previous dispensation.

'Listen, Alex. I don't know what you're working on but you'll have to drop it for the moment because the editor's got a very interesting special he wants you to get involved in.'

'Oh?'

'Do you know much about science?'

Alex realised that a resounding negative would be reckless in this instance, but fortunately Lois was not waiting for an answer.

'Because there's a piece by Brent Southern – quite a reliable chap – about this company called AMCO. You might have seen his feature about them a few days ago.' She thrust a photocopy from the rival newspaper before him. 'They've got some sort of research establishment down in Slough and they seem to be getting up to some sort of fantastically hush-hush molecular biology breakthrough. The editor's terribly keen on this kind of story and we thought rather than have you sitting here twiddling your thumbs you might like to get stuck into it. Try to take the story on.'

'Right.'

Alex had tried hard not to look as though he was twiddling his thumbs. He was vaguely aware of the editor's obsession with scientific advances. A small irascible Scot, the man was conservative on religion, drugs, social policy and Europe, but a positive dinosaur when it came to science, exuding a general alarmism about anything involving a test-tube and a lab coat.

'I did see the piece actually. Fascinating stuff.'

He'd known Brent Southern when the man used to prop up the hotel bar back in Beirut. He was responsible for more fliers than an airline and anything he wrote had to be taken with a liberal dose of scepticism. Just then, from across the desk a secretary leant and said:

'I don't want to interrupt, Alex, but it's your mother on the line.'

He cringed, certain that receiving calls from family members constituted unprofessional conduct. There was probably a line about it in the staff manual. But the deputy editor was already moving away, like a grazing shark which dies if it stops swimming.

'I'll leave you to get on then, Alex, OK? And you'll have something for us by next week, hmm? Just pop in my office and let me know how you're doing.'

★　★　★

It was just too much. Jessica had been bounced into taking these children all Saturday in the full expectation that Steve would be coming up to share the load. Vaguely she had thought they could go to the zoo, or a puppet show, or a circus, or any one of those half-remembered features in the distant landscape of childhood. But when she had rung to tell Steve about it, instead of volunteering to come up to help her he'd apologised – no, almost boasted – that the interest in Edgar Avon had snowballed and he had been commissioned to contribute a treatment to a BBC documentary about literary pretenders. Unfortunately the meeting with the producers was next week so he'd have to stay down in Sussex over the weekend and get working on it. When she suggested driving down with her nieces he had said it would not be 'fair' to the delegates to have children milling around and she had replaced the receiver with a clang that she instantly regretted.

Almost immediately the phone rang again and she seized it with relief and remorse.

'Now that's what I like to hear. A woman sitting by the phone waiting for my call.'

It was terrible to want one brother and keep getting another – like some Platonic process where you attained only the shadow of the ideal. And Alex's voice was so different from his brother's, so irritatingly upbeat. Steve would never resort to that sort of crude sexist remark. Indeed he would be mortified to be accused of discriminating against women in any way. Steve claimed he was often oblivious to the difference between his male and female students, except of course that women's minds were so interestingly cross-disciplined and broad-ranging, whereas men were often more narrowly focused. Steve was fully versed in gender politics and certainly not afraid to call himself a feminist.

'Oh. It's you,' she said. 'I was expecting a call actually, so I'd better ring off.'

'Hey. Wait a minute. It's about Friday.'

'What about Friday?'

'We're having dinner, remember? Except I've got a bit of a problem.'

For an instant she was dismayed, but the sensation was far too transitory for her to bother tracking it down for analysis.

'That's fine because I've got a problem too. I've got my three nieces turning up at the crack of dawn on Saturday so it's probably best if I rest a bit in preparation.'

'No wait, I'm not crying off. It's just that my mother wants me to go down to her place. She's got some friends coming or something and wants some input from the younger generation.

Apparently Steve's too busy, as you probably know, so I couldn't really abandon her.'

'So, what?'

'So what I'm saying is, would you like to come too? I admit we would be the only two there who don't hold a buspass, but most of her friends are fairly pleasant old crocks. They may ramble and dribble a bit, but they're not positively senile.'

'Oh, I'm not sure.'

Jessica had met Steve's mother Etta a couple of times before. Hardened by early widowhood and long independence, she was the kind of person who took pride in 'speaking her mind'. Etta had been unconventional in her youth and decades later a few bohemian traits still lingered – she smoked like a man, drank neat Scotch and would not be seen dead in Jaeger or any of the usual tweedy, senior-citizen garb. She wrinkled and withered unashamedly, shunning make-up and all Canute-like resistance to the encroachments of age.

On their first meeting she had emerged from the garden in trousers and filthy sweatshirt and seized Jessica's hand in a firm, earthy grasp before enfolding her son in a hug, during which a huge dog came leaping up, raking its muddy paws down Jessica's clean shirt and insinuating its hairy body against her legs.

Etta lived in the real country, as opposed to the pastoral suburbia in which Jessica had been raised, where flora were pruned and barbered to within an inch of life, and she was hearty and countrified in a way that made Jessica nervous, as though at any minute she might be quizzed on hedgerows or silage or crop rotation. Jessica didn't know how country people managed to do that to urban dwellers. It wasn't as though Londoners thought other people inferior for not understanding the nature of the Circle Line or being unable to navigate their way from Covent Garden to Trafalgar Square. Further exposure to Etta had caused her initial cocktail of anxiety and hostility to dissipate, though only a little. To her credit Etta did not drone on endlessly about rural affairs and did ask a lot of probing questions about both Jessica's job and Steve's, and there were signs that she kept at least half an eye on current affairs. It also emerged that she had not always lived in the middle of nowhere. She had once owned a flat in Chelsea and reminisced quite entertainingly about her life in wartime London, where she had worked for the Red Cross and moonlighted as an artist's model before eventually marrying Steve's father and retreating to the country. The walls of the house were studded with pictures by artists she had known and the furniture was tasteful, though battered and covered in doghairs. The dog belonged to Alex and was predictably badly trained.

Jessica sighed politely. 'Well, it's kind of her to ask me but I'd rather not all the same, Alex.'

'Tell you what. If you help me out, I'll come and entertain your nieces on Saturday. I'll show them my magic tricks.'

'Do you do magic tricks?'

'Sort of,' said Alex. In truth his fumblings with cards and coins were generally received with derisive hilarity by the under tens, who watched him with unbecoming scepticism, scornfully pointing to the concealed card behind the palm or prising open the trick box with disdain.

But to Jessica, any adult assistance in the unmapped terrain of child care was an invaluable aid to survival.

'Who else will be at your mother's, then?'

'Actually, there's one fascinating old bird. She's a former journalist. She's retired now, of course, but she was at it at a time when there were hardly any women in the profession. You know. Before it was a positive disadvantage to be a man.'

'Oh, my heart bleeds. And you know how I love meeting journalists.' In the self-referential world Alex inhabited, any encounter was bound to be of more interest if it included another journalist.

At the other end of the phone Alex was momentarily distracted by the sight of his secretary returning with an imposing stack of files on AMCO, homework which had plainly been ordered up for him by the deputy editor.

'So you'll come?'

'If I do come, I'll need to get away early.'

'Did anyone ever tell you you were an angel?'

CHAPTER TWENTY-THREE

ALEX UNFOLDED THE clippings and read through the stuff on AMCO. Whatever else, the company was certainly used to being at the centre of controversy. Even if he failed to establish just what they were up to at the moment, there would certainly be a lot of past history to pad out his piece, and that might just be enough to satisfy the editor. After all, it was a field the man knew nothing about, or at least as little as Alex, which was practically zero. Reading through the files was something of a relief.

Since their first appearance in the mainstream press around a decade ago, AMCO had displayed an unerring ability to keep abreast of advanced molecular genetic techniques and they had also, by riding high on the crest of the biotech boom, acquired a reputation as the mercenaries of the gene world, aggressively pillaging the forefront of science for its commercial potential. It was AMCO that had heavily researched mutations on the p-53 gene that were linked with cancer in smokers – research that was sponsored by tobacco firms, who hoped pre-existing genetic susceptibility would reduce their liability in legal cases. AMCO had also been pioneering the attempt to create human body parts from cloned organisms originated from an individual's own cells and it had been AMCO which obtained substantial business sponsorship to study the implications of the news that gene IGF2R, on the long arm of chromosome six, was associated with high intelligence.

Exactly what they were up to now was harder to tell. Brent Southern's feature last week – the article which had attracted Alex's editor's attention – referred only to what Southern called a 'ground breaking' venture, which he said had been code-named Project Mars. Other than that, there had been no mention of AMCO in the press for months, except for a few paragraphs from the foreign pages of another newspaper – part of a larger focus on the forthcoming biodiversity conference in London to be attended by the American president.

According to the piece the Brazilian government, at the prompting of a group called Rainforest Watch, had registered a protest with AMCO and a number of other companies over the 'exploitation of natural resources'. One of the companies involved had been researching the analgesic qualities of a forest periwinkle, so that was none too exciting.

What he needed to know about was this Project Mars thing, and they did seem extraordinarily secretive about it. Alex was also keen to delay for as long as possible the point at which Jessica discovered that far from being immersed in the political reporting he had spoken of, or crafting a profile of Lewis Appleby, he was exploring one of her own client companies. When he put through the obligatory calls to AMCO he was redirected to Jessica's firm and was vastly relieved to get not her but a minion, who gave out a standard statement. He had been prepared to hang up if he heard Jessica's voice on the line.

After a day of flicking through the cuttings and scouring the Internet for AMCO's past history, propelled by what seemed like concrete action, though it was as much an urge to escape the office, he decided to drive to Slough to visit the company itself.

Alex was not clear what he was expecting, though he had envisaged that it might involve security fences, breeze-block outhouses and barbed wire. What there was came as a surprise. By its architecture, the AMCO headquarters was distinctly unintimidating. Having passed through the gate – which Alex accomplished by giving the name of a spokesman he had noted from the cuttings – visitors proceeded down a gravelled drive surrounded by fields of grazing sheep to a cluster of low-rise, redbrick buildings, grouped round a cloistered forecourt, projecting an open, 'community' feeling. Alex disliked it on sight. It was the kind of loathsome place in which the workforce were required to practise Tai Chi or aerobics or some sort of nonsense at eight o'clock in the morning, where there were wind chimes and organic food and group jogging and you got sacked on the spot for smoking. It was also the worst sort of place to appear without an appointment.

Once inside he glanced impotently round the lobby and at the few employees coming peaceably in and out. It was clearly impregnable. Glass doors leading off to laboratories and offices were accessed by code and card, steel lift doors opened and closed noiselessly and everywhere the lidless eyes of the security cameras regarded him dispassionately. The receptionist was predictably friendly.

'Can I help you. Are you visiting someone?'

'I'm Alex Irvine. A journalist from *The Nation*. I've come to ask a few questions about Project Mars.' Pathetic. A five-year-old could have done better.

'Please take a seat. Someone will be right down to assist you.' She added: 'I'm afraid this is a non-smoking environment.'

His assistor appeared almost instantly through the lift doors, a tall, pock-faced man with an air of suppressed irritation. Alex pretended to be diverted by the hideous modern sculpture that dominated the foyer.

'Frank LeRoux.' The man extended a hand briefly. 'I'll endeavour to help you, Mr Irvine, but I'm afraid you may have come to the wrong place.'

'Hello.' Alex tried to sound as unthreatening as possible and crouched down on the low leather sofa, taking out his notebook to suggest a lengthy stay.

'I've just got a few questions about your business here. I'm sure you know *The Nation* takes a keen interest in the bio-technology field.'

Frank LeRoux remained standing. 'I'm going to have to interrupt you. All newspaper enquiries are handled from London by Hughes Associates. Would you like the number?'

'Well, the thing is, Mr LeRoux, we're very excited and proud that an American company like AMCO chooses to locate here and we're looking at a special report on the whole biotechnology boom. I'd really prefer to talk on a more direct and . . . er . . . sympathetic basis about the company and what we feel is really quite exciting work, like the Mars Project, and . . .'

'I've told you already, Mr Irvine. Press enquiries are being handled by Hughes Associates. Please direct your questions to them. We're grateful for your interest but just now we really have nothing else to say.'

Alex was secretly gratified by Mr LeRoux's irritation. At least he was getting to him.

'Have you any idea when you might be ready to talk about Project Mars?'

'At the risk of repeating myself, Mr Irvine, press enquires are not my responsibility. Now I have to go, so I hope you can seen yourself out.'

He began to leave so Alex threw out at him: 'What are you going to do about the Brazilian problem?'

He could not miss the flash in LeRoux's eyes, the suppressed rage breaking through momentarily before the stonewalling façade descended.

'What problem? There is no problem. That problem is completely resolved.' LeRoux turned on his heel. 'Goodbye.'

★ ★ ★

It wasn't until the fourth attempt that Alex got through. It was a scratchy line to São Paolo, and sounded as though he was ringing in a hailstorm in the middle of the night, but the voice on the other end was reassuringly English – public school, calm, slightly terse. Alex explained that he was calling Rainforest Watch with reference to a company called AMCO.

'I should think so too,' said the man.

'I'm sorry?' Hope bounded madly in Alex's chest.

'Well, it's about time some of you lot woke up to the bioprospecting going on out here and AMCO's one of the worst. We were expecting some press interest with the bio-diversity conference coming up next month.'

'Right. What's bioprospecting, or whatever you called it?'

'Or biopiracy. Basically it means plundering the folklore and knowledge of indigenous people. It's a big issue. You must have heard of these pharmaceutical giants that come out here, find plants and organisms which have been used for centuries in local remedies and then take them back and patent the genetic content, on the spurious basis that isolating its properties counts as their own "invention". They then make millions from the discovery and the ethnic people have been effectively robbed of their own remedies. I thought this was what you were writing about. Didn't you ask about AMCO?'

'Yes. Yes, I did. But what exactly have they been up to?'

'Well, it's been in the press already. We helped some Indian people out in the Amazon region formulate a complaint to the Brazilian government which was then forwarded to AMCO. That was a couple of months ago.'

'AMCO said that problem was solved now.' Deliberately Alex injected a note of bored scepticism into his voice.

'Ha! Did they indeed?' The sardonic, reproving tone, just like a prep schoolmaster. 'Well, it's not.'

'What exactly was the problem?'

'It's all to do with shellfish.'

'Shellfish?'

Alex's excitement, which had risen so swiftly on finding someone to speak readily about AMCO, was dashed again. He didn't want to know anything about shellfish. Nor did the editor, he was sure.

'Well, not exactly shellfish. They're a kind of mussel. They're native to a particular stretch of river deep in the Amazonian rainforest and they're pretty much found nowhere else in the world. The tribe who cultivate them is known locally as the Guerreros and they regard the shellfish as part of an ancestral remedy. It seems they contain certain properties.'

'Medicinal?'

'No. More . . . behavioural, I suppose. Drinking the stew of the mussels is said to give this people their particular characteristics, which is to say it supposedly makes them courageous and fearless, and they've always guarded the ingredient very jealously from the other local tribes. AMCO heard about these mussels and went in and persuaded the Indians to let them take some samples. They also took some blood samples from the Guerrero warriors and their wives after they'd consumed the mussels. Most of them had never seen a syringe before but they were very stoic about it because they were under the impression they were about to make a huge profit from their special shellfish. Fortunately we came by and told them what AMCO would probably do with the mussels.'

'Which is what?'

'They'll take them back to the lab and if they find anything remotely useful they'll come out here and harvest the lot, and then go and patent whatever special ingredient they contain and make millions from it while giving the Indians absolutely nothing in return. When we told the Guerreros this they were quite rightly livid that they were about to be cheated out of their ancestral potion. In fact, I wouldn't like to be an AMCO representative going back there. They've all got poison blow-pipes and they won't take this raid lying down.'

'They might have to.'

'Not this lot. They're a very particular people. Very proud and isolated. There aren't many of them, and they tend to have very small families, so we reckon they'll have died out in a few generations. But they're legendary for their courage and fighting prowess.'

'Well, it sounds like they can manage without you, then.'

'I only wish they could. Unfortunately, without groups like ours to raise ethical questions about the racist and imperialist polices whereby multinational corporations think they can rob indigenous people wherever they choose, this kind of pillage will go on throughout the third world pretty much unchecked. The Guerreros have our full support and if AMCO think their little Brazilian problem is solved, they'd better think again.'

★　★　★

Shellfish. Local remedies. It didn't sound as though it was going to excite the editor. Quite the opposite. The editor hated The Environment. He said it was too 1980s. Even the bio-diversity conference was to receive only the barest coverage and that was happening on his doorstep in London. Reluctantly Alex flicked through the files for more about this bioprospecting issue. It was certainly widespread. There was a company making $100 million annually out of two drugs derived from a primrose from the rainforests of Madagascar. Another drugs giant had taken out fifty separate patents on the use of substances from the same species of Indian tree. There were patents out on everything imaginable, from soil bacteria in the heather forests in Africa, to Mexican fungi which had proved invaluable in manufacturing male hormones and a Namibian earth organism which could be used in treating manic depression. The rain-forests seemed to provide particularly rich pickings. AMCO's shellfish find was probably just part of a routine trawl through the vast numbers of still undiscovered plant and animal species there.

What had all this to do with the promising-sounding Project Mars? Nothing probably, thought Alex ruefully. But if he was to cobble anything together on AMCO in the near future, he might as well get back and tease them a little. It would annoy them that he'd spoken to the local Brazilian activists. Big companies like AMCO hated environmental opposition. He remembered the fury of Frank LeRoux at the mention of Brazil and dialled his number.

★　★　★

LeRoux's voice was deeply, professionally bored.

'You have been doing your homework, Mr Irvine, haven't you? I'm so sorry you've been wasting your time. As I said before, we have no interest in Brazil. We have no further interest in the Guerreros people.'

'And their shellfish?'

'I suppose you've been talking to the Rainforest Watch, or whatever they call themselves.'

'Could you just answer me. Have you an ongoing interest in the shellfish you found there?'

'No.'

'No?'

'Your hearing does you credit.'

'Then I assume AMCO won't be undertaking any further bioprospecting in the region?'

'I couldn't possibly comment on an area of commercial sensitivity. Nor would you expect me to. But for a little off-the-record guidance, the answer would be no. Now if that's all . . .'

★　★　★

The prospect of spending Friday evening with Jessica had been at the back of Alex's mind all week, like a forbidden treat to be savoured. As he ploughed on fruitlessly with the AMCO story, the notion of a night out with his brother's girlfriend increasingly seemed more than a treat – it was a just reward for the dispiriting task he was engaged on.

Given the amount of time he had spent fantasising about her over the last few days, it was astonishing how quickly she managed to dampen his expectations. She looked beautiful enough as she came running down the steps of her flat at seven that evening. Though she was still wearing a jacket and trousers from her usual brutal wardrobe of what he believed were called classic neutrals, her hair, which she usually wore tied ruthlessly up, was free and flowing and she wore a low-necked lace shirt underneath. When she got in beside him she smelt all clean and scrubbed, scented with a heady, citrus perfume which made his senses prick. But the sexiness was strictly cosmetic. Jessica herself, it was immediately obvious, was in what might be termed a withdrawn mood, though Alex would have called it sullen. She sat tense and distant, making only sporadic additions to his conversation, like someone randomly adjacent to a mad, garrulous stranger who should not be encouraged. After a while the effort, coupled with the traffic, reduced him to a similarly monosyllabic state.

Having lived abroad Alex was totally unused to London's Friday evening rushhour and horrified to find himself part of a creeping train of estate cars and jeeps packed up with clothing and provisions for the weekend away, like extraordinarily affluent refugees fleeing a warzone. At one point, when he was barely out of first gear on the motorway, a hatchback sped past him down the hard shoulder, narrowly missing his wing mirror.

'Bloody women drivers.'

'I can't believe I heard that.' Jessica hadn't spoken since Hammersmith but now she shifted with disdain in her seat, the way some women did, as though they were ring-fencing an invisible, antiseptic atmosphere around them to protect against male contamination.

'Oh, I'm sorry. I can't help it. It's because I'm a man. Aggression and sexism are genetically predetermined social behaviours.'

'You what?'

'That's what they say, isn't it? In the genetics business.'

'I don't think it's that simple.'

'But if it's all in the genes I can't help it, can I?'

'I assume you're referring to one of the oldest arguments in science? Nature versus nurture. Except everyone now knows there are a number of influences which have to be balanced. It's not just one or the other, it's how they interact.'

'I thought the genetic side was emerging as by far the most important predictor of behaviour?'

'Really.' She sounded cool. 'You seem to know a lot about it.'

'And even if you can dilute the influence of your genes, you can't escape them.' He made an attempt at jollity. 'So, your honour, in the eyes of modern science, I'd say my road rage is almost totally excusable. I rest my case.'

'Technically you could argue it either way. Either you're not responsible for your behaviour because you can't avoid your genes or you're totally responsible for your behaviour because you're genetically predisposed and other influences, like being well brought up and whether your mother ever taught you it was unacceptable to shout at female drivers, are much less important.'

'So which is it to be? Am I guilty or not guilty?'

'How should I know.' She shrugged and gazed out of her window, noncommittally. It was an exquisite evening, with a light breeze slicing through the humidity and the sun hanging red and pendulous in the west. Jessica wondered what Steve was doing now. She had tried to call him just before she left, but the woman who answered the phone at Fallings said he could not be found and gave an unconvincing commitment to pass a message on. Beside her Alex chattered away, disrupting her train of thought.

'I thought you were working for this genetics company.'

'I'm only doing the public affairs side of it.'

'That's not like you.'

'What?'

'I mean, you usually like to get into your subject, don't you? You get really involved.'

'Sometimes I do, sometimes I don't. You don't know me that well, Alex, so leave out the psychoanalysis.' Realising she had been a little sharp, she turned and smiled. 'Look, I'm sorry. I've haven't unwound yet. I've had a tough week. How's yours been?'

He gave a mock grimace. 'Don't ask.'

★   ★   ★

Practically the second they reached the top of the tiny lane that led to Etta's house and opened the car door, the enormous grey-haired dog shot out of the house and moulted all over her black trouser suit. Rearing on to its hind legs to reveal a bald pink belly, it attempted to place its matted paws on her shoulder and lick her face. Jessica grappled with it, digging it sharply in the ribs, but even then the animal did not desist, winding madly round her legs, snuffling obscenely, banging its meaty tail against her shins. Alex watched this encounter unperturbed, doing absolutely nothing to restrain the dog.

'Hey! Muddy likes you!' he observed.

'I can see that,' she replied, brushing down her suit as the creature halted momentarily and panted, its deadpan brown eyes fixed on her face, its foamy tongue lolling from its mouth. 'Appropriate name.'

Alex caressed the dog's head. 'It's after Muddy Waters. He used to be my favourite singer. I used to sit up at that top window there looking out over the empty fields playing "Bright Lights Big City Went to My Baby's Head". It used to drive Steve mad.'

'I can imagine.' Steve hated music, even background classical, when he was trying to work.

Etta appeared at the door in her eveningwear, which was exactly the same as her daywear except for the Chanel Number Five trailing sluggishly in her wake. Her hair was nestlike, her face a deflating balloon of bad skincare. She held a tumbler of whisky and a cigarette.

'How wonderful to see you, my dear,' she said, preparing to clasp Jessica to her pillowy chest. She had a sardonic voice, a sort of husky drawl suggesting late nights and gambling, which was strangely out of place in this rural setting. Jessica gave her an air kiss.

'Very nice of you to ask me.'

'Well, let's not stand here waiting. Come in quick. Everyone else is here.'

In the drawing room Muddy took pride of place, stretching its thin hairy legs out on the sofa. Nobody seemed to think anything of it and Jessica was obliged to make do with a low cane chair which forced her uncomfortably forward, into a position somewhere between a squat and a crouch. Looking round she saw that Alex's description of the other guests as elderly was no exaggeration. There were three of them, the Fortescues, an ancient couple who knew Etta from the local art historical society and a plump old woman with wiry platinum hair and sharp green eyes set in a round, grandmotherly face.

'This is Mrs Chumley,' said Etta, 'a very old friend of mine.'

'Old being pretty much the operative word there, I'm afraid,' remarked the woman, with a feistiness that surprised Jessica.

Alex was pumping her hand. 'You remember I was telling you about Mrs Chumley's exploits.'

'Oh, I do hope not.' The old lady laughed, obligingly.

'Jessica was fascinated to hear about your days in Fleet Street. Weren't you, Jess?'

'Mmn.' Jessica smiled like a royal on a hospital visit.

'They were exciting times. Very exciting. But it all seems a long time ago now.' In the absence of any encouraging noises from Jessica, the old lady smoothly switched tack. 'And do you work, dear?'

'Yes. I'm in public affairs.'

'Oh.'

Almost instantly Alex butted in.

'She's looking after a big biotechnology client.'

'How interesting. What sort of thing is that?' asked Mr Fortescue.

'Molecular genetics mainly. Research,' said Jessica.

'They did the first transgenic rabbit,' added Alex.

'Ooh, I read about that in the paper. Is that cloning?' said Mr Fortescue.

'No,' said Jessica.

'All this cloning nonsense. I don't see what all the fuss is about frankly,' drawled Etta, dispensing huge slugs of whisky to the older guests, and warm white wine for Alex and Jessica. 'Who says we're all so different from each other, anyway? Look at the number of people who watch *Coronation Street*, or play golf. So many people are exactly the same. Individuality is pretty thin on the ground, I'd say.'

'Actually my client has nothing to do with whole-human cloning,' interjected Jessica, keen to clarify the situation. But they were not to be distracted.

'The fact is, you're right, mother. I think there's nothing to be afraid of,' said Alex. 'I believe fear of cloning springs from a fear of the mass. It's like one of those science fiction things. People think we're going to get a huge army of people all the same. Like a lot of Adolf Hitlers.'

'Or Marilyn Monroes,' added Mr Fortescue.

'Or Elvises,' said Etta.

'Actually cloning another human being is currently outlawed in Britain,' said Jessica.

'But in reality,' continued Alex, 'it's nothing like that. For a start, you need to persuade women to carry the clones. I mean we don't have effective artificial wombs yet. And then, a clone is only the same as an identical twin and no one's scared of them.'

'Oh, I used to dread twins,' said Mrs Fortescue. 'All that washing twice over. Do you have children, Mrs Chumley?'

'No.'

Etta rose abruptly from her chair. 'May's husband was injured in the Spanish civil war,' she said briskly by way of explanation. 'Now dinner's up. I hope everyone likes pheasant.'

'Jessica's vegetarian,' said Alex, as though apologising for some mild but embarrassing disease.

'Oh dear.' Etta looked at her with irritation, projected as sympathetic concern. 'How could I have forgotten something like that? Could you just eat the vegetables then, do you think?'

Jessica was annoyed to find herself so instantly in the wrong. 'Of course. Please don't worry. I don't want to make extra bother.'

'It stands to reason she can eat vegetables,' observed Mr Fortescue reasonably. 'That's why they call themselves vegetarians.'

⋆　⋆　⋆

'Are you two planning a holiday this year?' asked Mrs Fortescue. Jessica regarded her over a plate heaped punitively with vegetation.

'I'm not. Alex might be.'

'Oh, I thought . . .'

Alex laughed quickly. 'No, Jessica's Steve's girlfriend actually. I'm entertaining her while he's away.'

'I'm so sorry. I didn't realise. I thought . . .'

'Don't worry. Easy mistake to make.'

'Is it?' said Jessica.

'What am I talking about? No, of course not. What a *faux pas*, Mrs Fortescue,' said Alex, turning on her in pantomime reproach and causing the others to laugh politely.

Jessica realised the dinner party was going wrong and she knew it was her fault. She had noticed the cautious way Alex was looking at her, as though she were an imperfectly tamed animal who was liable at any moment to return to its feral state. She was ashamed. She knew she had behaved like a sulky child from the moment they set out that evening, but she did not know why. What urge made her want to appear as unpleasant as possible in his company?

'We have just come back from a holiday, though,' she volunteered. 'Alex has been staying down in a place called Fallings in Sussex with us. The house used to belong to Sir Lewis Appleby.'

It was as though she had thrown a stone into the conversation.

'I say! Lewis Appleby. Didn't you used to know him, May?' said Etta.

'Now that's what other people might call coincidence and we journalists call good planning.' Alex's face lit up. 'Did you know him well, Mrs Chumley?'

'Fairly well. But we lost touch years before he died.'

'Well, you can solve this mystery for us then. Did you know he had a wife?'

'Of course I knew,' she said quietly. 'I went to their wedding.'

'Then what happened to her?' demanded Alex. 'Have you any idea why she vanished?'

'Now that is a question.' Her face seemed to reflect on something she had contemplated many times before. After a little pause she said: 'It's so hard to know what goes on in other people's marriages.'

'But it was so sudden.'

'Yes, it certainly took everyone by surprise. The summer after the war, it was; she simply disappeared.'

'And weren't her friends worried? You must have been suspicious.'

'Well, at first we were. Of course. But then Lewis assured us that she had gone of her own accord, and really it seemed interfering to take it any further.'

'But people don't just vanish,' objected Jessica. 'Weren't the police involved?'

'Heavens, no.'

'You can't just disappear,' protested Jessica.

'You can, my dear. It was different after the war. Things were quite fluid then. There were people coming and going everywhere, men being demobbed and coming home to find their wives had started up relationships with other men, or that their families didn't know them. It wasn't at all surprising to find a stranger had moved next door to you.'

'So what do you think happened to her?'

'This was all a long time ago. Why are you so interested?'

'I'm writing a piece about Lewis Appleby, as it happens,' said Alex.

Mrs Chumley seemed startled. 'Really. Surely no one's much interested in Lewis anymore. He died several years ago.'

'Now, Mrs Chumley, far be it from me to tell such a pioneer about journalism, but the fact is, there's a huge interest in the lives of these early English socialists. The development of the left. The pre-war thinking, the post-war planning, how these men's ideas helped shape the political landscape of today. And Appleby's so appealing as a thinker – very provocative and yet humane, the stuff about genetics, race and language, and the later analysis of the impact of genetics and evolution on culture. Don't you think?'

May Chumley was evidently not to be drawn any further. 'I'm afraid I never read much of it.'

★   ★   ★

Later, when the others returned to the drawing room for coffee, Jessica lingered in the dining room and looked surreptitiously through the photographs of Steve on the mantelpiece. There was a whole range, from babyhood right up to the time when he had grown the prickly beard that she had eventually persuaded him to shave off. As young children the two boys were always pictured together. There was Steve as a prep schoolboy with his arm round his brother, the two of them in the woods, staring down from the branches of a tree, and in swimming trunks on holiday. Then there was the grown-up Alex dressed in fatigues and holding a gun in some African-looking landscape and there was Steve collecting one of his degrees. He was so handsome. Just looking at his image made her physically ache for him. Suddenly the evanescence of his childhood and youth – a time that did not involve her at all – seemed to echo a sense of passing within her. She felt a nostalgia for her own life. When was the last time they made love? She tried to think but she could not even remember. Weeks ago, maybe months.

'They're nothing like each other, are they?' Etta was leaning against the doorjamb, smoking a thin black cigar and watching her.

'I suppose you'd know better than me.'

'Well, they're not.'

'Not to look at, perhaps. Steve is very tall and Alex takes after you more, I'd say.'

'They're chalk and cheese!' She padded towards the pictures and looked at them fondly. 'Steve has always known what he wanted and he has always worked towards that, even as a little boy. He has always been very ambitious and determined and he thinks about what would be good for him. Alex, on the other hand, never has a clue about his life. He rides along like a passenger, expecting someone else to make decisions for him, thinking that his fate will shape itself. He messed around at school and now I'd guess he hasn't got much idea what the future holds at this newspaper.' She replaced his photograph. 'He'll go nowhere, but he is a very giving boy. He has a good heart and he thinks about other people. He has empathy, which is I suppose what makes a good journalist.'

'I suppose.'

'What about you?'

'What? Do I have empathy?'

'No. I mean, do you know what you want?'

Jessica gave a brief, professional laugh. 'Not in every aspect of life, I have to confess. But then to me, Steve doesn't actually seem to know what he wants either.'

'Oh, I think he does.'

'Really.' She turned away. The last thing she needed was a dissection of Steve's character from his mother, who saw him at the most only a couple of times a year now. Etta leant towards her.

'I wouldn't interfere for anything, dear. I don't believe in it. I'm a fanatic for personal privacy, but if you asked my advice . . .' She waved her cigar, speculatively.

'About what?'

'If you asked me to choose between my boys, I couldn't do

it. No mother could. I love them both. But if I were a girl, I know which one I'd want to be loved by.'

Jessica felt herself stiffen in embarrassment at the misapprehension that Etta appeared to be under.

'I don't know what you must think, Etta, but I don't want you to imagine for a second that . . . Alex only invited me down here because he knew I was stuck in London with nothing better to do and he wanted some company.' She was aware that sounded rude so tried to patch it up, continuing: 'I mean, I was very pleased to come, but he and I are just friends. Not even close friends.'

'Of course, of course.' Etta was soothing, discreet. 'Heaven forbid I meant anything like that. Blame it on an old woman in her dotage. Still it's nice to have the chance for a little chat. Now, my dear, come and have some coffee. You're not against caffeine, I take it?'

★   ★   ★

It was dark when they left, stars peppering a clear sky, and the unlit road layered with shadows. It had been an awkward evening but as they climbed into the car, Jessica could not forget Etta's comments. She looked at Alex, frowning in concentration as the car lurched over ruts in the road, and tried to picture Steve's face in his. It was impossible. The profiles didn't fit. They were too different – their mother was right about that, though she wasn't right about much else. As he turned and caught her eyes upon him, Alex broke into a smile. She was expecting that he would say something about her demeanour during dinner, but instead he said:

'It was a good evening, wasn't it?'

'Yes . . . I'm . . .'

'Wasn't it amazing that May Chumley knew him? Though I think her explanation of the wife's vanishing leaves a little wanting.'

'She didn't seem very curious about the whole thing.'

'You know, I got the impression she knew more than she was saying.'

'Perhaps she had an affair with Appleby herself.'

'Without wanting to repeat my sin of chauvinism, Jessica, to look at Mrs Chumley, I rather think not.'

It seemed he was not going to mention her behaviour. Could it be that he hadn't noticed?

Jessica said: 'So the paper's keen on this Appleby piece then? I thought you were supposed to be writing about politics.'

'There isn't any politics in the summer.'

'Oh, yes there is. That's the first thing you should learn. That's when it all goes on, behind the scenes. Away from Westminster. You should be thinking about what legislation is coming up in the next session.'

'Like the human genetics bill?'

'That certainly. And you have to consider what issues are going to be big.'

'All right. You tell me.'

'You really want me to?'

'Of course.'

The rest of the journey passed in animated discussion of the political landscape and Jessica barely noticed their progress until they pulled up outside her flat. He switched off the engine and looked at her expectantly.

'Door to door service.'

'Thanks.'

'No. Thank you for coming. I hope it wasn't too dreary for you.'

Jessica was not sure whether this was outright sarcasm, or merely an oblique reference to her attitude that evening. She knew she should apologise, but she just couldn't think of a convincing excuse. Apologising on its own didn't seem quite the thing somehow. She stared out into the road in front of them, a slight frown creasing her brow and in her hesitation something quite confusing happened. Alex leant over and kissed her.

Despite his awkwardness in every other aspect, his kiss was gentle and deft. She felt his fingers stroking the hair out of her eyes, tasted the wine on the soft cushion of his mouth and smelt the warm, comforting smell of his flesh as though she recognised it, though it was quite unlike Steve's. Experimentally, she responded until eventually he pulled away, entwining his hands in hers.

'You have no idea how long I've wanted to do that.'

'No? How long?' How cool she sounded.

CHAPTER TWENTY-THREE

'Probably from the time I first saw you.'

'You mean the time you told me my job was worthless and I was the paid lackey of people standing in the way of a free press?'

'Mmm. Yes. That time. The time you told me I was dysfunctional, irresponsible and immature.'

'Well, aren't you?'

'I think if we're going to discuss this further you should at least invite me in.'

Chapter Twenty-Four

In the hall the light didn't work and she struggled to find her doorkey in her bag.

'Aren't you supposed to offer me coffee?'

'Oh, there's an etiquette to intimacy with your boyfriend's brother is there?'

'We can always make it up as we go along.'

She disappeared into the kitchen and Alex heard the sounds of kettle and cups, followed by the distinctive clink of an answerphone button. There was no difficulty identifying the slow rasp which came next.

'I'm calling to tell you, Miss Leigh, that we had another visit from a journalist today . . .' Alex froze as LeRoux continued. 'Can I remind you that we have expressly requested you keep the press away from our base and off our backs. It is our very strong wish that we are not bothered with questions about Project Mars until we choose. If you have a difficulty with that, then perhaps we should talk more seriously. Otherwise, I don't expect to be hassled again. On the issue of your request for more extensive background on our current work, I have authorised the release to you of an updated brief on the current situation, including guidance responses to media questions, which you would do well to read and refresh your memory with. I'm having it biked round tonight. May I remind you that this information is highly commercially sensitive and it is imperative that it goes no further. Have a pleasant weekend.'

So his name had not been mentioned. Alex felt almost faint with relief. But his joy was soured at the sight of Jessica walking back into the drawing room. From the excited, teasing woman who had been responding to his kisses a moment ago, she was entirely transformed. Her expression was defeated and down-cast, her shoulders sagged.

'Oh God.' She plumped down next to him. 'That was AMCO. First it was that horrible drunk Brent Southern and now another journalist has been bothering them. The media are supposed to come to me directly but you can't lay down rules. That man who phoned – Frank LeRoux – he simply hates the press.'

'Listen,' Alex placed an arm round her and clumsily caressed the shoulder blade, thin as a bird's. 'Forget him. Don't let him ruin your evening. He sounds like an uptight American who hasn't got a clue about the British press. You know what bandits we all are. We don't toe the line like the Americans – we can't afford to without the kind of freedom of information they take for granted.'

'No. LeRoux's right. They've got important business and they've got to get the timing right. They're paying my company a lot of money just to handle the press and I should be capable of it. The trouble is, they won't agree with my strategy.'

'What is that?'

'I think we should buy the media off with a little briefing which gives them the idea that they know what's going on without giving anything away. That's what all papers want, when one of them has the hint of a story.'

'Do you know what's going on?'

'Not exactly, I admit. AMCO seem absolutely neurotic about how much they tell me. I think I've finally persuaded LeRoux to let me have more details. But frankly I shouldn't be talking to you about it at all.'

'You're not exactly letting out state secrets.'

'No. And it's not really your area this, I suppose.'

He removed his arm from her shoulder. 'What if some journalist does find out what's they're doing?'

'Oh, they couldn't possibly.' Jessica frowned abstractedly into her coffee cup.

Had she had been anyone else, Alex would have found the conversation tantalising. He could have eked information from this dejected girl as easily as ejecting an oyster from its shell. Instead, the situation was more complicated, if not positively uncomfortable. Facing such a clash of objectives, and in the absence of any alternative plan, he leant forward to kiss her again.

'I love it when you talk corporate media strategy.'

But this time her mouth was reluctant, her body stiff and unyielding before his hands.

'Actually, Alex, let's forget about that. It was a mistake. Not a good idea.'

'It feels like a good idea to me. One of my best.'

She got up and stalked across the room, raking her hand through her hair. 'I'm tired. I've got these children coming tomorrow. You promised to help, remember?'

Alex's body ached with thwarted desire, but this was too important to neglect the importance of timing.

'Fine.'

Obviously surprised at his ready retrenchment, she came over and kissed him lightly on the cheek. 'Thanks for being understanding. Can you let yourself out?'

'Of course.'

He went out and closed the door behind him. Down in the hall a band of light from the street lamp outside illuminated the darkness and he noticed a stack of mail on the table, on the top of it a thick envelope marked for Jessica. It bore no stamp but the franking on it read 'AMCO: For a Better Beginning.' It had to be the updated information that LeRoux had biked round.

Alex pondered only momentarily the quandary he found himself in. Having effected one betrayal in an evening – a pass at his brother's girlfriend – this one seemed infinitely simpler. It was almost effortless to pick it up and tuck it under his arm as he went out into the road.

★ ★ ★

Back in his Pimlico flat Alex spread the contents of the envelope out before him on the cheap, stained coffee table. It was a thick sheaf of papers, bound together in a clear plastic folder, entitled: *AMCO and The Media*. Alex guessed that it was a subtle form of insult on the part of Frank LeRoux to send out such an idiot's guide to Jessica – probably a punishment for her failure to prevent the British press doing its job. The document took the form of questions about the company, followed by information and then qualified answers to be given out to broadcasting organisations and newspapers.

'*How did AMCO's biotech business begin?*'

'Answer: AMCO was co-founded in 1953 by Hubert Wagner, chairman of the Texas pharmaceutical company Wagners, and Axel Müller, a German biologist resident in

Virginia whose initials gave the company its name. In the late 1980s the company began specialising in biotechnology, and now occupies the vanguard of the biomolecular revolution. AMCO co-ordinates a number of research and development facilities, employing 2,700 people who use state-of-the-art technology to provide services, including transgenic animal-based protein products, automated DNA sequencing and DNA synthesis, and personalised genetic profiling services as well as innovations in many other areas of molecular biology.'

Then, following this was a qualifier.

'Response to press enquiries: Any of the above.'

'*What position does AMCO hold now in the biotech marketplace?*'

'Answer: AMCO is among the top ten companies in its field and has been tipped for further growth by the business press. See enclosed clips from *Wall Street Journal* and *International Herald Tribune*. Among recent achievements, last year AMCO was the first company to synthesise the protein implicated in Archer Syndrome, a muscle wasting condition affecting 5,000 in the US, which attracted huge medical interest.'

'Response to press enquiries: AMCO is rapidly expanding its base in the biotech field, and hopes to initiate further exciting work at its recently established base in Slough, England.'

He flicked through further corporate waffle and there, though he could scarcely believe it, was the question he wanted – the one that had been ricocheting around his brain all week.

'*What is Project Mars?*'

'Answer: Project Mars is among AMCO's most exciting work to date. It arose from study of the Guerreros tribe, a 300-member hunter-horticulturist group from Northwest Brazil which has been noted for its aggressive and risk-taking behaviour. These characteristics have been known for centuries – they may have influenced the naming of the Amazon river after warlike females of antiquity – and were locally attributed to the freshwater shellfish diet obtained from Amazonian mud banks. But on examining the molluscs AMCO found them to be a close relative of *Modiolus capax*, the brown-shelled capax horse mussel common to the region and showing no substantial deviation.

'Researchers turned to the possibility that the behavioural

anomalies stemmed not from the diet but from the biological make-up of the tribe itself. Blood samples from the tribe were taken and, after two years work, AMCO detected a significant anomaly – all members of the tribe screened shared an unusual form of a gene on the X chromosome found in only three per cent of the control group. The gene in question has been code-named Mars. AMCO's work relates it to the processing of dopamine and in this particular form it predisposes carriers to certain heightened behavioural traits including risk-taking, aggression, competitiveness, sensation- and novelty-seeking. It is also expressed in a dearth of empathy, leading to inhibited social skills. It should be remembered that environmental influences – notably the relentless rivalry of tribes in the region and the warrior tradition – may play an unquantified part in magnifying the effect of the gene.

'In women possessing two copies of the X chromosome and of the gene, similar effects are observed, but a potentially more interesting behaviour is also manifest. Mars appears also to be associated with an absence of so-called "maternal instinct". The women of the Guerrero tribe are noted for weak bonding in child rearing, a high rate of infant rejection and a small number of offspring in comparison with other indigenous peoples of the Amazon region.'

'*How is AMCO developing this discovery?*'

'Answer: AMCO has applied for a patent to this gene, with a view to exciting commercial applications. Its potential in future germ-line therapy cannot be overestimated. It is particularly important that no media comment about the project, or the patent application, enters the public arena before the bill passes in the next British governmental session – at the earliest six months from now.'

'Response to press enquiries: AMCO has no knowledge of Project Mars.'

★   ★   ★

The whole thing was bewildering to Alex. First, what could be the relevance of some dodgy factor in the bloodstream of a distant Indian tribe? And then there was the idea that anyone should have commercial rights to human DNA or that a multi-national company could patent people's genes. He knew all this went on, of course, but 'commercial applications'? What on earth could that mean?

He realised he had been sitting staring at the documents for some time. He should go and make some coffee. In the fridge the milk carton was torn and wilted and its contents sour so he decided to drink the coffee black. He stood in the kitchen under its trembling neon light as the acrid liquid slipped down his throat, mulling over the meaning of Project Mars.

Warlike men and aggressive women. He'd certainly seen enough of them to last a lifetime. Like that bastard with the machine gun in Burkina Faso. Thinking of the angry boy-soldier as he surveyed his dingy surroundings, something became clear to Alex. It was the answer to the question which had been bothering him – the particularly acute motivation, which he had not been able to fathom on his knees at the end of a guerrilla's gun, that he had for staying alive. It was this, or rather the opposite of this, that he craved. It was a home, with a woman and children in it.

No sooner did he have the thought than he felt an immediate sense of clarity and relief. There. He'd admitted it at last. The next thing was to try and talk himself out of it.

CHAPTER TWENTY-FIVE

IF ALEX WANTED to forget about the procreative urge, spending a day with Jessica's three nieces was a good place to start. He suggested a visit to the aquarium, so the five of them queued to descend a deep slope to a vast watery maze beneath the South Bank. The cool, aqueous beauty of the place enthralled Jessica. As she drifted among the cliffs of glass, each one a silent sea with its own enclosed world, the sheer indifference of the fish relaxed her. The way they veered and turned their backs as one when they approached the sides of the tank, threading away through the murky fronds. How clever of Alex to think of this. As she watched him pushing the buggy containing the youngest child, she found herself wondering who else he had taken there, and then stopped herself, realising she should be grateful that he had turned up at all – he had looked so much the worse for wear when he appeared at her flat bleary and unshaven that morning. The children had loved his dishevelment, jumping up to touch his stubbly face as though it was designed precisely for their entertainment.

However much Jessica liked the aquarium, though, it was not a success with her nieces. The weak-chinned, drifting sharks, looming past the glass with their cold, amoral eyes, frightened the four-year-old. The rays' stealth bomber bodies aroused little interest and the great ghostly shoals of silver-sided fish left them unmoved. The crabs in their scuttle and hurry repelled them. No one wanted to stroke the lobsters in the 'seashore zone' or search for limpets in the vinyl rockpools. In the end they sat on a wall defiantly as Alex disappeared for refreshments.

'Why couldn't we go to the zoo? This isn't nearly as good.'

Jessica looked at them apprehensively, their small natures as unplumbed to her as the depths of the dark sea tanks around them. Their wants were foreign to her, and she was uncertain of the exact extent of their sophistication.

'What do you want to do, then?'

'Go home,' said the middle child.

'Apart from go home?'

'Watch television.'

'We could pretend we're watching television,' said the oldest, creatively, peering into the 'Mediterranean' tank as though viewing an exceptionally dull wildlife show. The children stood momentarily, awaiting some dramatic flourish to the marine events before them, but the flicker of interest aroused by this idea rapidly wore off and they resumed their seats again, aggrieved, regarding Jessica with dumb, judgmental eyes.

Fortunately, at that moment Alex returned with ice-creams and they clustered around him excitedly, their ennui evaporated.

'D'you know what my favourite fish is?' he enquired of them.

'No,' they chorused, enchanted with him.

'Fish and chips!'

They yelled with delight.

'So let's go and find some!'

'Always does the trick,' he smiled deprecatingly at Jessica as they made their way out of the aquarium. She sighed.

'God. Who'd be a mum?'

'Your sister seems to enjoy it.'

'Yes,' she said. 'She does. And you know it was such a surprise. Rosie was the most promising of all of us. She got a first, and had a brilliant career. She was a lawyer specialising in medical negligence and she was absolutely committed to it. She'd work till all hours every night and she never talked about children, or if she did it was only to say how they wouldn't fit into her lifestyle. Then she went and met Pete and had Lucy, but even then it was fine and she was back at work in six weeks. Now look at her.'

'What happened?'

'Oh, nothing new. Women at our firm are forever pretending they don't want children and then they meet the right man and go off and get pregnant. They come back, usually, until they have another and find they can't cope with the hours and then they just go and leave. It's a familiar pattern. It's happening with one of the associates in my office at the moment. She's gone off and left us very short staffed. Frankly, if there was a way of finding out definitively who wanted children and who didn't the implications would be enormous.'

She fell into a pensive silence but her remarks stirred in Alex a sudden realisation. What was the phrase AMCO had used about the Mars gene? 'Commercial applications'? Might it be that companies – large firms or corporations – wanted to find out more about the people they were hiring? To discover whether a man or woman had that rare X factor which made them unusually adventurous and aggressive. Or to pinpoint through a genetic screen those few, valuable women with absolutely no maternal instinct to slow their upward progress on the career ladder? It wasn't the sort of thing any company could admit to. It could even be against the law. But it might be information worth having.

Even as the thoughts ran hurriedly through his head, the problem was clear to him. The problem was walking right next to him, her arm lightly encircled in his as the children quibbled and squabbled ahead. The situation was already so difficult, he could not bear to think about it for any length of time. On the one hand all his hungry senses were on alert – scouting for the casual gesture, the laugh, the confidential smile, all the usual semaphores of sexual attraction. Yet behind them the thought of his brother was a dragging weight, a calliper hobbling the smooth path to seduction. There had, according to Alex's primitive instincts, been promising body language from Jessica that morning. Yet there had been no repeat of last night's kiss and she had let slip several nostalgic references to places she had travelled with Steve.

Then there was AMCO. While Jessica seemed not to have missed as yet the envelope he had removed the night before, she would certainly know where it had gone when she read the piece he intended to write about her biggest client. As the deadline for the piece approached, it loomed like a mounting barrier between them, even more threatening than the invisible presence of his brother.

The children stayed all day and left, inexplicably protesting, at seven that evening. Alex reached gratefully for a bottle of wine.

'How about I make you some dinner?' He could not bear the idea of leaving.

'No.'

'Oh, go on. Just a quick pizza or something?'

'No. I mean, I want to cook for you.' She came over and gave him her wry smile. 'You were brilliant today. You went far beyond the call of duty.'

He wondered if he was falling in love with her. He loved the smooth, clean lines of her, and the doubts and hesitations that lapped deep beneath her bold, bright exterior. He loved the way she intimidated some men with her edge of hostility and her uncompromising challenge – after all, those same qualities that had once repelled him now, perversely, seemed to attract. And now, he knew he could not desire anything other than such confidence, such exhilarating warfare.

Hesitantly Alex stepped forward and kissed her and while she did not respond, neither did she resist. His hands devoured her hungrily, feeling out the form of her body like Braille. Instead of being clouded by desire he felt exceptionally alert, almost removed, as though he were viewing this experience from outside, or as though he were watching something he wanted to memorise, because it might never happen again. He began to unbutton her shirt, delivering kisses to her white throat, then dipping down to the swell of her breasts confined in their soft net of lace.

The doorbell rang. He watched in slow motion as she froze, mystified, and, fastening her shirt, went to answer it. Then he watched how her face broke out into a smile of sheer, un-mistakable delight as she stepped forward to hug the caller.

'Steve! What a wonderful surprise!'

CHAPTER TWENTY-SIX

SURELY THE MISERABLE fag end of the week was at its worst in the city. At least when Alex had lived in the country it was legitimate to be bored stiff on a Sunday, it was the natural state of rural existence, but here at the hub of things one was supposed to feel alive.

He got up and peered vacantly out of the clouded windows of his flat. It was going to be another scorching day but as yet the street was deserted, the only activity a litter of chip wrappings and fast-food cartons, the detritus of other people's Saturday nights, shifting listlessly in the gutter. It seemed there was nothing for it but to work on his piece today. Lois would get her article after all. And the Project Mars story was really astonishing stuff – he could see the headline already. '*Company Uncovers Secret of Maternal Instinct. Genetic tests could allow companies to screen out the motherly type.*' If he just allowed his journalistic instincts to take over he could forget Jessica, and the thought of how she would view him when the story about her biggest client was splashed all over the paper. The image of her face when she saw Steve at her door the night before spurred him on. Though she had been practically buttoning her shirt as his brother strode in, Steve had not even had the grace to suspect anything, judging by the warmth of his greeting and the way he begged Alex to stay for another glass of wine and rambled on about his forthcoming documentary. Alex had made his escape as fast as he could.

But now that he was sitting there at home, with the laptop on the table and the pilfered document in his hands, he did not have the heart to go on. After all, he was not entirely sure he understood the implications of AMCO's plans for Project Mars. Ideally this sort of story should be talked over with an expert, but given the need for secrecy he could hardly go calling up the usual rent-a-quote scientists. Then, in a rush of inspiration, he remembered Leo Jones.

Leo was one of the few constants in Alex's life. Their

friendship dated from the first day at university, perversely, perhaps, given that Leo's chosen course was medicine and Alex's was languages. They had been assigned adjoining hutches in the college's modern block and the porous nature of the walls ensured they rapidly knew all the incriminating details of each other's private life. Practically two decades later their friendship was just as close and easy as ever. They might see each other only once or twice a year, but their sporadic meetings seemed to pick up exactly where they left off. What made Leo ideal as a friend, Alex thought, was that nothing really changed with him. He had gained about two stones in weight, several professional qualifications and a prestigious job in a London teaching hospital, but everything important about him could more or less be counted on to remain the same. The same wiry garnish on the balding skull, same slow grin that split his big face, the same unvitamined complexion and grubby-collared shirt bespeaking the single male existence. And the same ready availability to come out for a few beers whenever Alex happened to call out of the blue.

They agreed to meet in a pub in Covent Garden whose mock Tudor beams and 'traditional' bar food offered a notion of Olde England concocted in the 1970s for the Japanese market. Outside, the pub looked on to a dusty central square where mime artists and rap dancing acts came and went randomly, like channel-hopping on bad television. As Leo went off for drinks Alex sat next to a group of desultory lunchers, watching a man eating fire as they forked over their scampi salads. The fire-eater, a diminutive Indian, gulped down the flames with effort, as though grappling with a giant kebab.

'So you're still a sad bachelor,' said Leo pleasantly, returning from the bar with a couple of foaming pint jars in his hands. 'What happened to that masseuse you were hanging around with?'

'Aromatherapist,' said Alex. 'She's history, I'm sorry to say. In fact I'm not sorry at all, but forget my sex life, Leo. I rang because I've got something to ask you. It's a work issue, something a bit technical.'

'That's right. Who needs a sex life with a job like yours.'

'Well, the job's changed a bit actually, but I'll get round to that in a minute. The thing is you're a doctor, you know about genetics . . .'

'Some,' agreed Leo cheerily. 'Is this an embarrassing medical problem you've got then, Alex?'

'Just listen, will you?'

Leo leant back, as Alex imagined he might for his patients, a slight upward curve of the lips signifying a professional mien of tolerance, interest, and support. As Alex told him about Project Mars, Leo's surprise was only detectable from the tiny frown furrowing the fat folds of his brow.

'Amazing,' he murmured when Alex had finished. 'The effort these people put in – you have to take your hat off to them. The sheer laboratory slog involved in isolating that gene. And if it's true – what an intriguing discovery.'

Alex leant towards him urgently. But what intrigues me, Leo, is the way AMCO is planning to use it. They talk about commercial applications. At a guess I suspect it could be in the workplace, in that they may offer some sort of genetic test to companies who would value people with this rare X factor. You know, City banks, aggressive law firms, the kind of place where the killer instinct really counts. Outfits which like the idea of hyper-competitive males and would prefer their female employees to devote themselves entirely to their careers. So what I wanted to ask you is, is genetic screening of employees technically possible?'

'Of course it's possible. You've heard of DNA fingerprinting for catching criminals. You only need a cell from anything – saliva or a bit of hair – and you process the DNA from it, effectively separating out certain genetic markers which are pretty much unique to that individual. It's been going for decades now. The difference is, now there's so much more knowledge of the genome, you can tell so much more. Before long they'll be able to give everyone their own personalised DNA sequence with the low down on every gene in the body.'

'And what can you tell from that?'

'Pretty much everything really. What colour eyes you have, what hereditary diseases you're susceptible to, whether you're going to go bald in middle age, or become a mad alcoholic.' He laughed. 'All the things your mother could have told you to start with.'

'But surely the more this kind of thing develops, I mean sophisticated genetic screening, it's going to lead to unfair discrimination?'

'So? There's nothing new about unfair discrimination on the grounds of your genetic inheritance. I don't recall dwarves ever getting a particularly warm and compassionate reception from the public at large. No mediaeval society for the protection of hunchbacks.'

'But those are visible, obvious things, Leo. Knowing every tiny detail about a person – I mean what diseases they're going to get twenty years down the line, for God's sake – is a different thing altogether.'

'Maybe. But there's plenty of insurance companies already refusing to insure people who carry genes for certain inherited diseases.'

'Discriminating on grounds of behaviour, though. I mean, if you can tell whether someone is aggressive or competitive or maternally inclined because of a particular configuration of genes and you can test them for that . . .'

Leo raised a stubby, nicotined finger to interrupt him.

'I'd better stop you there. In fact there's something I should have mentioned from the word go. You remember me telling you I was thinking of taking a break – going into research for a while? Well, it's a bore, Alex, but the fact is AMCO is one of the companies that has approached me to sponsor the project I'm contemplating. It's the usual kind of thing – a generous offer of funding, use of their facilities in return for a first look at the research results. It would mean a move, but I think it's the right time for me. AMCO's offer is a pretty fantastic one and I'm minded to take it, so although I'll help you all I can, I don't think I'm the right person for you to be confiding your doubts in.'

Leo's smile did not waver, but behind the mild eyes it was as though a door had slammed shut. Never before in their friendship had either Alex or Leo declined to discuss an issue that was important to either of them. Now he took off his smeary spectacles and bent his head, cleaning them energetically.

'Oh. I see.'

'And as it happens I need the money because I'm getting married.'

Alex's sense of disorientation increased and his face, un-fettered, registered momentary dismay.

'Christ. I mean, congratulations, Leo. This is very sudden. It's great. Who's the lucky lady?'

'She's called Melanie and before you ask she's a psychiatric nurse. Yes, I know, very fitting and all that. She's a single mother with an annoyingly intelligent kid – he's banned smoking in her house, so either the kid goes or I take a job where I can smoke in the office – anyway the wedding's next year. We were going for something unconventional but, as the kid says, the mere sight of me and his mother together is unconventional enough, so we'll probably make do with a white dress and a church. I was going to call you.'

★   ★   ★

Alex wandered back through the West End. The hot streets were busy with Sunday shoppers and their cars, shards of bright sunlight bouncing off the bonnets. Alex's old, familiar feeling of dislocation from the people around him – a sensation that in the past he had always prided himself upon – had been intensified by the encounter with Leo. Passers-by slid around him like a river round a rock, diverging and inter-twining, their eyes travelling over him unseen. He noticed several young couples, their bodies locked together in a mobile embrace and for a second a sheaf of bright hair and a laugh convinced him he saw Jessica, but the face was a crude travesty of her original. On an impulse he stepped into a callbox and dialled her number. She answered on the second ring.

'Hi? Steve still there?'

'No.' She sounded dispirited.

'What's the matter,' said Alex grudgingly, 'missing him already?'

'No.' There was a pause, then from her end of the phone came something that sounded like a stifled sob. 'If it makes you feel any better, he's left me.'

'What?' Alex's heart scarcely skipped a beat, before told her: 'Listen. Don't go out. I'll be right round.'

★   ★   ★

Mourning did not become Jessica. She looked woeful and hardly sexy at all. Her sleek hair was matted, her lovely, translucent skin blotched and reddened from crying, her nose swollen and her eyes puffy with tears. She greeted him stiffly but after a few sympathetic comments from Alex she fell into his arms, wailing out her sorry tale between sniffs, with no prompting and much repetition. Unerotically Alex patted her back and viewed the undented duvet through the opened bedroom door, though even his instincts were sensitive enough to tell him that it was likely to stay like that.

Jessica's story was a mess, but however askew her narrative, it was immediately clear that Steve's visit, far from being a romantic surprise, had been a courtesy call to terminate their relationship.

'I just don't believe it,' she sobbed. 'At first he gave me all this . . . crap . . . about communication and lifestyle differences and how he hoped I wouldn't allow acrimony to spoil things. Then it turned out he has been carrying on for . . . months.'

'No!' Gently dabbing at her tears, Alex was genuinely surprised. Though his brother was highly successful with women, serial monogamy had always been his preferred style. It was as though the mess of infidelity would add time-wasting emotional complexities to his life and impute, however unjustifiably, a scintilla of moral error.

'He said the more I nagged him to move from Cambridge, the more he realised that we had very different lifestyle goals. He needed someone who genuinely shared his aspirations for his work. Then, when I asked exactly what he meant, he got nasty and said I subscribed to a bourgeois, suburban vision of life that he personally eschewed – I think I've got that right. He said it wasn't my fault, I was a victim of my hormones and my cultural conditioning but I secretly wanted a family and was trying to trap him into it.'

'And now he's met someone who doesn't?'

'Yes. That woman Sarah. I can't believe it.' She sniffed. 'She's far older than me and she looks like the back end of a bus. We used to laugh about her, for God's sake.'

The story was interrupted by a fresh torrent of tears and Alex continued making circular, rubbing movements across her back as she huddled next to him. He fetched her a large drink, and an even larger one for himself. Then eventually, long after he had tired of the platitudes slipping from his lips, something he said seemed to work.

'Look, this may seem hard coming from me, but if that's the way he treats you, he's not worth bothering with.'

'You're right.' She sat bolt upright as though a button had been pressed and he saw the old, defiant glint re-enter her eyes. Helpless grief was being replaced by the purging fire of anger and indignation. Pretty swiftly too, it looked like. Perhaps she was less traumatised by the break than she realised. She blew her nose.

'Oh, don't look at me. I bet I look terrible.'

He performed a mock-serious scrutiny of her face. 'My mistress' eyes are nothing like the sun.'

'Very funny.'

'That's Shakespeare. Or Sir Edgar Avon, of course, or whoever else he's supposed to be this week.'

They laughed raucously, united in their treachery, then she turned to him.

'You know your mother said something bizarre to me when we went down on Friday.'

'Uh huh.'

Jessica took another sip of wine. 'She said that if I had to choose between her two sons, I should choose you.'

'Very bizarre.'

Privately Alex was aghast that his mother should make such a disloyal intervention but it was not the first time that her reputation for being outspoken had embarrassed him. He had suffered for years from her casual assessments of character and her reckless revelation of his most intimate confidences before schoolmasters, friends, employers and anyone else he allowed her to come into contact with. This time, however, he was also grateful.

'She may have been right, you know,' he said.

Jessica's face clouded again. 'Oh, sorry, Alex. I shouldn't have told you that. I don't want to give you the wrong impression after you've been so . . .'

'I hope you're not going to say kind.'

'No. But you are considerate.'

She smiled, reaching to pat his hand but just her touch was enough to make a jolt of desire lurch through him again. To check himself he sat back and took out a cigarette.

'As it happens, I've got a confession for you.'

'Mmm?'

'I was going to tell you, but there never seemed a good moment.' Nor, he realised latterly, was this one. 'Last week the paper asked me to write about AMCO. You know, about Project Mars. I mean it's pretty much out in the open already and if it wasn't me it would be someone else. There's a lot of people following the story. I've got to do a piece by next week.'

'But I thought . . .?'

He continued, in a rush of justification. 'It's an important issue, Jessica. From what I understand of it they've isolated one particular gene. The men who have it possess hyper-competitive natures – they're aggressive, novelty-seeking, risk-taking – but the women who have it manifest something else entirely. It seems they have absolutely no maternal instinct. And when you consider it, that's an astonishing finding. Quite apart from the social implications, companies would pay for that sort of information about their employees. Think about it – no maternity leave, no long breaks. Women should mind about that. And whether you want children or not, you should mind about it. And AMCO intend to make money out of it.'

She regarded him stonily. 'How on earth do you know all this?'

'That's what I was getting round to.' He paused, painfully. 'You know the envelope of stuff from AMCO you were being sent?'

'Yes. But it never came. The courier screwed up.'

'It did come. I took it.'

As he watched the incomprehension in her face turn to rage he realised he had broken his own golden rule – he had forgotten the importance of timing.

She wrenched his arm away from her, marched across the room and flung open the door.

'That's enough. It's all I need. I should have known it. Your brother cheats on me and you steal my post. You're unbelievable, you two. You're both untrustworthy liars. You're exactly alike. Just leave me alone. Get out.'

★ ★ ★

There seemed nowhere else to go but back to the office. To be among the dispossessed who inhabited the twilight working world when others hurried home to their families. Below him the windows of the ersatz, breeze-block cityscape glinted against a violet sky. The office was quiet on a Sunday, a few workers sitting in pools of halogen light at their desks, others gliding in and out. In the evening everyone was more focused. It was a question of getting the work done, putting the newspaper to bed and getting out of there. Someone offered Alex a take-away hamburger and he refused, queasily.

Now there was no excuse not to finish the story and have it on Lois' desk by the following day. It really couldn't wait. And the story was all there. All Alex needed were a few standard 'no comments' from Frank LeRoux. In truth, that was the only part of the job he actually looked forward to – the thought of LeRoux's purpling, pock-marked face when he realised his top secret story was out in the open. And then Alex thought of that same face venting its rage on Jessica.

Brave, beleaguered Jessica. Wasn't she worth more than a story? He knew the longer he held on to the truth about Project Mars, the longer he allowed rivals like Brent Southern the chance to get to it. But then he remembered Jessica's scorn and her contemptuous jibe that he and his brother were alike. Once he would have taken that as the greatest compliment. Now it was an insult and it stung.

He thought of ditching the AMCO piece and going back to the place he laughingly called home. But the prospect of a dismal take-away in front of the television in Pimlico kept him at his desk. Eventually, his head physically throbbing from the clash inside it, he turned to the Lewis Appleby profile. At least a little literary homage wasn't going to upset anyone. And the disappearing wife certainly gave it some interest. There was nothing for it but to ring May Chumley. She had plainly been reluctant to talk any further, but she was, after all, the only person he'd found who actually knew Appleby.

When he reached May Chumley, after calling his mother for her number and apologising for the late hour, she was surprisingly chatty. The old lady did not sound remotely startled to hear from him and after a few niceties she volunteered that there was another acquaintance of Lewis Appleby's who was keen to talk to him. If Alex called now, they would certainly be in. He should ask for Tom.

Alex took a slurp of coffee and dialled. The man at the end of the phone sounded friendly, but younger than he'd expected.

'Ah yes. Mr Irvine. May said you would ring. Look, you don't know me, my name's Tom Fisher. But I heard you were trying to contact Katherine Appleby.'

'I . . . er, I had no idea that I could. But I'd very much like to. Is she still alive, then? Do you know where I could find her?'

'Yes, she's alive. But first I'd like to know why you want to contact her.'

'Well, I'm aiming to write a piece about Lewis Appleby.'

'What sort of piece is this you're planning?'

'Um, an affectionate retrospective. A look at his life and work kind of thing.'

'So this would be . . . respectful, then?'

'Yes, highly respectful. Look, who . . . ?'

'In that case, she'd like to meet you. Can you take down this address?'

Alex reached for a pen and scrawled an address in Kent.

'Can you make tomorrow?'

'Er yes, I suppose so.'

'Let's say two o'clock.'

'Mr Fisher, you didn't mention, who are you?'

'Oh, I'm sorry, I didn't make it clear. I'm Lewis Appleby's son.'

★　★　★

He was a tall man, with blazing blue eyes and thick wavy hair, which although it had gone grey with age, did not seemed to have thinned. He walked with a slight limp as he made his way down through the cottage garden on a path bulging with banks of silvery lavender. Jasmine and honeysuckle intertwined luxuriantly around a picket fence. Alex, standing at the gate, wondered where he had seen that face before, until he remembered the portrait of Lewis Appleby in Jessica's bedroom at Fallings. The one his wife had painted with its thin, contemplative mouth and slight sardonic turn of the lip.

A bad night's sleep and a long, sweaty journey had not helped Alex's mood that afternoon. Tom Fisher had not mentioned on the phone that the road leading to the house was unsigned and the place would be incredibly difficult to find. Alex had had to stop in two villages to coax specific directions from surly locals who might have been imparting information to enemy aliens for all their co-operation. But as he entered the house, its stillness, the cool, stone-flagged hall and the loud ticking of the grandfather clock immediately soothed him. Ducking to avoid low beams, Tom Fisher showed him into a small, chintzy parlour.

'She'll be right in. She's making a cup of tea. I'll be in the garden if you need me.'

Alex took out a cigarette then thought the better of it. Over the fireplace hung a painting of a large, grey house and he stood up to get a better look. It was a handsome place, painted in full summer, judging by the blaze of roses in the foreground, and with a start of recognition he realised it was Fallings. Of course. It was only a few days since he had seen that view for himself, sitting at the top of the hill by that curious shell house, with Steve's neglected, enigmatic girlfriend by his side. As he peered at it, Katherine Appleby came in behind him. She was white-haired and upright, dressed in an elegant navy dress and bearing a cup of tea and a slice of fruitcake. She gave him a dazzling smile.

'That's one of mine. I did it from memory,' she said, following his gaze. Briskly, she sat down and motioned to a seat opposite.

'It's so kind of you to come all this way, Mr Irvine. May said you were writing a piece about Lewis. And that it would be a respectful piece. It was that which did it really, I suppose. We had a long talk, and then I came home and chatted to Tom, and I've decided after all this time, that people might as well know what happened.'

PART FOUR

Chapter Twenty-Seven

Sussex, 1945

IT SEEMED, IN those few bewildering months after the war, that the shell house was somehow to blame. Obviously such an accusation was absurd, and yet Lewis spent so much time supervising its reconstruction it was as though he was being taken away from her a second time. He'd been absent after all for most of the war, engaged in secret work that Katherine knew meant something to do with intelligence and only returning, in unheralded breaks of a few brief days, frustratingly unable to give his news, which was confidential, and having instead to hear her news, which was trivial or non-existent, to do with the corn, or the potatoes they'd been growing on what used to be lawn. She had spent most of the war working the land around Fallings. It was fulfilling but exhausting work, though Bill's extensive kitchen garden at least ensured that they ate well. Now that it was over and the nation was adjusting to peace again, there was a new beginning for Katherine too. In June 1945 she gave birth to Tom, a child whose placid gaze had seen only peace, and it seemed that surely now their life together could properly begin.

All over Europe shattered cities were being picked up from the dust and slowly rebuilt, but the restoration of the shell house struck Katherine as excessive. It seemed such a small place, a frippery, to demand so much of his attention. She told herself Lewis' enthusiasm to restore it was a reaction to the months he had spent in windowless rooms talking about codes and sabotage and undercover agents. He had always been driven by his enthusiasms, so Katherine tried hard not to mind when he spent long afternoons, then whole days, on his project.

Deep in Fallings' library he had found a set of faded, folded papers detailing the original construction of the shell house, with a sepia-inked architect's drawing and precise, eighteenth-century writing listing the numbers and positions of shells required. He announced that he was going to need several thousand shells of particular specifications – mussels, razorbacks, scallops, mother of pearl and tiny pink Caribbean conches with a tabby mottling on their backs. Katherine objected that with everyday groceries still rationed, surely obtaining something as exotic as foreign seashells would be impossible. Yet it emerged that Lewis' marine biology laboratory in London regularly threw up some of the more unusual species and the rest could almost certainly be found at the local coast. So great brown sackfuls of mussel shells and little boxes of rarer specimens began to arrive at the station and Bill insisted on collecting them by horse and cart to avoid using up the petrol ration.

Katherine might have spent more time with Lewis were it not that her main view of the outside world at that time was framed by her bedroom window. After almost ten years of trying for a child, Tom's birth had been an overwhelming, but also an exhausting, experience. She was two whole days in labour with him and for weeks afterwards she felt the life sucked out of her like a blown egg. To begin with he fed and slept badly, which meant that she did too, drifting in the grey, solipsistic hinterland of the sleep-deprived. In the end she gave in and lived entirely by his rhythms so that when he had fed and fallen asleep, lolling against the breast, a bead of milk on his small, pursed lips, she would collapse and curl around him on the bed, feeling the novelty of his nudging and stretching coming from without her, rather than within.

Tom's deformity, his tiny club foot, had also been a blow. Not to the baby, of course, who kicked the small turned limb unheeding in sheer delight at life, and not to his mother, for whom the soft solidity of his flesh, the slick licorice of his hair, his sparrow chest and grave little indigo eyes were the sum of perfection itself. But Lewis, she knew, was troubled by it. He was charming, of course, towards the child, but greeted him with jocular distance, as though they had been introduced at a cocktail party. The imperfection bothered him greatly, Katherine could see.

A couple of months after Tom's birth, in the glorious week that the whole country, including the local village, held street parties, lit bonfires and held thanksgiving services to celebrate VJ Day, a visitor came to stay at Fallings. He was a foreigner, a refugee from Europe, whom Lewis said needed temporary shelter. Katherine need not bother herself with him one bit, Lewis would cope on his own.

They had got used to people coming and going throughout the war. To start with there were the evacuees from London, a whole trainload of them, who had descended on the village in 1940. Mostly they were unaccompanied children clutching their gas masks and tiny little parcels of emergency rations and wearing signs round their necks giving their names and ages, but there were some mothers too, who had sat in a large, disgruntled group in the village hall, their noisy, grubby children running round them, truculently objecting to the billeting arrangements and the camp beds and the food until the vicar arrived and directed them to their new homes. Fallings had been assigned a little family of three, two sisters and a brother, who had never before seen a house with carpets, and could not believe they had been given a bed each, rather than one between three. At first it had not been easy – the children were full of scoffs and raucous hostility at the way life in the country was run, hiding their amazement at such exotic things as cows and sheep and the availability of plentiful fresh food with a confident urban assertion that life in London was infinitely superior. But Katherine had still felt a pang of regret when, soon after the Blitz, their parents in Limehouse decided the children would be better use down in London and sent for them to be returned.

Then there were other refugees, like the couple of Jewish girls from Czechoslovakia who had been taken in by old Mrs Foster, a rich widow in the village. She had sent money for their passage in 1939 and although they were supposed to be employed in domestic work for her, the girls had supposedly become so close to their benefactress that there was no question of them returning to their homeland and instead they were to be sent on secretarial courses for a new life in England.

This new refugee, however, seemed less keen to be integrated into the community. Katherine watched him from the window of the bedroom as he accompanied Lewis to the shell house, politely admiring the work. He was a handsome young man, studious-looking, with short cropped hair and small wire-framed glasses. From what Lewis told her she gathered that he was a scientist too, one whose work in the field of heredity Lewis had admired. They spent much of their time in the laboratory that had been constructed from an outhouse in the grounds, and in the evenings he tended to take dinner in his room.

He was scrupulously polite, always greeting her in his accented English and tipping his brown trilby hat to her when they passed on the rose walk during one of Tom's turns in the pram. If she had to put her finger on anything unusual, it was the way he looked at the baby. She tended to tuck the odd foot under a blanket, but he had spotted it at once, unlike most other people who bent over to admire Tom, but when he did no look of sympathy crossed his brow. Instead, it was more like curiosity, even perhaps distaste.

★ ★ ★

At the beginning of autumn she decided she needed a break. She would go up to London and visit May. May's famous love of babies meant she had raced down to Fallings soon after Tom's birth to see him, so she would not mind indulging a besotted mother who chattered a little too much about her child.

Re-entering the dirt and clamour of London, however, was almost enough to make Katherine forget the newly minted joy of motherhood. The war may have ended, yet the Londoners in their utility clothing and demob suits, picking their way through the rubble of bomb-damaged buildings, seemed soured by austerity, their skins sallow with deprivation. Even May, though she greeted Katherine as affectionately as ever, was thinner and graver somehow, as though her usual jocularity had taken a serious dent. Despite clinging to the crumpled sartorial style she had always favoured, May was now an important professional with her own staff and office high above Fleet Street, the walls decorated with large, blown-up photographs that had featured in past issues of the magazine. She enfolded Katherine in a huge hug and shut her door.

'It's the only way we'll get to talk. I'm afraid I'm madly busy today. It's press day, so don't be offended if I disappear but it's just so good to see you. You look tremendously well, it must be all those eggs and milk. Now's certainly the right time to be living in the country.'

Between them the conversation bubbled freely as ever, with

May talking about her job, about the war and about James Chumley, who was back in England and living in digs near her flat. James had been through a deep depression following the death of his friend Will Mason.

'I think he'll never stop blaming himself for it,' sighed May.

James had gone off to fight in the Spanish civil war and had somehow persuaded Will to accompany him as an unofficial war artist.

'Will never intended to fight at all, he loathed that kind of thing, but he didn't take it seriously enough. He was hit by a stray bullet as he was sketching on a hillside. The awful thing is, it was one of their own side,' said May. 'Anyhow, James was injured too, and that, as well as his communist past, meant he was rejected for active service in '39. He was working in the Information ministry, writing propaganda pamphlets to be dropped by planes, when I had an absolute brainstorm and commissioned him as a war reporter for the magazine. He did a brilliant job. We keep him on staff in fact, though it's hard getting him to write anything.'

They were interrupted by May's secretary.

'Oh, hold on, it looks like I've got a visitor.'

A tall, gangling soldier with a dark crew-cut and a portfolio under his arm edged into the room.

'I'm sorry, you're busy. I can come back.' He was young, with a west country burr, slow as treacle.

'No no, Arnold, this is Katherine Appleby.'

Shyly he shook her hand: 'Pleased to meet you, Miss.'

'Arnold has some pictures for our latest issue. I'm afraid they're pretty shocking, Katherine.'

That was an understatement. The photographs were the most horrifying that Katherine had ever seen. They had been taken by Arnold in his capacity as an official photographer with the British army as it moved across Europe liberating the concentration camps.

Katherine had heard about the camps where Jews had been taken but this was the first time she had focused on them. She saw piles of corpses stacked – there was no other word for it – like so much yellow firewood in a yard, small children standing alongside them. There were women, somewhere between the living and the dead, whose faces seemed to have travelled far beyond anger or defiance. A crush of bodies, with eyes heavier than their whole flesh, watching and waiting against a wire fence.

'How terrible.'

Out of the canvas portfolio he pulled a second sheaf of pictures, which he said had been taken by the Germans themselves, documenting life in the camp. He fanned them out on May's desk.

'There, that's work going on in the camp's hospital, so called.'

He spoke slowly, sparingly, as though comments were superfluous. May passed them over with a few murmurs about where they might be used and then bustled out to attend to a crisis on another of her pages. But one photograph had Katherine transfixed. It was of a man wearing a white coat, holding the arm of a tiny, naked child. The doctor smiled to camera. The child, who could not have been more than three, also gazed into the lens, her thin limbs knotted as stripped flotsam, a tuft of dark hair and eyes wide with fear. Next to her, staring identically at the camera, was the child's double, her twin.

'That man, who is he?'

Arnold looked over. 'That fellow is called Herr Doktor Albrecht Abelmann. A specialist in inherited conditions. Apparently he had a teaching post at some institute down in Munich but he asked to come to the camp because there were people who could be used in his experiments.'

'What did he do?'

He weighed her up, as though wondering what to tell her.

'He took deformed children and those with congenital conditions. He was especially interested in identical twins. He operated on them. Infected them to see how differently they would react. Explored their organs. Subjected them to vile things in the name of research.'

'And where is he now?'

'He was arrested. He was one of the lucky ones. A lot of the rest were lined up and shot.'

Katherine could not take her eyes away from the picture.

'Hey.' Arnold took her arm. 'I can see you're pretty affected.' Gently he removed the photograph from her sight. His gestures were calm and deliberate, as though a dense weight within him slowed his movements.

'Would you . . .' she said, then faltered. May was nowhere to be seen. 'I mean, I wondered if you'd like a cup of tea? There's a café just across the street.'

They went across the road and sat behind steamy windows drinking dark brown, sweetened tea as Katherine asked Arnold relentless questions about his life, and he talked readily, without embarrassment, as though being grilled by this attractive, intense woman with her beautiful clothes and gentle manners was perfectly natural for him. He had been born in Somerset, of a British mother and a Polish father who ran a small dairy farm. Arnold was always destined for a job on the farm until the war broke out and then, though he might have gained exemption from active service as an agricultural worker, he swiftly joined up. By the end of the war his passionate hobby of photography had redirected his path and he had been appointed as a photographer accompanying Allied troops across the continent.

His Polish father had always talked of his country with great pride, but until the war came Arnold had never really given much thought to actually seeing it for himself. Even then, when he was assigned to photograph the liberation of concentration camps and prisoner-of-war camps, he could not have guessed what horror would accompany his first visit to his paternal homeland. Across Europe the troops moved and Arnold and his box of equipment went alongside them, squashed in a jeep or crammed into a van. The first time he had seen a camp had been back in April when British soldiers found 40,000 sick and starving people near a place called Belsen. Even as the liberating troops arrived SS guards were shooting prisoners trying to take potatoes from a pit and Arnold stood and worked, trying to shield his horror behind his lens. In the months since then he had journeyed constantly, his camera freezing images which seared the mind.

Katherine gazed at him as he talked. The Polish ancestry gave him a handsome, distinctive look, quite unlike the Somerset farmboy he was. He had a broad, high-cheekboned face and his eyes were widely spaced, with great dark lashes from which he looked up at her with a gaze whose steadiness gave a semblance of placidity, but was occasionally shot through with acute, anguished intelligence.

When he talked about the atrocities he had seen she expected him to be evasive, but instead he was direct and descriptive, making no concessions to her gender in the way of other men, who hated to talk of their war experiences, or filtered them for a female sensibility. Looking at him she realised how young he was – surely he couldn't be more than twenty-five? He had a muscular body and broad, farmer's hands, which looked more accustomed to ushering life into the world than witnessing appalling death.

At one point he said: 'You want to know a lot.'

'I need to know.'

He nodded in acceptance, and she added: 'You said I was affected by those pictures. But how could anyone not be affected? It must have had a pretty deep effect on you.'

He offered her a cigarette, then lit one. 'You're right. I take these pictures and I encourage people to look at them but there's no cure on earth for seeing these things.'

★ ★ ★

When she returned she went straight to Tom's room. The baby was deep in sleep, pale as marble, and as always she reached to feel the flutter of his invisible breath. He lay in the old Appleby cot, a hundred-year-old oak rocker lined with worn white linen, for which she had sewn a new blanket with a scatter of yellow flowers. His arms were thrown above his head in the newborn gesture of surrender, his shell-pink eyelids tight shut, his small pursed mouth moving and sucking as though dreaming of the breast. Even at this age, when his baby features were scarcely formed, she could tell he would resemble Lewis, from the high, clear forehead and the fine pencil line of eyebrows with their interrogative arch.

He had only existed a few months, yet his arrival had changed her more profoundly than any experience, the love she felt for him infinitely more powerful than any emotion she had felt before. Nor was the change she had undergone an introspective one. It affected everything, her whole perspective was awry. When she looked at the world now she saw it peopled with parents and children, fraught with peril and pain. It was as though this love was an acid that did not blind, but allowed you to see clearly for the first time.

★   ★   ★

She was in the cool gloom of the flower room, stripping some white roses of their thorns, when Lewis found her. The flower room's shelves were stacked with vases and boxes of shells and its centre was dominated by a huge marble slab for chopping and trimming the floral harvest of Fallings' gardens. Even given the amount of flower beds which had been turned over to vegetables during the war there was still a glorious abundance of roses and daisies to be picked and the air in the flower room was sweet and heavy with the scent of them.

Lewis came in to store some shell sacks, full of talk about the next book he planned to write and how one of his closest friends, elected as an MP in the new Labour government, had suggested that Lewis may take a formal role as a scientific consultant.

'It would mean us taking a house in London but you'd like that, wouldn't you? You'd get to see more of your friends. You're far too isolated here.'

She went on, cutting and slitting the rose stems.

'I'm OK.' She plunged the flowers into icy water.

'And how was your day?'

She gazed up at him, her hands in the dark leaves, her face intense above the white petals.

'Lewis who exactly is that man? Your visitor?'

'I told you. His name is Herr Müller.'

'Are you sure about that?'

'Well, of course I'm sure. What on earth are you talking about?' He stood over her for a second, gently tracing the violet shadow beneath her eye with his finger, as though he could brush away fatigue. Then, with an abrupt movement he turned to leave, adding: 'I know you're tired with the baby but you can get very querulous sometimes, darling. Why don't you have an early night tonight? I'm sure the journey's worn you out. And I'll be working late in my study.'

CHAPTER TWENTY-EIGHT

A POOL OF coloured light from the stained-glass door bathed Katherine in an unnaturally rosy glow as she stood in the narrow hall. It was a tall town house, in a not particularly smart part of Fulham, where a scrubby, dog-ridden little green and a line of sooty plane trees seemed to be the sole representatives of the natural world. Yet the house's modest proportions belied the class of its domestic furnishings. From where the maid had instructed her to wait she could see the drawing room, decorated with some fine pieces of silver and china and a collection of Alfred Munnings on the wall. Over the fireplace there was a large portrait in oils of a young woman, and a set of photographs, including a wedding group, stood on the baby grand piano in the far corner.

As Katherine stood there, there was a sudden gust of giggling and a tiny girl ran out from the kitchen, then stopped stock still in her tracks at the sight of her. The child had a mass of strawberry blonde hair, and wore a light blue dress with white socks. She fixed Katherine with a stringent stare, strangely piercing for one of her age, before scampering away. Behind her, her mother's languid voice could be heard.

'There's absolutely nothing wrong with the Sutton-Clarkes. It's just as snobbish to object to them on grounds of their class as it would be to like them for it. Geordie's a fiendish dancer and Patricia says this new club is wonderful. I don't care if you don't come. I shall go alone. I'll have an excellent time and you can stew at home thinking of all those handsome officers flirting with me like mad.'

There was a rich laugh and a man's voice said: 'Go then. Geordie Sutton-Clarke is what you bloody well deserve.'

Then she came out and saw Katherine.

'Darling, how wonderful to see you.'

Katherine kissed her cheek. 'Meredith. How are you? It's been a long time.'

The Kingslands had moved to Fulham after their marriage,

Ralph having refused the offer from Meredith's father of a grander establishment on the south side of Cavendish Square. Katherine had missed the wedding, but then so had everyone. It had been very small and quiet, because of the war of course, though some people suspected it was on account of the mutual disdain between Meredith's family and their future son-in-law. Now, despite her own abstraction, she was curious to see them. Everyone said Meredith's hauteur persisted, but it had been blunted and mellowed by happiness. The couple were known to bicker like crazy in public, though no one denied they were as devoted as honeymoon sweethearts.

She looked the same as ever, slender and immaculate with her sleek rope of hair and a fine, pink jersey suit that was surely beyond the reach of any clothing coupons. After she had been ushered into the drawing room and sat down, Katherine was perversely relieved to discover that even Meredith was unable to get proper coffee and served the usual, bitter mixture with chicory which everyone else was obliged to drink.

'It's so good to see you. How are all your family? And how is that wonderful house?' If there was envy in Meredith at her friend's good fortune, she hid it well.

'Everyone's fine and so is Fallings. The garden's a bit destroyed, though. We dug it all up.'

'And you've just had a baby! You should have brought him, Katherine. Isobel would have loved to see him.'

Isobel did not look like the kind of child who would be unduly ruffled by the chance to cuddle a baby. Even at two she was as self-possessed as her mother ever was, sitting across from them with her ankles neatly crossed, lecturing a toy doll and bear in fierce, alternate whispers. Suddenly she tossed them to the ground and jumped up, running to embrace the knees of her father who had just entered the room.

From what she could observe, Ralph had changed far less than his wife. A sardonic reserve surrounded him still, but he kissed her politely, patted the child's head and then went to stand behind Meredith. As they talked, Katherine noticed that his hands caressed his wife's shoulders with fine, sensual movements, as though he could hardly refrain from touching her.

'You wouldn't believe my husband. There's this absolutely

terrific club opened just off Berkeley Square and I've fixed up a fun set of people to go dancing but he'd rather stay at home drinking with my brother Hugo. I tell you what, Ralph. I'll make Hugo go, then you can both slump in a corner together.'

'You don't give up, do you?' His gaze lingered on her, amused.

She narrowed her eyes at him in mock menace. 'You should know that by now.'

'Well, leave Hugo alone. I need him. You see, I thought I'd get Martin over tonight. He rather wanted to meet your brother.'

Then he turned to Katherine. 'Before you get drawn too deeply into the tawdry story of our social life, perhaps it would be better if we talked first.'

He guided Katherine into his library, which was stacked floor to ceiling with his precious first editions and they sat in deep leather wing chairs, facing each other, like men at a London club.

'You should have visited us earlier. We've thought about you. How's Lewis?'

'Fine. Or rather, that's what I'm here for. Ralph, there's something I'd like to ask you about. You're the only person who might be able to help me, but I know that you probably can't. I mean . . . you know . . . war secrets and all that.'

'I'll help if I can.'

Katherine felt his keen eyes upon her and hesitated. It had taken her days before she plucked up the courage to phone Ralph Kingsland. Like Lewis, Ralph had been in Intelligence during the war, though his work had involved going abroad a lot, and it occurred to Katherine that he might be the only person who could explain to her what she needed. She'd left it until Saturday, telling Lewis she was on a shopping trip up in town, of which he seemed to approve.

She took out a cigarette and he drew out a gold lighter for it. Sitting there, eyes fixed on the small fire Ralph had lit in the grate, she spilled out the events of the last few weeks, of the photograph she had seen and how she was certain the same man was now staying in their home. Only Lewis had said that the man was someone entirely different. As she rehearsed her doubts, every word was weighted with bewilderment and behind it the shadow of something more bitter – a sense of betrayal.

'Don't tell anyone about this, Ralph, will you? Please? I feel dreadful enough coming to see you without his knowledge.'

'More than that,' he leant towards her, as though to emphasise the gravity of his own words. 'Whatever I say must stay totally confidential. I'm sure you understand how important that is. I'm taking a huge risk speaking to you.'

She nodded mutely.

'You know that Lewis was in touch with . . . the government . . . before the war?'

'You mean Intelligence?'

'Exactly. Well, as I understand it, and I'm not at all close to this, as a result of that contact Lewis was asked if your home, Fallings, could be used as a safe place.'

'Safe for whom?'

'For certain German scientists and engineers whose expertise Britain and the United States wanted to hold on to. They needed somewhere secluded to put them while they were interrogated.'

'But why the secrecy?'

'These men are Nazis, you see – some of them quite senior.'

'I still don't see why the interrogation or whatever couldn't be done in Germany. I mean that's where they're going to be tried, isn't it?'

'Not necessarily.'

He waited, while the implications of his words sank in.

'In some cases these people may never go back to Germany. Some are being given so-called "special treatment", which means essentially that their files come here and their wartime activity and Nazi past is disguised and they go on to a new life with a new name on their visa, generally in the United States. Without a trial.'

'Surely not. I don't understand.'

He steepled his fingers beneath his chin and sighed. 'It's hard to, I know. You see there's tremendous competing pressure from the Soviet Union. They know as well as us that some of these doctors and engineers and scientists are the most brilliant in their field, and in some cases they're working on the cusp of great new ideas. Ideas which could be very valuable – in fact it's not too grand to say, ideas which could change the way we live. Whatever other people may like to believe, in terms of technical innovation the Germans have been leaders for years and some of their scientific knowledge is outstanding. So what do you do with these men? Do you leave them to fester in jails, knowing that one day they may emerge and regroup behind a newly dangerous aggressor, or do you let them fall into the hands of the Russians, or do you debrief them and let their technological and scientific brilliance work for your own nation?'

'But surely nothing could justify people who have done such terrible things evading justice?'

'The justification is that they become reparations. The spoils of war. It's an age-old idea.'

'This man, the one at our home, do you have any idea if he is the same person I saw in the photograph?'

'Herr Abelmann? Yes. From what I have found out he was known to your husband before the war and admired by him. He worked at the Kaiser Wilhelm Institute of Genealogy in Munich and he and Lewis had corresponded about certain issues including his experiments on genetic resistance to certain infectious diseases. That was the main reason your husband was approached in this regard. It was known they shared some views on genetics and . . . other things.'

'What other things?'

'Eugenics.'

'You mean his national nutrition plan?'

'Not exactly. There was an idea Lewis was pushing a few years ago for a nationwide programme of voluntary sterilisation for the feckless and unemployed. It impressed quite a few of the people who count, but the war intervened and it all came to nothing.'

'But that's nothing like . . . I mean it has nothing in common with the terrible things this man did. For God's sake, Ralph, he experimented on living children.'

'The Nazis have been very interested in exploring methods of resistance to deadly diseases, both for the well-being of their own country and – in terms of biological warfare – for the destruction of others.'

'But Lewis would never have known what this man was involved in.'

Ralph met her imploring face impassively. 'Without doubt. As I said, your husband's specialist knowledge of genetics is one of the things that qualifies him to debrief Herr Abelmann about the implications of his recent experiments.'

Suddenly her reserve broke, the blood rushed angrily to her face and she burst out: 'No, you're wrong! He would never have agreed. I don't believe you.'

Ralph regarded her silently for a moment, then clasped his hands together decisively and stood up.

'Well, there's nothing more I can say, Katherine. I've already said more than I intended to. Obviously I don't know what you will discuss with your husband but you must remember that our conversation has to be strictly private. You give me your word on that?'

As she locked into his gaze Katherine felt the infidelity surge up and take possession of her. As clearly as a soldier crossing to the opposing camp, she felt herself step forward and leave her old loyalty behind her. Yet although she was embracing what she knew to be right, the dull ache of desertion remained.

'You seem very well-informed about my husband,' she said quietly.

'I am.'

'And what about you, Ralph?'

'Let's just say I'm one of a number of people who would prefer that these arrangements came to an end.'

As she bid farewell with forced brightness to Meredith and the child, promising to bring Tom to visit them soon, and walked back through the dusty Fulham streets to the underground, she wondered why Ralph had taken such a gamble. Why had he decided to tell her so much? Surely he had breached all kinds of secrecy laws? He could probably be had up for prison if Katherine were to let on that she had spoken to him. What was it he had said? That there was a group of people who were against Lewis' arrangement? And he had seem pleased – almost relieved – to be telling her about it. It was evident that he deeply disliked what was going on, but it was almost as though, quite apart from that, he disliked Lewis too.

CHAPTER TWENTY-NINE

THE EVENING WAS still fine when she got back, hot for the time of year, and the long light slanting from the west turned the windows of Fallings momentarily to panes of fire. She decided to walk in the garden to clear the confusion of her thoughts. She wandered slowly, barely aware of her surroundings, through the orchard where the windfalls lay soft and corrupted in the long grass, past the fruit beds where she plucked some raspberries from a bush and crushed them absently in her mouth, the crimson staining her lips. As she went her arm, bare in her thin cotton dress, scratched against a trailing bramble and drew blood, a precise, surprising track of drops against the brown flesh. She meandered on, directionless, until she found herself heading up the hill to the woods.

The shell house was almost finished now and Lewis was hugely proud of it. It was perfect, like a tiny, exquisite cathedral, with a classical statue of a nymph to cup the water from the small, underground river beside it. The last touch was to add a mother of pearl motif on the floor, making up the linked initials L and K. The ground around the shell house had been cleared of the brambles and bindweed that once overwhelmed it and the grass was now short and trampled. Her heart pounding from the climb, Katherine lay down on her back and turned her head, her ear to the hot grass so that she could almost feel the earth spinning beneath her. She was still lying like that when she heard footsteps and, realising it was too late to move without attracting attention, she stayed where she was.

Lewis and the visitor were each carrying a sack of shells up the hill. Grunting with effort they laid them down on the floor of the shell house and Lewis knelt to begin fitting fragments to the pattern he had designed. Katherine could see his back through the window bent to the task, the visitor standing by, his hands in his pockets. She heard the soft mumble of their voices, then Lewis stood up and rested his hands on his back.

'Almost there. What do you think of that then, Albrecht?'

'It is the most charming construction. Your wife, I think, is a fortunate woman.'

★ ★ ★

She waited until they were gone before she left the wood, then hastened to find Tom. The nurse had already put him down and he was deep in sleep but she picked him up and sat in the nursing chair, cradling him in her arms. She was still sitting there when Lewis passed.

'What is it, Katherine? What's the matter?'

Without looking at him she said: 'I know who that man is.'

'Not this again.'

'He's Albrecht Abelmann. You can't deny it. I saw a picture of him in May's office. He was working in a concentration camp.'

'This man hasn't been to any camp. He's an important scientist and his work has to be saved. He won't be staying here much longer.'

'Lewis, he experimented on people. On children.'

Between them their sleeping son stirred and punched out a fist to the empty air. Lewis watched him silently and in that moment she knew that he knew. He turned away from her and spoke tersely, as though the words were being dragged out of him.

'I knew of this man before the war and I'd read his work with great admiration. He's a leader in the field. Even in the past few days, I've learned from him. His work on disease resistance has been extremely valuable. It could save thousands of lives.'

'You can't see what I'm saying, can you?'

'You know the rules. This isn't something we can discuss any further.'

'He should be facing trial. Like the others will.'

Lewis never lost his temper. Not in all the years of their marriage had his composure been shaken. Now he took the baby from her arms and replaced him in his cot. Kneeling down so that his eyes were level with hers he took her face between his hands he said: 'I can see you're upset. You're young. You feel things too deeply. But you simply don't understand what's going on and you shouldn't interfere. You know we shouldn't be talking like this. What I can say for this man is that he has great ideas.'

'You never used to think ideas were more important than people.'

He looked at her strangely, then got up, his expression hardened.

'It must be perfectly clear that sometimes of course they are.'

'Tell him to go, Lewis.'

'I can't.'

'Not even for my sake?'

'No.'

He closed the door behind him.

In the vacancy she felt her love ebbing, her old admiration for his vitality and his pure, high-minded intelligence dissolving entirely, as the tide washes clean a lover's message on the sand. Her sadness was as huge and salt as the sea, and her tears were lost within it.

Supper was a silent affair. Herr Müller was taking dinner in his room, and between Katherine and Lewis an air of cold formality descended. They passed each other dishes with precise, exaggerated care, as though handling unexploded bombs. Their cutlery scraped and clinked like tiny weapons. The sound of the birds in the garden singing out their evensong reminded Katherine of her first visit to Fallings, when the perfection of the place had seemed overwhelming and she had longed for the aesthetic satisfaction of something awry.

Later that night when Lewis was having his coffee in the library, she pleaded an early night and went upstairs. Then she picked up her suitcase, placed her sleeping baby in one of the long wicker baskets Bill used for cut flowers, crept out into the car and drove out of Fallings for good.

CHAPTER THIRTY

ALEX STRETCHED OUT his stiff limbs as the old lady paused.

'It must have been a huge decision for you. To leave with a young baby.'

'Yes. It was very difficult – mainly in a practical sense. I was terrified what might happen when people found out that I'd left. That I might be accused of breaching secrets, or Ralph might.'

'So where did you go?'

'To my mother. It was the only place I could go. At first I thought when I approached her that she would tell me to go straight back to my husband, but she took me in and even without me explaining anything, she was a great support.'

Katherine recalled the numb weeks in which Syrie had set about feeding her and the baby, never probing too far, bringing tea, bathing Tom and carrying on the practicalities of life with her usual pursed face and the occasional thin smile.

'What about Lewis?'

'Lewis saw my leaving as a terrible betrayal. I think he could just not forgive me for having a different perspective. He believed in ideas, you see, and in the ends justifying the means.'

'But what did everyone think?'

'I think they assumed I'd had some kind of affair. I didn't want to explain why I'd gone and nor, of course, did Lewis. He didn't tell anyone where I was and I didn't want to be found. I resumed my maiden name.'

'He never remarried?'

'There was no one else. After I left he threw himself into his work. He finished three books in the following four years and that was really the start of the radio broadcasts and the talks and the political speeches and him becoming well-known.'

'So where did you go?'

She smiled awkwardly. He saw that as a young girl she would have blushed.

'Oh, didn't I mention that? The photographer, Arnold Fisher, the one May introduced me to. He had this flat, but he was going to be working on the continent so he let us stay there. Lewis found out from my mother where we'd gone and came there, shortly after I'd moved in, to order me back. But by then it was too late.'

'Why?'

She stared ahead for a moment, pensively.

'By then I'd realised what I wanted in my life.'

'What happened to the photographer?'

'He came back.'

Tom leant his head round the door.

'If you'd come a few years ago you could have met him. He and my mother were together for forty years. My own father didn't want to know, so Arnold brought me up.'

★ ★ ★

Alex was aware he must get Katherine photographed. The piece needed its illustration – a picture of the anonymous old lady who had made an emotional decision. A poignant shot of the forgotten wife of Lewis Appleby, icon of the left and the man who shielded Nazis. Yet however touching it might look when it appeared in the newspaper, Alex knew there was little lingering sadness here. Katherine's contentment was palpable, and it was hard to disagree that things had turned out well for her.

They went outside to take a picture in the late afternoon light. The garden was a glory – just a small patch but every inch of it cultivated and bursting with its own fertility. Fat marrows gleamed on the ground, swollen, fiery tomatoes dangled from their bush and overripe pears lay smashed on the ground, their fermenting flesh alive with wasps. A little way beyond the far gate a river slid by, its surface splayed by a willow's languorous fingers. Even the air seemed slowed and rich with the scent of warm earth, as though the day itself had reached its own pitch of ripeness. Alex was reminded of the definitive holidays of his childhood, the long, sun-filled days on the cusp of summer just before he and Steve returned to school when the colours in the fields around them were at their most vivid and the air intense with the smells of cut grass and mown hay.

He pictured Katherine against an apple tree and she pulled down a couple of hard green fruit, handing them to him.

'They're Bramleys, so you'll have to have them baked.'

The image of him baking apples for himself in the grubby kitchen of his Pimlico flat brought a wave of self-pity to the surface. When the pictures were finished and it was time for Alex to leave, he found himself prevaricating, packing his tape recorder slowly and re-checking his notes, as if he could not bear to depart. Eventually he said his goodbyes and went out to the car, but before he climbed in he hesitated. Something was bothering him.

'The scientist. What did Lewis tell you his name was?'

'Müller, it was. Yes, Axel Müller.'

PART FIVE

CHAPTER THIRTY-ONE

IF HARRY EVERETT craned his neck just a few inches from his comfortable reclining position on the sunlounger he could see a sprawl of olive groves tumbling gloriously down the hillside towards an ancient castellated town. The view from this villa certainly was fabulous. Misty and mediaeval, the Tuscan landscape extended before him, a vista seemingly unchanged either by time or by the encroachments of visiting Britons, expensively ensconced in their rented farmhouses. But Harry leant back and kept his eyes closed luxuriously. It was too hot for sightseeing.

Lulled by the slow gurgle of the swimming pool beside him he was dozing off when his wife Valerie stumped out of the villa and came to stand in front of him, casting a chill shadow across his browning flesh.

'There's a call for you. Some woman, ringing from London.' Her face, already burnished by the fierce Italian sun and fiery with local wine, seemed to glow with displeasure.

Harry removed his sunglasses and squinted defensively up at her massive form bandaged in a brightly patterned sarong.

'Didn't they say who? Was it someone from the constituency?'

'Some girl.' The noun, for Valerie Everett, was loaded as a gun. 'I told her we were on our holiday and didn't like to be disturbed but she wouldn't be put off.'

'Really? I've got no idea . . .'

'Just take it, Harry. She's holding for you.'

He stumbled inside to the phone, frantically calculating, mentally preparing an alias for his unknown female caller.

'Yes. Who is it?' he said aggressively, in case Valerie was listening in. Then his tone changed. 'Oh, Jessica. No, I haven't had a chance to go through those papers yet. I really wasn't expecting to see you till next month. Can't it wait? . . . Oh, I see. Well, fire away, then.'

★ ★ ★

275

Alex took the scenic route home, lingering along B roads, idling at amber lights. He was in no hurry to return to London. After a whole summer of drought, thunderstorms were at last promised and already he could see the first of the pewtery clouds, swollen with rain, massing on the far horizon. A chill breeze began to blow and the first drops spattered on his windscreen. Well, they could do with a change.

He wondered what Jessica had done about his revelation that he had taken the AMCO briefing documents and was planning to publicise Project Mars. Professionally, he supposed, she should have informed her client already. But if he could reach her, before she did, and tell her what he now knew. That Axel Müller, the German scientist who co-founded a pharmaceutical company in 1950s Virginia, giving his own initials to make its name, was almost certainly a former Nazi doctor who experimented on children in the camps. And that Müller – as he styled himself – was sheltered in Britain by Lewis Appleby, an admirer and himself a proponent of eugenics in the thirties, before it became a dirty word. How would she react to that?

It might be that she would forewarn AMCO of the unwanted publicity and the company would be certain to stop it any way they could, perhaps by giving Brent Southern an exclusive interview or by any other trick that might prevent their company being thrust involuntarily into the spotlight, losing dozens of points off the share price, and having their ethically dubious screening technique uncovered prematurely, just as the new human genetics bill was about to be debated. Or just maybe Jessica would not want to work for AMCO when she heard what Alex had to tell her.

Instinctively he knew it would be no use calling her, but Alex had never been any good at obeying his instincts so he pulled out his mobile phone and tried Jessica's office.

'She's out.' It was her assistant, normally flirtatious on the phone, now terse. Perhaps Jessica had confided in her.

'Out, or avoiding me?'

'Out,' said the assistant. 'And she didn't say when she'd be back.'

What did that mean? Perhaps she was in a meeting with AMCO right then. He hoped that at least she would understand why he had to use the story. But perhaps, he thought wearily, understanding him simply wasn't in her make-up.

★　★　★

Perfunctorily he put in a call to his own office and Ray, the laconic hack with the desk next to his, picked up the phone.

'You at last. You're very popular.'

'What do you mean?'

'There's an awful lot of people trying to get hold of you. I explained I wasn't your secretary and that due to staffing cuts secretaries are like hen's teeth round here, but some of them have been really quite rude.' Ray's long service in a newspaper office had led to his treatment of all triumphs, disasters, and impending crises in the same sardonic fashion.

'Let me have it.'

'Well, there's a man called Frank LeRoux shouting curses down the phone, who seems to believe you're hiding from him and is promising to sue us, then there's his lawyer talking about getting an injunction against the newspaper, threatening all kinds of things, theft of documents, breach of commercial privacy, multi-million-pound lawsuits, and there's our lawyer and of course there's the editor. He's mad as a snake, wants to see you immediately to know what's going on. And an MP rang too. Harry Everett, a very pompous man. He wanted to give you a quote – I think you're supposed to be honoured by that – but I explained he'd have to wait in line. I think that's it. Oh, and a friend of yours called Leo. Said he wanted to explain.'

'Leo Jones? *He* wanted to explain?'

'That's right. He left a number.'

★　★　★

'Alex Irvine. I've heard of you,' said the chippy kid who answered Leo's phone. 'You're the journalist. Can you get free tickets for gigs?'

'Just get Leo.'

Leo came on to the phone sounding as mellow as he ever did but the tension and anxiety that had been building up in Alex overflowed in an angry outburst.

'It was you that told them, wasn't it, Leo? You told AMCO

277

about my story, you unprincipled bastard, and now they're trying to get the piece stopped.'

'Hold on a moment. Cool it.'

'Of all the sly, disloyal acts . . .'

'Wait . . .'

'When I thought you were a friend.'

'Actually, Alex I didn't say a word. As it happens I'm not taking AMCO's offer anyway.'

'Really?'

'Sure.'

'All right I'm sorry. Was this because of what I told you?'

'Oh no, mate. Someone came up with a better offer actually. Though I admit AMCO's plans for the Mars gene sound a little on the unsavoury side. It was the bit you mentioned about germ-line therapy that would concern me. You know what that means? Effectively altering a human being's genetic structure for future generations. You can introduce all the legal bans against it you like, but as long as the technology exists it will happen. And it's worrying stuff.'

'Well, AMCO certainly seem pretty worked up about me knowing.'

'They've got a lot to lose. It's a great find – the first behavioural characteristic traceable to the functioning of a single gene – and if it gets out before they patent it, or their plans prompt some kind of new restrictions, AMCO could miss out on a helluva lot of money.'

'So if it wasn't about AMCO why did you ring me, then, Leo? You said you wanted to explain something.'

'That's right. It was about what you were saying. About genetics. I thought I should clarify a bit. You see there's about 100,000 genes makes a human being and soon we'll have tracked down all of them. In terms of biology it's one of the most important advances of the century – at last we know man's genetic code – the implications are amazing. But knowing all Alex Irvine's genes doesn't mean I understand what makes him the tough guy he is. I mean I can know all the notes in a Mozart symphony, but I won't know how to play it. So what I wanted to say Alex is, it's important, but don't get carried away. The way people behave is always going to be far more complex than you imagine. You've been out with enough women to know that.'

CHAPTER THIRTY-TWO

JESSICA HAD RESIGNED from the AMCO account that morning. She resigned before she was fired, which would certainly happen, whether or not LeRoux knew that the information for Alex's scoop had come from her. She had contemplated the delight of telling Frank LeRoux to his face about the forth-coming publicity, but then realised it would be better to leave it as a surprise on his answerphone. She didn't know what resigning the account meant for her future at Hughes Associates, though it could scarcely be seen as an astute career move. When she'd told David, her boss, about AMCO he had protested incredulously at what he called 'an eccentric decision' and urged her to reconsider. But just doing it made her feel free, floating off like a balloon from the ballast of professional respectability.

After that she had called Harry Everett, and then, not knowing who else to tell, she phoned Rosie. The thing about having a sister, everyone said, was the way they always understood when you needed support.

'Is this going to be a long call?' enquired Rosie. 'Because it's not a very convenient time.'

Jessica persisted with her news, but it was still barely dramatic enough to distract her sister from her own predicament.

'Well, if you're at a loose end you can always come and help round here. We've got another two weeks of school holidays to go and the kids are climbing the wall.'

Behind her a menagerie of sounds rose, small, sharp sisterly quarrelling which Jessica knew was liable to last – off and on – for another few decades.

'Though if you want my opinion it sounds like you've done just the right thing,' Rosie added grudgingly above the noise. 'You're always telling me about being rung up by head-hunters so you won't be out of work long. And, you know, you could do with a change.'

'You're right,' said Jessica. 'I could do with a change.'

'By the way, thanks for taking the children the other day. They loved their day out with you. They thought the aquarium was brilliant and they simply adored your boyfriend.'

'He's not my boyfriend.'

'Oh, whatever. He seems like a good thing. He obviously has a way with kids.'

'He does,' said Jessica.

'Well, anytime you two want more contact with mine . . .'

'I'll bear it in mind. Listen, Rosie, I have to go.'

Craving something else eccentric to do, Jessica left the office and set off for a walk. No one she knew ever walked far in London except in the park or the gym and Jessica barely recognised the feel of the City's streets beneath her feet, or the view, outside a car or taxi. On a whim she bought an ice-cream as she strolled along. It was like stepping into another person's life.

Turning left out of Kingsway she walked down to the Strand, along Whitehall to Westminster, skirting the House of Commons. She looked up at the windows of the distant wing where Harry Everett's office was situated and thought about the debate to come that autumn when MPs would consider further loosening restrictions on human genetic research. She wondered whether Harry meant what he said about putting the work of AMCO UK in the spotlight.

Down Millbank she skirted the shrunken Thames, its parched tide dappled with foam and oil, and soon found herself walking through a hinterland of pubs and travel agencies and cheap hotels which served the shifting population of Pimlico. The demographic mix here, with shabby bedsitters up against smart, white, stuccoed addresses, gave the place a provisional, transitory feel. It was a district for the deracinated, served by late-night convenience stores selling vegetables in pairs and one-portion meals. As the sky above her grew dark and dramatic with impending rain, Jessica quickened her pace and felt glad she had somewhere to go.

★   ★   ★

Alex pressed a key and his e-mail flashed off across the green electric networks of the globe. At least he had tried to explain to Jessica. And by e-mail, which appeared to be her preferred method of communication. Outside, the rain was beginning to slap against the windows and fetching himself a beer he decided it was too late to return to the office. The editor, who had been poised between rage at the legal furore Alex had unleashed and the grudging acceptance that he may be breaking a major story, had insisted he finish the AMCO piece as soon as possible. It was a question of speed, now that the company knew about it and were mobilising their lawyers to stop it.

In the thundery afternoon gloom the flat looked more neglected than ever. He considered cleaning the place up, but did not have the heart. Perhaps he should be on the move again. He leant back and contemplated his experience to date, the countries he'd seen, the battles he'd been at, all the rage, the implacable hatreds and fighting. How odd to think that all these came down to the delicate dance of DNA, that slim twist with its scribble of chromosomes, wrapped in a tiny translucent shell. The way companies like AMCO were going, perhaps every atavistic urge, all the deepest human instincts like aggression, violence and procreation could soon be tagged, controlled, directed and in some cases dispensed with.

God knows what that said about his own existence – the random trajectory he called a career, the sexual desert and desultory social life of an unfulfilled thirty-eight-year-old living in a rented cupboard. Was that destiny written blindly in his blood? Somehow, Alex argued to himself, there had to be things biology couldn't account for. Where was the blueprint for unrequited passion, or hopeless attachments to unsuitable girls? What, after all, did his genes know about love?

These melancholy reflections were interrupted by the buzz of his broken doorbell. It was Jessica, but quite unlike her usual self. Her customary sophistication was drenched, her hair flat and dark against her head and stray raindrops coiled like tears down her cheeks. Instead of striding in as he might have expected, she hesitated, one hand on the door frame, looking around her as though peering into unpredictable or dangerous terrain. As he glanced behind him Alex saw the detritus through her eyes, the rubble of abandoned papers and boxes in corners, the tilt of dishes in the sink, all the signs of a life in hiatus.

'Great flat you've got here,' she smiled. 'Ever thought of moving out?'

'I wasn't expecting you.' He gestured to his laptop. 'I've just sent you an e-mail. I wanted you to know how I felt.'

'Should I go home and read it?'

'I could be more direct.'

He went across to where she was standing and pulled her damp body around him like clothes, kissing her, easing off her dress and running his hands over her shivering flesh. She cleaved to his hard, warm body, seized by a febrile urgency which surprised her, feeling the sparks of attraction she had so long suppressed catch and flare within her. This much, she knew, was beyond her control. It was beyond anyone's control, this fusion to a strange flesh fired by all the cells in her body, and the deep ache within her, ready to receive him.

Some time later they lay naked and breathless, fingertips touching, as the room's paltry furnishings crept back into focus. He propped himself up on his elbows and smiled at her: 'I can't really move out. Where would I go? Executive bachelor pads of this calibre are not that easy to come by.'

'There's this place in Notting Hill I had in mind.'

He looked down as she turned to him, the beautiful face unabashed, the eyes with their clear, uncompromising blue.

'You know something, Jess?'

'What?'

'You never cease to surprise me.'